PETER RALPH

THE CEO

IT WAS 10:00 a.m. and the heat was already oppressive, pushing 30 degrees when Douglas Aspine parked his black BMW Z3 at the front of the Federal Bank branch in South Yarra. He checked his hair in the rear-view mirror and turned his cell phone off, before putting a coin in the parking meter.

As Aspine was shown into the branch manager's office, a little, balding man with thin pursed lips glanced up before dropping his eyes back to a thick file on the desk in front of him. The branch manager, Jonathan Bardon, got up from a visitor's chair and said with a tinge of nervousness, "Hello, Doug, I'd like you to meet one of our head office lending managers, Colin Sarll."

Sarll did not get up or extend his hand, but instead just nodded, "Take a seat, Mr. Aspine," as he continued to examine the file.

An uncomfortable silence descended over the compact room. Bardon stared down at the cheap carpet, and his chair creaked as he shifted his large, overweight body uneasily before asking, "Coffee, Douglas?"

Before he could respond Sarll looked up. "So you'd like to borrow another $100,000, Mr. Aspine?"

"That's right; I've discussed it with Jonathan. I thought I'd get the documentation out of the way today."

"What documentation? We're not even close to approval. Why do you need the loan?" Sarll frowned.

Fuck! Jonathan hadn't warned him about this prick, and now refused or was too scared to make eye contact. "Well, the value of my house has risen by $130,000 in the last year, and I wanted to realize some of the increased equity. Is there a problem?" Aspine asked, through perfectly capped white teeth.

"Mr. Aspine, we lent you $350,000 to help you buy your house for

$400,000 nearly six years ago. You've increased the loan every year since, and you now owe us $750,000. That's right, isn't it?"

"Look, the house is worth a million dollars now. What's your problem?" Aspine nonchalantly drawled, trying to keep the terseness out of his voice.

Sarll paused, perusing the file again. "You're general manager of Biotech Products Limited and earned $400,000 last year."

"That's right."

"And you owe the bank $100,000 on your credit card. What do you do with your money? With a salary like that you should be reducing your loans, not increasing them."

Fuck again. Jonathan had probably been thinking about his forthcoming retirement and hadn't warned him about this ambush. What could he say? There were the lease payments on his wife's Mercedes, three sets of private school fees, other credit cards the bank didn't know about, and $10,000 in private golf club fees. Then there was his mistress, Charlie, and the cost of renting her apartment and MGB. Didn't this guy realize the suit he was wearing was an Armani? Everything was essential; there was no scope for savings. "I pay a huge amount of income tax, and the company takes a lot in superannuation contributions," he muttered. "I've got a few applications in for CEO's positions which I'm confident about. If one of them is successful, I'll be on a million dollar plus salary package."

"You can't save anything on a $400,000 salary? What you're telling me is simply not possible. You don't need a higher-paying job, but you do need to cut your expenses," Sarll said, his face filled with righteous indignation. "Besides, you've been unsuccessfully trying for a CEO's positions ever since you started banking with us, and at forty-five, you're not getting any younger."

Aspine felt himself color, and wanted to slam his fist into Sarll's sneering face. Instead, he pushed his large toned body back into his chair, ran his hands through his thick, black hair, and sighed in exasperation before saying, "Do I have to go to another bank?"

"You aren't going to find another bank. Not when they know, what we know." Sarll sneered, flicking through the file.

Anger and desperation welled up inside Aspine. There was $15,000 in overdue school fees, other household bills of $10,000, and he owed his stockbroker $35,000 on a losing trade. "That's what you say," he said contemptuously. "Are you going to give me the loan?"

"No, we're not, and you'll have to enter into a debt reduction program with us."

Aspine had taken enough. He jumped up, gripped the desk and eyeballed Sarll. His Grecian nose and handsome features, now contorted in rage, looked ugly as he shouted, "Why don't you go and fuck yourself, you beady-eyed little bean-counter?"

Jonathan Bardon leaped up and placed his pudgy wrinkled hands on top of Aspine's arm as if to restrain him.

"It's all right, Jonathan, I'm not going to hurt him."

"Hurt me? We have laws to stop thugs like you. Lay a hand on me, and I'll see you in jail," Sarll said, his eyes blinking rapidly.

"I'll have all of my accounts closed within sixty days, and you know what you can do with your bank," Aspine shouted, as he turned and stormed out of the office.

The heat off the bitumen was stifling as he sat in the Beemer listening to the messages on his cell phone, of which only the last held any interest. He hit the ignition and felt a gust of hot air before the air conditioning kicked in. He sighed with relief as he punched the recall button. "Jeremy Smythe," the refined English voice responded.

"Jeremy, it's Doug Aspine returning yours."

"Hello, Douglas. I had a call from Mercury Properties regarding their CEO's position. I'm sorry, they liked you, but you don't have any CEO experience and, well, they've gone with a proven performer."

"Who did they appoint?" Aspine asked, trying to conceal his disappointment.

"William Norton? Do you know him?"

"Fuck, Bill Norton, he must be pushing sixty. What are they doing?"

"As a matter of fact he's sixty-one, but he's still very fit, switched on and, more importantly, he's been a CEO for the past twenty years."

"Don't give me that shit! I'd buy and sell him ten times over on my worst day. Jesus, what are you doing letting them appoint a bloody geriatric?"

"Settle down. You were close, and I pushed hard for you because I thought you were the best candidate. However, in the end, it's the client who makes the final decision."

"And you still get your big fat fee no matter who gets the job, don't you?"

"Douglas, Douglas. That's offensive, but I'm going to overlook it, because of your obvious disappointment," Smythe responded.

Don't lose it Aspine told himself. He needed these pricks, but one day he wouldn't, and then he'd no longer have to put up with their bullshit. "Sorry, Jeremy, I was letting off steam. You did a great job for me. I appreciate it."

"Do you have anything else on?"

"Yes, I've applied for the CEO's position with Genilab through one of your competitors, Sainsbury & Co."

"Oh, I know about that. They've already made an appointment. I'm sorry."

"How do you know?"

"The head-hunting industry is small and, how might I put this? Incestuous. We all know about each other's assignments. Douglas, I know you're disappointed, but you're getting closer. Keep your chin up, old boy."

"Sure, thanks again, Jeremy."

Aspine had barely finished the call when *The Sting* tone that his youngest son had downloaded to his cell phone echoed around the car.

"Aspine," He growled.

"It's Ricky Renshaw, from Euro Sports Cars, Mr. Aspine. I just wondered if you're still interested in the Ferrari because we've got another party showing interest."

A bloody car salesman trying to hustle a sale. Could the day get any worse? "Ricky, if you've got a buyer, then sell the thing. Don't waste my time."

"I didn't think I was. Don't you remember saying that if anyone else showed interest, I should buzz you?" Renshaw said, his angst apparent.

Fuck, I did say that. That little prick at the bank screwed up my memory. "Sorry, you're right. I'm still interested, but I've had a temporary change of circumstances. I'll have to put it on the back-burner for now."

"That's okay, Mr. Aspine. You know it's a one-off and, if they don't import another one, this will be your only opportunity."

"Thanks, but I'm going to have to pass. If you've still got it in a few months' time, I might have another look. I have to fly. I'm running late for an appointment. Stay in touch, Ricky."

Charlie's sexy sugary voice resonated from her answering machine, but Aspine didn't leave a message. He needed to see her — right now. Her cell phone rang twice. "Hello, darling," she answered.

He ignored her greeting. "Where are you? I need to see you."

"Where do you think I am? It's nearly 40, and there's not a cloud in the sky."

"You're at the pool."

"That's right, darling."

"I'll be there in fifteen minutes," he said, unable to hide the tenseness in his voice. Christ, he was desperate for some relief.

The building was a typical high-rise glass edifice that bordered the upmarket suburbs of Prahran and Toorak. He stopped in the driveway, swiped his security card and waited for the roller door to the basement car-park to rise. Charlie's bright red MGB was next to the lift well, and he parked alongside it, before inserting his security card in the slot next to the elevators. He hit level twenty, the rooftop, and alighted onto artificial grass surrounded by potted palms. There was a small gymnasium to the right and a sauna, spa and twenty-five-meter pool with the customary deck lounges, and a barbecue area to the left. She was lazing in the shallow end and, he could see the striking contrast between her dark brown skin and white micro bikini. She heard his footsteps and gazed up at him. "Are you coming in?" she smiled mischievously.

"I need to see you in the apartment."

She climbed the steps of the pool, and his eyes followed every movement. She was superb: long ash-blonde hair, a provocative, teasing smile, a tiny waist and a lean, tight body, disproportionately large breasts, and slender, toned legs. As she slipped her feet into a pair of sandals, he ogled her still-dripping body and the tiny thong that was meant to cover her private parts.

"I can't."

"Can't?"

"My Mom's coming over for lunch in about fifteen minutes. We can't go to the apartment," she said, smiling at his obvious discomfort.

"Fuck! How long has this been going on?" he scowled, his face ugly with frustration.

"It's her birthday. She's fifty-two today. I haven't seen you for a week, and you didn't say you were coming, so I organized lunch. Doug, I can't plan my life around what you might do. You have to tell me; you have to let me know."

He silently cursed. Christ, the apartment, the MGB and her other expenses set him back sixty grand a year, and now she was saying that he'd have to give her notice when he wanted a screw. Fuck that! "Why don't you call and tell her you're not feeling well?"

"It's too late and, besides, that'll only make her want to come over even more. Why don't you throw your clothes off and jump in? I'll make you feel good, real good."

"Yeah, and what if some prick comes around the corner and sees me starkers, bonking you in the middle of the pool?"

She was totally uninhibited and giggled. Maybe it was the twenty-year age difference, but he knew that he couldn't perform, knowing someone might decide to use the pool while they were hard at it. He glared at her. "Fuck this. When I found you no other prick would've paid for your abortion, no other prick would've set you up in a life of luxury, and no other prick would've looked after you like me."

"Yes, and no other prick promised me that he'd ditch his wife and marry me as soon as he could," she said, for the first time not smiling.

"Fuck this," He growled, heading toward the elevators. He hoped she would call him back, and say she was going to get rid of her mom, but he heard nothing.

He hadn't thought it possible, but the day was getting worse. Stress and frustration were synonymous with his psyche, and it briefly crossed his mind to go home and try it on with Barbara. It had been ages since they'd had anything resembling sex, and her life now seemed to revolve around the kids, her girlfriends, and extreme gym workouts. She was still a good-looking woman but held no appeal for him. He cursed Charlie, slamming his fist into the passenger seat. He pointed the BMW toward Elsternwick where the only publicly-listed brothel in the world, The Daily Planet, was located in the appropriately named Horne Street. The shares had come on the market at $2.05 but now, some eighteen months later, were trading at a measly 40 cents. *Who says sex sells,* he thought? It was just after two o'clock when he pulled up in Horne Street, and the heat shimmered off the near-melting bitumen. As he was getting out of the car, his cell phone rang and, while tempted not to answer, the name on the screen was that of his boss, Bob Dwyer. "Yeah. Bob, what's up?"

"Where are you? You haven't forgotten we've got an appointment with the drug people from Sigma at two-thirty have you?"

"Of course not," he lied. "I had some private business with my bankers that over-ran a little. I'm on my way."

"Well make it in a hurry, because you're going to have to brief me on the key points that we'll be covering."

"I'll see you in fifteen minutes," Aspine said, casting a longing look at The Daily Planet before hitting the accelerator and burning rubber. In the semi-peak hour traffic, it was a thirty-minute drive to Biotech's offices.

The meeting with the Sigma executives went well, and Aspine managed to bluff his way through it with no preparation. He was more worried about why Bob Dwyer, the seventy-year-old founder, majority shareholder and CEO of Biotech, wanted to see him the following morning. Dwyer was lean, fit and could easily pass for mid-fifties. More concerning for his employees was that he was still sharp, and had an uncanny knack of detecting bullshit.

Aspine thought about visiting Charlie on the way home, but he was still pissed off with her, especially about what she had said about his marriage promise. Christ, she couldn't have been stupid enough to believe him. He had been half-pissed when he said it and just presumed that she would realize he was talking crap. If she didn't watch out, she'd find herself replaced by a younger more appreciative mistress.

The attraction of The Daily Planet had passed. It would now be packed with desperates all looking for a fix, and the thought of batting second or third or even further down the list had no appeal. The drive along the glorious tree-lined St Kilda Road promenade toward his house in Malvern was relaxing, but the image of Colin Sarll would not leave him, and he felt the stress and tension starting to return. His thoughts were interrupted by the ring tone of his cell phone.

"Hello, Jeremy. Why the late call? Have the people at Mercury Properties had second thoughts?" he laughed.

The pompous voice that came over the speakerphone was unusually restrained. "That's not funny. William Norton had a heart attack while running around the Botanic Gardens today, and dropped dead."

"Fuck! It's over 40. What was he doing running in that type of heat?"

"I told you he was a fitness fanatic. I guess he never anticipated going like that. Anyhow, the people at Mercury called and told me that I mustn't lose you."

"Christ, it's the last way I'd want to win a job," Aspine said, thinking something had finally gone right in what had been a shithouse day.

"Yes, I know, Douglas, but it's not as straightforward as it seems. They've appointed another firm of headhunters. It seems you're not their ideal candidate, but if they can't find anyone better, you've got the job."

"Pricks!"

"Take it easy. You're close, very close."

"Are you going to continue to look for other candidates?"

"Of course, that's what they've hired us for."

"I don't want you to. I want you to act for me solely. What do you get out of an assignment like this? Eighty to a hundred thousand?"

"We can't just act for you. You're not the client and, as you know, our fees are a secondary consideration. We're primarily interested in the quality of the candidate," Smythe said, sounding like a cross between the Pope and the Virgin Mary.

"I want you to act for me solely. If I'm successful, I'll pay you a further fifty thousand from my funds. After I'm appointed, I'll use my influence to ensure all senior appointments at Mercury are handled exclusively by your firm. Jeremy, this is an opportunity for both of us. Don't blow it."

"Yes, we might be able to do that. After all, we do think you're the best candidate, and doubt we'll find better. You realize of course this has nothing to do with money. It had no influence on my decision."

"Yes, of course." Aspine smirked. "When will you get back to me?"

"I'll aim for tomorrow. I'll use the ploy that you've had another offer, and they'll have to move quickly. Don't worry, Doug, I know how to close."

"Thanks, Jeremy. I look forward to hearing from you."

If I get the job in the next three days, I might even send some flowers to poor old Bill's funeral, Aspine thought. *Perhaps it might motivate a few of the older public company CEOs to throw in the towel before it's too late.*

When he pulled into the garage, he could hear the pounding of heavy metal music coming from the house and young voices arguing.

"Dad, Dad," his eldest son, Trevor, shouted. "Jemma's being a bitch. Make her turn the stereo down, I can't hear the cricket."

"Daddy, he's being mean." the tall, olive-skinned brunette pouted.

As Jemma was speaking, the television commentator screamed, "Gilchrist's hit another six," and a roar of approval went up from Trevor, and his younger brother, Mark.

Aspine couldn't hear himself think. How could Barbara live with this day after day?

"Where's your mother?" he heard himself yell, just as Mark shrieked, "Get off the phone, Jemma, you know I was about to use it."

"She's in the kitchen, Dad," Trevor responded.

"Daddy–"

"Jemma, get off the phone and turn the sound system down. Trevor, turn the bloody cricket off, and you can all tidy up before dinner."

No-one moved.

"Now!" Aspine shouted.

Jemma reluctantly put the phone down, and Trevor stared at him defiantly before turning the television off.

"Hello, darling, I heard you shouting," Barbara said, her lips brushing his. "Is there something wrong?"

She was petite with fine features and high cheek bones and, while only a year younger than him, had no noticeable wrinkles. He had often thought that the kids were blessed when they got her looks and his stature.

"Christ, Barbara, how do you live in this bloody madhouse? Why don't you stop them?"

She laughed. "I'm used to it, and I like the noise. Come on, let's have dinner."

"Dad, year seven is going to China for five weeks. Can I go?" Mark asked, his mouth half full of steak and chips. "Mom said it'd be okay."

"How much is it?"

"Six thousand dollars, plus I'll need some spending money."

Before Aspine could respond, Trevor interrupted, "Will you have time to look at cars this weekend, Dad? You know it's only three months to my eighteenth, and I'm booked in for my license that day."

"Daddy," Jemma said, "my cell phone allowance is not enough. I'm losing friends. Can I get an increase?"

Jesus, why isn't that little prick from the bank here to listen to this? Then maybe he would understand why I can't save anything. As he mused, the phone rang, and chairs went everywhere in the charge to answer it.

"I'm expecting a call," screamed Jemma. "It'll be for me."

A moment later she returned looking despondent and said, "It's for you, Dad. Some guy called Jerry, with a funny, snooty voice."

"Not Jerry, Jeremy! I'll take it in the study. Hang up after I answer."

"Hello, Jeremy. That was quick. What news do you have?" Aspine asked, struggling to keep the excitement from his voice.

- 2 -

"MERCURY'S CHAIRMAN, Sir Edwin Philby, wants to meet with you at nine o'clock tomorrow morning at the Victoria Club. Can you make it?"

"I've got a problem. I have a meeting with my CEO at the same time. No, forget that, I'll email his PA tonight. Yes, I can be there," Aspine said while moving books and papers to the side of his desk so that he could rest his legs in the cleared space.

"That's a wise decision. Now bear this in mind: Sir Edwin is very conservative and very busy — he's on at least ten boards and is heavily involved in philanthropy. He's anxious to resolve the appointment of a new CEO at Mercury and, if you impress him, the position's as good as yours." Jeremy said, oozing confidence.

"What about money? How much am I going to be paid? What about bonuses? How many stock options will I get, and what hurdles will there be before the cash is in my pocket? And what about benefits; you know, car, travel, entertaining and club fees?"

"Douglas, Douglas, my boy, you can be quite crass at times. Make sure you don't upset Sir Edwin and leave the salary package to me. And Douglas, don't say anything remotely favorable about the Labor Party or the trade unions if you know what I mean."

"Don't worry, Jeremy. I'll get back to you after I've met with Sir Edwin."

"Good luck."

Aspine finally found Mercury Properties Limited's latest annual report among the unpaid invoices, statements, final demands and second letter from the school seeking arrears of fees of fifteen thousand seven hundred dollars. Mercury was a long-established top-two-hundred-company with an impeccable reputation. It owned quarries and warehouses, manufactured bricks and cement, developed land, built offices, apartments, and houses and managed properties. It was rich in assets with minimal borrowings, but financially it had performed poorly. The balance sheet was lazy and the assets needed to be worked far harder, but that wasn't a problem — rather an opportunity. With a little downsizing, the sale of some assets and an increase in borrowings, it would be relatively easy to significantly increase profits. He flicked to the page on directors' remuneration, noting that the former CEO had been paid nearly two million for delivering mediocre profits. He hadn't paid much attention to Sir Edwin's remuneration as chair of the company, but two hundred and seventy-five thousand for chairing twelve meetings a year was a nice little earner. Aspine savored the thought of a CEO's big fat salary and the additional millions that he would make in bonuses and options — all his problems would disappear. Later he would be invited to join other public company boards as a non-executive director, adding to his esteem and financial resources. He smiled to himself; even if he stuffed up and got fired he'd be paid around five million dollars — a real no-lose proposition. Being a public company CEO left winning the lottery for dead and tomorrow was going to be a life-changing day. His pleasant thoughts were interrupted by Barbara.

"Are we in trouble?"

"What the hell are you talking about?"

"I had a call from the school today. The fees are nearly six weeks overdue. It was embarrassing."

"What did you say?"

"I said the check must have been lost in the mail. They asked me to put a stop on it and to drop another one into the school's administration by Friday. Are we in trouble?"

"No, we have a few temporary cash problems, that's all. Christ, Barbara, do you know what your Mercedes costs, what you spend on clothes, the cost of your tennis and golf clubs, not to say anything about the gym?"

"So it's all my fault is it?"

"I didn't say that, but those girlfriends you mix with have some bloody expensive tastes. Is it so important for you keep up with them?"

"I've known them all my life. Maybe if you had a decent job, I wouldn't have to worry about the kids getting thrown out of school!"

"Are you worried about *them* or the shame and embarrassment *you'd* feel?" he said, his mouth twisted in a cruel smile.

"You bastard," she responded before storming out.

Normally this would have been the cue for him to stomp out of the house, and spend a sex-filled night with Charlie. But he was still pissed off with her, so for once the stomping act was not an attractive option.

The Victoria Club was situated in Collins Street, Melbourne, on the forty-first level of the Rialto Towers; home to some of the most prestigious and influential professional firms in the city. The young receptionist said, "Hello, can I help you?"

"I'm looking for Sir Edwin Philby."

"Oh, you must be Mr. Aspine. He's expecting you. I'll show you to his table."

As they entered the dining room, he smiled. Only one table was occupied — by a slim, distinguished looking, gray-haired man in his late sixties. He was immaculately dressed in a three-piece pinstriped, navy blue suit with a large gold fob watch attached to the vest. His tie and handkerchief matched perfectly, and his stark white shirt looked like it had been pressed within the past five minutes. He stood up as they approached and extended his hand. "Good morning, Douglas, it's a pleasure to meet you. Thank you, Anne; could you please bring me another pot of tea? What will you have?"

"It's good to meet you, Sir Edwin. I'll have a skinny-cinno."

"So you're health-conscious. That's good. Look, I only have an hour, and we have a lot to cover. Take a seat."

"Thank you."

"Let's cut to the chase. We have a dossier on you that's nearly two inches thick, so I'm not going to waste time with small talk," Sir Edwin said, smiling warmly. "You have an engineering degree, an MBA, and you've held senior management positions since you were thirty, with an impressive record in some tough situations. Why then, in fifteen years, haven't you been able to make the jump to CEO?"

Aspine considered the question carefully before responding. "Many of the CEOs I've worked for have been of a similar age to me, or they've been founders who won't finish until they're carried out."

"Like your current boss?"

"Yes, Bob Dwyer's a good example. He's seventy, but he's still fit, sharp, ambitious and a great deal-maker, not unlike Rupert Murdoch."

"What happened when you looked outside your current employers?"

"I made the shortlists for a number of CEO positions but never quite made it."

"Did you ever try for a CEO's position with a privately owned company?"

"Never. I've only ever applied for public company positions."

"There are some large private companies, you know. Look at Visy Board — it's a huge private company."

"Yes, with the founder's son running it." Aspine laughed. "No thanks."

"So you don't think you've missed out because of your abrasive nature?"

"Abrasive nature?"

"Yes, according to our dossier you told one of your bosses to fuck off and walked out. Then you were in the Federal Court fighting the unions, and you've had some equal opportunity trouble as well. Worse, your wife applied for a restraining order and accused you of being violent toward her. Isn't that right?" Sir Edwin asked, pouring another cup of tea. "Would you like more coffee?"

"No thanks, one's enough. I was very young when I walked out and defeating the unions, and the equal opportunity people was critical to the culture of my employers. As far as my wife goes, we had a tiff which blew up, but I never laid a hand on her. I presume you know that she withdrew the application for the restraining order?" Aspine replied, surprised at the depth of information they'd managed to dig up.

"Yes, I thought the business with your wife was probably a storm in a teacup, but I needed to check. I agree with you regarding culture — it's critical. That's why you appealed to me, despite your lack of CEO experience. Mercury needs cultural change — massive cultural change."

"Why didn't the last CEO implement it?"

Sir Edwin chuckled. "Harry Denton was with the company forty years. He was an institution who was immovable until he finally retired late last year. He's still on the board as a non-executive director, which is a little sad."

"Why didn't you get rid of him?"

"I was appointed two years ago by the institutional investors who were unhappy with the company's performance, but so long as Harry was CEO, I was stuffed."

"Why?"

"The board has six directors, and I'm the oldest, but you'd never know it. The other four are dedicated supporters of Harry. Some are only in their fifties, but with their lack of flair you'd think they were in their nineties. Wait until you meet them."

Aspine found the last comment encouraging. "You're not making the job sound overly appealing."

"But you know it is, Douglas, and you're hungry, ambitious, and this is your stepping stone to breathing the rarified air peculiar to public company CEOs. What do you think of Mercury's balance sheet?"

"It's lazy."

"Lazy? It's moribund, and my supporters in the institutions want it fixed. If you haven't already guessed, I have a reputation to uphold."

"I can increase profits by at least fifty percent in the first year."

"How certain are you?"

"I'm positive."

"Good, good," Sir Edwin said checking his watch. "I have one last question. Am I anything like what you expected?"

"I'm not with you."

"Come on. Weren't you expecting an eccentric with a title, a houndstooth jacket, a pompous voice and hardly any business knowledge?"

"I hadn't thought about it."

"You're very diplomatic. Let me explain. My father was a successful inventor who was knighted for his contribution to science and the community. When he passed away, he left most of his money in charitable trusts under my stewardship, and I've spent most of my life giving it away. As a result, I was knighted for my philanthropic endeavors," Sir Edwin said, roaring with laughter. "Next time we meet, I'll be Ed, even though there will be occasions when it is more appropriate to use my title."

"So we'll be meeting again?"

"Yes, Douglas, I think we'll work well together," Sir Edwin said, extending his hand. "Sorry, I have to rush. Someone will be in touch. It was nice meeting you."

It was warm and sunny when Aspine left the Rialto Towers, and he bounced down the street with a fresh spring in his stride. He wanted to let out an almighty whoopee and share his euphoria with the rest of the world. It was a ten-minute walk to Biotech's offices, but in what seemed no time at all, he was sitting behind his desk replaying the interview. It'd gone almost perfectly, but he wasn't sure what his face had betrayed when Sir Edwin had raised the matter of violence with Barbara. That was over ten years ago, and he hadn't really hit her — at the worst it had been no more than a solid backhander. On reflection, he was confident his explanation had been accepted. He toyed with the idea of phoning Jeremy, but he didn't need him anymore — *other than to negotiate a big fat salary package, that is.* No, Jeremy could wait while he basked in the afterglow of the meeting and what was going to be a prosperous future. His thoughts were interrupted by his intercom buzzing. "Douglas, Mr. Dwyer, would like to see you in his office."

"Thanks, Sally, I'm on my way."

Bob Dwyer occupied the smallest of the executive offices. It was about three meters square, and there was barely room for a visitor's chair. Some said he liked to understate his importance, but others thought he liked to grill his underlings in a confined and inescapable space. The door was open. "You wanted to see me, Bob."

"Close the door and take a chair," Dwyer said, not looking up.

He was dressed in his standard attire of crinkled, open-neck, check shirt, old blue cardigan with holes in the elbows, gray pants, and black shoes that had been resoled many times. His shareholding in Biotech was worth more than five hundred million, but no-one could ever accuse Bob Dwyer of standing on ceremony. He looked up and peered over the top of his glasses; his large nose and thinning, fading, red hair reminded Aspine of a hawk — a very nasty hawk. "You faked the meeting with the Sigma people. You were a bloody embarrassment."

"You're wrong. They were impressed with my presentation."

"Don't fucking tell me I'm wrong! I've forgotten more about this business than you'll ever know. You're right about those Sigma bozos though; they had no idea you were snowing them, but that's no excuse for your abysmal performance. I shouldn't have been surprised because you're hardly ever here these days."

"I've worked countless weekends and nights. In the past few days I had a few personal matters to take care of, but don't try and hang some guilt trip on me."

Dwyer laughed, but his eyes were cold. "So you think I'm trying to hang a guilt trip on you? If I'd been doing that, I would've mentioned the thirty-five thousand bucks you hold your hand out for every month. You mightn't believe this, but you don't earn a salary like that working from nine to five."

"If it's not a guilt trip, what is it?"

"You're a smart man. I thought you would've worked it out. I want your resignation," Dwyer said, sliding a single sheet of paper across the desk.

Aspine picked it up and quickly skim-read it. He had prepared many similar documents for others, but never suffered the indignity of having one prepared for him. It was simple in content, and by resigning and accepting the sum of one hundred thousand dollars he waived all his rights, past, present and future, against the company.

"I'm not signing. Christ, I've been here nearly three years, I'm forty-five years old, and it might take me six months to find another position," he lied. *How good is this? It fits perfectly with the Mercury job* he thought.

"Then I'll sack you and pay you the minimum. Would you prefer to show that on your CV, or take the hundred thousand and we'll agree it's a resignation?"

"You've got a short memory. You've forgotten what I did to the unions in the Federal Court. Would you like some of the same and the accompanying publicity?"

A vein in Dwyer's neck started to throb furiously, and he partially lifted himself out of his chair. "Don't threaten me," he yelled. "You beat the unions because they had no money for legal fees. I've got plenty and if you take me on I'll tie you up in the courts for years."

"Bullshit! If you sack me and try to get away with paying the minimum, you'll lose. It could set you back half a million plus legal fees, and you'll need to spend hours, maybe days, maybe weeks, with your lawyers. Do you really want that?"

"How much would you like, Doug?" Dwyer asked, not trying to hide his sarcasm.

"I'll settle for one year's salary."

"You want four hundred thousand. You're mad! I'm never gonna pay that."

"I've got three kids at school, a bloody big mortgage, and no job. It's a fair figure."

Dwyer hit a button on the intercom and said, "Don, I'm with Douglas Aspine. Change the amount on his resignation to two hundred thousand. Get it retyped and bring it down with a check, including any holiday pay and whatever else is owed in respect of this month."

"I didn't agree to two hundred thousand. What are you talking about?"

"Here's the deal, Doug. Take it or leave it. The negotiations are over. I'm a good judge of human nature, and I'm guessing you're going to sign, take the money and leave us in peace. Only a fool would leave two hundred on the table and go to the courts, and you're not a fool," Dwyer said, the corners of his mouth turned up in a sly smile.

"You smug bastard! I ought to tell you where to shove your check. We both know I'll get more if I brief my lawyers."

"No, we don't. You're sitting there trying to work out how much you'll have to pay your legal sharks. Our lawyers are going to be arguing for a lot less than two hundred and, even if you're partially successful, there's no certainty you'll get costs. And don't forget, we'll drag the litigation out. It'll be years before you see any money, but your lawyers will bill you every month. Do you want to take me on that badly and, more importantly, can you afford to?"

Aspine knew everything Dwyer said was true, and that he was going to sign. Despite this, he scowled, thrust his jaw out and said, "I don't know. If you increase the amount to two hundred and fifty, we can shake hands and walk away, knowing we've struck a fair compromise."

Dwyer burst out laughing. "You must have a hearing problem. I told you the negotiations are over, and I'm already being more than fair. Oh, and Doug, I don't care if I never shake your hand or set eyes on you again. I want you to pack your personal belongings and get off the premises."

As Dwyer was talking, Don Terret, the company's financial controller, came in with the amended letter of resignation and check. Dwyer quickly perused it and pushed it across his desk to Aspine. "Sign it. Don will witness your signature, and then you can have the check," he said.

"I'll sign, but it's not right."

"Goodbye, Douglas. Don will accompany you to your office, and then escort you from the building."

It was lunchtime and the city streets were crowded with office workers enjoying the warm weather. Aspine walked to the nearest branch of the Federal Bank, deposited the check for a little over one hundred and eighty thousand after tax had been deducted, and paid the bank fee for a quick clearance. His immediate money problems were over, and he'd go on the internet later in the day and pay his bills. He wondered if the day could get any better and smiled when he thought about the extra hundred he had screwed out of Dwyer. If the silly old goat had waited a few more weeks, he wouldn't have had to pay anything. As he pondered this, his cell phone rang, and he looked at the screen. "Hello, Jeremy."

"Good afternoon, Douglas. Things must have gone well this morning. Mercury's principals have asked me to make an offer on their behalf."

"Go on," Aspine said, taking a deep breath.

"Well, needless to say, they wish to offer you the position. The commencing salary is eight hundred thousand, plus an incentive bonus that will allow you to more than double the salary component, plus options, a generous expense account, and a car allowance. What do you think?" Jeremy said, his voice filled with pleasure in anticipation of receiving profuse thanks.

"Eight hundred thousand! That's fucking terrible. Christ, you've been screwed. My predecessor was getting more than two million."

"Settle down, Douglas. Sir Edwin was your only supporter on the board, and he had to use all his influence to get them to make you an offer. They wanted to appoint the company's financial controller, Neil Widge. Harry Denton, the former CEO, was pissed off with your claim that you could increase profit by fifty percent. Let me tell you the basis of your incentive bonus. If you increase operating profit by twenty-five percent you'll get one hundred thousand, and for each five percent after that you'll get another one hundred thousand, but, and this is a big but, if you can increase it by fifty percent, they'll pay you a bonus of one million dollars. It seems Harry Denton said you have no chance of doing it. I lie — I believe his exact words were that you must be living in cloud cuckoo land." Jeremy sniggered.

"Yes. I understand the politics. I can force myself to live with the eight hundred to start with, and I'll enjoy asking Harry to counter-sign my check for a mil at the end of the year. What about the options and car?"

"Mercury's shares are languishing at $1.80. They propose issuing you two million free options, exercisable after you've been with the company for a year. You'll have a window of two further years to exercise them at a price of $2.50. Your car allowance is fifty thousand per annum — you can choose any car you like, but you'll have to meet any additional expenses yourself."

"Lousy pricks! I have to increase the share price by more than twenty-five percent before the options are worth anything. I've seen public companies issue options to executives to acquire shares at a figure less than the current market price."

"Isn't it clear to you? Sir Edwin used your comment about

increasing profits by fifty percent to extract the offer. If you can do it, by the end of the year Mercury's shares could be trading at $4.00, which will make your options worth three million. That makes your total remuneration about five million in the first year," Jeremy sighed in exasperation. "Contrast that with the four hundred thousand that Biotech's paying you."

"Yeah, okay Jeremy, you're right. I can live with their offer," Aspine said, chuckling at his greed.

"Sir Edwin would like you to start as soon as you can. He asked if you could convince Biotech to let you go without working out your notice. I told him that probability was remote, and it would be at least a month before you could commence."

"Go back and tell him I can start on Monday."

"What? Biotech isn't going to let you go on three days' notice!"

"Just do it and let me worry about Biotech." Aspine smiled. "Oh, and Jeremy, make sure the offer is couriered to me tomorrow. I'll fax my acceptance to Sir Edwin. I want to make sure there are no loopholes."

Aspine was still on a high when he called Charlie.

"Hi, darling," she answered. "I'm glad you called. I thought you might still be in a shitty mood about yesterday."

"I'll see you in half an hour," he responded. "I'm bringing a bottle of Dom Perignon, so chill a couple of glasses."

"What are we celebrating?"

"I'll tell you when I get there."

"Doug, I can't do anything. I'm sorry, but I'm really sore."

"Fuck, what's wrong with you?"

"I had a Brazilian this morning, and I lost more than intended. I'm going to be tender for the next few days. I'm sorry."

"That's okay. You didn't go to the dentist too, did you?"

"I'm not with you," she said, and then giggled. "Oh, you dirty bastard."

- 3 -

HARRY DENTON WAS born and bred in the country town of Wangaratta. He had come to the big smoke forty years earlier and joined Mercury as an apprentice carpenter when it was still owned by brothers, Les and Patrick Dalton. The Daltons were gentlemen and good bosses and had pushed Harry into doing a civil engineering diploma at night school — a task that took nearly ten years and which was testimony to his determination. Harry was a dedicated, loyal, hardworking employee and a natural leader, so it was no surprise when the Daltons appointed him CEO of the company. Unfortunately, after they passed away, their children showed no interest in owning the business. Harry with the help of the company's accountants and lawyers floated Mercury as a public company, allowing the Dalton children to sell their shares without affecting the company's management or future. Harry reluctantly accepted the additional role as chairman. Many loyal employees bought shares, including Harry, and the two percent he still owned was now worth twelve million dollars.

Under Harry, Mercury was like a large family with the utmost respect paid to its members. There was no such thing as downsizing or retrenchments and, in the absence of gross incompetence; a job at Mercury was a job for life. Sackings were few and far between and usually related to marriage breakdowns or alcoholism. In many instances, Harry picked up the cost of marriage counselors out of his own pocket and made large donations to Alcoholics Anonymous. Long before makeup pay came in, Harry paid any worker injured on the job, in full, and introduced superannuation for every employee, twenty years before it was legislated. Employees who were sick were treated with the same benevolence and there were no limitations on the payment of sick leave. Many employees had been with the company for decades and, in thirty years as CEO, Harry had only had two PAs.

Harry didn't believe in borrowing to fund expansion and didn't like or trust the banks, having watched them sell up many farmers and primary producers when they had fallen on hard times. He'd seen Mercury's competitors increase their sales by selling off-the-plan, and then later by accepting bonds from insurance companies, and it had made him sick. The marketing methods of Chris Skase, Alan Bond, and Bill Farrow were not for Harry Denton. Mercury grew steadily under his stewardship, and the credit squeezes and recessions that had killed companies in their thousands were little more than speed humps in an otherwise smooth road. As the company became more prominent, insurance companies and banks started paying attention to it and buying large tranches of shares. Then they agitated for higher profits and larger dividends. Harry's focus had always been on the long-term, but these institutions looked no further than the next profit report or dividend. There had been a time when institutions had been loyal, long-term shareholders of public companies. Now they would sell their shares at the first hint of bad news, and would salivate at the thought of a takeover bid. Harry didn't like them, but they controlled more than fifty percent of Mercury. When they approached him seeking his resignation as chairman on the basis of good corporate governance, and the appointment of Sir Edwin Philby, he didn't object. Harry thought that corporate governance for a company run as honestly as Mercury was a waste of resources. However, he was glad to be no longer chairing meetings where shareholders were far more aggressive, greedy, and noisy than they had been in bygone years.

Harry had married his childhood sweetheart, Mary, and they had three children and were now the proud grandparents of five grandchildren. Every Sunday morning the family met at the Presbyterian Church in Melbourne to worship. He never swore or blasphemed, either at home or the company. He drove a six-year-old Holden and insisted Mercury buy only Australian-made vehicles. He and Mary had lived in Armadale for thirty-five years, in the marital home that he had built.

It was 8:00 a.m. and Harry and his friend, company lawyer and co-director, Stan Pettit, waited in Mercury's offices on the upper level of a two-level building that fronted a large warehouse. Harry was a small man with strong features, many wrinkles, a jutting jaw, a full head of curly gray hair and bright blue, piercing eyes. He was dressed in an ill-fitting dark suit, and the collar and sleeves of his once-white shirt were frayed.

"I thought he'd be here by now, Stan," Harry said, to the slightly younger man.

"Did you tell him you were going to be here to meet him?" Pettit asked, slumping into the closest chair.

"No. I've never met or spoken to him. Ed said we had to get him, as he was about to accept another offer, and I went for it. I've got a nasty feeling that I was snowed. If I'd been starting a new job, I'd have been here at seven."

"Yes, but that was in the good old days." Pettit gasped.

"Stan, you need to be careful, because you're stacking on weight. I thought your doctor put you on a diet because of your blood pressure," Harry said, his concern obvious.

"He did, but I've got clients always wanting to discuss deals over lunch or dinner. I'll have to get out of the law if I'm ever going to lose any weight." Pettit chuckled.

"It's not funny. I'm finding the air conditioning a little cold, but your face is red, and you're sweating. Are you sure you're all right? Why don't you undo the top button of your shirt and loosen your tie? Would you like a glass of water?"

Before Pettit could respond, Harry pressed the intercom for his former PA. "Shirley, please bring me in a glass of chilled water."

"Certainly, Harry."

"I'm all right. I can't stand for long periods of time, but now I've got a chair, I'm okay. How much longer do you think our man will be?"

"Don't know." Harry frowned. "If you want to go to your office, then do so. There's no need for both of us to wait."

"I cleared my appointments. I don't have anything on until after ten. I'll wait. You don't think he's changed his mind do you?" Pettit grinned.

"No, I don't," Harry responded, without mirth.

"Oh, would you like a glass of water too, Stan?" Shirley asked as she entered the office.

"It's for him," Harry said. "I don't want one."

"Thanks, Shirley."

After she'd left, Stan said, "She's a great PA. How long has she been with you?"

"Over twenty years and yet it seems like I hired her yesterday. Where'd the time go, Stan?"

Aspine sat stuck in bumper-to-bumper traffic in his new pre-owned Ferrari Maranello, which could go from 0 to100 kph in 4.2 seconds and had a top speed of 325 kph. It had set him back six hundred thousand, and his fifty thousand per annum car allowance didn't cover the insurance and servicing. But he was about to earn five million, so the cost paled into insignificance. It had taken him just five minutes to make the decision to buy it on credit. The upholstery was black, the body was Ferrari red, and he reveled in the many admiring and envious glances that came his way. The traffic cleared for a second, and he hit the accelerator. The Ferrari responded, and he smoothly went through the lower gears using the F1 Paddle Shift. Finally, he could see Mercury's offices and he gunned the powerful red car through the gates, pausing in the middle of the car-park, looking for a vacant space.

Harry looked out the window. "Stan, come over here. I think Satan's arrived."

They watched as the Ferrari reversed across the car-park, to the far fence, where it was parked on a rough strip of gravel. The man who got out was tall and strongly built.

"He doesn't look happy, Harry."

"Mercury's never allocated parking spaces for its executives, and it's not about to start now."

Aspine was annoyed about having to park his new toy so far away, and he took the stairs to reception two at a time. He knew from the photos in the annual report that the poorly dressed little guy was Harry Denton and the bald, fat, sweaty man with the horn-rimmed glasses was Stan Pettit. "Well this is a surprise," he said, shaking Harry's hand before addressing Stan. "It's a pleasure to meet you, Stan. I take it you both know who I am."

"Yes, Douglas, we know who you are. Welcome to the company," Harry said. "We thought we'd brief you about the business and then introduce you to the people you're going to be working with."

"That's nice of you, Harry, but I already know more than enough about the business, and I'll introduce myself when I'm ready. Just show me where my office is and let me know how I can get some signwriting done."

"Signwriting?"

"Yeah, I need to get the car parked closest to the offices moved so that the space can be painted. I don't intend to park in the outback again."

"We don't allocate car-parks to executives."

"Harry, I don't give a fuck what happens with the other executives, but I'm the CEO, and I don't intend to park a hundred meters away just because it's convenient for the office girls."

Harry's face flushed, and he fought to hold his tongue.

"Why don't you point me in the direction of my office? Then you and Stan can get going. I'm sure you're busy men, and I don't want to hold you up. Besides, I've got a lot to get through today."

"You know you're responsible to us," Harry said, peeved at the way he'd been treated.

"No, I'm not. I'm responsible to the board and then only through the chairman. Harry, you're a non-executive director and, seeing you've raised it, I'd appreciate it if you'd confine your role to just that."

"Come on, Harry," Stan said. "It seems Douglas doesn't want or need our help."

Aspine walked down the corridor, past offices that he guessed were occupied by the company's executives. The office at the end was obviously his, and adjacent to it was a glass-fronted office occupied by a frumpy, frizzy-haired, middle-aged woman who he knew to be his PA, Shirley Bloom. He did not acknowledge her but entered his office. It was small, ill-lit, and was furnished with an old L-shaped desk, a brown fabric swivel chair, and three matching visitors' chairs, all badly worn and in varying states of disrepair. There was another door to the right of the desk that opened onto what was obviously the boardroom, comprising a large board table and twelve leather chairs. He sat in the swivel chair, looked out the window and saw his car. "Shirley," he shouted. "Come in here."

She waddled in and sat down, saying, "So you already know my name."

He ignored her comment. "Arrange to get the closest car-park sign written, and have a sign erected behind it *Reserved CEO*."

"Oh, Douglas, we don't have alloc–"

"It's Mr. Aspine to you, and I don't give a stuff about what's occurred in the past. Get my car-park sign-written today." He watched her large flabby cheeks turn red, and he held her stare until she lowered her eyes.

"Is there anything else?"

He looked at his watch before responding. "I want to see the manager of human resources at ten o'clock and the financial controller at eleven. And get me a coffee, white with none. If I need anything else, I'll shout."

She didn't move and appeared to be deep in thought. "Mr. Aspine, Harry used to buzz me on the intercom and, well, he used to get his own coffee."

"Shirley, listen, because I'm only going to say this once. I'm not interested in what Harry did or whether he buzzed or sent for you by carrier pigeon. If you do what I say, we might get on well, and if you don't, you won't be here much longer. Is that clear?"

She turned bright red again and stood up to leave. "Yes, Mr. Aspine."

"Hang on, Shirley." Aspine reached inside his briefcase and handed her a page of the *Financial Review*. "Photocopy the article about my appointment, blow it up to double size, and put it in an envelope with a with-compliments-slip marked private and confidential, to Bob Dwyer at Biotech." He smirked, knowing Dwyer would go ape shit when he found out that he had been screwed.

Before commencing, Aspine had spent days reading the company's annual reports, announcements to the Stock Exchange, press clippings, board minutes and management reports that Sir Edwin Philby had couriered to him. He had a solid understanding of the company, its current projects, and its personnel. He'd been elated to learn that the company banked with the Federal Bank. He could hardly wait to meet the bank executive handling the company's account.

Kurt Metzger was a strapping young officer in the Munich Police Force at the nineteen-seventy-two Olympics and bore close witness to the Munich Massacre. He had been profoundly affected and shortly after left his home country bound for Australia. Within a month of arriving in Melbourne, he was working with Mercury Properties as a builder's laborer. He had only been employed six weeks when an enormous concrete beam crashed down, crushing him and two of his co-workers. Displaying immense strength, he had managed to move the beam and save the lives of his fellow workers, but by the time it was lifted off him, his back was shot to pieces. Harry Denton, visited him every day in hospital and, as he recovered, offered him the newly created job of health and safety officer. Kurt had grown with the company, culminating with his appointment as human resources manager ten years earlier. He knocked lightly on Aspine's office door and entered. "I'm Kurt Metzger. You wanted to see me," he said, in a guttural Germanic accent, as they shook hands.

"Sit down, Kurt. I presume you know who I am."

Kurt was still slightly stooped from the accident and curled his lean body into the chair. His once-blonde hair was gray and thinning, and his face bore deep worry lines. "Yes, Mr. Aspine," he said, in the same way an army private addresses his sergeant.

"Kurt, Mr. Aspine, was my father. My name is Douglas or Doug. What I need from you are summaries of the company's four thousand employees, firstly by department, secondly by location and thirdly by age categories in bands of five years. When can you let me have them?"

"Four thousand two hundred and eleven. All of that information is in the system. I can have printouts for you within two hours. Is there anything else?"

Aspine smiled. *This guy's been in Australia for thirty years but still gives the impression that he wants to jump up, click his heels and salute.* "I'd also like to see status reports on all WorkCover claims and employees who've been receiving sickness benefits for longer than two weeks."

"Yes, Mr. Aspine, that's not a problem. I can let you have them with the other information."

"How did you address Mr. Denton?"

"Everyone called him Harry. Most of us grew up with him as CEO."

Aspine let it pass. "Is there a strong union presence in the company?"

"We're property developers and builders, so yes, there is, but we work well with the union organizers. You'll be pleased to know that we haven't had a strike or union dispute for over five years," Kurt said, smiling for the first time.

"In my experience, that usually indicates that the company's management is negotiating after having bent down, grasped their ankles, and dropped their pants."

That wasn't the response Kurt had expected. Harry never drew crude analogies like that. "We like to think of ourselves and the unions as being equals."

"Fuck! You guys are playing with yourselves. Those union organizers must be pissing themselves laughing. Well, we'll soon change that." The buzzing of the intercom interrupted him. "Yes," he snapped

"Neil Widge is here for his eleven o'clock appointment," Shirley said.

"Tell him to wait."

Kurt had had time to think, and he spoke in a slow, measured tone. "It's a strong union. You need to be careful before doing anything precipitous."

"Precipitous?" Aspine smirked. "I all but broke the last union that took me on. I'm looking forward to dealing with these commie pricks."

"Harry used to delegate industrial relations and negotiations with the unions to me," Kurt responded, looking miffed.

"You and I will work well together if you remember one thing: I don't give a fuck about what Harry said or did. This company has underperformed for the past ten years, and I intend to fix that underperformance. Make sure I have that information by one o'clock."

"Yes, Mr. Aspine."

Aspine sighed, "On your way out tell Neil Widge to come in."

Neil Widge had commenced with Mercury as an accountant over twenty years earlier and worked his way into the position of financial controller and company secretary. In his latter role, he attended all board meetings and saw himself as a defacto director. As he entered the office, it hit Aspine that he was an older version of the Newman character made famous in the hit sitcom, *Seinfield*: curly gray hair, little piggy eyes, large glasses, fat jowls and thin, unsmiling lips. His handshake was soft and sweaty, and he was trembling, not with fear, but with pent-up aggression. He glared at Aspine. "You shouldn't be sitting in that chair. After Bill Norton's death, they promised me that I'd be CEO," he said, eyes, blinking rapidly.

"Why didn't they appoint you?"

"The institutions, that's why. They appointed Sir Edwin Philby as chairman and he appointed you. Not one other director wanted to appoint you. How does that make you feel?" Widge sneered.

"I don't give a fuck. The institutions own more than sixty percent of the shares, so a majority of shareholders support my appointment. Anyhow, we're not here to discuss my appointment. I'm CEO, and you'd better get used to it in a hurry."

"And if I don't?" Widge snarled, tears of anger welling up in his tiny eyes.

"I'll reluctantly have to sack you, and at your age you'll be lucky to ever work again," Aspine responded, hoping Widge's pride might make him do something stupid.

"Sack me? You prick! I'll save you the trouble. I resign!" Widge yelled, standing up and smashing his fist on the desktop. His face was contorted, and he was trembling uncontrollably. "When the board hears about this they'll sack you and reinstate me."

"Well, you give me no choice. I accept your resignation. You don't have to worry about working out your period of notice. We'll pay you for that, but I want you off the premises within the hour." Aspine smiled. It would have cost another three hundred thousand had he sacked Widge, but the fool had resigned. He hit the intercom. "Kurt, Neil Widge, has resigned. Help him clear his desk and show him off the premises."

Widge hadn't moved; his anger had receded and been replaced by shock. "I-I might have overreacted," he said. "I-I think I might reconsider."

Aspine laughed. "I'm sure you know the law of contract. You made an offer, and I accepted. For you, I'm afraid it's game set and match." *One down, five hundred and ninety-nine to go* he thought.

Within minutes of Widge's departure, Aspine was on the phone to Jeremy looking for his replacement. "I need a financial controller, pronto. I won't tell you your business, but there are two things I want. He's got to be under forty-five, and he can have any color hair so long as it's not gray."

"You've sacked Neil Widge already?" Smythe gasped.

"No, he resigned, but I eventually would've had to fire him. He saved me the time, trouble and expense."

"You said two conditions, but you referred to three. There are some clued-up females in the market. Does your financial controller have to be male?"

"Yes, make that the third condition. I'm not into that affirmative action crap, and I want to be able to say 'fuck' anytime I want to, without being hauled up before some lefty feminist, equal opportunity tribunal."

"You have a callous way with words, but I wouldn't express that opinion in public," Jeremy said, a trace of disgust in his refined voice.

"I'm not stupid. I think you're going to be busy over the next few months."

"Shirley," Aspine shouted. "Who's our relationship manager at the bank?"

"Phil Kendall."

"Get him for me."

A few minutes later Shirley said. "I have Mr. Kendall. I'm putting him through."

"Congratulations, Douglas. You've got some big shoes to fill," Kendall said.

"Christ, I hope you don't mean that. Don't you read the company's financials or track its share price?"

"It's always been a conservative company run by morally responsible people."

"So you think low returns on equity, decreasing earnings per share, and a lousy share price is moral? We're going to have to agree to disagree."

Kendall was taken aback by the aggressive tone of Mercury's new CEO and resolved to tread with more care. "You called. How can I be of assistance?"

"I'm looking at all existing relationships, including banking, and I want to see if you can deliver on our needs."

"Mercury's banked with us for fifty years. The relationship is solid."

"Phil, understand this: I'm a catalyst for change, and a lot of long-term relationships are going to be severed. Particularly ones where I think we've been screwed or under-serviced. Now, this has been a great account for you, low risk and high yielding; almost the perfect bank customer."

Kendall didn't like the way the conversation was going. He'd been fast-tracked for big things in the bank, but if he lost a top-two-hundred-company, there'd be hell to pay with his bosses. He didn't need this. "When can I come and see you, Douglas?"

"I have some time next Tuesday morning. I'd like you to bring your South Yarra branch manager, Jonathan Bardon, and one of your lending managers, Colin Sarll, with you. Can you arrange that?"

"Yes, of course, but they won't have anything to do with Mercury's account, so may I ask why?" Kendall said, choosing his words carefully.

"I'll let you know on Tuesday morning. Is nine-thirty okay for you?"

"Yes. I'll get back to you if there's a problem with the other two."

"There won't be a problem, Phil, but if there is make it go away. That's what good managers do you know. Goodbye."

Neil Widge had been terribly upset and suffered a dreadful shock. In less than ten minutes, twenty-six years of loyal service had disappeared. Kurt listened to him and was sympathetic, but the new CEO was not to be messed with, and he still had a deadline to meet. He was a good manager and had delegated the reports to two of his assistants while he escorted Widge off the premises in a tactful, but efficient manner. At exactly one o'clock he knocked on Aspine's door and said, "I have those reports."

"Good. Let me have them."

Aspine quickly perused them, and they were as expected. Eighty percent of the company's employees were based in Victoria. He paused and reread one of the reports, before letting out a low-pitched whistle.

"Is there something wrong?"

"Half our employees are over fifty, and we only have two hundred under twenty-five. Jesus, we're a company full of geriatrics. How did that occur?"

"We have many long-serving employees. Mercury has been a good and fair company to work for, so we lose very few employees."

"Fair or cushy?"

Before Kurt could respond, Aspine let out another whistle. "We've got nearly a hundred employees on light duties, WorkCover or extended sick leave. Christ, we're a nursing home for the old and infirmed."

"We're a caring company and our employees repay us with loyalty and hard work."

"Bullshit! I'll take these reports home with me, and we'll talk again tomorrow. You can take me around the offices and warehouse now, but don't introduce me to anyone unless I ask. I don't want to be meeting those who mightn't be here on Friday."

"You're going to make some retrenchments?"

"Yes. Six hundred," Aspine replied, not batting an eyelid.

"Si-six hun-hundred. You-you ca-can't be serious. Are you-you going to cons-consult the unions?"

"Why should I? Come on, Kurt, I'd like a tour of the warehouse."

The intercom buzzed, and Shirley said, "It's Harry Denton, Mr. Aspine, he wants to talk to you about Neil Widge."

"Tell him I'm busy, and get him to call me at home tonight."

"He won't like it."

"Just tell him, Shirley!"

- 4 -

DUSK WAS SETTING, and the street lights were flickering, as Aspine swung the Ferrari into his driveway. He got out and patted it like it was a dog that he loved. The door from the house to the garage opened, and Barbara said, "Harry Denton's on the phone. He's called three times. He sounds agitated."

"Shit! Did he give you a hard time?"

"No. He's been a perfect gentleman, but he sounds stressed."

"What a pity."

"I don't understand."

"Pity he didn't insult you."

"I'm still not with you."

"Don't worry about it. I'll take it in the study."

"Yes, Harry."

"I want you to take Neil Widge back as financial controller."

"He resigned and, as far as I'm concerned, that's it."

"He was under stress, and you baited him. You know what you did. You coerced him into quitting."

"So he stuffed up, and then ran to you to fix things."

"I don't want to argue about it. I'm telling you to take him back."

"You're telling me." Aspine chuckled. "Understand this, Harry, you're no longer CEO and the resignation of executives, other than me, is not your concern. I've accepted Widge's resignation, and I've already instructed management consultants to find a new financial controller."

The phone went quiet, but Aspine could hear heavy, labored breathing. "Harry, are you still there?"

"If you won't reinstate him, I want him properly compensated."

"We've done that. We paid him every cent he was legally entitled to."

"You know what I mean. Don't play games with me. I want you to pay him what you would've, had you sacked him."

"For the third and last time, this has nothing to do with you as a non-executive director. Now butt out and let me get on with my job."

"I'll raise it at the next board meeting, and I'll get the board to approve payment. There's more than legalities involved, there are morals."

"You do that. Look, I'm tired, I'm hungry, and I don't want you calling me at home."

"That's not what you told Shirley."

"Sorry, Harry. What I meant was, don't call me again anywhere. If you want to talk to me, do it through the chairman," Aspine said, slamming the phone down.

"Bad call?" Barbara asked, brushing her lips across his.

"No, it's fine. Where are the kids?"

"School barbecue. I'm picking them up in an hour. Would you like dinner now?"

"Yeah, get me a toasted ham and tomato sandwich. I'll have it in here. I've got a lot to get through. Oh, and don't prepare dinner for me until I say. You should eat with the kids until I get on top of this company."

"That's fine. Mark asked me about the China trip again today. Do we have enough money to let him go? His heart's set on it, and all his friends are going," Barbara said, her face drawn.

Aspine smiled. "I told you that our money problems are over. If they weren't how could I afford that red monster in the garage?"

She looked down at the floor. "You've had expensive cars on finance before, and we've still been in trouble."

"Fuck. You never let up, do you? Listen to me! I'll arrange a credit card for you next Tuesday with a hundred thousand dollar limit. In the meantime anything the kids' want, which you approve of, is fine. If that's all, I've got heaps to get through."

"I'm sorry," she said, sniffling, "the school's call chasing fees last week freaked me out."

"Sure. You'd better get going if you're going to pick the kids up on time."

"You're right. I'll get your sandwich and coffee when I get back."

Aspine spread the summaries of the company's employees across his desk and with a yellow marker began running lines through age groups and locations. His preference was simple but not practical. He wanted to sack all employees over sixty, then all those over fifty-five, working his way down until he had six hundred. However, this would provide the grounds for a discrimination action, which he wanted to avoid. No, there would have to be a cross-section of employees terminated, but he only intended to retrench a minimal number below the age of twenty-five. The thirty employees on extended sick leave could be terminated, or their wages could be stopped, without recrimination. He mused: these would be the easy thirty. The remaining seventy employees on this list were on light duties and WorkCover, and their removal would be tougher. In theory, bringing employees who had suffered workplace injuries back to work on light duties for a few hours a day was fine. In practice it was diabolical; as most of these employees soon realized that working in the store or a site office, was far cushier than laboring on a construction site. The effect being that far too many employees ended up in these soft locations and couldn't be removed because they were on WorkCover. Experience told Aspine that if injured workers weren't back working full-time within six weeks of an accident, they would most likely have forgotten how to work. He sure as hell didn't want to keep them on the payroll.

Aspine smirked when he drove into Mercury's car-park and saw the yellow lines, and the sign behind it — *Mr. D Aspine CEO*. Shirley's job was safe for another day.

She greeted him confidently. "Good morning, Mr. Aspine."

She obviously thought her longevity, and connections with the other directors made her flame-proof. She was in for some sad news, but not while he still had a use for her. "Do you think so? Get me a coffee and then organize a meeting for ten o'clock in the boardroom. Jack Gillard, Tim Farmer, Brian Eppel and Anthony Keen. Ask Kurt to come and see me at nine forty-five."

"Yes, Mr. Aspine," she said while answering the phone. She looked up, putting her hand over the mouthpiece. "Mr. Dwyer for you."

"Put him through."

"You thieving bastard!"

"I'm sorry, I'm not with you."

"You already had a job when you were crapping on about your kids, and taking six months to find another position," Dwyer snarled. "I ought to sue you."

"Read your waiver agreement, Bob. We both waived all past, present, and future legal rights, so there's nothing you can do — except bleed that is," Aspine laughed. "I didn't think you'd call. Don't you have any pride? Now you have a good day because you've made mine. And Bob–"

The sound of dial tone echoed down the line.

Kurt knocked on the door. "You wanted to see me, Mr. Aspine."

"Kurt, listen to me carefully. My name's Douglas, and that's how I want you to address me. Now tell me about Tim Farmer."

"He's been with the company for forty years. Started as an apprentice, then went into sales as a liaison clerk, then out onto the road as a sales representative, and finally, he was appointed sales manager about ten years ago."

Aspine groaned, "You mean he's never had another employer, and the only sales managers he's ever worked for were employed by Mercury?"

"Yes, that's right. He's a good man."

"Yeah, I'm sure. What about Anthony Keen?"

"He's been our supply manager for nearly twenty years."

"How old is he?"

"Mid-fifties, but he's very fit. He's into orienteering."

"Brian Eppel?"

Kurt looked down at his feet and shifted uneasily. "Fifty-one. He's headed up design and engineering for twelve years, and before that was employed by Leighton."

"God, is there anyone in the company under fifty? Give me the bad news about Jack Gillard."

"He's senior project manager. He's been with us about six years, and you'll be pleased to know he's only thirty-eight."

"Shit, some good news. How did that come about?"

"When the vacancy arose, we couldn't convince any of our project managers to apply, so we had to advertise. Jack was the best applicant."

"Why?"

"I'm not sure. They probably didn't think they had the necessary skills."

"No, that wasn't the reason. Their jobs were too cushy to run the risk of taking on something more demanding. Do we have one on-site project manager under fifty?"

"No, the youngest is fifty-two."

"Why doesn't that surprise me? Before the others join us, I want to brief you on how we're going to handle the retrenchments. The thirty on extended sick leave are the easiest. I want the remaining five hundred and seventy to predominantly be the over-fifties, but not to the extent that it looks discriminatory. We need to be discreet."

"But it is discriminatory."

"You obviously didn't hear me. The retrenchments will be across the whole workforce. I saw a lot of fatties when we went for our walk around the offices and warehouse. Get rid of them; they're candidates for heart attacks and more bloody WorkCover claims. And make sure your people don't employ fatties in the future."

"That's shockingly discriminatory. Are you going to give that to me in writing?"

"Don't be fucking stupid and don't you put it in writing either.

And make sure your people know we're no longer in the business of employing fat, unhealthy bastards."

The intercom buzzed, and Shirley said, "The others are in the boardroom."

"Let them know we'll be a few more minutes," Aspine said.

"One last thing, Kurt. We need to reduce the seventy employees on WorkCover. They've either got to get back to their normal duties or get out. No more pussyfooting around. Do you understand?"

"You can't sack or retrench employees on WorkCover," Kurt responded indignantly.

"There are ways. I'll let you know. Let's join the others in the boardroom."

Aspine took the chair at the head of the boardroom table. "Gentlemen, as you know, I'm Douglas Aspine, your new CEO. I've called you together because we're about to make some retrenchments, and–"

The white-haired man with the ruddy complexion and large stomach interrupted. "We've never retrenched anyone. Not in the forty years I've been here. Harry, would never let it happen. Does he know?"

This is the excuse for a sales manager Aspine thought. "Tim, don't interrupt me again, or you'll be the first one out the door. As I was about to say, we need to reduce our workforce by five hundred and seventy. Of that number, seventy will come from our interstate branches and five hundred from Victoria."

Tim Farmer let out an audible gasp but didn't say anything; Brian Eppel stared blankly at the wall; Anthony Keen looked down at the table. The young man with the transparent white skin, freckles and bright red hair, who Aspine knew to be Jack Gillard, displayed no emotion.

"Kurt has the numbers and the areas where they're going to come from, and he'll brief you. Jack, you're going to have to get rid of three hundred from our sites."

"This is shocking," Tim Farmer moaned. "It's never happened before. I feel sick."

"The number of employees should have never been permitted to rise to this level, but the problem has to be fixed," Aspine said coldly.

"But we've been making money," Farmer insisted.

"Tim, the profits have been shithouse. Not much better than bank interest. I'm going to fix that."

"Douglas, you haven't said when the retrenchments will occur."

"This Friday, Jack, but I want to stress the need for secrecy. If the union finds out before then, it'll cause trouble. Outside of this office no-one knows, so if word leaks out, it'll be very unpleasant for the leaker."

"But...if that happens you won't know who–"

"You're right, Tim, but I'm sure I'll be able to narrow it down to one or two, who I'll have no option but to remove. Are you clear on that?"

"I won't say a word," Farmer sniffled.

Brian Eppel was twisting his mustache and nervously tugging at his ear. "Is there no way of avoiding the retrenchments?" he asked, standing and pulling himself up to all of his one hundred and sixty centimeters, as he started to pace around the table.

"No, Brian. For Christ's sake sit down, I'm getting a sore neck," Aspine barked.

Anthony Keen, the tall distinguished-looking gray-haired supply manager, finally spoke. "Do we work on the basis that last on is first off?"

"Of course, we fucking don't. We work on the basis that you keep the good employees irrespective of when they started and get rid of the deadwood. Fuck, Anthony, you sound like a trade unionist, not a manager."

In twenty years Harry Denton had never spoken to him like that, and the smooth, urbane Anthony Keen, bit his tongue and seethed.

"We have an Enterprise Bargaining Agreement with the construction workers, and there's going to be hell to pay with the unions on Friday. Don't be surprised if they close our sites down."

"Yeah, I know, Jack. I can stand a little bit of pain for an awful lot of gain," Aspine said, grimacing. "Is there anything else? If not, you should liaise with Kurt about the administration. Tim, don't go. I have a few things I want to discuss with you."

Tim Farmer's hands twitched nervously, and his eyes blinked rapidly. He knew what had happened to Neil Widge, and had no intention of being sucked into resigning.

"Tim, what did your highest paid sales rep earn last year?"

"Eighty thousand."

'That's fucking terrible. How can that be? What's the breakdown between salary and commission?"

"We don't pay commission. Never have."

Aspine rolled his eyes. "Christ, please tell me you're joking. The only way to pay sales reps is by minimal retainer and generous commission. Your star rep should be earning at least three hundred thousand, and anyone earning eighty or less should be shown the door. Haven't you heard about the Kevin Dennis Motors sales incentive plan?"

"No," Farmer responded, starting to sweat.

"The lowest earning salesman for the month gets sacked — each and every month. Do we sell finance?"

"No."

"Urban's a major competitor, and it does. How do we compete?"

"We sell on quality and price."

"And Urban doesn't? Jesus, we're trying to compete with one arm tied behind our back. Do we sell off-the-plan?"

"No. That'd be catering to the sleazy end of the market."

"Do you know some of Australia's wealthiest people buy penthouses and apartments off-the-plan?"

"No," Farmer said, flushing and wishing the interrogation was over.

"Do we accept insurance bonds as deposits?"

"No. We only take checks, bank checks, and cash."

"Why doesn't that surprise me?" Aspine groaned. "I've heard enough. We'll talk again after the retrenchments are behind us."

"Shirley, who do I talk to at our PR firm?" Aspine bellowed.

"We don't have a public relations firm, Mr. Aspine. Harry could never understand what use they were."

"Shit!"

He picked up the phone and hit Jeremy's speed-dial number. "Jeremy, it's Doug. Do you have a contact in a top notch public relations firm?"

"Of course, old boy. Wesley Bracken at Bracken & Methven. Give me five minutes to clear the way. He may not take a cold call from you."

"Okay, Jeremy. Give me a buzz if there's a problem. Oh, and keep a lookout for a good young sales manager."

"You haven't sacked Tim Farmer?"

"Not yet. Early next week, I expect."

"Are you looking for someone in the industry?"

"Preferably, but an ex-used car salesman would be fine."

Jeremy laughed. "You're joking."

"No, I'm not. I want someone who's innovative and knows how to sell."

"I understand. I think I have someone on my books who you'll find interesting."

Barely five minutes had elapsed before Wesley Bracken called. "You're going to retrench six hundred?"

"That's what I said."

"It's going to be national news. The unions will go crazy, and you're going to be under severe pressure. I don't think the prime minister or treasurer will say anything, but the Victorian Premier will no doubt castigate you."

"I'm not worried about the unions. They'll bleat and carry on for a while. They might even threaten to, or go on strike, but in the end, they'll come to heel."

"That's operational. I'm not concerned about that, but we need to plan what you're going to say to the media. What are you going to say when they ask you why the retrenchments took place?"

"That's easy. The company's overstaffed and inefficient."

"Wrong. You'll say you don't look at it as retrenching six hundred workers, but saving the jobs of three thousand six hundred."

"I like it."

"You'll have to say it with sincerity. The journos will crucify you if they think you're bullshitting. You have to express regret and show compassion."

"So you want me to take calls from them?"

"No, I don't. We'll set up a press conference, and I'll be sitting next to you. I want you to come into our offices on Thursday night, and we'll role-play it. We'll try and anticipate every question you're going to be asked, and provide you with the politically correct responses. We'll advise you on what you should wear, how you should act, and we'll show you videos of media conferences where matters like this have been successfully handled. You're in good hands."

"Will we hold it here?"

"Shit no. If we do, the media will try and interview retrenched employees. There'll be tears, stories about not being able to meet mortgage payments, loyalty and past service counting for nothing, and anything else that makes you look bad. They still might interview disgruntled employees, but we don't want to make it easy for them. We'll book a meeting room in the city."

"Thanks, Wes. I'll see you in your offices on Thursday night."

Aspine could hardly wait to call his chairman with the news. "Ed, it's Douglas Aspine. I thought I should give you the courtesy of letting you know that I'm instituting the first cultural changes this Friday. I'm retrenching six hundred."

The phone went quiet. "You've moved a little faster than I thought you would," Sir Edwin eventually said, coughing nervously. "I had Harry Denton on the phone complaining to me that you tricked Neil Widge into resigning. But six hundred; he's going to be uncontrollable when he finds out."

"It has to happen, there's no sense procrastinating."

"You're right, but the fallout's going to be nasty. I'm glad you've let me know. At least I can be prepared for Harry. Do you want me there on Friday?"

"No. I've briefed a PR firm, and it'll be better if you're not around."

"Yes, you're right. Good luck, Douglas."

It was dull and overcast on Friday morning, and Aspine sensed the gloom as he climbed the stairs. Word had obviously leaked, as he'd known it would — perhaps it was the payroll department when they'd been instructed to prepare the final wages, or the project managers, or the quarry managers, or the branch managers. He was surprised that Harry Denton hadn't called him. Perhaps Sir Edwin had headed him off? He was wearing a charcoal gray suit, white shirt, a conservative tie and black shoes — just as Wes Bracken had instructed him. He'd been surprised by Wes's youth, but quickly realized that the young, good-looking man with dark hair, piercing brown eyes and a flashing smile was savvy and street smart. It'd been a long night, and he had been grilled with every conceivable question the media could ask. Wes had told him when to look sad and serious, when to drop his eyes, when to express compassion, and when to lower his voice to a near whisper. He'd been told not to fidget, shift his eyes from side to side, argue with the media or be smug and sarcastic. A meeting room had been booked in Collins Street, near the Stock Exchange, and the media conference was scheduled for four o'clock. Wes had said that he had some favors owed to him, and he'd get his contacts to ask a few tame questions.

"Kurt," Aspine yelled into the intercom, "is everything going to plan?"

"Yes, Mr. A…Doug."

"That's better. Now that wasn't so hard, was it? Keep me in the loop. As soon as you've completed the retrenchments, I want a full report."

"Don't worry," Kurt replied, his voice heavy with resignation. "I have teams at each site, and I've instructed the branch managers. It'll be over by two o'clock."

- 5 -

NEWS OF THE retrenchments was across all of the popular Melbourne radio stations by three o'clock. The secretary of the Construction Employees Union expressed outrage that the union had not been consulted, and the Enterprise Bargaining Agreement had been breached. Sympathetic talkback jocks took calls from angry retrenched workers and milked their rage for all it was worth. The Victorian premier criticized the management of Mercury and said the government would look at providing short-term assistance to the retrenched workers. The prime minister declined to comment but expressed sympathy and concern for the workers.

Aspine met Wes and his assistants in the car-park of the building where the media conference was being held, and they took an elevator to the sixteenth floor. Aspine found the room surprisingly large, but only half a dozen chairs were occupied, and only one television station was in attendance. "Why's the room so large, Wes? How many do you expect to attend?"

"Don't worry, about thirty or so. I don't like small intimate rooms where these bastards can feed off each other."

"Yeah, I understand," Aspine said, ambling toward the front table.

"Not too casual, Douglas. Look down at your feet, and when you sit down don't look at the pricks; drop your eyes to the table. I've got a few of my contacts here, and they'll feed you some easy questions," Wes said, his face drawn in mock concern.

There was a flurry of activity at the door, and they looked up to see two Channel Sixteen cameramen followed by an attractive woman wearing a smart mauve suit and oversized sunglasses. She was smaller than she appeared on television, but well put together and her dark black hair shone.

"What's Fiona Jeczik doing here? Her stories are about fashion, food, health and diet. Why would *Your Family Today* have any interest in this?" Aspine muttered, under his breath.

Wes was unconcerned. "Don't worry. She's probably having a quiet day and looking to fill in a couple of minutes on her show tonight."

There were close to forty in the room when Aspine stood up, introduced himself and read a prepared speech. His face was solemn as he told of his anguish and concern for those who had been retrenched. As he was sitting down, the first question came from the floor.

"Why'd you really sack 'em? To cut costs and increase profits?"

"No, no. I had no choice. Had the retrenchments not taken place, the positions of the remaining three thousand six hundred employees would have been in jeopardy," Aspine responded, brushing a large white handkerchief under his eyes.

"Why didn't you consult the employees or their union?"

"There wasn't time. I had to be decisive if I was going to ensure the continuity of the company and its ongoing employees."

"The company had over twenty million in cash at last balance date. Why don't you admit that you made the sackings to preserve it for your shareholders?"

"No, that's not right. I thought about our stakeholders, our suppliers, the people who we owe money to, our customers, the community, the charities we support, and of course the employees who we'll go forward with. Let me assure you, Mercury is a good corporate citizen."

"So the company's not broke then?"

"No, but that's not to say it wouldn't have got into trouble had this action not been taken," Aspine said somberly while smiling to himself. This was far easier than he had anticipated, and he felt himself relaxing.

Fiona Jeczik's voice was sweeter than it sounded on television. "Is it true that you've only been with the company five days, Mr. Aspine?"

"Yes, that's right."

"Do you have a company car?" She smiled.

Bitch! He knew where she was going, and he kicked Wes hard under the table.

"What's the point of the question, Ms. Jeczik?" Wes said, sharply.

She ignored him. "It's a million dollar Ferrari isn't it?"

A few gasps came from the other journos, and the mood of the meeting noticeably changed.

"No, it's not," Aspine snapped.

"What the million dollars or the Ferrari?" She smiled, her perfect white teeth contrasting with her flawless olive skin.

Aspine felt himself staring directly into the cameras and his eyes shifting from side to side. He quickly dropped them to the table.

"Does anyone else have a question?" Wes asked.

Again she ignored him. "Is it true that your salary and bonuses will exceed five million this year?"

Fucking bitch! Who leaked? "No!"

"Isn't it true that you're on a million dollar cash bonus if you can increase profits by fifty percent?" she asked, her dark eyes twinkling.

"That's confidential. I'm not going to answer that."

"You just did, Mr. Aspine. You just did." She laughed. "How does it feel to have the blood of six hundred families on your hands just to increase your personal wealth?" Her smile turned to a sneer of disgust.

Aspine was sweating, touching the knot of his tie, feeling his shirt cuffs, and twitching; no matter where he looked, those fucking cameras followed him. He nudged Wes hard in the ribs.

"Ms. Jeczik, what you said is untrue and defamatory," Wes blustered.

"Sue me then. I'd love to stay and ask more questions, but I have a deadline to meet."

As she stood to leave a flurry of questions came from the journos all related to Aspine's salary, bonus, and car. The media pack smelled blood and were baying for more.

"Ladies and gentlemen, I think we've been more than fair, but we only booked this room for an hour. I thank you for your attendance, but we have to bring this conference to a close," Wes said.

One of Wes's assistants punched the elevator button to the car-park. The mood was tense, and Aspine was black with rage as he muttered, "Fucking bitch, fucking bitch." Then he turned and glared at Wes. "I was told you were the best, but you let me get ambushed. You ever do that again, and you can shove your public relations firm up where it best fits."

"It wasn't our fau–"

"Yes, it was. You were blindsided. You never anticipated that bitch being there. You goofed up."

There was a piece of paper under his windscreen wiper. 'I was right about the Ferrari, but not the million dollars? How much was it? Nine hundred and ninety-nine thousand?' *Bitch. Bitch. Bitch* he thought, tearing it into pieces. He turned his cell phone on and listened to his messages. There were three from Harry Denton, which were barely decipherable and sounded like he was having a heart attack. Two were from the union's secretary, and one from the organizer. There were three anonymous calls, probably from ex-employees, threatening to kill him. The only one he'd return was from Sir Edwin, but even he could wait. His head was aching, and he felt a migraine coming on. He needed to see Charlie — desperately.

He hit her speed dial, and dispensing with any cordiality, snapped, "Meet me in that wine bar off Chapel Street in thirty minutes."

"You mean the Greville Bar?"

"Yeah, and, Charlie get a cab or walk there."

"Sure, darling. I'll see you soon," she murmured nervously. She knew he'd had a bad day and that she was about to hear all about it while he drank himself senseless. She far preferred it when he visited, had sex and went home — sometimes she even enjoyed it when he was in a buoyant mood, but that was rare. When he drank, he became morose, evil tempered and sadistic. She showered quickly, not wanting to be late, and threw on a yellow blouse, white slacks and flat sandals that wouldn't hurt her feet on the fifteen-minute walk. The Ferrari was parked in front of the Greville, and when she entered the small intimate bar, he was sitting at one of the tables, sipping red wine while staring vacantly over the top of his glass.

She bent down and kissed him. "Hi, hon."

"What are you drinking?" he grunted, pushing his car keys over to her. "Make sure you don't dent it or there'll be hell to pay."

"Mineral water," she replied, a sense of dread coming over her.

For the next two hours, he related his day over and over, his face becoming darker and darker while he drank two bottles of red. She'd seen him like this before when the only effect the alcohol had was to drive him into a rage. "Fucking bitch," he growled, for the tenth time. "What do you think?"

She knew she couldn't say anything that would appease him. "Why don't we go home and go to bed, Doug? It'll make you feel better."

"Later. I need a drink," he said, catching the barman's eye. "Let me have another bottle of the same."

She excused herself to go to the toilet and every male eye in the bar ogled her. When she returned he was seething and imagined her hair was jet black, her skin dark brown, her nose more aquiline and that she was wearing deep red lipstick.

"Fucking bitch," he shouted, and the bar went silent.

She put her hand on his arm. "Doug, Doug, it's me."

He shook his head, and the image of Fiona Jeczik faded.

"Let's go home, Doug. Come on, hon."

A big, strapping, blonde-haired man, who'd been drinking at the bar, sauntered over and asked. "Are you all right, Miss? Is he annoying you? Can I do anything to help?"

Before she could answer, Aspine snarled, "Fuck off!"

The big man ignored him. "Miss?"

"I'm fine," she lied.

Charlie hoped that Aspine would flake on the drive to her apartment, but he sat bolt upright, muttering words that were indecipherable, other than bitch. She parked near the elevator and went around to the car's passenger side to help him.

"I'm all right," he slurred, pushing her away.

He slumped out of the elevator and stumbled down the corridor to the apartment, collapsing on the sofa and using the remote to flick on the television.

"Would you like coffee?"

"Get me a Jack Daniels."

She waited for her coffee to brew and hoped he would be asleep by the time she returned to the living room. He wasn't. Instead, he was sitting on the edge of the sofa with his eyes glued to the television, watching the late night news. She heard the word Mercury, and Fiona Jeczik was smiling from the screen, before the camera panned to Doug, his eyes shiftily darting from side to side.

"Doug," Charlie said, reaching out to hand him his drink. She moved her head at the last moment and his fist clipped her shoulder before glancing off her forehead. She was dazed and staggering when he stood up and threw her on the carpet, crashing down on top of her. "Fucking bitch," he shouted as he started tearing her clothes off. She didn't struggle, but lay still, closed her eyes, bit her lip and prayed it would be quick. She felt his full weight slump on her and knew it was over. His breathing became heavy, and he fell into a deep, drunken sleep. She lay trapped under him, tears running down her cheeks. Hours later she awoke — he was gone — all she was wearing was the yellow blouse, and she felt cold and dirty. She shuffled into the bathroom and took a near boiling shower in a futile attempt to physically and mentally cleanse herself.

Barbara shook her husband hard. "Wake up, wake up, Sir Edwin's on the phone."

His head was thumping, and it felt like someone had thrown glass in his eyes. His throat was parched, he couldn't remember anything after leaving the wine bar and had no idea how he had got home. "What time is it?" he rasped.

"It's just gone nine. You didn't get home until five. Where were you all night?"

"Pass me the phone and get me a glass of water," he grunted, trying to generate some saliva to ease his burning throat. "Good morning, Ed."

"Douglas, you didn't return my call."

"I was flat out all day. I ran out of time."

"You should've made time. Harry's called an emergency board meeting. They want to remove you. They wanted to hold it on Monday, but I said I wasn't available and pushed it out until Friday. Harry's as mad as hell."

He sipped the water and felt it lubricating his throat. "Is that all?" He laughed.

"You're not worried?"

"It's too late. There's nothing they can do. I'm going to enjoy teaching them the business facts of life."

"You're remarkably calm. They have a majority on the board, and they're going to sack you. I'm not sure I can save you."

"Don't lose any sleep over it, Ed. They're not sacking anyone. Thanks for the call. I'll see you on Friday."

"I wish you'd call when you're going to be late. I was about to start phoning the hospitals and police stations. Is one call too much?" Barbara asked.

He thought about bullshitting that he'd been out with clients, but she knew about his extra-marital affairs and, so long as he didn't flaunt his conquests in front of her precious girlfriends, she ignored them.

"No, it's not. I'll try and remember next time. Is Trevor home?" he asked, anxious to change the subject.

"Yes. Why?"

"I thought I'd take him out and buy that car he's been pestering me about."

Barbara visibly brightened. "That'll be nice. I'll tell him. How long will you be?"

"As long as it takes to shower, have breakfast and skim-read the papers."

"You won't be skim-reading them. Your photo's in *The Age* and *Financial Review*, and the commentaries aren't flattering. I'll tell Trevor you'll be ready by midday."

The sackings were front page news, and Aspine was castigated by reporters, unions, employees, social groups and the state government. Everyone was against him, except investors and traders who engaged in heavy buying of the company's shares pushing their price up by seven percent. He mused that the silent people with the money must approve of his strategy. The articles were no more than what he had expected, and luckily only one reporter raised the discrimination issue about the over-fifties, and what he described as the overweight. Andrew Lawson, the secretary of the union, was reported as saying that he would meet with Mercury's management and demand the reinstatement of all workers. Failing this, the union would seek four weeks retrenchment pay per employee for each year worked. The hangover was wearing off, and Aspine grinned — he'd tell Lawson to fuck off. With luck, the dopey prick would take the rest of the workforce out on strike, or do something equally stupid. There was an article hidden at the back of the *Financial Review* about Russell Ridgeway, CEO of ANQ Insurance, and the salary package he had negotiated, that amounted to nearly fifty million over three years. Ridgeway had done a mighty job turning the ailing insurer around, but as Aspine read the article he felt sick with envy.

"This is a terrific car, Dad. Have you tested it out yet?" Trevor asked.

"I haven't, and I don't intend to," Aspine replied, dropping the gears back a cog, as he changed lanes and accelerated to pass a slower vehicle hogging the passing lane.

"Shit! Did you feel that? You passed him like he was standing. Can I have a drive?"

"No, you can't. You couldn't handle a car like this. Maybe in twenty years or so. Have you got your mind set on any particular car today?"

"Yeah, I'd like a WRX or a good second-hand Nissan ZX."

"They're far too powerful. I was thinking of a Corolla or Pulsar."

"Shit! They're girls' cars. The guys will take the piss out of me if they see me driving that crap. Who are you to talk anyhow? How fast does this thing go? Three hundred and fifty clicks an hour?"

"Mind your language or you'll get nothing. I've been driving for twenty-seven years, and all you've done is take a few lessons. I should buy you one of those old boxy Volvos. Now there's a good, safe car."

"You do that, and I won't drive it. I'll stick it in front of the house, and it can sit there," Trevor responded, his eyes angry and defiant.

"Son, I was joking about the Volvo, but forget about the grunt cars. We'll find a well-maintained Ford or Toyota for about ten thousand, and get it mechanically checked before buying. How's that sound?"

"Yeah, a Ford's okay, but I'd rather a WRX."

"Forget it. When you're twenty-one and have your own money you can choose what you want. I'm not buying a WRX for you to go out and kill yourself. End of story. Do you want to look at Fords, or not?"

"I suppose I'll have to."

The Sting phone tone echoed around the car. "Hello."

"Mr. Aspine?" A male with a distinctly Cockney accent asked.

"Yeah, who is this?"

"Andrew Lawson, from the Construction Employees Union. I need to see you."

"Make an appointment with my PA."

"I need to see you today, Mr. Aspine, today. You don't think you can breach the Enterprise Bargaining Agreement, sack more than four hundred of our members, and expect that we're not going to do anything about it, do you?"

"Listen you Pommy bastard, I don't care what you do, but we're sure as hell not meeting today. Your members weren't sacked, they were retrenched; they're not going to be reinstated, or paid one more cent than they've already received. Do I make myself clear?"

"What about tomorrow then?" Lawson responded, ignoring the insult.

"Call my PA on Monday. If I can squeeze you in, I will."

"You know we can close Mercury down, don't you, Mr. Aspine?"

"You do that, and I'll retrench another four hundred by the end of the week. You have no idea how bad the business is going, so I'd be careful if I were you."

There was a long pause. "I'll see you on Monday then. I'll have one of our organizers, Henry McBain, with me. And understand this, Mr. Aspine; our lawyers will be seeking orders restraining you from making further sackings."

"If I can fit you in, I will. Goodbye."

"What was that about, Dad?"

"Just a whining Pommy commie. Jeez, how come you never run across an American shop steward or organizer?"

- 6 -

SUNDAY'S NEWSPAPERS WERE filled with tear-jerking human interest stories and the hardship facing Mercury's retrenched employees. *The Age* cartoonist depicted a crowd of slaves surrounding a prancing black stallion, pulling a Ferrari red chariot driven by a Roman Centurion, a caricature of Aspine, with the caption *Throw them to the lions*. Aspine stared at it and cursed Fiona Jeczik for what must have been the hundredth time.

As Aspine drove along St Kilda Road in peak hour Monday morning traffic, he reflected on the events of the prior week. Try as he might, he couldn't remember anything about Friday night after leaving the Greville. He had flashbacks where he was punching that bitch Jeczik in the face, but he knew they were just pleasant daydreams. He also sensed that he had upset Charlie, but couldn't remember how. He'd send her flowers when he got to the office and, no matter what he had said or done, he was sure that she would forgive him.

He was still two hundred meters from the gates to Mercury's offices when he saw the placards, tents, barbecues and a large group of former employees and their families. As they saw the Ferrari, they moved to block the entrance and he heard booing and hissing before an egg splattered across his windscreen. He angrily pushed the door open, his flashing eyes searching for the egg thrower; but before he could do anything, he caught sight of the television cameras and checked himself. "This picket's illegal, and if I have to call the police to remove you I will," he said, not addressing anyone in particular.

This resulted in another burst of catcalls, and a closing of the ranks to completely block the entrance. He cursed, knowing that he would have driven straight through the picket, had the television crews not been there. As he pondered his next move, someone said, "Let him through. We're stopping ingoing and outgoing deliveries, not employees."

There were howls of protest, but the tall, gangly man who'd issued the command walked toward the gates, and the picket parted.

Aspine didn't thank or acknowledge him as he climbed back into the Ferrari and drove through the gates, hearing the sound of hands slapping its body. As he got out, he saw a small, youthful looking man sporting a distinct mop of red curly hair wearing a disheveled cheap suit. "We've been waiting for you, Mr. Aspine," he said, the Cockney accent even more pronounced than it'd been over the phone.

"Andrew Lawson, I presume. Are you responsible for this illegal little blockade?"

"Illegal? What's illegal? I don't see anyone on your property. I don't see anyone trespassing. I don't see anyone damaging equipment. What's illegal?"

Before Aspine could respond, the tall man who'd cleared the picket walked up and held his hand out saying, "Henry McBain, union organizer, Mr. Aspine."

Aspine ignored the extended hand and glared at McBain before refocusing on Lawson. "What do you want?"

"I told you on Saturday. We want to meet with you to discuss having our members reinstated and, if that's not possible, we want them adequately compensated."

"No-one's being reinstated, and we've paid them their full legal entitlements."

"Mr. Aspine, you're new to the building industry. Do you know what it does to your costs when you're midway through a concrete pour and the trucks stop delivering, or the men walk off the job?"

"Don't fucking threaten me, you Cockney git. If the CEU takes me on it'll get what the Maritime Worker's Union got from Chris Corrigan. Now let me give you some advice. I'll have security guards with German Shepherds here tomorrow morning to make sure the gateway's kept clear, so you'd be wise to remove your picket,"

Aspine whispered menacingly, his hand covering his mouth as he eyed the television cameras.

"Keep that kind of talk up and we'll shut your business down."

"Do that and I'll retrench another four hundred workers every week of the shutdown."

"No, you won't. Our lawyers are in the Industrial Relations Commission right now, obtaining orders restraining you from making further dismissals."

"We never had these problems with Harry," McBain said. "We worked well with management. We'd like to have the same relationship with you."

Aspine laughed. "Henry, what you mean is that you were screwing poor old Harry, and you'd like to screw me in the same way. It ain't gonna happen, not ever! Look, I've got work to do, so if you're finished, I'd like to get on with it."

"We've hardly scratched the surface. If you think you can treat our members like this and get away with it, you've got another think coming," Lawson snapped.

Aspine had recovered his composure and sarcasm. "You don't give a shit about them. You're more worried about losing members' subscriptions that fund the union-provided car you're driving, and your other little perks."

"I resent that. I look after the brothers like they're family."

"Brothers? Christ, you sound like a follower of Marx."

"I am."

"Harpo, I guess," Aspine said, as he started to walk to the office.

"We're not finished yet," Lawson said, ignoring the slur.

"Yes, we are," Aspine shouted, as he closed the door to the office.

The offices were quiet like someone had just died. There was an absence of conversation; employees were hunched over their desks with their heads down and their bums up. Aspine smiled and wondered if there was another motivator remotely close to fear for effectiveness. He stopped at Shirley's door. "Come into my office."

As she waddled in, Aspine was barking instructions. "Get someone to give my car a wash. Make sure they get all the egg off the windscreen."

"Egg?" she said, the edges of her mouth turning up.

He glared at her. "Did I say something amusing?"

She turned red, and he watched her squirm, before saying, "Get two dozen long-stemmed red roses sent to Charlene Deering. Her address is in my Teledex."

"I have to have an account number. Do you want them charged to you?"

His nostrils flared. "Charge it to advertising or general expenses. Christ, it's a chicken-shit amount. I don't care where you charge it, so long as it's not to me."

She started to say, "But Harr–," and then bit her tongue.

"Type this and let me have it in fifteen minutes," he said, passing her a draft of Tim Farmer's resignation. He enjoyed watching the color drain from her face. "After you've finished, get him up here."

"Is there anything else?"

"There is. Did you see the board minutes of the meeting where I was appointed?"

She gulped and looked down at her feet. "Yes, yes, I think I did."

"And you also saw the letter of offer?"

"Yes."

"Did you tell anyone about the Ferrari?"

"The Ferrari?"

"Yes," he growled. "Did you tell anyone that I drove a Ferrari?"

Her flabby face turned crimson, and her hands were trembling. "I might have mentioned it to a few girlfriends."

He didn't say anything and the tension built, as he watched her shift uncomfortably, the underarms of her blouse stained with perspiration. "Is-is that all?" she asked, unable to stand the silence.

He nodded. He hadn't been sure who had leaked his salary package to that Jeczik bitch, but now he knew. Shirley stood to leave, and her legs nearly went from under her, but still he did not speak. His lips were closed in a thin, grim line as she backed nervously out of his office.

The boutique legal firm of Sly & Vogel had acted for Aspine when he had crushed the Vehicle Builder's Union in the Federal Court ten years earlier, and he'd maintained a passing relationship with the firm's senior partner. The receptionist answered, "Good morning, Sly & Vogel."

"It's Douglas Aspine, for Mr. Vogel."

"Will he know what it's about, Mr. Aspine?"

He sighed loudly, "Just let him know who it is. He'll take my call."

"Yes, Mr. Aspine, I'll put you on hold."

He was listening to the tape espousing the legal firm's services when Max Vogel said, "Congratulations, Doug. I've been reading about you in the *Financial Review*."

"Thanks, Max. I'd like you to handle the company's legal work, but first we have a small hiccup that needs to be settled." Aspine then went on to explain his position and the convening of the special board meeting.

"They'd like to terminate my services, but they won't after we teach them the business facts of life."

"What do you have in mind?"

"I want you to prepare a writ, and statement of claim on my behalf, for three years' salary, bonuses, and profits foregone on the conversion of options. Fifteen million dollars! I want copies by Thursday night, and I want you to be ready to issue on Friday."

"No problem. You do understand we'll be acting for you personally."

"Of course. I also need you to prepare a notice to the Stock Exchange regarding my dismissal. If I'm dismissed, I want you to fax it and a copy of the statement of claim to the Exchange immediately."

Vogel emitted a low whistle. "Shit, the share price will go through the floor, and the institutions will go crazy."

"Yeah, that's why they won't sack me."

"When can you get your employment contract to me?"

"I'll leave a copy of it in a sealed envelope at our reception, and you can arrange for a courier to pick it up."

"I'll do that."

"Max, I need you to do something else for me. The CEU's before the Industrial Relations Commission today. They'll claim that I breached the Enterprise Bargaining Agreement, and be seeking reinstatement of the retrenched workers, or an increase in termination benefits. Can you represent the company?"

"Given the circumstances, there's a conflict between us acting for you and also acting for the company. We could instruct someone else on the company's behalf."

"I don't want that. I want you to act for the company."

"You're making it hard. How confident are you that you're not going to be sacked on Friday?"

"There's no possibility that I'll be sacked. Not the remotest." Aspine chuckled.

There was a long pause before Vogel responded. "We'll act for the company against the union, Douglas, but please make sure you don't get sacked."

"I won't. Needless to say, I want you to oppose everything the union puts up."

Tim Farmer tapped lightly on Aspine's door. He looked nervous; his face had lost its ruddiness and was white and drawn. "You wanted to see me."

Aspine didn't ask him to sit down but pushed the letter to the edge of his desk. Farmer picked it up and started to read. His eyes watered, and the whole of his body began to shake. "So...this is the end after forty years," he said, his voice shaking. "And you expect me to accept two hundred and fifty thousand dollars."

"It's generous."

"For forty years' loyal service?" Farmer sniffled.

"I'm giving you the opportunity to resign rather than being fired. If I sack you, we'll be paying you the minimum legal entitlement. Sure you might get more in court, but the legal action will drag on for years. Do you want that?"

"And you want me to sign this and waive all my legal rights," Farmer said, crumpling the letter in his hand. "Do I get to take legal advice?"

"Not if you want to walk out of here with a check for quarter of a mil."

"And if I don't sign?"

"I'll fire you. Tim, understand this, in one hour you'll be off these premises. Whether you resign or are sacked is up to you."

Farmer's eyes were running, and his bottom lip was quivering. "I'll sign, you bastard. I hope you rot in hell."

"Shirley," Aspine shouted, "come in and witness Tim's signature," while buzzing Kurt on the intercom. "Kurt, Tim Farmer's resigned. Arrange payment of his final entitlements and then escort him off the premises. After you've done that, come and see me."

"Thanks for being so discreet," Farmer said, his eyes burning with rage.

The Phoenix Security Company was founded by a smart, never-convicted criminal and stand-over man, Marvin Adler in Sydney in 1965. Its genesis had been putting down the anti-Vietnam riots on University Campuses, in a manner that could've never been contemplated by the police. It was a natural extension to expand into labor relations, where Phoenix acted for employers to end strikes in a way best described as coercive, but which Marvin called persuasive. It also provided investigation services, crowd controllers, and bodyguards. It had been linked to racketeering, blackmail and the selling of protection, but had never been successfully prosecuted. The business had expanded nationally and often acted as a third party negotiator for weak employers that lacked the wherewithal to negotiate with militant unions. Phoenix's fees were outrageously high, but were justified by its short mission statement — *we deliver what we promise!* Aspine remembered how effective Phoenix had been in persuading striking employees of the Vehicle Builders Union to terminate their union memberships and return to work. As he picked up the phone, he wondered whether the Victorian manager and part-owner, Tom Donegan, would still be with the company.

"Tom Donegan, please."

There was a pause as the receptionist put him through, then he heard wheezing, followed by a raspy voice that hadn't changed in ten years. "Douglas, it's been a long time. I thought I might hear from you. You've made quite a splash in the media."

"Hello, Tom. I thought you'd be retired by now. I'm glad you're not."

"I'm too busy to retire. Too busy helping people like you." he coughed. "Sorry, bloody cigarettes are killing me."

"I have a small job for you. I need a picket cleared. I think a few of your guys with dogs will be able to handle it. You'll have to be careful though, because there are televisions crews on the picket line."

"We don't have dogs anymore. They projected the wrong company image. We now see ourselves as intermediaries, negotiators, and mediators."

Aspine laughed. "Are you saying you've become respectable and can't help me?"

"Oh, we can still assist you. I can send two of our negotiators out this afternoon who'll remove the picket and, by the way, they'll be as well dressed as you. It'll set you back forty thousand, though."

"Hell, for that type of money I might as well wait them out."

"Yeah, that'd be wise, but you want to send a message, don't you? You can't afford to let that picket line linger for another week. You're worried about losing credibility, aren't you?"

"Yes, I need to act decisively."

"Leave it with us, Douglas. As you know, we can be very persuasive."

Aspine put the phone down, and Shirley buzzed. "Jeremy Smythe wants you to call. He said it was urgent. Andrew Lawson also wants you to call him."

"Jeremy, what's the problem?"

"Thank you for returning my call, Douglas," he responded, the nervousness in his voice palpable. "I'm worried. The publicity's not good. Are things getting out of control?"

"Why do you ask?"

"They're going to try and sack you on Friday."

"Who told you that?"

"Sir Edwin called. He's worried too."

"Oh, I understand. You made the recommendation, and Sir Edwin supported it. Now you're shitting yourselves about looking stupid."

"You have to understand our position."

"Bloody nervous nellies. No-one's going to sack me. You have nothing to worry about."

"How can you be so certain?" Jeremy moaned.

"You don't need to know. Have you found me a financial controller and a sales manager?"

"You've sacked Tim Farmer?"

"Yes, this morning."

"I have two candidates for the finance position. I interviewed a young man this morning who is clever, but lacks poise and experience. I only have one candidate for the sales position, but I think you'll like him. I haven't advertised either position. Do you want me to?"

"No. Fax their CVs to my home and I'll let you know who I want to interview. Oh, I nearly forgot, I need a PA."

"You've fired Shirley?"

"Not yet; she doesn't know it, but she's going on Friday. Her replacement will be young, attractive, modern and well-presented. I don't want anyone who resembles Shirley."

Aspine looked up to see Kurt standing sheepishly at his door. "Come in and take a seat," He snapped. "How was it with Tim?"

"He's bitter and upset, but he's not going to take any action. He's not the type to fight."

"No fire in his belly. That was probably his problem."

Kurt stared at the floor, not saying anything, but letting his body language register his disagreement.

"Anyhow, that's not what I want to talk to you about. I'll be tied up most of Friday, so I need you to do something for me."

Kurt looked up, his face filled with apprehension. "What?"

"I want you to get rid of Shirley. Work out something that'll give her no grounds for legal action, but make sure it's not over the top."

"Why?"

"That's none of your damn business. I've made the decision."

"Why can't you do it before Friday?"

"Because I have an important board meeting to attend, and I don't want to give Harry any more ammunition than he already has."

"So you want me to handle her dismissal and her final remuneration."

"That's right. I have a figure in mind so it'll be interesting to see what you actually pay her. Consider it a test, Kurt. It'll tell me something about you."

-7-

FIONA JECZIK'S WEEKLY drive to the nursing home in Warburton was a time to enjoy her yellow Audi TT and reflect on the past. The only child of a beautiful English mother and a doting Polish father, she'd been raised in a happy household on the outskirts of London. They weren't poor, but needed to work hard for the added luxuries. Her father often toiled sixty-hour weeks as a compositor on Fleet Street, while her mother took in washing and ironing to supplement the family's income. As a young girl, she would sit on her father's knee while he fired questions at her: "What is the capital of Sweden? What is twelve times eleven? How do you spell myth?" To her, it was no more than playing a wonderful game with a man whom she dearly loved but didn't get to see enough. Some weeks he would work seven days straight, leaving before she awoke and arriving home after she'd gone to bed. As she grew older, her father stressed the need for education and pushed her to study, the result being that she was always at the top of her class. By the time she was ten she was fluent in English, French and Polish, knowledgeable about world affairs, and had more than an elementary grasp of politics.

As she entered her teenage years, her idyllic world crashed around her when Rupert Murdoch closed his Fleet Street locations and relocated to new high-tech premises in Wapping, where compositors were no longer needed. There was violence on the streets as News Corp sacked thousands, and the print unions took their members out on strike — a strike that lasted for nearly a year, and all but bankrupted the unions. During this time, Murdoch's newspapers, aided and abetted by Maggie Thatcher, never missed a day's publication.

Fiona's father had been a devoted servant of the *Times* and *Sunday Times* for nearly twenty years, but this counted for nothing, and he became unemployed overnight. Fiona had never seen him drink before but, as the strike dragged on he would have his first vodka by ten o'clock in the morning and still be sitting in the same chair at midnight nursing a glass. Often he was incoherent, and his rambling became indecipherable. Her mother would plead with him, "Petrosh, you can find another job in another industry."

He would slur, "Too old, too old...I'm forty-six. I'm too old to learn something new."

Fiona's mother took in more washing and ironing, cleaned houses, and even babysat in a desperate but futile attempt to make ends meet. As she toiled on relentlessly, she aged; lost weight and her once full face became lined and drawn. Fiona had never seen her mother and father fight before, but arguments and shouting became an every-day occurrence.

Against this background, in November 1987, the Jecziks' spent the last of their savings and boarded a BOAC Jumbo at Heathrow, bound for Melbourne and a new life. They rented a small two-bedroom apartment in North Melbourne, and her father got a job with the *Melbourne Age,* and a little of the family happiness returned. It didn't last, as the previous two years had turned him into a bitter man and, worse, an alcoholic. At night, vodka in hand, he would ramble on about Murdoch the bastard, the loss of their savings and how unfair it had been. The following morning he would rise late for work or would call in sick. Inevitably he was sacked, and the cycle repeated itself until he'd worked for all the local newspapers and none would tolerate him. Fiona's mother was lucky enough to get a job in a super-market, and her wages, plus what she made from washing and iron-ing at night, was just enough to allow them to subsist.

Fiona enrolled in a local high school where her academic brilliance again shone through, culminating with her being dux of the school in 1993. In 1994, on a full scholarship, she commenced an Arts Degree — Media and Communications — at Melbourne University. It was a strange but considered choice, because she had already determined that the media was the most powerful and influential forum known to mankind, and she intended to use it. To help supplement the fami-ly's income, she took part-time jobs at McDonald's and Woolworth's, before stumbling across an ad for a casual receptionist clerk with

Channel Sixteen. The advertisement called for written applications, but this was not for Fiona, so, with CV in hand, she took the luxury of hailing a cab to Channel Sixteen's offices. The receptionist coldly informed her, "The human resources manager doesn't see anyone without an appointment."

"Please, let him know I'm here," Fiona pleaded.

"I'm sorry he's not in." the receptionist said, as the reception doors opened and a good-looking young man entered. "Oh, Mr. Bentine, this young lady would like to see you. I've informed her that she'll have to make an appointment."

Fiona could feel Bentine looking her up and down, and she flashed him a brilliant smile. "Please, Mr. Bentine, I only need five minutes."

"Mr. Bentine's my father, I'm Maurice or better still, Morrie. I can give you five minutes and not a minute more, Miss ...?"

"Fiona, Fiona Jeczik."

An hour and a half later she left Bentine's office having secured the position.

Fiona's role at Channel Sixteen was at the bottom of the food chain: she ran errands, did the filing and filled in on reception. She stayed long after her designated working hours, chatting to the script-writers, mingling with the production staff, watching live current affairs shows and sitcoms, all the time learning. Some of the channel's stars and executives were drawn to her looks, and in the early weeks, she was continually hit on. She became adept at fending off those who she thought might help her in the future with a radiant smile, but those she assessed as of 'no account' were met with an icy stare which said, 'stay away from me'. After completing her degree, she joined Channel Sixteen on a full-time basis. Appointed as a sales executive, which was a fancy television description for a sales representative, she soon found out first-hand the power of ratings and the power of the stars fronting the top-rating programs. In the evenings she hung out with the camera operators and the sound technicians on the sets of live productions, just waiting for an opportunity.

One wet, murky night, just before six o'clock the channel received a call from the Cabrini Hospital advising that Martha Stern, the creator, and presenter of *Your Family Today,* had been involved in a serious car accident. With less than an hour to find a replacement, the management and production staff panicked, and someone suggested Fiona. "Look, it'll only be for one night, and we'll use one of the news presenters tomorrow night. We just have to get over tonight."

So Fiona fronted the cameras for the first time, her radiant looks, flashing smile, impeccable dress and precise presentation beaming into thousands of households around the nation. By noon the following day the worst was over for Martha Stern, but she would not be well enough to host *Your Family Today* for at least another eight weeks. Executives and production staff were unanimous in their praise for Fiona, and it was decided that she would continue to host the show until Martha returned.

Fiona had never been a fan of *Your Family Today* and thought it lightweight, banal and boring. The stories were repetitive; typically about weight loss, diets, women's issues, fashion, health, fitness, and well-being. She was amazed that it occupied the prime six-thirty time slot, but not surprised that it was being killed in the ratings by its two commercial competitors, which televised genuine current affairs programs. Halfway through the eighth week, Fiona was summoned to a senior executive's office and informed that the channel's CEO and significant shareholder, Barry Seymour, had been impressed by her performance and wanted her to continue to anchor the show.

"What about Martha Stern?"

"She's past her 'use-by' date." The senior executive laughed. "Besides, you managed to gain a few rating points. Mind you, it's nothing to boast about because you're still running last."

"Has Martha been told?"

"Fiona, don't worry about her. She'll be well looked after, and so will you. From this Monday, your salary will be quadrupled, and you'll become the permanent host of the show. How does that sound?"

"It's acceptable," she said, knowing that Martha had been paid far more. "Will I have input into the production of the show? Can I change the format? Can we make it more current affairs based?"

"Whoa! Slow down. *Your Family Today* was created to differentiate us from the others. We don't want to copy what they're doing."

"But we're getting killed in the ratings. Why can't we do some investigative journalism, and start breaking stories?"

"Fiona, let us worry about the ratings. Just present the show in its existing format," he condescendingly said.

She bit her tongue hard. "I'll do that," she said, knowing she wouldn't.

During the ensuing two years, Fiona, and a small team of investigative journalists led by her brilliant young producer, Craig Chisholm, broke major stories on loan sharking, prostitution in the suburbs, pedophilia, corporate greed, government rorting, real estate fraud, stock manipulation and insider trading. The day after the stories were aired, she was invariably summoned to a senior executive's office and read the riot act. She would apologize, kowtow and promise that it wouldn't occur again while at the same time planning her next *exposé*. She didn't understand management, as ratings had increased every month since she had first presented *Your Family Today*. It now rated second, although it was a long way behind Roy Merton, who anchored *The Front Page* on Channel Five. Fiona became a slave to the ratings, knowing management might criticize her for changing the format, but wouldn't fire her so long as she continued to pick up points.

The phone call from her father was rambling, teary and slurred. "Yo... your mother has passed away. Victoria has died."

He had never called her Victoria. It had always been Vicky. It was like he was talking about someone else. Fiona felt the sting in her eyes as she fought to maintain her composure, and her voice quivered. "How?" She heard herself ask.

"Heart attack. You muss come home, Fiona. We need to be together," he slurred.

She felt the tears welling up and blinked rapidly, in a forlorn effort to stop them. She was angry. Her mother hadn't died of a 'heart attack', but from overwork as a result of her father's drinking. "I'll be home right after seven.

"You're still going to do your show? You can't."

"I have to. They can't get anyone to replace me in half an hour," she lied, fighting back the urge to choke. She had seen what had happened to Martha Stern and didn't intend to give anyone else the opportunity to impress.

Her father somehow managed to stay sober until the funeral, but later drank himself senseless, wallowing in guilt, self-pity, loss, and anger about the man who had brought this dreadful ill-fortune down upon him.

Despite management's edicts, Fiona continued to take *Your Family Today* deeper into investigative journalism and current affairs. She was at the forefront in condemning the banks for mass retrenchments when they were making record profits; she delivered scathing rebukes on Roy Walton for destroying the lives of thousands of FIF insurance policy holders; and Sydney Filder and Gene Askin for insider trading. Night after night she bombarded the Australian Securities and Investment Commission (ASIC) and the Director of Public Prosecutions (DPP) for what she saw as their weak-kneed efforts in bringing Mike Blizzard to justice. Ratings soared and *Your Family Today* finally knocked Roy Merton and *The Front Page* from its number-one spot. The criticism from senior executives ceased, and some of those who'd been caustic and outspoken now feared for their positions. Rumour had it that Barry Seymour had given her carte blanche regarding production and content. She was one of the nation's highest paid television presenters and Channel Sixteen's most valuable property. Ratings equated to power, and huge ratings equated to huge power.

Fairhills Nursing Home was about an hour from Melbourne, and Fiona enjoyed putting the Audi's top down and letting the breeze run through her hair. The driveway to the home was flanked by towering cypresses and, as she drew closer they thinned and were replaced with beds of roses, tulips, azaleas and rolling manicured lawns. She had placed her father in the home shortly after the death of her mother when his attacks on the vodka had become uncontrollable. He could hardly walk, and it was only on his good days that he could even remember her. The reception was peaceful and filled with beautiful flowers from the grounds. She spoke briefly with the receptionist and then went and sat in one of the many chairs on the long veranda. A few minutes later, a male nurse wheeled her father out, and she took his hand and kissed him gently on his almost transparent forehead. His hands were bony, his face gaunt, and the few strands of hair he still had were stark white. He looked like he was a hundred years old, and she found it hard to believe he was the same man whose knee she had sat on less than twenty years ago. There was no sign that he recognized her. "Leave us please," she said, looking at the nurse.

"Yes, Ms. Jeczik."

She took her father's hands, placing her own around them, massaging gently. "Do you recognize me, Daddy?" she said, staring into his blank eyes. "Daddy, it's me, Fiona." The tears welled up, and she gently touched his face, hoping he would respond. He didn't, and she sat holding his hands, staring at the beautiful gardens. After an hour, she looked deeply into his eyes, but there wasn't even a flicker. "Poor, Daddy. They've hurt you so badly. Now I'm going to hurt them."

- 8 -

TOM DONEGAN WAS as good as his word. As Aspine drove out of the car-park, there was no sign of the picketers, the barbecues or the tents. *Did Donegan bribe Lawson and McBain, or did his representatives intimidate the picketers, to such an extent that they'd packed up and gone home?* No matter, they were gone, and Donegan had confidently undertaken they would not be back.

Charlie hadn't called, which was surprising, as she always did when he sent a present or flowers. He knew he must have said or done something to upset her on Friday night, but didn't know what. The traffic was at a standstill, so he called her, but got the answering machine, and she didn't answer her cell phone either. He left a message, "Hi Charlie, it's me. Hope you liked the flowers. Call me."

He returned Trevor's wave as he entered the driveway, and his thoughts turned to a larger house with a four-car garage. Trevor's Ford had to be parked out in the street, and he always seemed to be in it, counting the days to when he could drive it by himself.

The Mercedes wasn't in the garage and when he entered the house it was strangely quiet. Jemma was sitting cross-legged on the sofa watching television, with a soft drink on one side of her and chips on the other.

"That looks healthy. Where's Mark and your Mom?"

She held her fingers to her lips and whispered, "Just a second, Daddy, I don't want to miss the last of Home and Away." The channel panned to an advertisement and Jemma said, "They're at school. It's China Orientation night. Mom's left sandwiches in the fridge for you, and there's coffee in the percolator. She told me to tell you that you received a lot of faxes today. They're on your desk." She'd hardly looked at him, her concentration focused on the box, even during the advertisements.

"Thanks, darling," he sighed.

The covering fax from Jeremy set out his recommendations and apologized for forwarding the CV of a young accountant, Kerry Bartlett. He was highly qualified, obviously bright, but only twenty-nine and lacking experience. The position of financial controller would be a quantum career leap for him. The recommended candidate was forty-two and vastly more experienced, having worked for public companies in senior financial positions for most of his working life. He came across as being strong-willed, savvy, confident and competent, and just the type of financial controller Aspine didn't need. There was room for only one king at Mercury Properties, and he sure as hell didn't want any princes. He skim-read the third applicant's CV, but already knew he would only be interviewing one candidate. Jeremy described Brad Hooper as a long shot for the position of sales manager and suggested that he run extensive advertisements to attract better-qualified candidates. He was thirty-two, and his CV stated that he had sold life insurance, used cars, home loans, funeral plots and tax schemes, but had never managed a sales team. He had been the leading salesman in every company he'd worked for, and Aspine knew he was going to employ him. Maybe not as sales manager but, if not, as the company's gun sales rep who would set the standard for the rest of the sales team.

He pushed the CVs aside, closed his eyes and smiled, as he thought about the meeting with the bank and Colin Sarll in the morning.

"That must have been a nice thought," Barbara said, kissing him lightly on the lips. She was dressed in snug-fitting black slacks and a turquoise silk blouse, and he momentarily appreciated how attractive she was.

"I didn't hear the garage door. How was the Orientation night?"

"Oh, it was wonderful. You can't imagine how happy you've made Mark, and Trevor loves the car you bought him. How was your day?"

"The same."

"I thought it might have been a little better. You were only on one television station tonight. They showed those thugs blocking you this morning, and the eggs smashing on your windscreen."

"It wasn't that bad, and it was only one egg." He grinned. "They make it look worse on the news." The removal of the money pressures had obviously brightened Barbara's life, and she was expressing support for him. He wondered what the sting would be.

"Jamie and Sue Wallace have invited us to a dinner party on Saturday night. I said we'd be there."

"You said what? Christ, Barbara, how many times do I have to tell you I can't stand your snooty-nosed friends? Besides, I can't go. I have to be in Sydney this weekend," he lied.

"We never do anything together anymore," she groaned.

"Hey, it's a bit late for happy families. You have your friends and your life, and I have mine, and we've both got the kids. You can go to the Wallaces' dinner party without me."

"You know I can't do that. I'll be the only one there without a partner. How do you think I'll feel?"

"If memory serves me weren't you and Jamie Wallace once an item? It could be an opportunity for you to get reacquainted." he smirked.

Her eyes welled up. "We went out a few times. We were never an item, and it was long before I knew you."

Aspine started to shuffle through the papers on his desk. "I've got a lot to get through. We'll talk after," he said, knowing they wouldn't.

"All right," she sniffled. "Would you like coffee before I go to bed?"

"No thanks. Goodnight," he said, his tone polite but cold.

There was no sign of the picketers as Aspine eased the Ferrari through the gates. Shirley had left him a long message from Max Vogel. It had gone well at the Industrial Relations Commission, and proceedings would continue today. The commissioner had been critical of the company breaching the enterprise bargaining agreement and, not consulting with the union before making the retrenchments. Despite this, the union's claims for reinstatement and increased retrenchment benefits had fallen on deaf ears. Max had, on behalf of the company, given the commissioner an undertaking not to retrench any more employees while proceedings were continuing. Aspine read the message again with satisfaction. It was going better than he'd anticipated, and he doubted there'd be any press or television coverage today. *Yesterday's newspapers are today's fish wrappers!* He thought.

Shirley buzzed, interrupting his thoughts. "I have Mr. Smythe for you."

"Good morning, Douglas. What did you think of the candidates?"

"I like the sales guy Brad Hooper a lot. I don't know about the sales manager's position, though."

"Yes, that's what I thought. What about the financial controller?"

"I was impressed by young Kerry Barrett."

"It's Bartlett, not Barrett. Yes, technically he's excellent, but he lacks confidence and aplomb. He'll be out of his depth addressing merchant bankers and stockbrokers about the company's prospects. He'd make a good assistant."

"I think he's the type who'll grow with and into the position. Besides, I'll be the one talking to the money men in Collins and Pitt Streets."

"Would you like to interview the others? They're vastly more experienced than Kerry."

"No. Arrange interviews at your offices this Monday afternoon for the two candidates I've nominated."

"Certainly."

"Do you have anyone on your books who fits my PA requirements?" Aspine whispered.

"Yes, I have two women who are clever, charismatic and well groomed. One of them has had twenty years' experience with–"

"Too old," Aspine interrupted. "Tell me about the other one."

"They're both in their late thirties. They're savvy, attractive, and have held senior positions in companies far larger than Mercury. I'm not even sure that they'd accept a position with you."

"They're old boilers! I thought I told you less than thirty but, if I didn't, I am now." Aspine chuckled, knowing that Jeremy would be cringing.

A loud sigh came down the phone line. "I'll get back to you, Douglas."

Shirley buzzed again. "Mr. Kendall from the bank is here for his nine-thirty appointment."

"Let him know I'm running a few minutes late." Aspine smiled. He was going to enjoy this meeting, but first, he had to call Charlie.

The phone rang twice before Charlie answered. "Hello."

"Why haven't you called me?" Aspine demanded.

"Oh, it's you. I didn't think I'd hear from you again after Friday night."

"Come on, I sent you flowers, didn't I?"

"You think a few flowers is a fair trade-off for punching me in the face and raping me on the floor," she said, her voice bitter and angry.

"I-I didn't know. Shit, it was the piss."

"You don't remember do you, you bastard! Don't you remember seeing Fiona Jeczik on television, and then going crazy? You need help. You're a sick, sick man."

"I was drunk. Charlie, you know I wouldn't hurt a hair on your head."

"Yes, you sure proved that."

"I'll give away the booze. It'll never happen again."

"I want you out of my life. I'm going back to work. I don't need you."

"Don't do anything rash. Think about it," he said, fighting back the urge to tell her that she would never earn enough to live in the lifestyle to which she'd become accustomed.

"You're always violent and nasty when you're drunk. How do I know you won't hit me again?"

"I told you, I'm giving up the booze."

"You've said that before."

"I'm going to Sydney on Friday night. Come with me. I'll take you on a shopping spree. Let me make it up to you. If you still feel like splitting after the weekend, I won't stand in your way."

"I don't know. I'll think about it and get back to you," she said. The annoyance was still in her voice, but the bitterness wasn't.

"I'll be waiting for your call." He smiled, confident that she'd say yes.

Aspine checked his watch. It was nearly ten o'clock, and he had kept the bankers waiting long enough. "Shirley, pick up the phone," he said into the intercom. "I want you to book flights to Sydney for Ms. Charlene Deering and myself, on Friday night, returning Sunday evening. Organize a rental car and book a suite at the Park-Hyatt for Friday and Saturday nights."

"Who will I charge it–?"

Before she could finish, he said, "Show Mr. Kendall in."

Phil Kendall was younger than Aspine had expected. Early thirties; tall and gangly, with sandy hair, freckles, and a boyish smile.

"Sorry to keep you waiting, Phil," Aspine lied, surprised at the strength of the young man's handshake. He shook Jonathan's hand warmly while ignoring Colin Sarll.

"That's okay, Doug. We know how busy you've been. How can we help you?" Kendall responded, taking a seat.

"I intend to expand the operations of the company significantly. We're a top-two-hundred-company, but by the end of the year we'll be top-one-hundred, and by the end of the following year, I'm aiming at top-fifty. I can't grow the company without having access to funds."

"I'm sure we can accommodate you with some of our loan products."

"You're holding a debenture over the company's assets, you've got mortgages over all its real estate, yet, other than a shitty little stand-by facility, you provide nothing. The other banks would kill for our account!"

"The company's never been a big borrower. Harry ran it conservatively and didn't like borrowing."

"Why then are you holding a shit-load of security when you're not providing anything for it?"

"It probably built up over the years, and the company never asked for mortgage discharges."

"And you never volunteered them. Does the company have an offset facility when you calculate interest charges on its various accounts?"

"No. It was never asked for."

"Let me get this clear. You charge interest on the company's overdrawn accounts, but don't offset it against the credit balances in its other accounts. So at the end of the day, you charge interest on a net credit balance while having the use of funds to lend to others. That's great banking. Why don't you tell me what other cute deals the bank has with the company, which aren't quite so obvious?"

"You don't understand. That was the way Harry, and Neil Widge, liked to run the company. They knew they only had to ask, and we would have been more than willing to provide increased facilities."

"What about the offset of interest?"

"That's something which was overlooked. I'll get it fixed when I get back to my office."

"I want it backdated, and I want a credit for every cent you overcharged."

"We can't–"

"Yes you can, and you will, if you want to retain the company's banking," Aspine interrupted.

"How far back do you expect us to go?"

"How long did you say the company's banked with you?"

"Fifty years."

Aspine smiled as he watched Phil Kendall shift nervously in his chair.

"We'll go back as far as our records permit. Probably about six years. It won't be a large credit. I doubt it'll be much more than a hundred thousand."

"So you don't consider a hundred thousand's a great deal of money, Phil," Aspine said, for the first time turning his gaze to Colin Sarll.

"I didn't say–"

Aspine cut him short. "Jonathan's been handling my personal banking. Would that switch to you?"

"Yes," Kendall replied, visibly tensing. "We like to have the banking of our major corporate clients, and their executives, under one roof."

"So if I needed a one hundred thousand dollar personal loan there'd be no problem?"

"Of course not. Look, what occurred with Colin was a misunderstanding."

"There was no misunderstanding. He point blank refused," Aspine snarled.

"But your circumstances have changed."

"What's that mean, Phil? Are you saying you would've refused the loan if I hadn't gotten this job?"

"No, no, I'm not."

"So you're saying he fucked up then?"

"Mr. Aspine, I'm sorry we got off on the wrong track," Sarll sniffled.

"No, you're not, you little prick. You're sorry I got this job, you're sorry you're sitting in that chair, and you're sorry Phil's here. Did you tell him you called me a thug?"

"What, what? You didn't say anything about that," Kendall said, eyeballing Sarll.

"I-I said it in the heat of the moment. That's right, isn't it, Jonathan?"

Jonathan Bardon had six months to go until retirement. He wasn't going to upset Phil Kendall and get sacked without all of his benefits. He moved uneasily in his chair before saying, "I don't think you should have said it."

Aspine smirked as he watched Sarll grovel. "Phil, I'd like a word in private."

Sarll almost jumped out of his chair, and Jonathan was also relieved to be out of the firing line. As the door closed, Aspine said, "You can see how difficult it would be for me to keep the company's banking with you. It's a shame because we're going to need access to significant loan funds."

"No, I can't. You won't deal with Colin Sarll again. I'll be handling the company's account and your personal account. We'd like to help you with the company's loan requirements."

"I'm sure you would, but I don't know whether I could deal with a bank that calls and treats its clients as thugs."

"You want me to sack him?"

"That's up to you."

"Do we get to keep the company's business if I do?"

"I can't give you a guarantee, if you don't you'll definitely lose it," Aspine said, his mouth set in a grim line.

Kendall grimaced. "I'll see what I can do."

"Do that, but don't think you can shift him interstate or overseas without me knowing."

"Is there anything else?"

"Yes. I want a platinum credit card for my wife Barbara with a limit of one hundred thousand. Can you arrange it?"

"Consider it done."

"Come back to me if you're interested in retaining the company's business." Aspine smiled, knowing Kendall knew what he had to do.

"I'll get back to you," Kendall said, standing and extending his hand.

Phillip Kendall cursed loudly as he opened the door to his car. Douglas Aspine was nothing more than a power-crazed egomaniac, and Colin Sarll had just been doing his job. He slammed the door, knowing that he had no choice if he wanted to remain on the fast track at the bank. If he lost the business of a top-two-hundred-company, his bosses would ship him off to Yarrawonga.

- 9 -

ASPINE ENTERED THE boardroom at 9:00 a.m. Sir Edwin was sitting at one end of the long table, Harry Denton at the other, with Stan Pettit on his left and Dawn O'Rourke, Neil Widge's former PA, on his right, with minute book in hand. There were three others whom Aspine recognized from photos in the company's annual reports. He smiled; the one thing they had in common was their hair color, which, he mused, might be described as Mercury gray.

"Good morning, Douglas," Sir Edwin said with a quiver in his voice, motioning him to take the chair to his right.

The tension was palpable and, as Aspine scanned the faces around the table, they refused to hold his gaze until he got to Harry. His eyes were bloodshot and angry, but did not drop, and his top lip curled in a sneer.

"Let me introduce you to Andrew Malone, David Cleary, and William Claymore," Sir Edwin said.

Aspine didn't stand or offer his hand. Instead, he nodded. They looked old and weak, and not looking forward to this meeting.

"Let's get to the business at hand," Harry snapped.

"I thought Sir Edwin was chairman." Aspine smiled, pushing his chair back from the table, stretching his legs and yawning while exaggeratedly covering his mouth.

This served to infuriate Harry. "We're not standing on ceremony," he snarled. "You sacked Neil Widge, retrenched six hundred good employees, ruined our relationship with the union, and brought the media down on us."

"Harry, you know that's not true. Widge resigned, the workforce needed downsizing, and the union's been touching up the company for years, but our lawyers, Sly & Vogel, are giving it a belting in the Industrial Relations Commission. Sure there was a bit of press, but that's the price of progress. You wouldn't know much about that, though."

"Our lawyers? Stan's our lawyer. What do you mean our lawyers?"

"He used to be. I thought there was a conflict, with Stan serving on the board and handling the company's legal affairs."

"What conflict?"

"I can't see Stan voting to sue his own firm if it stuffs up the company's legal work." Aspine laughed. "I solved the problem."

Stan's face was red, his forehead moist and his breathing labored. He placed his hand on Harry's wrist to calm him but was too late.

"Enough! Enough!" shouted Harry. "We met before and want your resignation. If you don't resign, we'll sack you."

"The board met?"

"Yes!"

"Were you at the meeting, Sir Edwin?" Aspine asked.

Before Sir Edwin could answer, Harry responded, "That's not relevant. Five of the company's directors resolved to terminate your services — one way or the other. We'll pay you your base salary of eight hundred thousand if you finish up today."

"Eight hundred thousand? I'll earn five million this year, and I've got a three-year contract. That's fifteen million by my reckoning."

"Fifteen million! Don't try and bluff us. You screwed your last employer out of two hundred thousand. You'll jump at eight hundred."

"Is that what Bob Dwyer told you? You've been busy, haven't you, Harry?"

"Harry, this is not a wise decision," Sir Edwin intervened. "The media will have a field day, and our shares will be hammered."

"I think Ed's right," William Claymore said. "Can't we find another way around this?"

"No." Harry scowled. "He's out of the company today. Make up your mind: are you resigning or do we sack you?"

Aspine reached down, picked up his briefcase, placed it on the table and slowly flicked it open, removing two documents. "Gentlemen this is a copy of a writ, and a supporting statement of claim for fifteen million dollars."

"You're bluffing," Harry growled.

Aspine stood up and picked up the phone from the bookshelves behind him, and hit the loudspeaker button. "Shirley, is there someone waiting for me?"

"Yes. Mr. Des Rankin, from Sly & Vogel."

"Put him on."

"Hello, Des, what are you doing here?"

"I have a writ to serve on the company."

"Thanks, Des. Don't leave."

"So much for conflicts of interest," Pettit muttered.

"Gentlemen, I'm not finished," Aspine said, holding up another document. "This is an announcement to the Stock Exchange that includes details of the writ and the interference by your former CEO in the performance of my duties. Would you like me to read it to you?"

"You're a real piece of work, aren't you?" Harry shouted. "It's not going to save you."

"Hold on, Harry," Pettit said. "If this gets out, it'll be devastating."

"That's right," Sir Edwin agreed.

"Think about it, Harry." Aspine smiled. "Do you think the institutions will let you and your friends survive when they know about this? You'll all be out, and the new board will settle my claim rather than see it dragged through the media."

"We can't do it," Andrew Malone muttered. "It'll set the company back years."

Harry's face was black with rage, exacerbated by Aspine's smirk. "You...you can't let him blackmail us,"

"I...I don't want to get into a fight," whispered David Cleary, a frail little man who looked twenty years older than he was.

Aspine caught Sir Edwin's eye and saw the trace of a smile on the knight's face.

"Gentlemen, will I call Max Vogel and ask him to remove his employee? Or would you prefer he served the writ?"

Sir Edwin glanced around the table at the defeated faces of Harry's supporters, before responding. "Tell him to call his Rottweiler off, Douglas, you have no reason to issue."

There were tears of anger and frustration in Harry's eyes, as he stood up and stormed out of the boardroom shouting, "This isn't over yet."

"Is there anything else anyone would like to raise?" Sir Edwin asked, glancing at his fob watch and then, after a short pause: "I declare this meeting closed at ten-fifteen."

"Dawn, don't minute anything about the writ or statement of claim," Aspine said. "It serves no purpose."

She looked at Sir Edwin, who nodded his assent.

After the others had left, Sir Edwin said, "That was a superb performance, Douglas, but you've made some bitter enemies."

"That's the price of change and progress."

"Yes, but don't you think you should slow down and, well how can I put this, use a little more discretion?"

"No, I don't. You're after a quantum improvement in the company's performance, and I'm going to give it to you. All you have to do is look after my back, and show a little more spine than you did today."

"What...what's that supposed to mean?"

"Ed, you thought they were going to get me. God, you even struggled to make eye contact with me. If I'd been relying on your support, I wouldn't be here now."

"I'm sorry. Harry confronted me before the meeting and said he'd already met with the other four, and the decision was a *fait accompli*. I never thought you'd thwart them so effectively. Were you bluffing or would you have issued that writ?"

"Oh, I would have issued, but that's water under the bridge. I want to get rid of the non-executive directors, and replace them with others who can make a contribution."

"You know you can't do that. Only two come up for re-election each year."

"Other than Harry, they're weak. I'll have their resignations soon enough."

"Slowly, slowly, Douglas. First, you need to deliver on your promise to increase profits by fifty percent. After that, you'll be in a much stronger position."

On the flight to Sydney, Charlie was aloof and told Aspine she was only with him because he'd said he wouldn't drink. She performed half-heartedly on Friday night but cheered up after an expensive day's shopping on Saturday. For dinner, she wore silver stilettos and a stunning black dress which showed just enough flesh to have most of the men in the Park-Hyatt dining room gawking, and their wives berating them.

"What do you think of me going back to work?" she asked, leaning forward and exposing the white of her breasts against her tan.

Fuck, he'd spent $8,000-plus on her today. That would be about three months' pay for her doing anything else other than what she was doing for him. "What do you have in mind?" he said, sipping mineral water while craving for a shot of Jack Daniels.

"I thought I might try for a PAs position or perhaps I could go into advertising. I'm very innovative and creative."

He wanted to say *Yeah, I know, but they don't pay for X-rated innovation.* "You could, but I doubt you'd earn enough to pay for the apartment and car on your own."

She looked puzzled. "I hadn't intended to. I thought we'd leave things as they are, but I'd get a job so I'll have something to do during the day."

He pinched himself. *She expects me to fork out $60,000 a year for the apartment and car, plus God knows how much on clothes and travel, without being available when I need relief. The lease on the apartment has only a few weeks to go, and if I stop the car payments, it'll be repossessed. She's just about outlived her usefulness, but I won't say anything yet. Why spoil tonight and tomorrow morning?* "I see." He smiled. "What about your mom's visits?"

"She'll be able to see me at night. That won't be a problem. I'm glad you're supportive. I thought you might be angry."

Later that night, she nestled into his shoulder and whispered. "Was that good?"

She had warmed to him a little, but was still restrained, and he wanted to say, *it was better than last night, but there's plenty of room for improvement.* "It was great."

She snuggled a little deeper into his chest. "Doug."

"Yeah, what is it?"

"How would you feel about a threesome?"

Maybe he had misjudged her. Some of her girlfriends were smoking hot. "Honey, if that's something you want to try, I'm up for it."

"You're too good to me," she said, kissing him.

"Who do you have in mind?"

"I don't think you know him," she said. "He's the new pool guy at the apartments."

"Guy?" he snapped, angrily pushing her away. "What the fuck are you talking about? You think I'm going to get into bed with another guy? You're a fucking lunatic."

"You hurt me," she said, rubbing her arm. "What's gotten into you? I was teasing. I knew what you'd think when I suggested a threesome."

She'd always been totally uninhibited, and maybe the pool guy had already comforted her after that lost Friday night. Well, fuck that! "Don't ever suggest anything like that again," he growled, turning his back on her and pulling the blankets tightly around him.

He thought he heard her say, 'If it had been another girl you wouldn't have gotten shitty,' but he ignored her. He'd had sex with Charlie for the last time, and his mind quickly turned to finding a replacement. He closed his eyes and smiled. *Perhaps Jeremy Smythe had someone on his books?*

-10 -

CHARLIE HARDLY SPOKE from the time they left Sydney to when Aspine dropped her off at her apartment. Barbara was petulant and pouting when he arrived home, and totally ignored him. He guessed that she'd gone to the Wallaces' dinner party by herself and was still expressing her displeasure. *As if I fucking care.*

On Monday morning, he paused at the door to Shirley's office. It was spotlessly clean: the personal photographs had gone, and there were no papers or files on the desk.

He flicked open his Teledex and called the real estate agents managing Charlie's apartment, and gave them one month's notice he was terminating the lease. The first she'd know about it would be when they made contact to seek her consent to inspection from prospective tenants. Then the shit would hit the fan.

After evicting Charlie, Aspine summoned Kurt to his office. "Tell me about Shirley."

"She was upset and emotional. It was difficult."

"I'm not interested in her feelings. How much did you pay her?"

"Four weeks for every year worked. It worked out to one and a half years salary plus statutory entitlements."

"About what I would have paid her. You did well. What was her reaction?"

"I told you," Kurt said, a trace of irritation in his voice.

"Not her emotional reaction. Christ, no female's ever been fired without turning on the water works. Surely you expected it? Did she say anything about suing?"

"She's not a fool. She said her dismissal was harsh and unfair."

Aspine laughed. "She left out unreasonable. Go on."

"She's going to see Gater & Salomon. I don't think we've heard the last of her."

"She'll expect them to act for her on a contingency basis and to take their fees out of what they extract. It's going to be sad news when they tell her they won't act — at least not without some upfront fees."

"How can you be so sure of that?"

"You got her final pay about right. Even if she wins, she won't get enough to justify lawyers being involved, and there's a good chance she'll get nothing. We'll get one letter of demand from Gater & Salomon, and I'll get Max Vogel to pen a response telling them to get stuffed. You did well."

"I felt terrible. It was like firing family."

"Get over it. Heading up human resources isn't just about employing people."

"I know, but we've never had retrenchments and dismissals like this before."

"And hopefully, they're over. We had to get rid of the fat, and those who didn't want to play on the new team. Now it's done, we can get on with the business of making money."

"Yes, Mr...Douglas."

Jeremy Smythe had converted a double-story mansion in upmarket Toorak into a contemporary office suite. He'd had it painted white, set aside the front yard for client parking, and packed the wide veranda with exotic potted plants. The inside was a mix of fine antique furniture, paintings, and artifacts, coupled with a sophisticated computer and communication system. The entrance was at the rear, where a family room had been converted into the reception area, complete with marble counter, leather reclining chairs and coffee tables. Aspine parked the Ferrari and got out just as a stunningly attractive brunette came down the steps from the veranda. He stopped and admired her legs and petite, finely shaped body as she walked toward her car. As she opened the door, she looked over her shoulder and caught him staring at her. He thought that he glimpsed a smile, before watching her drive out of the car-park.

His shoes sunk in the plush carpet as he entered the reception. Large gold letters on the wall behind the reception counter spelt out 'Smythe & Associates.' Two of the three receptionists' were answering incessantly ringing phones. The third looked up and asked, "How can I help you?"

"Douglas Aspine for Jeremy Smythe."

"We've been expecting you, Mr. Aspine. Can I get you a drink?

"No thanks."

"Please take a seat. Mr. Smythe won't keep you waiting long."

He'd just sat down when Jeremy came down the hallway. "Hello, Douglas, come through, we'll talk in my office. You mightn't believe it, but we have twenty offices and three boardrooms in this old house."

"It's impressive."

"We try to do our best," Jeremy sniffled as if to downplay the millions spent on the conversion.

"We're seeing Kerry Bartlett first. He's due in five minutes. Are you sure you don't want to interview either of the other candidates?"

"Definitely, and I'd prefer to interview him by myself. Do you have a spare office I can use?"

"Well, if that's what you'd like, you can use the office two doors down the hallway on the left."

"Thanks. Have you discussed salary?"

"No, he's currently earning $120,000 as a senior accountant. Are you sure you don't want me in on the interview?"

"Positive. What time is the sales guy due?"

"Brad Hooper's appointment is in an hour's time."

The intercom buzzed, and one of the receptionists' said. "Mr. Smythe, Mr. Bartlett is here for his two o'clock appointment."

"Get him a coffee, and show him down to the spare office in five minutes."

"Have you found me a suitable PA yet?"

"Not to your exact specification."

"There was a young, slim brunette leaving as I came in. Did you interview her?"

"I employ twenty consultants. Any of them could have interviewed her. How do you know she was looking for a PA's position?"

"I don't," Aspine grinned. "Find out who she is and what position she was interested in."

Jeremy exhaled loudly. Aspine stood up and strode down to the spare office where he wrote 160, 200, and 250 on a sheet of paper, and then tore it into three pieces. He then placed them in the drawers on the right-hand side of the desk. As he put the 250 piece in the bottom drawer, there was a knock at the door, and one of the receptionists' introduced Kerry Bartlett. He looked younger than twenty-nine; perhaps it was the slight acne, the smallness of his stature or the softness of his features. His handshake was limp, and his dark brown eyes couldn't hold Aspine's gaze. "Take a seat, Kerry, and tell me why I should employ you as my financial controller?"

"I have an Economics & Commerce degree from Melbourne University, and I'm a Chartered—"

"I know about your academic background and work history," Aspine interrupted. "I want to know why I should employ an untried financial controller?"

"I-I'm no-not really un-untried. I-I've b-been doing the f-financial con-controller's job in my cur-current pos-position for the pas-past four years. I...I ju-just don't have the title."

"Or the salary." Aspine chuckled.

Kerry blushed, and his eyes started to water. "You-you're right."

"Why is that?"

"I-I'm not su-sure."

"Is it because of the quality of your work? Have you failed to meet deadlines?"

"I work a hun-hundred hours a week when necessary, and the qual-quality of my work is be-beyond reproach," Kerry responded, a tinge of indignation in his voice.

"Do you think you can handle briefing merchant bankers and stockbrokers about the company's prospects?"

"I-it's not som-something I-I've done be-before," he said, his shoulders slumping. "I-I thin-think I might b-be able to han-handle it."

"Kerry, a 'might' won't cut it. I can't run the risk of the company being inadequately promoted. I'm sure you understand."

"Yes, yes I do, Mr. Aspine," Kerry replied, his disappointment obvious.

"It's a shame. You're obviously a skilled accountant, and I would have liked to have employed you." Aspine paused and placed his fingertips on his forehead, as if in deep thought. "I've got it. You could brief me on the figures, and I could handle the merchant bankers."

"You-you'd do tha-that f-for me."

"I don't know much about accounting or figures," he lied. "You'd have to help me get a better understanding of the numbers. Do you think you could do that?"

"Oh, yes. That wouldn't be a problem," Kerry replied, his eyes full of hope.

"It does create a salary problem, though because you wouldn't be handling the job in its entirety. How much are you earning now?"

"One hundred and twenty thousand."

"And how much would you expect to earn in this position?"

Kerry looked down at his feet and muttered, "I don't know."

He's perfect Aspine thought. *He's shy, lacking in confidence, nervous, and probably easily coerced and intimidated.* He reached into the top drawer of the desk and took out a piece of paper with 160 written on it, and placed it in front of Kerry. "When I was reading your application and CV, I thought this would be a fair figure."

"Yes, that's fair." Kerry smiled for the first time.

"Plus a company car, and 200,000 options to acquire shares in the company."

Kerry glowed. "That's very generous, Mr. Aspine."

"Call me Doug. When's the earliest you can start?"

"I h-have to give a mon-month's no-notice, b-but they may le-let me go in a we- week. I can ask."

"Do that, Kerry, and welcome aboard," Aspine said, extending his hand. "I'll get a formal offer couriered to you, but I believe in the honor of a man's handshake."

"Thank you, Doug. I-I'm looking fo-forward to w-working with you."

After Kerry had left, Aspine took the other two pieces of paper out of the drawers and tore them up. He felt smug. He'd bought Kerry for a lowball figure.

Brad Hooper was the antithesis of Kerry Bartlett. He wore a lemon-colored shirt with a tan tie, neatly-pressed, brown slacks, and bone Cuban-heeled shoes. He had short cropped hair, a protruding jaw, and hazel eyes that had a hardness that belied his age. There was strength and confidence in his handshake.

"How did you get into selling, Brad?"

"My Dad died when I was halfway through year ten. I left school and went out flogging vacuum cleaners door-to-door on a commission basis."

"You became the family breadwinner?"

"Yeah, and if I didn't sell, we didn't eat."

"Did you ever go hungry?"

"Never." Brad smiled, but his eyes remained cold.

"You've sold life insurance, funeral plots, and home loans. Why haven't you stayed with one product?"

"Shit, I've sold far more products than those. I look for the biggest commission earner at the time and flog it. Home loans were great, but now every prick's selling them, and the banks have cut back their commission payments."

"Have you ever managed a sales team?"

"Nah, and I've never wanted to. I've never trusted management. Every time I've made a shit-load of money, they've changed the rules to reduce my commission."

"What's the most you've ever made?"

"I've had quite a few years where I've made more than two hundred and fifty thousand."

"So you've set yourself up nicely?"

"I didn't say that." Brad laughed. "I like the good life. Fast cars, fast women and slow horses are expensive interests."

"That they are." Aspine chuckled. "You're not embarrassed to tell me about your weakn..., interests?"

"Why should I be? You're not looking for a rich salesman. You're looking for a hungry salesman with the ass out of his pants, who has to make sales or starve."

"You're selling to me right now aren't you? Find out what the customer wants and give it to him."

Brad crossed his legs and rolled up his shirtsleeves to expose his powerful forearms. "Look, I'm the best salesman you'll interview, but I'm not right for the sales manager's job."

"Why don't you let me decide that? I know you can sell finance, but what do you know about selling off-the-plan?"

"I bought a few apartments on the Gold Coast off-the-plan and sold them before completion. I made some nice money. Selling off-the-plan won't be difficult."

"Did you have to put down a deposit?"

"Yeah, ten percent. I would have bought more if I could have, but I had to borrow the deposits."

"What if I told you that you could have bought them without deposits?"

"How's that?"

"You haven't heard of insurance bonds?"

"Nah."

"Let me tell you how they work. If you want to buy an apartment off-the-plan you go to an insurance company that's in the business of issuing deposit bonds. You pay them between a half and one percent of the sales price, and they provide the seller with a guarantee of deposit. Of course, you still have to settle in full on completion." Aspine grinned.

"Shit! You're saying I could be selling your apartments without having to ask buyers for a deposit?"

"It's a little more complicated than that, but yes, in many cases you'll be able to make deposit-free sales."

"Jesus, I'd be making so much commission you wouldn't be able to pay me."

"If you're half as good as you say you are, you could earn more than three hundred thousand a year as a salesman."

"When do I start?"

"Not so fast. What would you say if I told you that you could make a million as sales manager?"

"You're not going to pay me a million dollar salary."

"You can be certain of that, but I am prepared to pay you a commission on every sale made by the sales reps in your team. All you have to do is teach them how to sell, and then crack the whip."

"How many reps?"

"Twenty-five, but you'll have to employ more."

"Do I have to keep the existing employees?"

"What do you have in mind?"

"I know some great floggers who'd jump at a deal like this, and they'd need minimal training."

"If you take on the sales manager's position, I'll hold you responsible for the company's sales performance. If you want to sack the existing sales team, that's fine with me. Just remember, if you can't generate sales, you'll go the same way as them."

"Are you offering me the sales manager's position?"

"Yes."

"I'll take it, Doug. I'm between jobs, so I can start tomorrow if you like."

"Welcome to the team, Brad," Aspine said, grasping his hand. "I'll see you in the morning. What are you going to do for the rest of the day?"

"I'm going home to Google insurance bonds. I'll know more than you by the morning." Brad grinned, but his eyes remained cold and hungry.

"I was hoping you'd say that."

As Aspine left the office, he bumped into Jeremy in the hallway. "Douglas, I'm sorry that girl wasn't here seeking employment. She's a Telstra customer service officer." Jeremy smirked.

"Did you get her name and phone number?"

"No. Why would I?"

"Because I damn well asked you to."

"Calm down. I'll find out and let you know."

"Before I leave?"

"Yes, yes, if you need to know so badly."

"Thank you. Oh, and hold off on looking for a PA for me until I get back to you."

"You're going to employ the Telstra girl? God, you have to stop thinking with your dick."

"Don't ever fucking talk to me like that. I never get involved in affairs with my employees," Aspine lied.

"I'm sorry, it's just that I think she's totally unsuitable. She's not even a PA," Jeremy whined.

"That's not important. She's got pizzazz, personality, charisma, and charm. She'll relate well to our major customers."

"And you can tell that by looking at her?"

Aspine yawned. "Yes, I can."

"Very well, I hope you're not making a mistake. There's another matter I'd like to discuss with you."

"Yes."

"I was wondering when we might expect the fifty thousand."

"What fifty thousand?"

"You know. The amount you offered to pay us if we acted exclusively for you in respect of the Mercury position."

"Oh, yes, but I recollect you saying that I was the best candidate, and it had nothing to do with money. Didn't you say that?"

"Yes, yes, I did, but you misunderstood. I didn't say we didn't need the additional fee. After all, we didn't interview anyone else."

"Why would you? You already had the best person." Aspine smiled.

"We had an agreement," Jeremy responded angrily.

"I hope you're not suggesting that I've gone back on my word."

"No-no, of course not bu-but I think you misconstrued our earlier conversation."

"Are you sure that *you* didn't?"

"Positive."

"I'll have to write you a check then," Aspine said, his tone cold and measured, "but I'll also have to put Mercury's recruiting out to tender."

"Bu-but you said we'd be handling it exclusively?"

"I'm sorry, you must have misconstrued our conversation."

Jeremy coughed loudly, and Aspine heard him mutter, "Bastard."

"What did you say?"

"Nothing, I got something stuck in my throat. Look, I don't want to sour our relationship over a misunderstanding. Let's forget the fifty thousand."

"Thank you, Jeremy. I'm glad we concur."

"Are you still going to put your recruiting out to tender?"

"Tender? What tender? Your firm handles our recruiting work."

As Aspine drove away from Jeremy's offices, he marveled at how easy it'd been to renege on the fifty thousand.

When Aspine called Kelly Jenner, she answered, "Hello, customer relations, Kelly Jenner speaking." She had a friendly, bubbly voice.

"Hello, Kelly. My name's Douglas Aspine. We almost met today."

She sounded puzzled. "How can I help you, Mr. Aspine?"

"You were at Smythe & Associates. You were leaving as I was arriving."

"The Ferrari."

"I'm pleased to see you remember me."

"You were staring," she said. "How did you get my phone number?"

"Jeremy Smythe."

"Do you have a Telstra problem?"

"No, but I'd like to see you."

"Oh, I'm sorry. I have a partner."

"Kelly, this isn't a personal call. I'm CEO of Mercury Properties. I have a proposition for you that I think you'll find interesting. Can you come and see me in the morning, at nine o'clock?"

"But you said you didn't have a problem." She paused. "Yes, I can, but I'm a little confused. Can you tell me what it's about?"

"I will in the morning, Kelly."

- 11 -

KELLY WORE A smart black suit and white blouse. She was smaller than he recalled, but everything was in proportion. More importantly, she exuded vibrancy. "Thank you for coming in, Kelly, Aspine said."

"Why do you want to see me?"

"We'll get to that shortly. Tell me about what you do for Telstra? Have you been there long?"

"Six years. I handle telephony complaints and problems for large commercial clients. If there's a problem, I liaise with our service divisions to minimize any inconvenience that our clients might suffer."

"What did you do before?"

"I worked in various sales positions, mainly in real estate."

"Have you always had a lot of people involvement?"

"Yes. Look, what is this about?"

"Bear with me. I only have a few more questions. In addition to your salary, do you receive any benefits?"

"Yes, a car."

"How much do you get paid?"

"How much do *you* get paid? I'm not telling you that."

"Kelly, I'm looking for a PA."

"So that's why you wanted to see me. You saw me for the first time yesterday and decided that I'd make a good PA. It's ridiculous. Is that how you find your employees? I type at twenty words a minute, my spelling is diabolical, and I make lousy coffee. You can do far better than me."

"Call me, Doug. And, Kelly, I checked your presentation and people skills with Smythe & Associates," he lied. "I couldn't care less about your typing and spelling, and we'll soon be shifting into more upmarket offices where we'll employ a tea lady. The job entails organizing my appointments, making sure I keep them, liaising with our major clients and financiers, and keeping the losers away from me. My PA will end up knowing more about the company than anyone, except me. Most importantly she'll look after my back."

"It sounds appealing. Would I have to travel?"

"You may have to accompany me interstate, and on rare occasions, there'll be some overseas travel. Is that a problem?" Aspine asked, trying not to leer.

"No. How much does the position pay, and is there a car provided?"

"Ninety thousand to start. We'll lease any car you want, but the cost will come out of your salary. I'm sure that's a lot more than Telstra are paying you."

"No, it's not a lot more. Where are the new offices going to be located?"

"That will be one of your first assignments. I'll let you know what I'm looking for, and anywhere close to the city will be fine."

"If I accept, that is." she said, frowning.

"If?"

"I won't switch jobs for ninety thousand."

"It's more than you're earning now."

"Yes, but you're the one who's buying. I want one hundred and ten thousand to start, and a review to one hundred and twenty after three months."

Aspine was torn between begrudging admiration and his hatred of being bettered in any business negotiation — particularly by a female. The money wasn't important, but he couldn't be seen to be a pushover. "One hundred thousand with a review to one hundred and ten after six months, subject to your performance."

"You won't be able to fault my performance. When would you like me to start?"

"Tomorrow, I'm sure you noticed that I don't have a PA."

"What happened to your last one?"

"That's a long story," he said, escorting her to the foyer.

"I'll be able to start on Monday fortnight. If I can do better, I will."

Aspine reclined in his chair and thought about his team, and smiled. A greedy sales manager, a weak financial controller, a savvy and stunning

PA, a puny design engineer, an ambitious senior project manager, an insecure HR manager and an indecisive supply manager. He would meld them together, ensuring that their very survival depended on him. He had ensured that there was no-one who could fill his shoes, so, in time; the board would also become totally dependent on him. The company would be described in the media as Douglas Aspine's Mercury Properties. He was interrupted by a loud cough and looked up to see Brad Hooper. "Hello, Brad," he said, standing up. "Let me show you around, and introduce you to your staff."

"That's fine, Doug. I've already found my office and met some of the reps. Christ, they're sales virgins — they have no idea how to sell! They're all on salaries and get paid whether they sell or not. Do you know that we've got two hundred completed, unsold apartments in the Docklands?"

"I knew we had unsold apartments, but not to the value of eighty million. Are you going to sack the reps and replace them with your guys?"

"I can't afford to. There's another seven partly completed high-rises, and that's two thousand units. Do you know how many have been sold? I'll need every rep I can get, and then some, but first, I've gotta get this lot on commission and show them how to sell. Oh, and there's three office buildings in various stages of completion, that I haven't been able to find out much about."

"I told you that we've never sold off-the-plan. Don't worry about the office buildings; they're pre-sold at fixed-prices to property trusts and insurance companies.

"Two of the apartment blocks in Richmond are ninety percent complete and not one apartment has been sold. It has nothing to do with selling off-the-plan. The sales guys are slack, and no-one's been pushing them."

"Shit! Let's get the Docklands apartments sold pronto and then you can hit Richmond. What's the competition like?"

"Urban pre-sell all their apartments and provide finance, so they don't have anything. Apartco have fifty to sell, and Vicland about thirty. You could say that we're the bunnies." Brad grinned. "We don't even have site sales offices."

"How the hell have we been selling anything then?"

"Potential customers' call and our reps arrange to meet them on site."

Aspine groaned, "They're order takers, not sales reps."

"Are we going to offer finance?"

"Of course. We're already financing the unsold and partly completed apartments. Try and get buyers to arrange bank or credit company finance but, if they can't, we'll provide it. And don't forget we're now selling off-the-plan, and accepting insurance bonds."

"I'm hardly likely to forget." Brad laughed. "I reckon I now know more about insurance bonds and selling off-the-plan than you do. I just don't think we should confuse the reps until we've sold the Docklands apartments. Remember, these guys have never sold finance before, so even that will be a learning experience. Luckily we still have two Docklands ground floor apartments. I've got a team of eight heading there this afternoon. They'll have phones, desks, and cubicles, and I'll show them how to close a sale."

"I'm impressed. You've certainly hit the ground running."

"Yeah, I worked out that the Docklands, plus the two partly completed Richmond buildings, will net me close to half a mil."

"Only if they're sold, and at full list price!"

"You obviously don't know that our prices are less than our competitors."

"God, it's getting worse. I'll need to review the pricing with you."

"If I get the opportunity to sell twenty apartments at wholesale prices to Henry Kaye, do you want me to take it?"

"Yeah, it'll cost us margin but give us cash flow, so don't offer finance. Henry can organize it, by selling directly to the suckers he's conned."

"Fine. I'll be at the Docklands for the next few days."

"You're not going to get any buyers out there without advertising."

"Yeah, I know. I've got reps from the newspapers meeting me later this afternoon. I'm running full-page advertisements this weekend. In the meantime, I'll try and show our 'virgins' how to sell."

"You've made a great start, Brad."

When Brad arrived at the Docklands, he noticed the small 'open for inspection' signs and resolved to replace them with larger, brightly painted signs. The building was quiet, except for the bustle of the eight reps setting up the sales offices. Surprisingly, there were three fully furnished display apartments of one, two and three bedroom configuration. Brad decided that he would nominate one rep to role play a sale to him, as a buyer, in front of the others. He would then show them how the sale should have been handled. As he was contemplating this, one of the reps, Rob Sorenson, said. "There's an elderly couple in the foyer who want to make an inspection. Do you want to handle it?"

"No. You do it. I'll tag along for support. Let's go and meet them."

Eric and Cynthia Cartwright were from the country, in their mid-sixties, and looking to move to the city so they could be close to their grandchildren. They had expressed interest in a one bedroom apartment, and Brad watched as Rob sold the features of the display apartment, before asking if they would like to see the views from the upper levels. "Hold on, Rob. I think Mr. and Mrs. Cartwright might like to inspect the two or perhaps the three bedroom display apartments," Brad said.

"We don't have lots of money," Eric responded. "We'll be struggling to even afford a one bedroom apartment."

"Oh, I thought you said you were shifting to be closer to your grandchildren. Where will they sleep when they stay with you?"

"That's a good point," Cynthia said. "It won't hurt to look at the two bedroom apartment. It's not as if we're going to be buying today."

As they inspected the larger apartment, Brad said, "Can you see your grandchildren sleeping over in an apartment like this? You could take them to the movies, football, or a restaurant, and they could come back and stay the night."

"It's a nice thought," Cynthia replied, "but we can't afford it."

"You'd be surprised at the finance packages we can put together, but we can talk about that later. Let's go upstairs and check the views. There's been strong demand for apartments in this building, and the after-market's strong. Rob, what's the highest level that we have a two bedroom on?"

"Twenty-one but it's the most exp–"

Brad interrupted. "Of course, it's the most expansive. It's a prestige apartment with views to kill for. Let's go up and inspect it."

"So there's been good capital appreciation?" Eric queried.

"Every apartment in the building will be sold by the end of the month, and you know what happens when there's no more supply." Brad winked.

The level twenty-one apartment overlooked Victoria Harbor, and the water views were breathtaking. Brad opened one of the large sliding doors to the balcony, and the Cartwrights followed him, cooing about how wonderful the apartment was. He could feel their desire growing. "Can you imagine your grandchildren up here? They'd never want to go home."

"It'd be lovely," Cynthia said, "but it's out of our price range."

"Perhaps not? Let's go down to the sales office and see what we can do for you."

Rob was quiet and looked embarrassed and uncomfortable. "Pass me a price list, Rob," Brad said and ran his eyes down the list until he reached level twenty-one, and saw $630,000. "Mr. Cartwright, you're going to be delighted. For just $650,000 that beautiful apartment can be yours. There'll be more than enough room for your grandchildren to sleep over."

Eric looked shocked. "We can't come up with that type of money."

Cynthia's face was filled with yearning. "We could sell our house in Shepparton."

"We'll be lucky to get three hundred thousand for it."

"But we could use our savings," Cynthia persisted.

"No, our savings have to last us for the rest of our lives. I'm sorry, it's too expensive."

Brad smiled at Cynthia. "Your husband's a tough negotiator. The pricing of the two bedroom apartments is very lean because we're marketing them to one-child families, but I can reduce it by ten thousand, especially for you, if you sign today."

Eric looked sheepish but proud. "No, we can't afford it and, even if we could, we'd still have to sell our house first."

"May I call you Eric?" Brad asked, his demeanor now serious.

"Yes, of course."

"Eric, I know you're a tough negotiator, but I can't reduce the price any further. My boss isn't going to be happy when he finds out that I've discounted ten thousand. In fact, he's going to be as mad as hell."

"I-I'm no-not trying to force your price down," Eric said, glowing with satisfaction. "We don't have the money."

"You don't have a thousand dollars?"

"Of course, we do, but not on us," Eric responded, looking puzzled.

"But you do have a credit card?"

"Yes."

"Eric, do you want the ten thousand you've haggled out of me?"

"Well, well–"

"Of course, you do," Brad interrupted. "Why don't you give us a thousand dollar deposit off your credit card and sign up? You can settle in ninety days. That'll give you plenty of time to sell and settle your house."

"Oh, that sounds terrific," Cynthia said.

"I suppose if I sign the contract note subject to finance, we can't get into too much trouble."

"Sorry, if I'm going to get the discount past my boss, the contract note will have to be unconditional. Don't worry, though, because if the banks knock you back, which they won't, we can arrange finance. You've got nothing to worry about."

"At the same interest rate as the banks?"

"Our rates will be a little higher, but no more than one to two percent. The difference is insignificant, but don't worry, because the banks aren't going to knock back solid citizens like you. Rob, draw up a contract note for Mr. and Mrs. Cartwright please."

"You haven't explained about the cooling off peri–"

Brad cut Rob short. "Look, these lovely people want to get back to Shepparton. Let's finalize the paperwork so they can be on their way."

"We're staying in Melbourne for another five days," Cynthia said. "There's no need to rush."

"Who will be doing your legal work?" Brad inquired.

"We'll see our lawyers as soon as we get back to Shepparton," Eric said.

Brad smiled to himself. What a stroke of luck: the three-day cooling off period would expire before they got to take any legal advice.

After the Cartwrights had left, Brad said, "That was easy, Rob. Did you learn anything?"

Rob shifted uneasily. "You didn't tell them about the three-day cooling off period. They don't know they can cancel."

"Why would they want to? Anyhow, details of the cooling off period are on the front of the contract note. There's no law saying we have to explain or spell them out."

"No, but it's the right thing to do. It's morally responsible."

"Rob, I'm not interested in morals. I'm interested in sales, and you'd better start thinking about making some." Brad scowled.

"You inflated the list price by twenty thousand, and then made such a big deal about the poor old guy screwing you down by ten thousand."

"The prices on the list are too low. I didn't do anything illegal. That is unless you consider smart negotiating illegal?"

By the time they take legal advice the cooling off period will have expired, and there'll be nothing they can do."

"They got what they wanted. We got what we wanted. It's a win-win deal. Under the new incentive plan, you just earned nine thousand in commission. How long's it been since you made that type of money in a day?"

"If that's how you make big money, I'm not sure I want to," Rob said, his voice shaking with emotion.

Brad groaned. *They're sales virgins; maybe it would be faster and more effective to sack the lot of them, and replace them with real hustlers.*

- 12 -

BRAD'S ADVERTISEMENTS WERE a cross between the most garish of those used by second-hand car dealers and the most persuasively slimy of those utilized by the major life insurance companies, but they got results. Most of the old sales team had resigned or been fired, and their replacements were made up of young, smartly dressed men, sharing two common characteristics — greed and hard, cold eyes. Despite the crassness of the advertisements, buyers rolled in, and within two weeks Docklands was completely sold. The apartments in the two near-completed Richmond towers were also selling fast, as Brad's team used any method to close a deal. Apartments were sold on one hundred dollar deposits, insurance bonds, pledges and, in one instance; a salesman lent a proposed buyer five hundred dollars to get his signature on a contract note. What was five hundred dollars when the commission was nine thousand?

There was an unhealthy vibrancy in the offices of Mercury. Reception couldn't cope with the incoming calls, and sales soared. A new vocabulary was adopted in the corridors, tea room and toilets. Words and sayings like, stitched up, stooge, wood duck, sucker, mug, chump, not the full twenty cents and moron, were common.

Aspine made announcements to the Stock Exchange nearly every day, reporting the sales successes. The financial press was quick to pick up on the company's change of direction, and *The Australian's* Marcus Easton labeled Aspine, a turnaround expert. He glowed with pride when he read the article, and jotted down Easton's name, for future favorable treatment. The market was stirring, and the share price was inching up.

Max Vogel called to say the union had all but caved in at the Industrial Relations Commission but was going to appeal to the Full Bench in respect of the thirty sick workers. Many were claiming that their ailments resulted from workplace injuries and were covered by WorkCover. The union also wanted to negotiate a new Enterprise Bargaining Agreement.

Everything Kelly said was true. She couldn't type, she couldn't spell, and the coffee she made tasted like shit. Aspine could live with the typing and spelling, but had given her a ten-minute crash course on how to make a good cup of coffee. Despite this, she proved to be sharp and savvy in her first week as his PA. He had bitten his lip when her bubbly voice came over the intercom saying, "Douglas, Mrs. Lensworth from the National Homeless Foundation would like to talk to you."

"Christ, don't interrupt me every time someone calls looking for a handout."

"She's not looking for a handout. She wants to talk to you about taking a position on their board."

"Oh, shit no! I'm far too busy. Piss her off, and don't bother me with this type of crap again."

Five minutes later Kelly came into his office and sat down opposite him. He watched the hem of her dress creep up and caught a glimpse of thigh as she crossed her legs. "Yeah, what is it?"

"I think you should reconsider that board position with the NHF."

"I told you I don't want to talk to losers. Hell, why would I want to get involved? I'd have to put in a heap of time and effort, and wouldn't get a cent out of it."

"Not everything's about money."

Her hem had crawled a little higher, and he was enjoying the view, but not the conversation. *Christ, doesn't she understand? Is she thick?* "Kelly, look–"

Before he could finish, she said, "I thought that you'd want to serve on a board with Russell Ridgeway."

"Not Russell Ridgeway, the CEO of ANQ Insurance?"

"Yes." She smiled.

"Oh, hell! You didn't tell that woman, what's her name to piss off did you?" Aspine groaned.

"Catherine Lensworth. I told her you were in a meeting, and that I'd get back to her when you were available."

"Shit! How'd you know Ridgeway was on the board?"

"I Googled the National Homeless Foundation while I was taking Catherine's call, and his name popped up. I assume you'd now like to say yes."

As Kelly left Aspine's office, he checked out her legs and tight little butt, while fantasizing about taking her on one of his interstate trips. Brains and beauty — he had chosen well.

Kerry Bartlett was quiet, diligent and hard working. He started early, finished late, and kept tight control of the company's improving finances. He prepared a profit & loss statement covering the first month of Aspine's stewardship, and the result was poor. Aspine wasn't fazed in the slightest. "Don't worry, Kerry, we hardly sold anything, and the cost of retrenchments is in the figures. I didn't expect to make a profit."

"Are you going to announce the result to the market?"

"No. They're only management accounts, and I don't want to spook investors."

"What about compliance with the Stock Exchange's continuous disclosure rules?"

"I have an obligation to keep the market fully informed, not misinformed. The result's a hiccup, a small ripple in an otherwise smooth sea. When you prepare the current month's figures, you'll see a huge increase in profits."

"Yes, I've seen the increase in apartment sales, but some of them have been sold on deposits as low as a hundred dollars. You wouldn't want to include those sales in the figures until they're settled, would you?"

Aspine frowned. "I thought you'd include all unconditional sales, irrespective of the size of the deposit. I don't know much about accounting, and would never consider faking the figures," he lied, "but I do want you to produce realistic results."

"Yes, of course. Of course," Kerry responded, a little too quickly. "I understand."

Aspine smiled. He hoped he'd never have to cook the books but, if he did, he had a deferential chef in Kerry.

Home life had also improved for Aspine. Whoever said, 'Money can't buy happiness,' had obviously never had any. Phil Kendall had sent the platinum card out to Barbara, and she'd been overcome with gratitude. It had momentarily crossed Aspine's mind to jump between the sheets with her, but he didn't want to create a precedent that he might later regret. Besides, it had been an easy week, and without tension, he could control his sexual urges. He had organized a dinner at Lynch's Restaurant in South Yarra on Saturday night for some of his senior managers and their partners and knew Barbara was looking forward to it.

Mark was in China with the school, Trevor was counting the days to when he could roll the Ford onto the road, and Jemma had her first serious boyfriend. She'd gone from being a tomboy to a beautiful young woman almost overnight. Fortunately, Barbara had schooled her on morals from an early age. He hoped that she'd also taught Jemma about contraceptives because if she had inherited any of his genes, her hormones would be starting to run wild.

Aspine was disappointed that he hadn't heard from Charlie. He knew that the lease had less than two weeks to run and that the agents would have contacted her. Perhaps she was going to vacate without saying a word, thus depriving him of the last satisfaction that he had hoped she would provide. He hadn't made the monthly payment on the MGB and knew that it would be repossessed. She was one of those quiet, unflappable people who rarely, if ever, lost her temper, but when she did was uncontrollable. He could imagine her kicking and screaming with rage, and a cruel smile crossed his face.

BECAUSE OF BARBARA'S penchant for punctuality, the Aspines were first to arrive at Lynch's. A waiter greeted them. "Good evening, Mr. and Mrs. Aspine. Would you like to have a drink in the lounge, or should I show you to your table?"

Aspine enjoyed the recognition and marked the waiter down for a generous tip. "I'll have a Jack Daniels neat, and Mrs. Aspine, a gin and tonic, at our table."

"Certainly. Follow me."

They had eaten at Lynch's frequently in happier times, and Aspine could tell Barbara was pleased. She looked stunning in a long black, off the shoulder number that seemed glued to her gym-buffed body, and her white pearl necklace accentuated her solarium tan. The table was set for eight, and Aspine took a chair at one end while motioning to Barbara to sit on his right. As she reached for the chair, the waiter deftly removed it for her.

"Thank you," she said, giving him a radiant smile.

"I won't be long with your drinks."

A few minutes later he returned with a tray of six drinks, and Brad Hooper and his girlfriend, Stacey, and Jack Gillard and his wife, Pam. Stacey was a buxom, attractive blonde with a wide, friendly smile, whose white dress was a fraction too short, and far too low. Aspine mused that she was exactly what he thought Brad would bring. Pam Gillard was a mirror of her husband, with white freckled skin, auburn hair and a trim, athletic body. After the introductions and they were seated, Brad inquired, looking at the two vacant chairs, "Who's missing?"

"Kerry Bartlett and his wife. I'm surprised, I thought they'd be first here," Aspine responded.

"Yeah, it's most unlike bean-counter behavior to be late," Brad grinned. Stacey burst out laughing at her boyfriend's comment, and her breasts bounced up and down in harmony with her mirth.

"What do you do, Stacey?" Aspine asked, trying to focus on her face. He thought she was coarse and loud but, despite this, found it hard not to stare at her voluptuous breasts.

"I'm a nurse and part-time dance instructor. Oh, and I look after Brad, and that's a full-time job." She giggled.

"And do you work, Pam?" Barbara asked, anxious to include everyone in the conversation.

"No, Jack's old fashioned, and thinks I should be home for the kids."

"That's interesting. Douglas is the same. How many do you have?"

"Three, from ages two to six. They can be tiring."

"So you're about due for another," Aspine said, displaying his usual lack of tact.

Pam felt herself color and was about to respond when the waiter showed Kerry Bartlett and his wife, Jasmine, to the table. Kerry was sweating heavily, his shirt was stained, and he looked nervous and uncomfortable. "Sor-sorry wer-we're la-late. Our ba-babysitter can-cancelled at th-the last min-minute, and we ha-had to find an-another."

Aspine paid no attention to Kerry but found it hard not to stare at his wife who, in contrast to her husband, seemed cool and totally in control. She was Eurasian, with large round eyes, a small, cute nose, and pronounced cheekbones, and the simple cotton dress she wore showed off her slender body. There was just a touch of cleavage, which made Aspine yearn to see more. He thought that she was one of the most provocative and beautiful women that he had ever set eyes on, and felt a stirring in his groin. He wondered what she saw in the pimply faced, nervous Kerry. She sat at the end of the table, directly opposite him. "That's all right, Kerry, these things happen," Aspine finally responded, without taking his eyes off Jasmine.

The waiter returned with glasses of mineral water for Kerry and Jasmine. "We'll order now," Aspine said.

"So you're hitting it hard tonight, are you, Kerry?" Brad guffawed, and as if on cue Stacey giggled.

"We're Rechabites, Bradley," Jasmine said, displaying no sign of admonishment in her feminine sing-song voice.

"Wreck a whats?" Brad laughed.

"We don't drink alcohol. Don't worry, we won't try and convince you to join us."

"I think that's admirable," Barbara intoned, wanting to interrupt her husband's fixation on Jasmine. "Don't you think so, Douglas?"

"Everyone to his own," Aspine said, draining the last of his Jack Daniels. "Gentlemen — and ladies — I'd like to say a few words, after which we can enjoy the night. I asked you here tonight to celebrate the rebirth of Mercury Properties. It is my intention to significantly expand the company's operations and to double its size within two years. Gentlemen, to achieve this goal I will need the help of you and your partners. You are the key members of my team and, if we work together, we can turn Mercury into a financial powerhouse. You might well ask yourself what's in it for me. If we're successful in meeting the targets that I've set, we can earn enough in the next three years to never have to work again. Since I was appointed CEO, the share price has climbed twenty percent, and yet I've barely scratched the surface. Within three years we'll increase it by five hundred percent."

"So we should race out and buy shares," Brad interrupted.

"No, you shouldn't. Why spend your money on shares, when I can ensure that you're granted free options, which have no downside, only upside. But to earn them, you'll have to work hard, very hard, to drive the company forward. We'll need to work as a team and support each other when the going gets tough."

"Greed is good," Brad grinned.

"How do these options work?" Jack asked.

"Simple. The shares are $2.45 now and, say, the company issues you 500,000 free options to acquire shares anytime over the next three years at $2.60. Assume the share price increases to $9.00, and you exercise your options and buy 500,000 shares for $2.60, and you then sell those shares for $9.00. That's a profit of over three million."

"Shit! Mercury never had anything like options under Harry," Jack said. "We got a turkey, a bottle of wine and his best wishes at Christmas. Who issues them?"

"The board issues mine as part of my salary package, and also authorizes me to issue a quantity to you, my key executives. They don't know it yet, but they're about to increase that quantity five-fold."

"Who pays for these options?" Jasmine asked.

Aspine smiled. She might be a Rechabite, but she's greedy, and greed was the key to many other vices he already had planned for her. "No-one; that's the beauty of options, they're free."

"I understand that. I have a brother in Singapore who's something of an entrepreneur, and I've heard about deals like this before. Who pays the three million profit that Jack's going to make?"

"No-one. We increase the value of the shares, and we're rewarded for it," Aspine said condescendingly.

"Yes, but isn't it the existing shareholders who are paying the profits on the options, and aren't you already rewarded by your salary?"

She was stunning, and also smart. She was going to be a challenge, and again he asked himself what she saw in Kerry. "No, Jasmine, that's not right. We have to increase the value of the existing shares before our options become valuable."

"We don't need convincing." Brad grinned. "That's right isn't it, Jack?"

"I'm not about to look a gift horse in the mouth."

"Can we forget business and enjoy the rest of the night?" Barbara said.

"Good idea," Aspine responded. Two of his three key executives had swallowed the bait, but Kerry had hardly said a word, and his wife seemed opposed to the idea of making money. Everyone had a price, a weakness, a desire — he'd just need to find Kerry's. Right now, even without tension, Aspine had one desire — Kerry's wife.

The entrees arrived, and Aspine popped a Tasmanian oyster into his mouth. "They say these things are aphrodisiacs."

"God, just as well you didn't order them, Brad. You're horny enough as it is." Stacey laughed, knocking down her fourth beer.

"Settle down, Stace. I'm sure no-one wants to hear about our sex life."

Jasmine giggled, and Aspine thought *at least she's not a prude.*

"How are the prawns, Kerry?"

"They'r-they're fi-fine," he stuttered. Jasmine rested her hand on his forearm and squeezed it gently.

"Jasmine, what do you do to fill in the day?" Aspine asked.

"I have the kids, and I'm involved in charitable work," she said. She was polite but short, and he sensed that she hadn't been impressed with his little speech on greed.

"So am I. I've recently accepted an invitation to join the board of the National Homeless Foundation. Do you know Catherine Lensworth?"

"I do; she's lovely and works so hard. It's such a good cause. Not many people realize how many homeless people there are in Australia. It's a shame in such a wealthy country. I'm so pleased to hear of your involvement. Big business is generous, but active participation, like yours, is rare. How did you become involved?"

"Catherine approached me, and I never gave it a second thought before accepting. I'm not all about greed, you know."

"I didn't say you were," Jasmine said, blushing.

Barbara rolled her eyes, knowing that her husband never did anything for anyone else unless it benefited him. She was grateful when the main courses arrived, and the conversation turned to the food and the ordering of more drinks.

"Kerry, what are your interests, besides work?" Barbara asked.

"I-I don-don't ha-have mu-much time wi-with work and all."

"He loves spending time with our two boys," Jasmine said.

"I-I do. I wi-wish I had a pla-place in the mountains whe-where I could take them fl-fly fishing, canoeing, hor-horse riding, and whi-white water rafting."

"That's easy," Aspine said. "You can have the best place money can buy in the high country if we can turn Mercury around."

"I thought we'd finished talking business," Barbara groaned.

"I wasn't talking business," Aspine growled, stuffing a large piece of barramundi into his mouth.

"Jack's not going to have to sack anyone else is he?" Pam asked.

"Sorry, Pam, that goes with the territory of being an executive. If Jack's got people working for him who are underperforming, they'll have to go."

"I didn't mean that. I meant sacking three hundred employees for no reason."

"You mean the retrenchments. No, unless there's a massive

slow-down, the retrenchments are over, but you're wrong when you say that there was no reason. They never should have been employed in the first place. We didn't create the problem, but we had to fix it. It's one of the hardest decisions I've ever had to make," Aspine said, directing his last comment to Jasmine.

"No more business talk," Barbara moaned, looking at Stacey for support.

"Yeah," Stacey slurred. "Are we having dessert or port?"

"We have to go," Jack said. "We told the babysitter we'd be home by midnight. Thank you, it was an enjoyable night."

"We're the same," Jasmine said. "It was lovely to meet you all and thank you, Barbara and Douglas, for your hospitality."

Aspine escorted the two couples to the door and stood at the entrance leering at Jasmine's legs and her perfectly proportioned body as she walked down the street. It could take a long time, but he intended to have his way with her.

When he returned to the table, Stacey had ordered port and was slurring at the waiter to leave the bottle. Brad looked nearly as bad as his girlfriend, and there were two empty glasses in front of Barbara. "I thought you were driving," he said, angrily pushing his glass away. "I can't drink this if I have to drive."

"Oh, I'll have it," said Stacey, downing it in one gulp.

"How are you going to drive, Brad?" Aspine scowled; annoyed that he couldn't participate in destroying the bottle of port.

"We didn't drive. We never do. We got a taxi. Don't worry about us."

"You're smart. Come on, Barbara, we're going."

Stacey's speech was almost indiscernible. "Bu we're jusssss gerring started."

"I'll sign the bill, Brad. You and Stacey can stay as long as you like, but we have to go."

"I wanna stay too," Barbara said. "We never go out anymore."

"You're free to stay, but I'm leaving now."

"Spoilsport, all right I'm coming. You're not fun anymore." Barbara stood up and stumbled, grasping for her husband's arm, but he pulled away from her in disgust.

Aspine climbed in behind the wheel of the Ferrari, and Barbara flopped into the passenger seat. Despite the alcohol, she had held up well, and looked closer to mid-thirties than forty-four. He wondered whether she was spending his money on Botox, or maybe having fat pumped from her thighs into her face. "What was it like mentally undressing your financial controller's wife?" she said angrily.

"You're pissed."

"You leered at her all night. No female's safe from randy Douglas Aspine."

"Shut up." He glared at her, taking his left hand off the wheel.

"Are you going to hit me? Try it and you'll be in jail in the morning, and this time I won't withdraw the complaint. God, she wouldn't be twenty-five, and you're nearly fifty. What do you think she's going to see in you? You're a joke," she said, the anger turning to tears.

He gritted his teeth, pursed his lips, and hit the accelerator.

"You'll end up losing your license," she taunted.

He ignored her, but as the red monster closed in on 200 clicks, he stole a quick glance at her face. It was white, and her eyes were locked on the road and the intersections that they were flying through.

"Slow down. Slow down. I'm sorry, Douglas, please slow down," she screamed.

He eased off the accelerator, the corners of his mouth imperceptibly turning up.

As he turned into his driveway, a red MGB blocked the entrance. "Shit!"

"Don't get angry. It's probably one of Trevor's or Jemma's friends," Barbara sniffled.

Aspine got out and walked over to the MGB when he noticed one word carved in the side doors and hood. It had obviously been done with a coin or screwdriver. The letters were about thirty centimeters high, and spelled out 'CUNT.' The car was locked, and there was no sign of the keys. Now he knew why he hadn't heard from Charlie. Bitch! It was far more effective than phoning to tell him that he was a mean bastard.

"Who'd do something like that?" Barbara gasped. "What does it mean?"

"Probably bloody hoons with nothing better to do."

"The car must have been stolen, but why would they dump it in our driveway?"

"I don't know. I'll get up early in the morning and contact the police, and organize a tow truck."

"No! You have to get it towed away tonight. What will the neighbors think if they see it in the morning? It's disgusting."

"All right, all right. I'll call someone, but I don't know why it can't wait until the morning." He was actually relieved that Barbara had insisted on getting rid of it. The fewer people who saw it, the fewer awkward questions there would be. He would call the finance company on Monday, tell them where they could pick it up, and agree to pay any shortfall on the eventual sale.

"Wake up, Douglas, there's a real estate agent on the phone who says she needs to talk to you urgently."

"What time is it?" he groaned.

"It's just after nine. Don't forget you have to call the police about that car."

"Yeah, yeah, pass me the phone, and get me coffee."

"What did your last slave die of?"

"Hello."

"Mr. Aspine, it's Karen Phillips from Kaye & Burton. We manage the apartment you've been renting."

"I gave notice of termination of the lease a few weeks back," he said, anxious to finish the call before Barbara returned with his coffee.

"I know. We went to do a cleanup this morning, and the apartment's been vandalized. Do you know anything about it? When were you last there?"

"Christ, you don't think I did it," he growled, wondering what Charlie had done. "What's the extent of the damage?"

"Someone's used lipstick to scrawl one word on all the walls and mirrors. It's disgusting and difficult for me to say."

"Then don't," he said, impatiently. "See if you can clean it off. If you can't, repaint the apartment. Send the invoice to my post office box. You have the address; it's where you sent your rental invoices."

"Thank you for being so cooperative, Mr. Aspine."

"That's all right, but don't call me at my home again. I can be contacted at Mercury Properties. Goodbye." He slammed his fist into the pillow. "Bitch!" He had underestimated the anger of a *woman scorned*.

Barbara brought him his coffee as he was finishing the call. "Did that real estate agent say something to upset you?" she smirked.

He grunted and ignored her.

"Don't forget to call the police about that car. I still don't understand why it was dumped in our driveway," she prattled.

"Me neither," he lied, "I have to go into the office for a few hours." *At least there's nothing more that Charlie can vandalize. She's obviously forgotten that I have a very revealing DVD in which she features. Perhaps I should send it to her mom.*

- 14 -

KERRY BARTLETT HAD been a brilliant student with uncanny numerical skills, but he'd never been accepted by his peers at Colac High School. He was awkward, gangly, pimply faced, didn't play sport, and could hardly put two words together without stuttering. A devout Catholic, he attended Sunday school and church every week, didn't smoke, didn't drink alcohol and, unlike most of his peers, had never tried recreational drugs. He wasn't unpopular but was ignored and thought of as a nerd.

Midway through year eleven a beautiful Eurasian girl, who had recently emigrated from India, joined Kerry's class. Her father had been an officer in the British Army, and her mother was a tall, willowy Indian model. Her accent was refined, her command of English perfect and she spoke in a delightful, almost musical form. She had large pale blue eyes, light brown skin, long dark hair, and a flashing smile that seemed to captivate every boy in the class. She was equally popular with the girls and was always surrounded by a large group of friends. Jasmine George was attractive, charming and charismatic — everything that Kerry Bartlett was not.

Kerry fell in love with Jasmine the instant he laid eyes on her, but the competition for her affection was fierce, and he thought that he had little to offer. The class Don Juans and sports jocks were all over her, but she was dismissive of them and didn't find their often crude jokes funny. She was fun, but didn't like pranks, and had a low tolerance for stupidity and shallowness. Four weeks after joining the school, she attended church with her family. After the service was over, she introduced herself, saying, "Hello, Kerry, you're in my class at school, but we haven't met. I'm Jasmine George."

His heart pounded so hard that he thought it would burst. "He-hel-hello, Jas-Jasmine."

"You're the class brain." She giggled. "I've read about your academic achievements in the school magazines."

"Un-unfortunately, ye-yes."

"Why, unfortunately? Kerry, God has given you a gift. It's something to be grateful for, and to be proud of." she frowned.

"I-I tho-thought you li-liked the oth-other bo-boys at school."

She placed her hand on his arm. "They're fun, but they're fools. I like intelligent people and the more intelligent, the better."

His face flushed bright red. "Th-thanks," he blurted out.

On Monday, he went to the chemist and bought a tube of Clearasil that he painstakingly applied to his pimples, night after night, with little success.

For the next few months, they had brief conversations at school and longer ones every Sunday. Kerry rehearsed asking Jasmine to McDonald's or Subway, but he could never quite pluck up enough courage to get the words out. He need not have worried. "Kerry," she asked one Sunday, "I'm having trouble with math, and wondered whether you'd be kind enough to come over to my home and help me?"

"I-I'd like th-that," he shouted in excitement, and Jasmine burst out laughing. He hung his head, his face bright red, and then, for the second time, felt her hand on his arm.

"Don't be embarrassed. You're kind, spontaneous, honest, caring, and nice. Don't be ashamed of those qualities, very few people possess them."

As time went by, they spent more and more time together, and by year twelve Kerry was totally besotted with Jasmine, despite her being his main competition for dux of the school honors.

After leaving school, Jasmine and Kerry joined The Salvation Army and became Rechabites. Their lives revolved around their university studies, the church and helping others. Kerry completed a Commerce Degree and started studying for his CPA qualification, while holding down a position as an assistant accountant with a large retailer, as well as being the church's treasurer. Jasmine completed an Arts Degree, majoring in philosophy, before obtaining a position with a human resources firm.

They married just after Kerry's twentieth birthday and made love for the first time that night. He was clumsy, inexperienced, and had been too embarrassed to buy any books that might have helped him on his wedding night. Fortunately, Jasmine's mother had given her a thorough education about love-making, and she had read many books on the subject. It had been painful and unenjoyable, but she loved Kerry so much that she gave no outward sign of discomfort, not that he would have noticed. Two years later their first son Jack, was born and three years after that Jasmine gave birth to his brother Sam.

Kerry was a brilliant accountant, well-schooled in Australian and International Accounting Standards. If he'd been blessed with communication and people skills, he would have been one of the financial rocket scientists employed by the Macquarie Bank, on a million dollar a year salary. As it was, his roles were confined to that of assistant accountant or accountant, reporting to financial controllers and finance directors, who were not nearly as smart as him. Jasmine listened patiently each evening, as he poured out his frustrations about how unfair it was when he was overlooked for promotion. It was not the money but the lack of recognition that irked him. They lived comfortably on his salary, and occasionally had something left over for a little luxury. The night Kerry was offered the position with Mercury they hired a babysitter and went out to an expensive restaurant, where he'd gushed about his future. Three months later Jasmine was not so sure that he had made the right decision. The boys rarely saw him during the week — he worked most Saturdays — and he'd become tired and withdrawn. Worse, she didn't like his boss — he was loud, greedy, arrogant, and had openly ogled her in front of his wife, Kerry, and other employees. She had a strange foreboding, and would have been more than happy if Kerry had gone back to one of his old positions. That was not going to happen and, when he talked, it was about buying a holiday house in Mansfield, a new car or some luxury that they didn't need.

- 15 -

THE BOARD OF the National Homeless Foundation comprised two social workers, a local councilor, a trade unionist, a doctor, a psychiatrist, Russell Ridgeway, CEO of the insurance giant, ANQ and Catherine Lensworth. "Welcome, Douglas, it's kind of you to join us," she said, wrapping her damp, pudgy fingers around his hand. She was short, middle-aged, overweight, and her face was caked with rouge. He guessed the NHF was probably her sole interest in life. "Let me introduce you to the members of our board."

He nodded, smiled and shook hands, until he reached the boyish looking, smartly dressed man, who grinned and said, "How'd Catherine rope you into joining us, Douglas?"

"I thought the NHF was a good cause, Russell. I think that we who are so well rewarded in business should give something back to the community."

"Is that why you sacked half your workforce?" the trade unionist sneered.

"Jesus, Clarrie, get off your soapbox," Russell said. "Douglas is a busy man. We should be thankful he's found the time to help us."

"Gentlemen," Catherine said, "can we get to the business of the meeting?"

There was a murmur of assent, and she proceeded to read the minutes of the previous meeting, which were long and boring, before moving onto other items on the agenda. Aspine found it hard to concentrate, and was thinking about Kelly, when Catherine asked, "Douglas, do you have any ideas about how we might handle this problem?"

He had drifted off and had no idea what the problem was, and again Russell came to the rescue. "Catherine, you can't expect Douglas to fund replacement soup vans every time one drops a gearbox, or blows an engine. He's here for his expertise, not his cash. Watch her, Douglas, or you'll never have your hand out of your pocket."

"How much are we talking?" Aspine asked.

"With the trade-in on the old van, only twenty-five thousand," Catherine responded.

"What about sponsorship?"

"Sponsorship?"

"Yes. I'll need a reason if I'm going to get the donation approved by my board. Would it be possible to sign-write 'Proudly donated by Mercury Properties' on the rear doors and side walls of the van?"

"Oh, yes," Catherine cooed.

"That being the case, you can go ahead and buy your van, Catherine." A gasp went around the table, and even Russell Ridgeway looked impressed.

"I thought you said you needed the approval of your board," Catherine queried.

"You misheard me." Aspine grinned. "I said I needed a reason, and you've given me one. I'll have a check couriered to you this afternoon."

After the meeting, Aspine walked to the car-park with Russell Ridgeway. "Watch yourself, Douglas. Catherine may appear like the friendly motherly type, but she's a hard-headed, determined executive, who'll gleefully take your money."

"I'm happy to help the homeless," Aspine responded, eager to ingratiate himself with Russell.

"Good man. Are you a golfer?"

"I play a little."

"Would you care to join me at my club for lunch, and eighteen holes?"

"I'd like that. Where do you play?"

"Royal Melbourne."

Aspine thought the meeting could not have gone better, and he was looking forward to establishing a solid friendship with Russell.

"So this is the famous Ferrari. It doesn't look like a chariot to me. Don't those cartoonists jack you off, but you know you've made it when they start taking the piss out of you."

"What do you drive?"

"A Lamborghini," Russell said, pointing to a beautiful car parked two rows away.

They shook hands warmly and promised to stay in touch. Aspine reasoned the twenty-five thousand had been money well spent.

Aspine was interrupted by a gangly, fresh faced young man tapping on his office door. *Christ, Kelly's meant to screen my visitors. Where the fuck was she?* "Yes. What is it?"

"Can I see you, Mr. Aspine? It's important."

"Who are you?"

"My name's Rob Sorenson. I'm a sales rep."

"Whatever it is, take it up with Brad Hooper. He's your boss." Aspine scowled.

"But it's about Brad and one of the deals he—"

Aspine cut him off. "I don't listen to complaints about my executives from their subordinates," he said, glaring at Sorenson, who stood shifting his weight nervously from leg to leg.

"It-it's not a complaint. It's—"

"Jesus, man, sit down and spit out whatever's on your mind."

"We sold an apartment to an old couple, the Cartwrights, who couldn't afford it. Anyhow, the old feller's been worrying himself sick and phoning me every day. He hasn't been able to sell the family house, and he's made himself ill."

"He should've never signed the contract if he couldn't complete."

"He had a stroke last night, and he's in hospital in a coma. His wife called me this morning and said the stress of not being able to settle had pushed him over the edge. He mightn't come out of the coma."

"That's bullshit. People have strokes and heart attacks every day that have nothing to do with us. It sounds like his wife's using her husband's misfortune as a convenient excuse to get out of the contract. Anyhow, what do you expect me to do?"

"I think we should let them out of the contract. It'd be a huge relief, and it's not like we can't sell the apartment again."

"What'd Brad say?"

Sorenson hung his head but when he looked up, his face was

determined and his jaw set. "He said the guarantee they signed was joint and several and, that if the old bastard died, his wife would have to settle."

"And he's right. That's why you have joint and several guarantees. I'm sorry for the Cartwrights, but a contract's a contract," Aspine said, displaying no compassion. He agreed with Brad but was wary because this was the type of story that the media would be all over. The type of story that shrew Fiona Jeczik covered, and the mere thought of her smartass questions and sneering face made him cautious and uneasy. "I'll talk to Brad, and if we can do anything to help, he'll let you know." He almost slipped and said 'if you're still here'. Rob Sorenson didn't know it, but his future at Mercury was going to be very short-term.

-16-

ASPINE COERCED AND cajoled the board into providing him with the authority to issue three million options to acquire shares in Mercury to executives, at his discretion. He promptly issued three hundred thousand to Brad Hooper and Jack Gillard, and two hundred thousand to Kurt Metzger and Brian Eppel, that gave them the right to acquire shares in Mercury at an exercise price of $2.60, anytime over the next three years. Harry Denton vigorously opposed the granting of options but, with Sir Edwin's help, Aspine convinced the board that it was in the company's best interests.

Profits were up thirty-seven percent for the first half, but Aspine had anticipated a far greater increase and was worried about how the market would react. Apartment selling prices were too low, the construction of buildings was too slow, and the purchase prices of materials were too high.

The new sales team had cleared the backlog of apartments, and hundreds more had been sold off-the-plan. Mercury had an embarrassment of cash and Aspine knew that he had to put it to work, or be faced with earning a lousy five percent bank interest. He also wanted to increase apartment prices but knew that he couldn't unless the company's competitors also increased theirs.

Dissatisfied with the amount of time it was taking to erect high-rise buildings, Aspine dispatched Jack Gillard to Las Vegas for two weeks to study the methods of builders in that city. He knew it was common in Vegas to add a floor per week, despite the enormous size of the buildings.

Aspine's main concern was the cost of materials and consumables, and he was convinced that he had made a mistake in not sacking Anthony Keen, who he now saw as a weak and ineffectual supply manager. The thought that suppliers were stitching him up, stuck in his craw and he summoned Keen to his office. Even as Keen was sitting down, he barked, "Anthony! What's happening? Our suppliers are screwing us blind, and you're letting them get away with it."

"That's not right. We get three quotes on all major items. Are you having a bad day, Douglas?"

Aspine was momentarily taken aback by Keen's insolence. "No, I'm not, but if you keep that up you soon will be," he growled. "What do you do after you get the quotes?"

"We take the lowest of course!"

"You don't call the supplier with the second best quote and provide a figure they have to beat? Surely you contact the supplier with the best quote, and get them to sharpen their pencil? Christ, there's a million ways you can bullshit suppliers to drive down prices."

"That's not the way we do business. We work in partnership with our suppliers. They hold stocks for us, deliver promptly, and we pay them within their trading terms. That's the way Harry set things up, and it's worked very successfully," Keen said, running his fingers through his silver hair.

"Successfully! Jesus, no wonder we're getting screwed. Anthony, do you have to work, or is it a hobby?"

"What do you mean?"

"People, who negotiate like you, don't usually have to work. They're not hungry, and the thought of screwing someone is abhorrent. That's your problem. Now answer my question."

"I don't need to work, but I enjoy it, have a lot of good years left, and have no intention of resigning. If you try to get rid of me like you did with Neil Widge and Tim Farmer, I'll drag you through the courts and the media," Keen said, a vein in his forehead throbbing furiously. "I knew what you were up to when I didn't get any options."

"I won't get rid of you, but your days as supply manager are numbered. You can stay on as a purchasing officer if you like, reporting to the new supply manager. In a year's time, we'll compare the prices we're paying then, with what we're paying now. If I'm right, and they've been slashed, I'll sack you for gross incompetence. Then see how you go in court."

"I won't accept a demotion and–"

Kelly's shrill voice echoed over the intercom. "Douglas, there's been a terrible accident at the Rowville quarry. One of our employee's, Bert Stuart, has been run over by a tipper. He-he's dead."

Aspine's first thought was about self-preservation. "Kurt, I need to see Kurt urgently."

"He's not here. He's already on his way to Rowville."

"Get him on his cell phone, then get me Max Vogel and, after I've finished with him, Wes Bracken."

"Aren't you going to contact his family first?" Kelly gasped.

"Just do what I tell you."

Anthony Keen's face was filled with contempt. "I'll get back to you," Aspine said, dismissing him.

Kurt sounded like he'd been crying. "A tipper reversed over him."

"How can that be? Weren't the warning beepers on the tipper working? Is it one of ours or a subcontractor's?"

"The beepers were working fine. Bert was deaf, and sometimes when it was excessively noisy, he'd take his hearing aid out. It was one of those times. He didn't see or hear the tipper," Kurt sniffled. "The driver's a subcontractor. He's in shock and too distraught to talk. He's not to blame."

"How old was he?"

"Fifty-nine."

Aspine restrained himself. He knew who was to blame. Fucking Kurt! Why had the dopey German prick let someone that old and deaf remain in the employ of the company? He also knew that it wasn't the time to take him to task. "You'd better stay put. The WorkSafe investigators and coroner will be there soon. Now I know you're upset — we all are — but it's important not to admit anything. Do you understand?"

"You-you're wor-worried about that," Kurt choked.

Aspine fought back the urge to say, *you fucking stupid Kraut bastard, this is your fault!*

Max Vogel's advice was brief. "Douglas, you could go to jail. Admit nothing. Say as little as possible. Refer all queries to me, and lie low."

"Christ, Max, I can't do that. The union's going to come after me.

They'll claim that the retrenchments reduced safety. Then the media will jump on the bandwagon."

"Did they?"

"No. We've got the same number of safety representatives at the quarry as we had before. But the truth's never stopped the unions from spinning their anti-business bullshit, when they've had the opportunity."

"So you're saying you provided a safe working environment?"

"Yes, of course. The driver's a sub-contractor. Surely you can get to him."

"I thought you said he wasn't to blame."

"That was before I knew I might go to jail. I don't care who you hang out to dry if it keeps me out of the clink."

"I'll have a copy of his statement tomorrow, and we'll run a check on his driving record. Before the week's out, we'll know everything there is to know about him — his secrets, his girlfriends, his affairs and his drinking."

"I've got a call into Wes Bracken. Depending on what he says, I'm going to see Bert Stuart's family this afternoon."

"Douglas, if you're going to disregard my advice, please be careful."

Wes suggested that his firm prepare a media statement expressing the company's condolences, and separate death notices that he'd submit to the *Herald-Sun* on behalf of Aspine and the company. "Do you think I should visit the family this afternoon?"

"You have to. Anything less will appear callous and uncaring. Don't drive the Ferrari though, and take someone with you. You don't want any misinterpretations about what's said."

"I'll take Kurt. He's been at the quarry all day. He'll know more about what happened than anyone else."

"Bad move. The family will want to know the specifics and, the less you know, the better. Why don't you take your PA — females are more sensitive than males. Express sympathy and concern and offer to meet any short-term expenses."

"Doug, Fiona Jeczik's been holding for ten minutes. She said it'd be in your best interests to talk to her. Will I put her through?" Kelly asked.

"Get rid of her, then come and see me."

"You're not in her good books," Kelly said, as she entered his office. "She told me to inform you that she wanted to give you the opportunity to tell your side of the story."

"Forget about her," he said, wishing he could take his own advice. "Find out where Bert Stuart lived. We're going to visit his family, and we're taking your car."

"Why am I going, and why are we taking my car?"

"You're my PA, I want you with me, and taking the fucking Ferrari would be inappropriate. Understand?"

"Is that what your public relations people told you?"

"Get the address and let's get going. Like you, I'm not looking forward to it, and the faster we get it over with the better."

The drive to Scoresby in Melbourne's outer suburbs was quiet and uneventful. Aspine felt the tension rising, the tightening of his chest and shoulders, and the dull thudding in his temples which would morph into a full-blown migraine. He glanced at Kelly, who was grim-faced, eyes only for the road on the thirty-kilometer drive. She was in her own world, pondering the grief that Bert Stuart's wife and family would be going through. Cars were parked on both sides of the small street that Kelly turned into, but she found a space and squeezed her Volkswagen into it.

"Wh-what would you like me to do?" She asked nervously.

"Stay close to me. I don't want there to be any misunderstandings about what I say."

"You want me as a witness," she gasped.

"Kelly, I want and expect your support. It's the last thing I wanted to occur, but it has, and I have responsibilities. So do you."

"I do?"

"Yes, to me."

Groups of family friends were milling around the nature strip and driveway of the small brick veneer house. Many of the women were red-eyed, and the men were grim, tightly grasping their cans of beer. Aspine and Kelly made their way to the porch amid much whispering and pointing. Many of the men worked for Mercury, and they all knew who Aspine was, however, he didn't know any of them. The group on the porch cleared and they entered the house. A small, tearful, auburn-haired woman greeted them in the living room. "I'm Bert's wife Rita, and this is our son, John."

John was also small, in his late twenties, almost bald, with a goatee and large spectacles. His eyes were red and his handshake limp. "I'm sorry for your loss," Aspine said, directing his comments to both of them while looking at Mrs. Stuart.

As he was about to introduce Kelly, she took Mrs. Stuart's hands. "I feel so sorry for you. I feel your loss so badly," she said, tears streaming down her cheeks

"There, there, love," Mrs. Stuart said, in the brave way that people suffering extreme grief seem to find in their darkest moments. "Can I get you a cup of tea?"

Before Kelly could respond, John asked, "How did it happen...how did it happen, Mr. Aspine?"

"I'm sorry, John, the details that I have are sketchy. It seems that a sub-contract driver reversed his tipper over your father," Aspine said, swallowing hard.

"Bu-but how?" John stuttered.

"We're not sure," Kelly said, placing her hand gently on his shoulder.

Aspine glanced around the warm, homely room, focusing on a cluster of photos on the mantel shelf. "Your husband was in the army, Mrs. Stuart?"

"He was a highly decorated war hero in Vietnam," John sniffled. "It's ironic, he survived the Viet Cong, but he couldn't survive your bloody quarry. What happened to your safety procedures?"

Aspine felt the thudding above his eyes, and the room suddenly became uncomfortably warm. He knew what John was building up to, and he caught Kelly's eye and moved his head subtlety toward the door. "I'm sorry, John; until I see the investigator's report I can't answer that."

"Mrs. Stuart took her son's hand and quietly said, "Calm down, son, today is for mourning, not vengeance."

"We won't stay, Mrs. Stuart. We wanted to pay our condolences. If there's anything I can do, please let me know," Aspine said, backing toward the door, wondering what she had meant about 'vengeance'.

Kelly squeezed John's hand, before kissing Mrs. Stuart on the cheek.

It was late afternoon when they got into Kelly's car. "Christ, I need a drink something shocking," Aspine said, turning on his cell phone. He had seven messages, but the only one he returned was from Wes Bracken.

"Douglas, Fiona Jeczik called. She's running a story on the accident on *Your Family Today* tonight, and asked us if you wanted to put your side."

"Put my side? What's she talking about? What's she got? It was a fucking accident," he snarled, his head pounding.

"She sounded smug like she knows something that we don't. I told her you were out seeing the family and were unavailable. What could she know?"

"Don't worry about the bitch, she's bluffing."

"Let's hope so, but you still better watch the telly tonight."

"Yeah, I'll be in touch, Wes."

He glanced at Kelly, whose face was pale and drawn.

"Turn right at Springvale Road, and we'll stop at the Novotel. You look like you could use a drink too."

"Don't put me through anything like that again. God, it was sad. It hasn't fully hit Mrs. Stuart yet; she's still in denial."

"It's about another three kilometers on the left-hand side," he said, ignoring her. She'd handled herself well at the Stuarts, but he wanted to tell her not to talk anymore, that he was longing for a drink — that he was under stress — that he badly needed sexual relief. Her dress had crept up a little, and he placed his hand over his eyes as if to massage his headache while squinting through his fingers to check her out. He briefly thought about hitting on her. In any other circumstance he would have, but he sensed that she'd be disgusted, and it would kill his plans for a future liaison. The image of Fiona Jeczik flashed through his mind, and he wondered how the bitch planned to ambush him. He wasn't worried about her — he'd visited the grieving family and done everything by the book.

There were plenty of tables in the lounge, and Aspine chose one where they could see the television. The news had just commenced, and the death of Bert Stuart was the second story. "Fuck, it's been a quiet news day," he cursed.

"Did you say something?"

"No. What are you drinking?"

"Vodka and orange juice, thanks."

He ordered a Jack Daniels too, saying, "I need this," as he gulped half the burning alcohol down in one swig.

The color in Kelly's face returned, but her eyes were still red. She could barely taste the vodka and couldn't get Rita Stuart's tear stained face out of her mind. God, this hadn't been part of the job description and, for the first time, she was having second thoughts about leaving Telstra.

"You'll get over it," Aspine said, tactlessly.

"What?"

"I know how hard it was for you today, but we didn't kill Bert Stuart — it was an accident — an unavoidable accident!"

"Then why did I have to hold your hand? Why couldn't you have taken someone else? I'll resign before I ever let you put me through something like that again."

He swished the remainder of his Jack Daniels around in his mouth before swallowing it, and the barman refilled his glass. The alcohol was kicking in, and the pounding in his temples was easing. Kelly's bitterness surprised him, and any lingering thought of propositioning her evaporated. "Hopefully, neither of us will ever have another experience like this," he said, taking care to remove the edge from his voice. As he was talking, the theme music for *Your Family Today* echoed from the television, and the tense face of Fiona Jeczik appeared on the screen. His stomach knotted, the pain above his eyes returned, and he scarfed his whiskey, immediately trying to catch the eye of the barman.

Fiona related the tragic death of Bert Stuart, and finished by expressing sympathy for his wife, family and the driver of the tipper, but omitted to say that he was a sub-contractor.

Deceitful bitch!

She then cited Bert's war record. He had been a highly decorated

Vietnam War hero, and one of the last soldiers to come home before the fall of Saigon in 1970. There were pictures of him in full uniform, his medals and ribbons taking up most of the front of his shirt. The camera panned back to Fiona wiping tears from her cheeks.

Hypocritical bitch!

Harry Denton's solemn face appeared on the screen. He spoke quietly and respectfully and told how he had employed Bert when he'd returned from Vietnam with severe deafness, the result of a Viet Cong mortar attack. According to Harry, he'd been an exceptional worker, a good friend, and a great man.

Suck-up bitch!

Fiona choked as she asked union leader, Andrew Lawson, if Mercury's safety procedures had contributed to Bert's death. Lawson knew how to spin lies while avoiding a defamation action. "Well as you know," he said, "Mercury recently retrenched four hundred of our members, and lost some good safety people, in doing so."

"So the risk of an accident increased as a result of the retrenchments?"

"Definitely."

"Were there any other factors that contributed to Mr. Stuart's death?"

"We suspect the plant noise levels might be excessive."

"Would excessive noise levels be painful for someone who had to use a hearing aid?"

"Extremely."

The camera panned back to Fiona's face, and she was rolling her eyes and shaking her head.

Frame-up bitch!

"We contacted the company to inquire whether its CEO, Mr. Douglas Aspine, wished to appear on this program, but unfortunately, we did not receive a return call." Fiona frowned.

Aspine's eyes were glued to the screen, and he muttered under his breath, "I'm too smart for you, bitch."

"We thought you'd like to know how Mr. Aspine reacted to the news of Mr. Stuart's death. He immediately started making calls. Not to Mr. Stuart's family, but firstly to his lawyers, then to his public relations firm, and then to his insurers.

We were informed by sources close to the company that Mr. Aspine's PA prompted him to call the family, but was ignored. We wanted to ask Mr. Aspine why he felt it was necessary to contact his professional advisers, rather than Mrs. Stuart. I guess this is how 'big business' treats its employees, and those who are close to them."

The camera panned to Fiona's face, and her eyes were flashing with anger.

Self- righteous bitch!

"Kelly, what did you say to that bitch while she was holding for me?" Aspine growled, his face black with rage.

"Other than 'Do you still want to hold?' Not a word. Do you think I'm stupid?"

"You didn't accidentally slip up and let her know who I was talking to while she was holding on?" he snarled, nauseous, head pounding, and the underarms of his shirt sopping.

"I just told you that I didn't say anything, other than to ask if she wanted to continue to hold. How many times do I have to say it?"

His glass was empty, and he couldn't catch the eye of the barman, so he shouted, "Hey," and when the barman looked around, he pointed to his glass. He ground his hands together as if trying to crush them, before mumbling, "Fucking prick."

"What?"

"It was that bastard, Keen. He was in my office the whole time. Other than you, he was the only one who knew who I called. I'll kill the prick!"

"What about the insurance company? You didn't call the insurers. What was that about?"

"That Jeczik bitch embellished what she already had, knowing there was nothing I could do about it." he sneered.

"Why has she got it in for you?"

"Ratings, of course."

"You think she's that shallow?"

"Her day will come," he muttered, wishing the intense stirring in his groin would go away. He checked out Kelly's trim-taut body once more but knew it was pointless. His mind turned to Charlie. God, why had he got rid of her?

"We better get going."

"I'll get a room here, Kelly."

She was relieved. She'd seen the charming side of her new boss, and now she'd seen the black side. "I'll see you in the morning."

"Yeah," he grunted.

Aspine booked the room in the name of Douglas Court and paid cash in advance on the pretext that he'd be leaving early in the morning. Once in the room, he flicked the Yellow Pages to Escorts, and punched the nearest agency's number into his cell phone, making sure his number would appear as 'private' on the caller ID. Two minutes later his room phone rang. "Douglas Court?"

"Yes."

"I'm confirming your booking. Natalie will be there in fifteen minutes."

She was young, skinny and nervous. Her face was pock-marked, and the tell-tale injection scars of a drug addict punctured her lower arms. He looked at her and felt sick at what he'd sunk to, but he needed to stop the pounding in his brain and the throbbing in his groin. He paid her two hundred and fifty dollars and told her to undress and get into bed, before turning the light off. He took his clothes off, put on a condom and closed his eyes tightly, before climbing into bed, mounting her, and thrusting wildly like a crazed stallion. She bit her lip and whimpered in pain until he finally exploded inside her and rolled off. His head was no longer pounding, and the tension had disappeared, but he was disgusted. He flicked the bedside light on and, without looking, pushed her out of the bed with his feet.

She gathered up her clothes and went into the bathroom. He heard the basin taps being turned on and the toilet being flushed. "Hurry up and get out," he shouted.

- 17 -

A TAXI DROPPED Aspine home at 6:00 a.m. and he told the driver to wait.

"Where have you been?" Barbara snapped. "Where's your car?"

"One of our men got killed yesterday. I visited his wife and family and had a bit too much to drink."

"You slept at his place?" she said, looking astonished. "The accident was on the news. They said that directors could be jailed for manslaughter as a result of workplace deaths. Did you leave your car out there?"

Why won't she shut up? "I slept at a nearby hotel. I didn't drive my car. It's at work."

"At least you showed some sense. I don't know why you can't call when you're not coming home?"

He pretended not to hear. "I've gotta shower and get to the office."

News of the possible legal action hit hard, and Mercury's shares opened at $3.00, down 50 cents from the prior day's close. The 50 cents knocking one hundred and fifty million dollars off the market cap.

Just before noon, Kelly lodged the company's half-yearly report with the Stock Exchange. Net profit was up thirty-seven percent, cash at bank was up three hundred million dollars, and full-year guidance was for an increase of fifty percent. Aspine would've preferred to make a lesser forecast, but to do so, would have meant admitting defeat and handing Harry ammunition. Besides, if he didn't achieve guidance he wouldn't get his million dollar bonus, and the value of his options would be severely reduced. He intended to move heaven and earth to bring in his profit forecast.

The market welcomed the result and the optimistic guidance. Bert

Stuart's death and the possible legal action was forgotten. The institutions waded into the market and bought shares, pushing them to a five-year high of $3.80. Stockbrokers and merchant bankers who hadn't shown any interest in Mercury for years came out of the woodwork. Aspine was invited into their plush offices, where he addressed them on the company's past results and prospects. He met with more than a dozen brokers and basked in their compliments while being careful not to provide them with any more information than that available to the public. The brokers asked the same or similar questions in different ways, always trying to find something out that their peers didn't know which they could use to their advantage. CEOs sometimes leaked information to a favored broker, without appearing to breach the Stock Exchange's rules or Corporations Law. A broker would ask a CEO. "Is it true that the company's going to increase profits by sixty percent over the next six months?" And the CEO might respond. "You know I can't answer that," while beaming effusively. Aspine would become an expert at this form of leaking.

The invitation to lunch, from Selwyn Lappin, head of research at the prestigious brokerage, Blaylor & Fitch, was a pleasant surprise. "This way, Mr. Aspine," one of the receptionists' said, showing him to the boardroom while he was still taking in the ambiance of the offices. The walnut reception counter; the deep leather Chippendale chairs; the paintings by Whitely, Boyd, and Nolan; the quiet order, calmness, lack of urgency; and the smell of old money. The boardroom comprised floor to ceiling windows with views encompassing Port Phillip Bay, the Botanic Gardens and the Melbourne Cricket Ground. The seventeen-seat mahogany table was set for four. Selwyn Lappin shook Aspine's hand warmly, before introducing him to Phillip Muir, the head of institutional broking, and Duncan Milgate, who was in charge of corporate. Two tuxedoed waiters served prawns, lobster and French Chardonnay, and the talk was largely confined to family, golf, politics and the state of the economy. After the table was cleared and coffee had been served, Selwyn Lappin said, "You've done a remarkable job, Douglas. How confident are you about bringing in guidance?"

"Thank you. It won't be a problem," Aspine responded, knowing it was going to be a real struggle.

"Have you got anything up your sleeve over and above the fifty percent?" Phillip Muir asked.

"You know I can't answer that." Aspine grinned. "But Mercury's a long way from firing on all cylinders. Look–"

"You're ten weeks into the second half. You must know how much you're going to beat guidance by." Duncan Milgate interrupted.

Other brokers had asked similar probing questions, but this was different. Blayloch & Fitch were influential and, if they initiated coverage on Mercury, their clients would start buying, pushing the share price even higher. "There won't be any upside surprises this financial year," he said, emphasizing 'this financial year'.

"Do you expect to exceed consensus forecast in the following year?" Milgate followed up.

"We haven't released any projections," Aspine smiled. "I'm not losing any sleep over broker forecasts."

"Look, Douglas, we're not trying to get information that's not available to the public," Milgate lied. "We're trying to better understand the business."

"That's right," Lappin agreed. "We're initiating coverage on Mercury with a buy recommendation, and want to make sure our clients are fully informed."

"We'd also like to help you manage the company's cash, pending you finding a use for it," Muir said. "You must have close to four hundred million?"

"Have you thought about making a takeover?" Milgate asked. "We could help with the advisory work, assist you to raise a little more capital, and you could take a competitor out of the marketplace. You utilize your cash, get cost saving synergies, and remove a competitor. Makes sense doesn't it?"

Aspine pondered his answer carefully. They'd done a lot of work, and most of what they'd said had been carefully planned and was just a little too pat, but he was pleased and didn't want them to lose interest. "Yes, it does, and it's something I've been considering for a bit further down the track. Right now I've got enough on my plate, and takeovers are always disruptive."

"Who did you have in mind?" Milgate asked.

"Apartco."

"So did we," Milgate said, smiling at Lappin and Muir. "So did we."

Duncan Milgate put his arm around Aspine's shoulders as he showed him to the elevators. "We've done a little work on Apartco, and it's a perfect fit for Mercury. Would you like us to continue on a formal basis?"

"What's it going to cost?"

"Not much. No more than four hundred thousand."

"What do I get?"

"A proposal that you can take to your board knowing it's almost certain to be adopted. You're going to struggle to grow Mercury in the longer-term, and this could be the answer to your problem."

"And what do you get, if it's adopted?"

"We'll raise some capital for you and do a little consulting work. We'll talk to the institutions and convince them to accept your offer for their shares in Apartco. Our fees and commission won't exceed fifteen mil."

"Christ, you know how to charge."

Milgate didn't blink. "Douglas, we'd also be pleased to handle your personal account on a minimal brokerage basis. As you know, we handle a lot of public company issues and, if you join us, we can get you into the good ones on the ground floor."

Aspine held his hand out and smiled. "It's been a pleasure meeting you, Duncan. Go ahead with your research on Apartco, but bear in mind I won't be ready to move for at least nine months. I'll ask my 'now former stockbroker' to forward details of my personal holdings to you. I hope this is the start of a mutually beneficial relationship."

Six months earlier, Blayloch & Fitch couldn't have cared less about him. Now he was being courted, being offered special deals reserved for *those in the club,* at token rates of brokerage. *No wonder the rich got richer* he thought. Blayloch's had been supportive but expressed concern about growth and profit increases — if they'd been totally satisfied they would have placed a 'strong buy' on the company's shares rather than a 'buy'. He knew the easiest way to increase profits was by price increases, but this strategy was only possible if the company's competitors also increased their prices. He'd toyed with the idea of contacting the other manufacturers of quarry products, cement, and bricks, suggesting an across-the-board price increase of eight to ten percent, but he knew they wouldn't be receptive. Boral, Readymix, and Pioneer had been caught by the Australian Competition & Consumer Commission (ACCC) for fixing the price of cement, and been collectively fined twenty million dollars. Aspine thought that they'd been staggeringly stupid, because they'd taken minutes of their illegal meetings, before fixing identical prices. The answer was obvious and lay in increasing the prices of high-rise apartments, where Mercury had three competitors in most of the geographical areas where it operated: Apartco, Vicland and Urban. The conversation about Apartco had refocused Aspine's thoughts on apartment pricing. He hit 'one' on his cell phone, and told Kelly to make sure Brad was in his office in ten minutes.

Brad was sprawled in a visitor's chair, reading the form guide. "No wonder you've never got any money, Brad. There's never been a punter who's kept a dollar, but there are plenty of bookies living in luxury. Doesn't that tell you something?"

"I'm not a big gambler. It's the women and cars that keep me broke, but they're two habits I'm not giving up. What is it that you want to see me about?"

"I want you to write a nice letter to Cynthia Cartwright cancel-ing the contract for the purchase of the Docklands apartment. Don't forget to refund the deposit."

"Why? We've got a watertight contract that we can enforce."

"If the old fella dies and the wife goes crying to the media, they'll crucify us."

"You're worried about Jeczik."

"I'm not worried about that bitch or anyone else for that matter. It's good business sense not to run the risk of bad publicity. Brad, it's not up for debate. Draft the letter and make sure it goes out today!" Aspine growled, angry at the mere mention of Fiona Jeczik's name.

Brad was surprised but unfazed by the ferociousness of the response and started to get up from his chair.

"Don't go! I'm not finished. I want to talk to you about the selling prices of our apartments."

"We're about the same as Apartco and Vicland, and slightly less than Urban."

"I want you to increase prices by seven-and-a-half percent across the board, effective from the end of October."

"Fuck! The sales guys are going to go apeshit. We've just *had* a price increase. It's going to make it tough to make sales, and what are we meant to do with outstanding quotes and apartments that we're negotiating on?"

"It's simple; you've got six weeks to close them at existing prices. I don't want you or your reps backdating quotes after the end of October. Do you understand?"

"Yeah, I told you at the interview that management always makes it harder to make sales when the sales guys start making too much money."

"You're management now. I want you to support the price increase. I'm going to make Mercury the market leader and price setter. It has nothing to do with saving commission and, if you shut up and listen, you'll understand why."

"I'll toe the company line, but sales are going to collapse. Our average price is going to be forty thousand more than our competitors for basically the same apartment."

Aspine exhaled, not trying to hide his contempt. "Maybe I'm about to find out if you really can sell. What's the after-market like for our Docklands apartments?"

"Falling. Buyers who paid $600,000 last year are trying to sell for $550,000."

"What about our competitors' apartments?"

"The same. Docklands is ratshit."

"We've got three more blocks of land at Docklands, and I want to start building."

"Shit! Why don't you sell the land?"

"Who'll buy? The scavengers, the bottom pickers, and the opportunists? We'll take a huge loss. That's not an option. How many pre-owned apartments of ours are for sale?"

"About ten."

"Listen to me carefully. I want you to create twenty companies at different lawyers and accountants' offices, with them and their nominee companies as directors and shareholders. Make sure your name doesn't appear on any record. Then I want you to instruct them to buy the pre-owned apartments in the after-market, making sure that the sellers make profits."

"Have you gone totally mad? Why would I want to do that? Where am I going to get the money? What are you on?"

"You'll have no difficulty. I'll provide you with the name and details of a finance company that'll lend the new companies the funds to buy the apartments on a non-recourse basis. You'll arrange to rent them out, and defray the costs of the loans."

"Non-recourse?"

"Yeah, in the event of default on the payment of interest or principal on the loans, the finance company's recourse will be against the apartments and, if there's a shortfall, it'll wear it."

"What finance company does business like that?"

"I'll let you know in due course."

"The rental income won't even come close to covering costs and interest."

"I know."

"I don't understand. Why are you doing this?"

"You'll buy all of our pre-owned apartments that are for sale. Then you'll make sure that we get newspaper editorials, saying that there are sellers of pre-owned apartments constructed by Apartco, Vicland and Urban, but that none of our apartments are available, and those that have recently been sold resulted in profits for the sellers. I also want you to foreshadow the seven-and-a-half percent price increase and our next Docklands high-rise developments, as a strong sign of confidence. Don't forget to mention we'll be selling off the plan."

"You're going to try and prop the market up, and create the illusion, that the prices of our apartments have held up against the overall market decline," Brad gasped.

"Yes, and I want you to follow up with a major advertising campaign emphasizing that our apartments increase in value, whereas our competitors apartments decline," Aspine grinned.

"Fuck, is it legal?"

"That's a moot question because no-one's ever going to find out."

Apartco Limited was a medium-sized public company capitalized at seven hundred and fifty million. Its shares were trading at 90 cents, with fifteen percent controlled by its founders, the Romano family. Aspine knew that Mercury would have to bid at least a $1.20 to mount a successful takeover. *He also knew that Mercury would be making a bid within eighteen months.* It was against this background that he pondered the regulatory risk of personally buying shares in Apartco, knowing that he'd make a guaranteed thirty-three percent profit. Gene Alder had gone to jail for insider training, and Stuart Vizrad had been disgraced, fined three hundred and ninety thousand dollars, and been barred from being a company director for ten years. Aspine considered setting up a blind trust that he would fund, and that would buy the Apartco shares, but this was what Vizrad had done and he'd still been caught. He toyed with the idea of buying in Barbara's name or perhaps Trevor's, but the trail would inevitably lead back to him, and the risk of jail and disgrace was too great. Because of this he decided not to buy shares in Apartco — it had nothing to do with honesty, ethics or morals, and everything to do with the fear of being caught. However, he resolved to form a company that could not be traced back to him so that, if other opportunities to use insider information arose in the future, he would be ready.

EIGHT PURCHASING OFFICERS and nine support staff reported to Anthony Keen.

Aspine painstakingly perused their personnel records, until he reached the recently appointed Steve Brogden's file. He was twenty-eight, married with two children and, more importantly, had previously been employed by Westfield and Lend Lease, which gave him better credentials than any of Mercury's long-term employees. Aspine's only doubt about Steve was his motivation for joining a laggard like Mercury.

"Kelly," he shouted, "tell Kurt, Anthony Keen, and Steve Brogden to come and see me right now."

Aspine mused about Keen's reaction to the changes he was about to make, and the corners of his mouth turned up in a cruel smile.

Ten minutes later, Kurt knocked nervously at his door with Keen and Brogden close behind him.

Aspine glanced up, directing them with his hands to sit down. "Gentlemen, I've called this meeting to discuss Anthony's future with the company."

As Aspine had anticipated, Anthony flushed with anger. "What are Kurt and Steve doing here then?"

"I'm not with you, Anthony," Aspine responded, feigning aggrieved innocence. "Kurt is human resources manager and your future falls within his area of responsibility."

"I'm a senior executive, and discussions regarding my performance and future were always held in private with Harry. Besides, what's he doing here?" Keen glared at Steve Brogden.

"I don't give a fuck what you did with Harry, and Steve's here because I've appointed him to take your place as supply manager."

Kurt's mouth was agape, and Keen looked like he would explode. Steve Brogden remained calm and apparently unaffected.

"I warned you that if you sacked me, I'd sue Mercury to the hilt. I'm going to enjoy watching you grovel in court."

"Anthony, Anthony, you've totally misunderstood me. I haven't sacked you, and I don't intend to. You'll remain on the same salary and benefits. You just won't be supply manager. I'm sure Steve will be able to use you as an expeditor or clerk. You'll have to vacate your office, though, and work with the other purchasing officers."

"Bastard! You're not going to get away with this."

"I'm sorry, Anthony, I don't understand why you're upset," Aspine said, expressing mock concern. "If you're not happy, you can always resign."

"You'd like that, wouldn't you? You can play your little games, but I'm not resigning."

"I'm glad to hear it." Aspine smirked. "You can leave us now and clear out your office for Steve. Can I assume you'll be out in an hour?"

Keen got to his feet, trembling with rage

"Anthony, Kurt will be circulating a memo this afternoon, to the effect that any employee who leaks company information to the media will be summarily dismissed. Shut the door after you."

"You can't do it," Kurt said.

"I just did." Aspine grinned, looking at Steve. "So what do you think?"

"I'm flattered, Doug, but you've never spoken to or interviewed me, so why did you choose me?"

"You were too young to have gray hair, and you've worked for some savvy companies. My only concern is why you left them to join Mercury?"

"I wanted to raise my family in Australia. Promotion at Westfield was only on offer in the US, so I decided to find a company with its operations in Australia, preferably in Victoria."

"Was that the only reason?"

"No. Mercury had a lot of older employees, and I sensed that I might get to be on a fast track."

"You thought you could shove the oldies out of the way?"

"Yes."

"See, Kurt, you should always back your hunches. I have good feelings about this young man."

"That might be the case, but Steve's going to find it difficult so long as Anthony remains with the company. And he's not going to resign."

"Steve, I want you to start screwing prices down. Suppliers have been pulling Anthony's pants down, and I want them crunched. I expect you to make a big contribution to our bottom line and give me the grounds to sack him. If you can cut costs by five to ten percent in the next six months, I'll fire Anthony and, if he's stupid enough to go to court, I'll bury him."

Kurt's body was motionless, and he slowly shook his head.

"Is there anything wrong, Kurt?" Aspine chuckled.

"No, Douglas."

Norman Pell was a highly successful but devious tax accountant, who'd acted for many notorious white collar criminals. Despised by tax office employees, he devoured tax law and case history in the same way that a prolific reader devours novels. He was also a petrol head with a love of fast European cars, and it was this interest that led to his close friendship with Aspine. The phone rang only once, "Pell & Pell, Jessica speaking."

"It's Douglas Aspine. Is Norman in?"

"Yes, Mr. Aspine. I'm putting you through."

"Hello, Douglas. You're not looking to sell the Ferrari, are you?"

Aspine ignored the question. "I need to see you. Do you have time for coffee this morning?"

"Sure. Do I need to do any research before we meet?"

"No. I'll head into the city now and meet you in the Hyatt at eleven."

"Okay."

Norman was sitting at a table in the dining room when Aspine arrived. As he strode toward the table, the little man with the disproportionately large head, receding hairline and horn-rimmed-glasses stood to greet him. Aspine extended his hand, wondering how many had under-estimated Norman because of his physical appearance, only to later regret it.

"Hello, Douglas. Now, what's so urgent that you had to rush in here?"

Aspine glanced around until he caught the eye of a waitress and beckoned her over to take their orders. "I want you to create a company for me with a stooge director. Someone who'll sign documents, applications for bank accounts, tax, and corporate returns, but who won't have a clue what the company's doing. Can you organize it?"

"That's easy. What's this company going to do?"

"It's going to provide finance to companies, who want to buy apartments from sellers of Mercury's apartments."

"Where's the money coming from?"

"Mercury will make loans to the new company."

"You're going to try and prop up the prices of your apartments," Norman said, his face lighting up in a huge grin. "It can't be done; the market's too big. Besides, how's Mercury ever going to get its money back?"

"When the market picks up the buying companies will sell the apartments and repay their loans to the new company, which will then repay Mercury."

Norman looked bemused and slowly shook his head. "That's so convoluted."

"Not really. We need a credible name. Something like Custom Credit, Esanda, or Mercantile Credits. You know what I'm looking for."

"More like Estate Mortgage," Norman laughed, "but the prestigious name still didn't save it from collapse. What you're proposing is illegal and dangerous. Are you sure you don't want to reconsider?"

"No. What about Balmoral Finance Proprietary Limited? It sounds classy."

"If it's available, I'll get it. You know Mercury's auditors are going to want to see documentation and confirm the loan at balance dates."

"You can prepare whatever they require and get our stooge director to sign it. Don't worry about the auditors, I can handle them. Anyhow, the amount of the loan will be immaterial in relation to Mercury's total assets."

"Who's going to sign checks on Balmoral's account?"

"No-one."

"No-one?"

"That's right. Get our stooge director to set up internet banking for Balmoral. Then you'll be able to log into the account at any internet café and transfer monies without there being any trace of who authorized the payments."

"Will Balmoral hold mortgages over the apartments it's financing?"

"No. I don't want some smartass reporter doing title searches and finding out that Balmoral's financing the purchase of all of the pre-owned apartments, or the cat will be out of the bag. Balmoral will hold the titles, but mortgages won't be registered against them."

"I don't like it, but I'm not at any risk, so I'll do it. How do I get paid?"

"I want you to review Mercury's tax position. I'm certain that you can reduce our liability. It's something the former management would've never considered, so I think you'll find plenty. When you submit your invoices, inflate them to cover the work you do for Balmoral. You worry too much." Aspine chuckled. "Oh, and set up a Hotmail address from an Internet café and check it daily but don't use your computers. I'll make sure requests for finance are channeled to that address."

"Is that all? I need to get back to my office."

"No. Make sure Balmoral makes an interest payment to Mercury at the end of every month. I don't want anyone getting suspicious. That covers everything," Aspine said, shaking Norman's hand warmly. "Thank you."

Aspine was on his way back to the office when his pleasant musings about the demotion of Anthony Keen were interrupted by his cell phone ringing.

"Doug, it's Phil Kendall. Have you looked at our proposal?"

"Is Colin Sarll still employed by the bank?"

"No. He took early retirement."

"Aspine laughed. "Is that what the bank calls it when it sacks someone? How'd he react when you told him?"

Sarll had broken down and cried when he'd been dismissed, and at fifty-four, knew that he'd never get a job at another bank. Kendall had no intention of letting Aspine have the satisfaction of knowing this. "He said that he'd been considering early retirement, and the misunderstanding with you brought it to a head."

"Is that right?" Aspine said, sounding miffed. "What about the credit for interest?"

"I've authorized a credit to the company's account of one hundred and thirty-six thousand. Is your wife happy with her new credit card?"

"Yes."

"And have you considered our proposal?"

"We'll keep our banking with you, Phil, but if I find out that little prick's still employed by the bank or any of its subsidiaries you can consider the account lost. Do you understand?"

"Doug, he's taken early retirement and won't be back." Kendall smiled, knowing that Aspine had wanted to hear something far more bloody.

"Goodbye, Phil," Aspine said, punching the steering wheel hard. Sarll had got off far too lightly, and Phil Kendall had spoiled a perfect day.

Kelly followed Aspine into his office with an armful of lease documents for execution. She had done a fine job negotiating the lease of luxurious new offices in Kew. The lessor had agreed to fit-out the offices to her demanding specifications, which included partitioning, floor coverings, sophisticated audiovisual equipment, and antique French furniture. Aspine's new office was twice the size of the one that he now occupied, and overlooked a green, heavily treed park. The boardroom was similar to Donald Trump's in The Apprentice and Aspine smiled, knowing that it would drive Harry ballistic. "You've checked the documentation?"

"Of course."

"And you've run it past Sly & Vogel?"

"Yes," She sighed, in exasperation.

"Settle down, Kelly. I just want to make sure the documentation reflects what we discussed. You've done an exceptional job. When do we move in?"

She felt herself blushing, as compliments from Aspine were rare. "Thank you. I've organized to have the files boxed and transferred by mid-November. We'll be fully operational on the 1 December."

"About seven weeks. That's good because I'm sure looking forward to getting out of this shit hole. Have you found a tea lady yet?"

"Not yet. Don't you like my coffee?" she laughed. "I had a skilled teacher, you know."

He smiled. It was the most relaxed that she'd been since the death of Bert Stuart. "Keep the next few weeks free. We might be heading to Switzerland and the West Indies."

"Fantastic. Will I have time for sight-seeing and shopping?"

"It's business, Kelly, but you can pack your bikinis," he said, running his eyes up and down her trim body. As he was ogling her, the phone rang in her office.

"Excuse me. I have to take that."

He cursed the phone. He'd got no response to his clear hint when even a giggle or smile would've told him all he needed to know.

"Douglas, it's Mr. Milgate from Blayloch & Fitch. He said it's urgent."

- 19 -

"HELLO, DUNCAN."

"Doug, it would be in your interests to invest in Philco Coal, but your investment can't exceed a hundred thousand. We don't want heavy buying tipping the market off before our other clients have bought."

"Jesus, I don't have a loose hundred thousand. How certain are you about this stock?"

Milgate sounded miffed. "Philco's shares are trading at $2.20. We expect them to be $3.50 within three weeks."

"You've got inside information?"

"That would be illegal, and this firm always acts within the law."

"Put me in for twenty thousand shares, but don't commit more than forty-four thousand dollars."

"You're a most unusual man. Our clients always want more, never less. Some have been stupid enough to buy more through other brokers, but we always find out, and dispense with them as clients."

Aspine smiled, at the less than subtle warning. "I'm not big on the stock market. You'll never have to worry about me," he lied.

"I wasn't suggesting that you'd do anything like that, Douglas. I'll be in touch."

As Aspine finished the call, Kelly said, "Wes Bracken's been holding for you. He said it's urgent."

Everything's urgent he thought. "Yes, Wes, what's the problem?"

"Fiona Jeczik's doing another exposé on you and Mercury tonight."

"How do you know? What's it about?" Aspine said, trying to keep calm.

"Channel Sixteen's been running ads all day about big business screwing consumers. Our accountant's wife works there and knows it's about Mercury, but doesn't know what Jeczik has. Do you have any idea?"

"Not the slightest," Aspine responded, feeling nauseous. *God, why does the bitch have it so badly in for me?*

"If I find out, I'll call you."

The house was strangely quiet. Mark was sprawled out on the couch watching *The Simpsons.* "How are you, Mark?"

"Good, Dad."

"Where are the others?"

"Mom and Jemma are shopping, and Trevor's out driving his car."

"Flick the television over to the Channel Sixteen news."

"Why can't you watch it in the study?" Mark protested.

"Because I'm going to watch it here, and that's all there is to it."

As the Channel Sixteen news came on Mark looked sullen and uninterested.

Five minutes later the solemn face of Fiona Jeczik appeared. "Today we have a shocking story about corporate greed; a story that will turn your stomachs, and which culminated in the death of a good man."

Aspine felt his chest tightening as he waited for the bitch to resurrect the death of Bert Stuart.

"This is the story of an elderly couple, Eric and Cynthia Cartwright, who were conned by Mercury Properties into buying an apartment which they couldn't afford. After they had realized they'd been duped, they tried to cancel the contract, but Mercury flatly refused. Because of the pressure that Mercury exerted, Eric suffered a stroke and was hospitalized four weeks ago. Sadly, he passed away this morning."

Aspine groaned, but this time, the bitch had gone too far. He'd instruct Max Vogel in the morning to sue her and Channel Sixteen for defamation. She couldn't prove that the sale of the apartment and the stroke were related.

The camera panned to the tear-stained, wrinkled face of Cynthia Cartwright. She was incoherent and rambling about Brad Hooper, and how he had insisted they complete the purchase.

"Were you ever told about the cooling off period?" Fiona asked.

"No, we found out after it had expired."

"And had Mr. Cartwright been in good health?"

"Oh, yes, he had a full check-up three months ago. It was only the worry of being unable to pay for the apartment that caused the stroke," Cynthia said, tears rolling down her cheeks.

The camera panned back to Fiona Jeczik shaking her head and rolling her eyes in disgust.

Cynthia Cartwright's merely surmising and can't prove anything. Aspine savored the thought of issuing writs. His initial nausea had passed, and he was now focused on vengeance. As he pondered this, the bitch reappeared after an ad break, and sitting opposite her was the young, innocent Rob Sorenson.

"You used to work for Mercury, Mr. Sorenson."

"I resigned this morning."

"You left in disgust?"

"Yes."

"Can you take us through the sale in detail?"

"Certainly."

Aspine felt the nausea returning. He needed a drink but was riveted to the screen. All thoughts of legal action and vengeance left him.

"Before Mr. Aspine's appointment, how much commission would've you have made on the Cartwright sale?"

"Nothing; I was on a flat salary."

"And how much would you make now?"

"Nine thousand dollars on settlement."

"Nine thousand dollars!" Fiona said, slowly drawing out the words through a thin, mirthless smile.

"Is it true that Mercury's sold six hundred thousand dollar apartments on deposits as low as one hundred dollars?"

"Yes."

"And is it true that some salesmen loaned clients deposits out of the commission they expect to earn on settlement?"

"Yes."

The camera panned to a close-up of Fiona Jeczik's anger contorted face. She had a document in her hand. "I'd like to read the letter Mercury eventually sent to Mrs. Cartwright, canceling the contract and refunding the deposit after they found out about Mr. Cartwright's stroke. *Dear Madam, Despite your failure to meet your contractual obligations, we have decided to waive our contractual rights. Your deposit for one thousand dollars is returned herewith. Bradley Hooper, Sales Manager.*"

Aspine's head was pounding, and he felt like he had been punched in the stomach. God, could Brad have written a more insensitive letter? He cursed, knowing that he couldn't sack him because he was imperative to the scheme to prop up apartment prices.

"Dad, are your salesmen crooks?"

He'd forgotten Mark was lying quietly on the floor.

"No, of course not."

"Is it illegal to pay commission?"

"No, Mark, it isn't. I'm not feeling well. Can you save your questions until after?"

"Why does that lady hate you?"

Before he could respond, the phone rang, and Mark jumped up to answer it.

"I'm home to no-one," Aspine said.

He heard Mark say, "No, he's not home."

"Who was it?"

"That Brad Hooper guy. Is he a crook, Dad?"

The phone rang again. Aspine went to the liquor cabinet, took a bottle of Jack Daniels, and stumbled down to his study. He did not take a glass.

The following morning the market wiped 50 cents off Mercury's share price, and the switchboard lit up. Two of Melbourne's most prominent talkback jocks picked up on the Cartwright story and ran tear-jerking interviews with Cynthia. Hundreds of irate citizens called in, attacking Mercury, Brad Hooper, and Aspine.

When Aspine walked into his office, Brad was already there. He looked nervous and was without his usual chirpiness. "I called you last night. Why didn't you return my call?"

"Brad, after that bitch read that letter, I wanted to kill you. There was no way I was going to talk to you until I'd cooled down."

"Are you going to sack me?"

"What for, doing your job? Not likely, but don't ever write another letter like that."

"There are a lot of people on talkback radio calling for my head."

"And mine," Aspine grimaced. "It'll blow over, but we're going to have it tough for a week or so. There'll be reporters chasing you. I don't want you to talk to them. Take the week off. By the time you get back, everything will have been forgotten."

By midday, Mercury's shares had fallen another 30 cents. "Mr. Lappin is insisting that he talk to you," Kelly said.

"Hello, Selwyn."

"Douglas, I've called four times."

"Sorry, I've been flat out."

"Many of our wealthier clients have, at our suggestion, already bought shares in Mercury. We've received a lot of concerned calls this morning."

Aspine smiled. The clients who'd already bought would be the most influential; the *special* ones who were tipped off before the buy recommendation was published, ensuring they bought at the lowest price. No wonder Lappin was nervous. "It's a storm in a teacup. There's nothing to worry about. Most of what was reported is unfounded."

"Are you going to sue?"

"What, and drag it out for years? No."

"Are you going to sack your sales manager?"

"That'd be tantamount to admitting we'd done something wrong. No, I'm not going to sack Brad."

"Is there any good news that you can release to the market, that'll negate the bad publicity?"

"That's an excellent point. I hadn't considered it, but there may well be something. Leave it with me."

"Let me know before you announce anything to the market?"

"Wouldn't that breach the listing rules?"

"I'm not asking you to read me the release verbatim. I'm just interested in the subject matter. Call me before making any announcement, Doug."

"Kelly," Aspine shouted, "tell Kerry Bartlett to come and see me."

Ten minutes later Kerry knocked nervously at his door. "You wanted to see me."

"Take a seat, Kerry. Have you got figures to the end of the third quarter?"

"No. I'm still working on them."

"But you have a fair idea of what the result will be?"

"Yes. Operating profit before tax will be between ninety-four and ninety-seven million."

"What's that as a percentage increase over the same period last year?"

"About forty percent," Kerry replied, looking down at his feet.

"Fuck," Aspine growled, placing his hands on his forehead, slowly pushing them through his thick hair. "We're between seven and nine million short."

"Yes."

"Kerry, you know how important it is for us to increase full year profit by fifty percent. What do we have to make in the last quarter to achieve it?"

"Forty million," Kerry whispered.

Aspine stood up and walked around the desk, placing his hand on Kerry's shoulder. "Don't be concerned. Sales are going to be strong. We could easily make forty million, but that's not the problem."

"No?"

"It's that Jeczik woman and the lies she's spreading about Brad and the company. It's putting pressure on our share price, and some investors are getting nervous. The brokers would like us to make an announcement to the market today."

"An announcement?"

"Yes, they want me to confirm the fifty percent profit increase, but it's so close to the end of the year that I can't afford to be wrong, or I'll lose all credibility."

"Bu-bu-but you can't d-do it because yo-you don't know."

"I can if you'll help me."

"I-I'll do any-anything I can, bu-but I don't know how I can help."

"Let's say that I make the announcement, but at the end of the year, we end up five to ten million short. I'm not sure how to put this, but is there any way that you can adjust the results, so we achieve our target?"

"Yo-yo-you want me to fal-falsify the fig-figures?" Kerry said, a nerve in his cheek starting to pulse.

"Hell no! I want you to help me if you can. Surely there's a way to massage the figures, where we take a little of next year's profit and put it into this year's figures? We've increased selling prices, we're reducing costs, and we're increasing efficiency. Next year's going to be a boomer, but I might need a little assistance this year."

"I-I don-don't know."

"Kerry, we're talking ten million out of a total profit of one hundred and thirty-five million, in a company with a market capitalization of more than a billion dollars. It's nothing and, besides, we still might make the forecast profit. I want to know if you'll help me if we don't."

"I-I'd like to be able to say yes."

"I'm sorry I didn't realize it was so difficult. I don't know anything about accounting, but all I'm trying to do is smooth the figures out over two years. I'd never dream of asking you to do anything illegal," Aspine lied. "I guess you couldn't conceal it from the auditors?"

"I could do it in half a dozen ways, and the auditors would be none the wiser. I'm not worried about the auditors."

Aspine mused that ego was a powerful motivator, even in the weakest of personalities. His suggestion that Kerry couldn't outsmart the auditors seemed to have struck a nerve. Aspine put his hand back on Kerry's shoulder and looked into his eyes. "If I need your help, will you come through for me? I'll be indebted to you forever."

"Yes. I-I'll do it if I have to, bu-but I hope you nev-never ask me to do any-anything like this again."

"Rest assured, I promise that it will never occur again. There are a few other matters I'd like to discuss with you. I'm bringing in a tax expert with a view to minimizing our tax liabilities. He's name's Norman Pell, and he's going to call you."

"That could be beneficial."

"And I'm going to put some of the company's funds out on short-term deposit with Balmoral Finance. They're paying seven percent."

"I haven't heard of them. Have you checked them out?"
"Don't worry, they're solid."

Aspine asked Kelly to prepare an announcement to The Stock Exchange, confirming previous earnings guidance, and then called Selwyn Lappin. Lappin asked if he could hold off for half an hour before transmitting to the ASX, and Aspine agreed. He guessed that Lappin would be organizing some moderate buying for favored clients of Blayloch & Fitch. Fifteen minutes after the announcement was made, Mercury's shares climbed 40 cents, recovering half of what they'd lost earlier in the day, courtesy of Fiona Jeczik. Her crusade against Mercury had not been all bad news though — Andrew Malone couldn't stand the pressure that he was under from friends and peers, and resigned as a director. Aspine wondered whether William Claymore and David Cleary would also resign, which, except for Harry and Stan Pettit, would clear the board of its deadwood.

By the middle of December, Mercury had deposited fifteen million dollars with Balmoral Finance Company Pty Ltd. Balmoral had made loans to a number of companies, to fund the purchase of pre-owned apartments built by Mercury in the Docklands. The prices paid were above market price, and very few of Mercury's Docklands apartments remained for sale by original buyers. In direct contrast, there were a large number of apartments available from sellers who'd purchased from Vicland, Urban, and Apartco. It appeared that Mercury's Docklands apartments were appreciating in value, or at least holding their own when the value of its competitors' apartments was falling. Brad placed double-page advertisements in the *Melbourne Age* and *Herald-Sun* stating that Mercury's pre-owned apartments in the Docklands were selling for more than their original purchase price and supported this by listing some recent sales. All showed healthy profits for the sellers. The ads were cleverly worded and inferred that Mercury's apartments were of a superior quality to its competitors apartments that were selling for less than their original prices. The message was clear — buyers wanting to watch their capital appreciate had to buy an apartment built by Mercury.

Aspine sold his shares in Philco Coal for $3.40, realizing a profit of twenty-four thousand, and two weeks later XStrata made a take-over bid for Philco at $3.80 per share. Blayloch & Fitch's information was excellent, and they also advised him to buy shares to the value of seventy thousand dollars in Carbotrim. He bought stock worth thirty-five thousand and sold it for a profit of fifteen thousand after Carbotrim announced the grant of a patent for a weight-reducing drug. He was then advised to put one hundred thousand into Ingotgold, but he only invested fifty thousand and was already ten thousand in front. Blayloch & Fitch certainly looked after their clients or at least their influential clients.

- 20 -

KERRY BARTLETT WORKED tirelessly during January to complete Mercury's Accounts, which showed an operating profit of one hundred and twenty-four million, an increase of thirty-eight percent over the prior year. He was sweating heavily when he related the result to Aspine.

"How much do we need to adjust the profit by, to achieve our forecast?" Aspine asked, knowing exactly what the figure was.

"Eleven million," Kerry gasped.

"Is there any problem?"

"I-I-I...nev-never knew the adj-adjustment would be so lar-large, and I'm not sure whether we should do it."

"Kerry, I made an announcement to The Stock Exchange in October because you told me there'd be no problem. If I go to the market and report a thirty-eight percent increase, I'll lose credibility, the company will lose credibility, and you'll lose credibility because the market will know that you were the one who came up with the figure."

"Wou-would you sa-sack me?"

"You're far too valuable. I wouldn't know what to do without you. I'd be disappointed if you went back on your word and let me down, but I don't hold grudges," Aspine lied. "What difference does it make whether it's five million or eleven million? We're only borrowing from next year's profits. It's not like it's going to happen again."

"I-I don-don't know."

"If you can't do it, you can't, but you're going to leave me high and dry. I thought you said you could conceal it from the auditors, but I must have misheard you."

"I can. They'd never find it, but that's not the point; it's the immorality of it."

"Immorality! Why didn't you raise it in October? Look, if you can't outsmart the auditors, that's fine with me, but don't bring up morals as an excuse."

"I-I can. It'd b-be easy. It's just–"

Aspine interrupted. "I can live with you going back on your word, but don't make out that you're smarter than the auditors."

Kerry's head was nearly on his chest, and he squirmed in his chair. "Ar-are yo-you sure you-you're only go-going to ask me this once?"

"I promise," Aspine responded, his face filled with sincerity.

"I-I I'll do it the-then, just this once tho-though."

Aspine smiled. He'd known that Kerry would cave in and knew he would again. "You'd better make the adjustment twelve million. If we make it exactly fifty percent, it'll look fishy. We don't want that, do we?"

The board met in the company's palatial new offices for the first time, to consider the year's results and to determine a dividend. Harry surveyed the antique furniture, the paintings, the artifacts, the plush carpet and the audiovisual equipment. "What a disgusting waste of shareholders' money," he muttered, to no-one in particular.

"It's the type of office that public companies wanting to project an image have, Harry. The management and staff are far more efficient than they were working from the cramped dog boxes you had them in."

"Hmmph, no-one ever complained to me about the offices. This edifice is more about your ego than efficiency."

Aspine was about to respond when Sir Edwin intervened. "Great result, Douglas, you delivered on your promise."

The other board members, except Harry, begrudgingly offered their congratulations. Harry shook his head and muttered, "Something's not right."

"The only thing that's not right, Harry, is the lousy result you brought in last year. You made it easy for me." Aspine smirked. "You must have been in cloud cuckoo land."

Harry's face turned scarlet. "You talk about projecting an image. You've lowered the image of a great and ethical company. You've got nothing to be proud of when you fleece senior citizens to make profits."

"That's bullshit. We refunded the Cartwrights money and rescinded the contract long before that Jeczik woman got involved. It was a beat-up."

"This board might be asleep, but Fiona Jeczik's not. She's awake to you and what you're doing. She's going to bring you down."

"You wish, Harry. You wish. It's a pity you're no longer a check signatory because I've got a million dollar check that needs signing." Aspine laughed. "I don't know what your gripe is; I've doubled the value of your shares."

"Let's move on," Sir Edwin interrupted. "Last year's final dividend was 10 cents. I think we should declare 15 cents this year."

There was a murmur of approval before Aspine said, "I don't think we should pay a dividend. We should conserve our cash."

Harry started to laugh. "You don't want to declare a dividend because you don't own any shares and think it'll reduce the value of your options. Conserve cash? You've sold everything that wasn't bolted down and the company's rolling in cash. You're a slimy piece of work."

Aspine smiled, but his eyes were hate-filled as he stared at Harry. An uneasy silence hung over the room, before Sir Edwin said, "I think the company can stand 15 cents, and the institutions are expecting it."

"Are we providing earnings guidance when we announce the results?" Stan Pettit asked.

"I'm glad you asked, Stan. I can increase operating profit by thirty percent this year, but to achieve it I'll need some new incentives. I've already discussed them with Sir Edwin."

"You-you've got a three-year contract," Harry said, almost choking. "What are you talking about?"

Aspine smiled. "You got paid two million to bring in a profit of ninety million. I'm going to make Mercury one hundred and seventy-seven million this year. I should be on four million."

"You've got a contract, and your options are worth three million," Harry shouted.

"My options are worth three million for one reason. Me! Your shares have doubled in value from twelve million to twenty-four million for one reason. Me! Mercury's going to make a record profit this year for one reason. Me!"

Harry snorted. "We'll hold you to the contract, and if you breach it, we'll sue you."

"I don't think the institutions would like to go down that road. After all, I've doubled the value of their investments."

"What did you agree to, Ed?" Harry snarled, emphasizing the 'Ed'.

"I haven't agreed to anything, but we did discuss an amended contract for Douglas's second year. Two million in salary, one-and-half million bonus if a thirty percent profit increase is achieved, with three million options to acquire shares at an exercise price of $4.00. Half of the options entitlement and bonus payable after six months, providing the pro-rata profit target is achieved."

"That's ridiculous. You're proposing to pay him three and a half million, and to top it up with three million options without any hurdles. The shares are already trading at $4.00. If you're going to issue options, they should be exercisable at $5.00, and the quantity should be reduced to two million. And what's this lunacy about paying half-yearly?"

"I agree with Harry," Stan Pettit said. "I can live with the salary and bonus, but the options and timing of entitlements are far too generous."

"I-I think I agree with Harry too," William Claymore mumbled.

"I've got half a dozen jobs that I can take that'll pay me more. If you haven't realized it, I'm hot property, and there are a lot of companies that'd like to have a CEO, who could increase their profits by thirty percent. You try and screw me, and I'll walk."

"Good riddance," Harry said.

"Hold on. Hold on," said Sir Edwin. "What if we increase the exercise price of the options to $4.25? How would you feel about that, Douglas?"

"Bloody unfair." Aspine scowled.

"No, it's still far too easy," Harry snapped.

"It seems fair to me," David Cleary whispered. "Surely we can reach agreement."

"Can we, Douglas?" Sir Edwin asked.

"I suppose so, but I'm not happy." He caught Sir Edwin's eye and gave him a subtle wink, as this was the scenario they'd agreed to before the meeting. By his calculations, he would earn seven million in his second year, and while not showing it, he was elated. "I have two other matters I want to raise. I want authority to issue a further three million options to my executives, on the same terms as those issued to me, should I deem it appropriate."

As expected, Harry opposed the proposition but, with a little pushing by Sir Edwin the other board members murmured their assent. Harry's power was almost completely eroded.

"What else, Douglas?" Sir Edwin asked.

"I'd like to invite Russell Ridgeway, the CEO of ANQ to fill the vacancy on the board left by Andrew Malone."

"That would be a coup. Do you know him?"

"He serves on one of the charitable boards that I'm on," Aspine responded, creating the impression that he assisted many charities.

"He's been very impressive in turning ANQ into an insurance powerhouse," Stan Pettit added. "I'd certainly support his appointment."

"What do you think, Harry?" Sir Edwin asked.

"If he's as smart as what the newspapers say, he'll decline. He'll know that you get fleas when you sleep with dogs," he said, addressing his last comment to Aspine.

"There's only one dog on this board, Harry," Aspine responded.

Aspine was elated with the outcome of the meeting and while Kelly was preparing the announcement for release to the market, he called Selwyn Lappin.

"What news do you have, Douglas?"

"We're announcing to the market this morning."

"Was the operating profit in accord with your earlier announcements?"

"Yes."

"What about guidance for this year?"

"That's included in the announcement."

"What increase are you projecting?"

"You know I can't tell you that."

The line went quiet and all Aspine could hear was Selwyn Lappin breathing. "I understand. Listen, I'm going to mention three figures, and I want you to say no to two of them. You won't be breaking any laws. Ten?"

"No."

"Fifty?"

"No."

"Twenty-five?"

"I didn't hear you, Douglas. Hold off making the announcement for an hour."

"Kelly, get me Russell Ridgeway," Aspine shouted.

"Hello, Douglas. What can I do for you?"

"Russell, a casual vacancy has come up on our board, and I wondered whether you might be interested in filling it?"

There was a long silence.

"Russell, are you still there?"

"Yes. Look, I appreciate your offer, but it's something I can't take on at present," Ridgeway said, sounding strangely subdued.

"Is there something wrong?"

"No, but the last exposé Channel Sixteen did on you was damning, and you've made some people at the top end of town nervous."

"I take it you're one of them?"

"No, but the insurance industry is very sensitive. I can't afford to be associated with anything that might be scandalous or improper."

Aspine cursed. Harry had been right, and Ridgeway was running scared. "I understand your decision, Russell," he lied. "I'd appreciate it if you'd keep this conversation private."

"It never happened." Ridgeway laughed, but he sounded relieved.

"When are we getting together for that game of golf?" Aspine asked.

"Golf?"

"Yes. Don't you remember? We were going to have lunch at Royal Melbourne, and follow up with eighteen on the east course."

"I'm sorry. It slipped my mind. I'll get my PA to arrange something, and get back to you."

"Do that, Russell."

As Aspine put the phone down, he cursed Fiona Jeczik. He was obviously on the nose with Russell Ridgeway, and it was all her doing. *Bitch!*

Mercury's shares rose 15 cents in the hour preceding the release of the full-year results, on steady but controlled buying. The market greeted the announcement of a fifty-one percent increase in operating profit enthusiastically and pushed Mercury's share price up another 25 cents to an all-time high of $4.40. Aspine's options were worth over three million and when added to his salary and bonus he'd earned more than five million for the year. Sir Edwin was happy, the institutions were happy, the stockbrokers and merchant bankers were happy. Only old Harry remained bitter and skeptical.

The morning newspapers were glowing in their commentary on Mercury's results and were unrestrained in their admiration for its CEO. Aspine read every word and basked in the afterglow. Marcus Easton, from *The Australian,* who'd already labeled him a turnaround expert, was lavish with his praise and called for the appointment of more proactive CEOs to manage the surfeit of staid and underperforming public companies. Aspine read the article for the third time before shouting, "Kelly, get me Marcus Easton."

Kelly had installed a sophisticated intercom between Aspine's new office and her own. He had only to press a button to talk to her but, to her disgust, he still insisted on shouting. A few minutes later she said, "I have Mr. Easton for you."

"Marcus, I want to thank you for your article today."

"It was richly deserved. You've done an excellent job," Easton responded, in a surprisingly immature voice.

"Thank you."

"What are your plans for the future?"

"Marcus, you know I can't answer that."

"You misunderstood me. I'm not seeking inside information, but rather the big picture of where you're aiming to take the company."

"Why don't you come to my office for lunch? Nothing special

— sandwiches and orange juice — and I'll let you know what I can about the company's direction."

"I'd like that. When?"

"How about midday tomorrow? Strike while the iron is hot, so to speak."

"That's fine, Douglas. I'll see you then."

For Aspine, it was time to reward those who'd helped him achieve the result, particularly the company's second most important person. "Kerry, come and see me."

Kerry's face was white and his pimples had flared up. Again, Aspine wondered what Jasmine saw in him. "Grab a chair. I want to thank you for the effort you've put in. You've worked hard and done a fine job."

"Thank you, I-I wi-wish we had-hadn't–"

Aspine held his hand up. "That'll never happen again, and it's not why I'm thanking you. It's the hundred hour weeks, the financial control, and your ability to produce accurate and timely results. I'm increasing your salary by sixty thousand, paying you a bonus of one hundred thousand, and issuing you another four hundred thousand options to acquire shares in the company, exercisable at $4.25. You realize that the initial options issued to you are now in the money to the extent of three hundred and sixty thousand."

Kerry sat glued to the chair, staggered by the magnitude of the numbers. "Ye-yes I know. Tha-thank you."

"Now you can afford that place in Mansfield for the boys. I want you to take this weekend off, so you can head up there, and buy it."

"Tha-thanks Doug," Kerry choked, with emotion.

"Get out of here." Aspine grinned.

Brad Hooper's bonus was five hundred and fifty thousand, and while he'd met all performance criteria, Aspine resented paying it. After all, it was more than half his own bonus, for which he'd had to sweat and cheat. As Brad sprawled in the chair opposite him, he silently cursed his generosity. "How are sales going?" he asked, already knowing the answer.

"Slowly. The price increase is killing us, and the others haven't followed."

"Have you been selling the fact that the price of Mercury's pre-owned apartments is appreciating, and the prices of our competitors are falling?"

Brad laughed. "Did you say fact? Of course, we are, and we've even managed to make sales to a few woodies."

"As far as the public's concerned, the price of our apartments have been climbing, and don't ever call our clients wood ducks."

"They're too expensive, and the reps are pissed off because they can't make sales. We're going to lose some of them once they've been paid their outstanding commissions."

"Tell them to hang in there. I want you to run those double-page advertisements again this weekend, and put them in *The Australian* as well because there's going to be an increase in demand."

"How do you know?"

"I know, and don't be surprised if our competitors have price increases soon. How are sales going in the three new Docklands projects?"

"There's been a few sold off-the-plan, but nothing of significance. They all seem to be going up at the same rate, almost like it's a race."

"It is. When Jack Gillard went to Vegas, he found that building teams competed against each other for large bonuses. That's how they build those bloody monoliths in such a short time. We're doing the same."

"I thought you called me in to talk about my bonus."

"I did." Aspine grinned, pushing Brad's check across the desk.

"What do you think?"

"It would have been close to a million if you hadn't raised apartment prices."

"You're not happy?"

"I didn't say that. Christ, it's the biggest paycheck I've ever seen."

"What are you going to do with it?"

"Don't worry. I'll find someone or something to blow it on."

"I've also allocated you another hundred thousand options exercisable at $4.25."

"How's that work? A lousy hundred thousand?"

"You're management, Brad, and it's time to start performing. Re-educate your team to sell at the right prices, and I'll look after you."

Brad was not appeased. "There are a number of our apartments on the after-market. What do want me to do?"

"Buy them. How much will you need?"

"About five mil."

'That won't be a problem. We have to hold the prices up. Have you got agents renting the ones you previously bought?"

"Yeah, but it's a struggle."

"Just make sure you get something to defray the interest costs."

- 21 -

INGOTGOLD ANNOUNCED THE discovery of a rich find in Tibet and Aspine sold his shares for a thirty thousand dollar profit; a gain of sixty percent in two months. He'd never made easier money and mused about Blayloch & Fitch's wealthy clients and the profits they must be making as a result of their broker's seemingly infallible recommendations.

Kelly showed Marcus Easton into the boardroom. There was a platter of sandwiches, a jug of orange juice and two glasses on the boardroom table. Aspine stood up and extended his hand. "Glad you could make it, Marcus." He was thin, pasty-faced, with long mousy colored hair, but his handshake was firm.

"Thank you for inviting me, Douglas. It's a little warm. Do you mind if I remove my jacket?"

"Make yourself comfortable."

Easton removed his jacket and hung it over the back of a chair.

"Help yourself."

"Thank you. Will any of your executives be joining us?" Easton asked, placing a recorder on the table, and flicking it on.

"No, a lot of what I'm going to discuss with you is confidential and off the record, so I'd appreciate it if you'd turn that thing off."

Easton looked embarrassed as he turned the recorder off.

"I'm sure you'll understand after you hear what I have to say," Aspine said, anxious not to upset the young reporter. "You're the first journo I've talked to since I accepted this position."

"It's been a remarkable transformation. You've taken an old, staid company into the twenty-first century. What's the biggest single change that you've made?"

"That's easy. Changing a slack culture to one of uncompromising quality," Aspine lied.

"I'm surprised. I thought that you'd say crushing the unions, downsizing, or implementing rigorous cost controls."

"I've done all of those things and more, but it's the improvement in quality that's made clients rush to buy our apartments."

"I didn't think anyone was rushing to buy apartments these days."

"We've experienced strong demand in our three new Docklands complexes. And you probably know that the few apartments available in our earlier developments are selling at a premium."

"I've seen your ads. I thought you'd highlighted a few apartments where the original buyers got lucky."

"We track the sales of our apartments by original buyers. In the past four months not one has changed hands for a price less than it was originally sold for. Contrast that with our competitors, where there's a plethora available and original buyers are sustaining large losses…and that's when they're fortunate enough to make a sale."

"Why is that?"

"Well, the design and quality of our apartments is superior to that of our competitors. We use the best materials, the finest tradesmen, and we're fastidious about the finish. Consequently, our apartments have increased in value, and those of our competitors have fallen."

"Are you saying the quality of your competitors' apartments is second rate?"

"Oh, I wouldn't say that." Aspine smiled.

"I thought you just did."

"Look, we're the only builder in the Docklands whose apartments are holding their value. We had a seven-and-a-half percent price increase at the end of October, but our competitors are reducing prices. Doesn't that tell you something? It's all about a superior product and superior quality."

"But if your competitors' prices are significantly less than yours, you must be struggling to make sales."

"Marcus, you grossly underestimate the intelligence of our clients. If you had the choice of buying a Docklands apartment tomorrow for seven hundred thousand dollars from us, knowing it will increase in value, or buying something from one of our competitors for six hundred and fifty thousand, knowing it will almost certainly lose value, which one would you buy?"

"So you are saying that your competitors' apartments are second rate," Marcus said, looking for a provocative headline.

"I'd never say that about my competitors' products. Maybe they're first-rate, just not as first-rate as ours. They'd be raising prices if they were. Instead, they're reducing them. If I were a buyer, I'd be worried."

"Worried because your competitors haven't put up prices?"

"Because of our commitment to quality, we have minimal maintenance and warranty work. Despite this, we have to include something in our price to cover contingencies."

"Are you suggesting that your competitors may not be able to service and warrant the apartments they've built?"

"Oh, I don't know, Marcus, you'd have to ask them." Aspine smirked. "Would you like more orange juice?"

The following morning, there was a full page article about Mercury in *The Australian* under the headline, 'A Quality Turnaround'. Marcus had written the article verbatim what Aspine had told him, and he glowed when he read the words, *Douglas Aspine's Mercury Properties*. He opined that if Brad's sales team couldn't sell now, they couldn't sell at all. He also knew that the article would infuriate the CEOs of Vicland, Apartco, and Urban.

The drive to Mansfield was fun, with Jasmine, Jack and Sam playing I Spy and singing while Kerry concentrated on the roads. It was the first Saturday that he'd taken off since starting at Mercury, and when he'd told Jasmine that he was taking the weekend off, she had been elated. He was still withdrawn and not himself. Jasmine put this down to the hours that he'd been working. Like Kerry, she'd been staggered by the size of his bonus and pay increase, and it worried her that his values were becoming more material. It was a clear sunny day, and the smell of freshly sawn timber hung in the air as they approached the outskirts of the town. Kerry had made appointments to inspect five properties, but the first two were old, run down, and not as they'd been described on *realestate.com*. As they sat in the bakery eating lunch, he couldn't conceal his disappointment, and snapped at Sam for playing with his food.

Jasmine placed her hand on Kerry's wrist. "Honey, he's only five, and he's been up since six o'clock."

"I'm sorry. Hey, Sam, come over here and sit on Dad's knee."

"When are we going home, Dad?" Jack asked. "I'm tired."

"We'll look at two more houses. Then we'll have some ice cream and go home. How does that sound?"

"Why are we going to live up here, Dad?"

"We're not, Sam. We're trying to find a holiday house where we can ride horses, fish, go boating, and maybe have a cow. You'd like that wouldn't you?"

"Will I get my own horse?"

"You sure will, Jack."

"What about me? I want a horse," Sam squealed.

"Me too." Jasmine giggled.

"We'll all have horses," Kerry said.

"Mine will be the fastest," Jack yelled.

"Will not. Will not. I want the fastest horse," Sam screamed.

"You're a bub."

"Am not, Jack. I'll hit you."

"We have another house to look at in twenty minutes. Finish your lunch, boys," Jasmine said, raising her voice just enough to settle them.

They drove out of Mansfield on a bitumen road, before coming to a gravel track meandering down to Lake Eildon. The agent had told them to take the last driveway off the track and, as they turned into it, they could see rays of sun bouncing off the lake. The property was neatly fenced, and the weatherboard house had been freshly painted. The real estate agent was standing by her car at the front of the house. "Hello Mr. and Mrs. Bartlett, I'm Kathy Lewis. Hello, boys, are you having a nice time?"

Sam cuddled Jasmine's leg and tried to hide behind her, and Jack looked down at his feet. Kerry did the introductions.

"Would you like me to come through the house with you, or would you prefer to look by yourselves?"

"We'll look by ourselves, thank you," Jasmine responded.

The house had five bedrooms, a large, renovated kitchen, two bathrooms, and appeared clean and well looked after. "What do you think, Jasmine?" Kerry asked, struggling to contain his excitement.

"The same as you." She giggled. "It's wonderful."

There was a bedroom with toy trains, cars and trucks on the floor, and Sam squealed, "This is my bedroom."

"It's on seven acres which borders the lake and has a small barn we can use for storage. Let's see if it's fully fenced," Kerry said.

"It's perfect." Jasmine smiled. "Are we going to buy it?"

"I think so."

The freshly painted barn was neat and tidy, and the timber post and steel strand fence was in good condition. Combined with the two hundred meters of lakeside frontage, it encompassed the property. There was even a small jetty, and Kerry imagined himself and the boys sitting on the end of it fishing, or perhaps launching a dinghy into the pristine water.

"How much is it, Kerry?"

"Three hundred and seventy-nine thousand, darling."

"Oh, wouldn't it be nice to buy a house with all this land in Melbourne for the same price?" Jasmine giggled.

As they were talking, Kathy strolled over to them. "Is it what you're looking for?"

"Very much so," Kerry replied. "We'd like to buy it."

"Are we going to buy it, Dad?" Jack cooed.

"Shoosh, Son, I'm talking to the lady."

"It's an exceptional property, and the owners aren't going to be very negotiable on price," Kathy said, in typical real estate salesperson speak.

"I thought it was three hundred and seventy-nine thousand?"

"Yes, that's right," Kathy replied, realizing that Kerry wasn't going to haggle and that the nine thousand she'd added to the asking price for bargaining, was going to be a bonus for the vendors. "The deposit is ten percent."

"That's fine," Kerry replied, removing his checkbook from his back pocket.

"When would you like to settle, and can I help you with finance?"

"Thirty days and, thank you, but I'll organize finance."

The boys were exhausted, and only the thought of ice cream forced them to keep their eyes open. Dusk was starting to fall as they left the town for the drive back to Melbourne. The boys were asleep, and happiness and satisfaction permeated the car. Jasmine glanced over at Kerry, and the stress and tension she'd noticed over the past few months had disappeared. She rested her hand on his leg. "Are you happy, honey?"

"Very, and looking forward to the first weekend we spend in our new house."

"But you work every Saturday. How are you going to get away?"

"I'm taking every second Saturday off after settlement."

"I'll believe it when I see it." Jasmine laughed.

Kerry took his hand off the steering wheel and playfully squeezed her arm. "You'll see."

Vic Garland, the sole owner of Vicland, was nearly eighty years old and had been building apartments for fifty years. In his prime, he'd been president of the Federal Liberal Party, and a behind-the-scenes kingmaker. He was brusque, impatient, and short with Kelly. "Put me through to Aspine," he croaked.

"You mean Mr. Aspine," she responded, annoyed by his rudeness. "I'm not sure if he's available."

"He'll be available for me, girly, now put me through."

Aspine picked up the phone but, before he could speak, Garland launched into a tirade of abuse. "I don't know how you got that journo to write that article in *The Australian*, but it's bullshit. What are you playing at? Apartment prices are falling, and yours aren't selling at a premium. It's crap! What are you doing? Selling them to mates, and agreeing to buy them back in three years' time?"

Aspine smiled. The article had had a bigger impact than he had anticipated. "Vic, I don't have mates with pockets that deep. Our apartments are holding their value because of their quality and finish."

"Don't give me crap. I don't know what you're doing, but I know it's a fix-up."

"Sorry, you feel that way, Vic. I'm a busy man, and if you've said your piece I've got work to do."

"I'm not finished. I want to know if you've really increased the list prices of your new apartments, or are you letting your salespeople discount back to old prices."

"I don't let my salespeople discount, and we're getting those increases on our new Docklands apartments. There are not many buyers, but at least when we make a sale, we make money. It's a tight market, but if you, Apartco and Urban were to increase prices, at least the sales that we collectively make will be profitable."

There was a long pause. "What you're suggesting breaches the Trade Practices Act and, if we get caught, we'll be up for millions in fines."

"I'm not suggesting anything. If I was, I'd suggest you raise your prices by seven or eight percent. We went up by seven-and-a-half percent, and you wouldn't want to match us exactly. Are you close to the management of Apartco and Urban?"

"I've already spoken to the decision makers in those companies. They'll do what I do."

"And what are you going to do, Vic?"

"I like making money, so I'm going to increase our prices but, if I find out that you're discounting, we'll bury you in a price war."

Aspine gripped his chair hard and fought back the urge to let out an almighty whoopee. 'Vic, we can control the market if we don't discount. We shouldn't be competitors or enemies because, when we are, it's the customer who wins. It's the customer who's the enemy and, if we all hold prices, no matter who wins the sale, the customer will have to pay up."

"As long as we don't get caught," Garland croaked. "I won't call you again at your office. How are we going to stay in contact?"

"Buy yourself and your contacts at Apartco and Urban prepaid cell phones. I already have one. My number's 0400 452 047. We'll talk soon."

The article in *The Australian* and the saturation advertising in the Melbourne newspapers had assisted Brad and his sales team to sell twenty-two of the Docklands apartments' off-the-plan, with the help of insurance bonds, easy finance, and minimal deposits. Compared to prior weekends, it was a good result, but Aspine was bitterly disappointed. He'd been expecting far better, and his mind turned to the first quarter's results, knowing they wouldn't be good.

- 22 -

YOUR FAMILY TODAY still presented human interest stories and this was the bait that Fiona Jeczik used to lure a successful suburban lawyer to appear on her show. His face had been made up and, as he sat opposite her, the cameras began to roll. "So you help the needy get started with their first house, Mr. Dowling?" she said, smiling sweetly.

"Yes, yes my firm does. It's about giving something back to the community." Dowling glowed.

"So you provide the initial finance and handle the purchase on behalf of the buyer?"

"Yes, our interest rates are a little higher than the banks, but we have to cover the additional risk."

"I understand. And the only other consideration that you receive is your legal fees?"

"Yes, but I try to keep my fees to the absolute minimum. I want to help my clients."

"And the money that you lend comes from your wealthier clients. Is that right?"

"That's correct. Their loans are protected by mortgage, and they earn a little more interest than they could from the banks."

"A win-win for everyone?"

"Well, yes. I hadn't thought of it that way," Dowling replied.

"It's a little strange that most of your conveyancing and finance work comes from one real estate agent, isn't it?" Fiona innocently asked.

Dowling stiffened in his chair. "I hadn't noticed. It's my clients who I'm interested in."

"Did you have a financial interest in any of the properties sold?"

"No, and I resent the question."

"Oh, I'm sorry. Did any company or trust in which either you or your family are involved, or are beneficiaries of, have any interest in any of the properties sold?"

"I don't know what you're getting at," Dowling responded, beads of perspiration appearing on his forehead.

"Didn't you or an entity associated with you purchase a house and land at 24 Salmon Street, Dandenong, for two hundred thousand dollars? And wasn't that property sold to one of your clients for two hundred and sixty thousand dollars one month later? Did you inform your client, when you were advising him and arranging finance, that you were the seller?" Fiona smiled, through compressed lips.

Dowling's face was red, and the lights in the studio were like hot coals on his face. "I-I don-don't know what you're talking about."

"Do you get sworn valuations on the properties you finance to protect your wealthy clients in the event of loan default?"

"Of course."

"Was 24 Salmon Street valued at two hundred and sixty thousand dollars?"

"I don't remember the property," Dowling lied, "but yes, there would've been a sworn valuation."

"And you only use one firm of valuers? How do you, the real estate agents, and valuers split the profits made on fleecing these poor people?"

"Tha...that's defamatory," Dowling said, sweat running down his nose onto his lips and chin.

"Sue me," Fiona replied, her lip curled up in disgust, as the cameras panned in for a close-up of her face.

"Where's Craig?" Fiona shouted to no-one in particular. "Where's Craig Chisholm?"

"Great show, Fiona." The baby-faced man responded, walking from behind one of the cameras. "I'm always on the set when you're doing your show."

"It wasn't a great show, Craig. It was the same as what I've been doing for weeks. The public's getting sick of seeing me frying small suburban professionals. I need a big fish. What do you have on Aspine?"

"Nothing new. He's an overbearing bully, earning a fortune to tear a company to pieces, in the name of downsizing and profit. He's a typical CEO."

"I value your opinion, but Aspine is far worse than that. You need to dig deeper. Talk to the people he's fired; old girlfriends, competitors, former bosses, and anyone else you can think of."

"I've got my two best researchers and our lawyers looking at him. We're running up huge costs and haven't unearthed anything other than that he's a nasty bastard, which we already knew. I've been waiting for the bean-counters to haul me over the coals."

"Tell them to come and see me," Fiona said, knowing that management wouldn't dare challenge her about costs. "Docklands is a disaster for all builders, but Mercury's running huge advertisements saying that everyone who's bought and sold one of their apartments has profited. It has to be lies. Check the selling prices, and then we'll expose Aspine for the liar he is."

"We already have. What they're claiming appears to be true. Are you sure this guy's any worse than most other CEOs?"

"Definitely, and somehow he's manipulating the Docklands apartment market."

"We thought of that. If that was the case, the sales would have to be to his friends and associates at inflated prices. He doesn't have many friends but, even if he did, why would they pay inflated prices?"

"You're missing something. Put another two researchers onto him. Don't worry about costs, keep digging."

Kerry Bartlett knocked nervously at Aspine's door. "Ca-can I-I see you, Douglas?"

"I always have time for you, Kerry."

"I-I've finished the first quarter's figures. Th-they're no-not good."

"I didn't think they would be." Aspine smiled, walking around his desk and taking a chair next to Kerry. "A small glitch caused by our price rises. Don't worry, the second quarter's going to be a boomer."

"Bu-bu-but the bud-budget was for-forty-two million, and we've only made twen-twenty-three million."

"Fuck! I didn't think they'd be that bad. How can that be?"

"We-well I-I had to rev-reverse the twel-twelve million adjustment we put through a-at the en-end of December."

"Oh, so that's what caused the blowout." Aspine smiled, placing his hand reassuringly on Kerry's shoulder. "You'll have to hold off on that reversal entry until we have a good quarter's figures."

The air conditioning was cold, but the perspiration stains under Kerry's arms were fresh. "Yo-you to-told me I would-wouldn't have to fud-fudge the figures again."

"And I'm not asking you to now. Look, we don't report quarterly figures to the Stock Exchange, only the board."

"Yes, bu-but we-we hav-have an ob-obligation to keep the mar-market ful-fully informed."

"And so we shall. In August, we'll report the half year's result to the end of June."

"Bu-but even wi-with the twelve million, we're still sev-seven million short of bud-budget. We-we're going back-backwards."

Aspine placed his hand on Kerry's knee. "You know we're going to surpass budget for the rest of the year, so what difference does it make if you increase the adjustment to nineteen million?"

"Yo-you wa-want me to fu-fudge the figures by nine-nineteen million dollars now?" Kerry gasped, barely able to talk.

"Don't panic, Kerry. It's not as if I'm asking you to fake the figures for the Stock Exchange. We'll exceed budget by nineteen million this quarter, and when you report June's figures, they'll be kosher."

"Ho-how su-sure are you that every-everything will b-be right by the en-end of June?"

"I'm positive. Besides, it's only the directors who'll see these figures, and they wouldn't have a fucking clue about anything. You've got nothing to worry about. Is there anything else you want to discuss? No? Good, ask Kelly to come and see me on your way out."

Kerry rose slowly from his chair without saying another word, his face stressed and drawn.

Kelly was wearing a short white dress, high heels, and a near-transparent lemon blouse. As she sat down, Aspine ogled her trim body. "You wanted to see me?"

"We're going to Hong Kong on Sunday for a week. Arrange the flights and make bookings at the Sheraton?"

"What happened to Switzerland and the West Indies?" She smiled as if to suggest that he'd been exaggerating.

"They've been deferred. Don't worry, if you're a good girl, I'll take you there as well."

"I've never been to Hong Kong. I'm so glad I'm going. Will I book business? Who are we seeing? Do I have any appointments to arrange?"

"I couldn't leave my right arm behind, could I? Book first class, I don't like flying with losers. Don't worry about appointments; I've already set them up." Norman Pell, the devious tax accountant, had set up his one and only appointment, with Hong Kong's leading firm of tax lawyers.

"What will I be doing? Will I have time to do some shopping?"

Aspine smiled slyly. Other than paying the airfares, accommodation, and expenses, Mercury had nothing to do with his business in Hong Kong. "I'm sure we'll be able to get some shopping in."

"It's so exciting," she bubbled. "Thank you."

Kelly's response was spontaneous, and Aspine had said nothing to suggest that the trip was for anything but business. "There are some great restaurants, and I'll show you the red light areas if you like?" He smirked. "You'll see sights that you won't see anywhere else in the world."

"I don't want to go into any sleazy places. I've seen Pat Pong in Bangkok, and I don't think that Hong Kong's red light areas will be any different."

"That's fine. So the only sleaze will be between you and me." Aspine laughed light-heartedly while intently watching Kelly's face.

"That's not going to happen." She frowned. "The door to my room will be securely locked."

"I thought we'd share a suite," he said, in mock seriousness. "It'd be much more comfortable."

"You put me in charge of hotel reservations. I'll book you a suite, and a room for myself."

Aspine was convinced that Kelly was teasing and that they'd be having a raunchy week in Hong Kong.

Jasmine was becoming more worried about Kerry. They'd gone to Mansfield to buy horses, relax, and spend some quality time together and with the kids. Kerry was morose, snappy with the boys, and had shown no enthusiasm or excitement when they'd bought the horses. Worse, she'd found two bottles of brandy in the bedroom that had been converted into a study for him. He'd never drank alcohol before and had expressed compassion for those who did. He was withdrawn, but she hadn't tried to get him to open up. In the few times that he'd been depressed in the past, she had tried to talk him back from his self-inflicted abyss, only to see him withdraw even deeper into himself. Eventually, he would snap out of it and, in an outpouring of pent-up emotion, tell her what was bothering him. She already knew — Douglas Aspine and Mercury Properties — but she didn't know why?

Craig Chisholm was excited. The whistleblower who they had labeled 'Mercury Rising,' and who had anonymously leaked Alpine's remuneration package, had made contact again. They knew that to have access to board minutes, she had to be a senior Mercury employee. Now she wanted to meet with Fiona privately, without cameras or recorders. She was asking for ten thousand in cash and said that she would call back at ten o'clock the following morning for Channel Sixteen's decision. "Hell, Fiona, we can't agree to the ten thousand without knowing what she's got."

"If she has anything like those minutes it'll be worth every cent. When she calls, agree to pay and arrange a meeting. I sense this could be the break we've been waiting for."

"It's all right for you. You don't have to account to those upstairs."

"I've told you before, that if you have any trouble with management or the bean-counters, refer them to me."

-23-

KERRY BARTLETT SAT in the corner of a dimly lit bar, nursing his third straight brandy. The dark amber liquid warmed him and seemed to ease the stress — even if only for a few hours. It had been twenty years since he'd tasted brandy, when his mother had used it to fight off the flu and bad colds. As soon as he swallowed it, she would hand him a tablespoon piled high with jam to remove the disgusting taste. It was only natural that he would turn to brandy, to ease his current ills, albeit the ones that he now faced were self-inflicted, and resulted in a tortured conscience. He had falsified figures submitted to the Stock Exchange, the Securities and Investment Commission, and to the board of Mercury Properties Limited. He'd signed a loan agreement and transferred millions of dollars of Mercury's monies to Balmoral Finance Proprietary Limited, on the verbal instructions of Aspine. He had authorized checks for tens of thousands of dollars payable to tax accountant, Norman Pell, for minimal services. It hadn't worried him, but now, as he stared at his empty brandy glass, he realized there was nothing to tie Aspine to the falsified figures, Norman Pell's invoices or the loans to Balmoral. Worse, he'd recently done a search of Balmoral, and found that its paid-up capital was only one thousand dollars; he'd never heard of its sole director; and its registered office was 'care of the offices of Norman Pell'. Try as he might, he could not fathom how he'd got himself into a position where he could go to jail for ten years. It hadn't been the money, but more of a desire to please and win the friendship and respect of the powerful and charismatic Douglas Aspine — a desire that remained largely undiminished.

QF29 departed from Tullamarine at 11:00 p.m. on Sunday, and touched down in Hong Kong on Monday at 6:00 a.m. The flight was smooth and uneventful. Aspine slept most of the trip, while Kelly watched movies, played computer games, and ate copiously. She had never traveled in the pointy end of a plane before and had no intention of wasting a second of it. Despite this, she was too excited to be tired and babbled incessantly during the cab ride to the Sheraton. "Where are we going? What do you think I should wear? Who will we be meeting?"

"We'll take it easy today." Aspine smiled. "The hotel's in Nathan Road, and we're staying in the middle of Hong Kong's most famous shopping strip."

"Yes, I know. I looked it up on the net before we left."

The cab pulled up at the front of the hotel, and two bell boys loaded their luggage onto a hotel trolley. They produced their passports at reception, and the attendant took an imprint of Aspine's credit card. "You have an exclusive suite on the eighteenth level, Mr. Aspine," the attendant said, "and Ms. Jenner, you have the adjoining deluxe room."

As the panoramic elevator rapidly ascended, they took in the magnificent views of Hong Kong and Victoria Harbor. "Let's take an hour to unpack and clean up, and then we'll do some shopping if you're up to it," Aspine said.

The suite Kelly had booked was huge and had separate living and office areas with all the mod cons. Aspine made one call to Crossley & Leyland, the tax lawyers and confirmed his 2:00 p.m. appointment for the following day. He showered and changed into a casual shirt, light cream slacks, and tasteful brown shoes. When Kelly responded to his knocking, she was wearing a silk tangerine blouse, brief black shorts, and sandals that accentuated her toned legs. "You look great," he said, mentally undressing her.

"Let's go," she said, uncomfortable with his leering.

It was hot and humid, and Nathan Road was teeming with a mass of endlessly moving humanity. Kelly wasted no time, and within two hours was carrying shopping bags laden with dresses, tops, shoes, makeup, lingerie, and gifts. Aspine enjoyed watching her change into a variety of dresses, but he was craving a drink and soon became tired and bored. He was also annoyed. He'd offered to pay for some items, but Kelly had politely declined. Worse, she had not given him the slightest hint that they'd be getting between the sheets. While peeved, he wasn't deterred. After all, she wasn't wearing those tiny black shorts for nothing, and she wasn't naïve.

"Let's go back to the hotel and get something to eat."

"Oh no, Doug, I've just started shopping." She giggled, "If we get busy, I mightn't get another opportunity."

"Yes, you will. I have some private meetings tomorrow, so you'll have the whole day to shop."

"Why am I here if I'm not going to be at your business meetings?"

"Kelly, I won't know if I'll need you until after tomorrow's meetings but, if I do, I want you to be available," he lied. "Do you understand?"

"Yes...yes, I think so."

When they arrived back at the Sheraton, Kelly claimed that she was tired and needed a few hours' sleep. Aspine wanted to say, 'How about I join you?' but, instead, bit his tongue, "I'm going to show you the sights of Wanchai tonight, so be ready by eight."

"Okay."

When Shirley Bloom, alias 'Mercury Rising', called Craig he agreed to pay her the ten thousand, on the condition that he also attended the meeting. He explained that it was for security reasons, and Shirley bought it. They agreed to meet at the rear of a noodle café in Mordialloc the following night at 9:00 p.m. Shirley said that the café was poorly lit, there was only one door to the rear and, if she got a whiff of a camera or a recording device, the meeting was off.

There was a faint refreshing breeze wafting off Victoria Harbor on the short ferry ride from Kowloon to Hong Kong Island. Aspine hadn't been in Wanchai for five years, but he knew that the red light district in Lockhart Road wouldn't have changed. The names of some of the bars, discos, and brothels might have changed, but the ingredients would be the same. Kelly seemed to be enjoying herself, looking inside the bars and discos. "Would you like a drink?"

"No thanks, I'm enjoying the atmosphere and the walk."

"See those girls in the red bikinis?" Aspine asked, nodding to a gaudily lit bar.

"Yes."

"They're not girls."

"No! They're beautiful."

"Bloody disgraceful if you ask me. There's nothing on this road you can't buy. You can get anything, from bestiality to conventional sex, that's if you can call anything in this place conventional."

"The thought of women and animals makes me sick."

"Not just women." Aspine chuckled, reveling in Kelly's discomfort.

"I knew about the sex, but–"

"That's nothing, Kelly. You want to see what some of these girls can do with a ping pong ball or a lighted cigarette."

"Stop it, you're making me ill."

Aspine had broken into a light sweat, and halfway down Lockhart Road, stopped in front of a bar named The Goddess. "Let's have a quick drink."

"I told you I don't want to go into any of these places."

"It's a bar, Kelly. It's tame; you're not going to see any deviant acts."

"All right, I am thirsty."

Aspine ordered a Jack Daniels, and a mineral water for Kelly. The bar was quiet, and there were a number of Filipino, Indonesian, Thai, and Korean girls lolling around looking bored. Because he was with Kelly, no-one approached him. Two young girls were dancing in front of floor-to-ceiling mirrors at the rear of the bar. They wore sarongs but were naked above their waists. Aspine leered at their innocent faces, their firm breasts, and the rhythmic but repetitive movements of their nubile bodies. His concentration was broken by Kelly tugging on his shirt sleeve. "Who's the old woman sitting in front of them?"

"That's their mama-san."

"Mama-san?"

"Think of her as a conventional western madam. She looks after the girls, negotiates their rates, and liaises with the Johns," Aspine responded, feeling a stirring in his loins as he focused on the smaller of the two girls.

"Can we go? I think the jetlag's starting to catch up with me."

It was after midnight when they got back to the Sheraton. "Feel like a night cap?" Aspine asked. "There's a well-stocked bar in my suite."

"No thanks. I need sleep," Kelly begged off.

As Aspine entered his room, he had a clear vision of the smaller girl dancing and wondered what Kelly's breasts looked like. Perhaps he'd find out tomorrow, he mused.

Crossley & Leyland had partners and managers fluent in more than a dozen Asian languages. They specialized in international banking, transfer pricing, and income tax minimization. Aspine's cab pulled up out in front of Imperial House at 1:45 p.m. and he alighted and walked briskly into the foyer. He entered an elevator, hit the button marked Crossley & Leyland, and it whisked him to the twentieth level. The doors opened onto a white marble floor, and a long black marble counter overlooking a small library, in which there was an array of deep, black leather chairs and accompanying coffee tables. There were three young women behind the counter, and a petite Chinese girl with beautiful skin, dark eyes, and jet black, glistening hair greeted him. "How may I help you, sir?"

"Douglas Aspine. I have a two o'clock appointment with Charles Ong."

"We've been expecting you, Mr. Aspine. Did you have a pleasant flight? Mr. Ong will be with you shortly. Would you like coffee or tea?"

"Yes. I arrived yesterday morning. I'll have coffee, white with no sugar."

"I'll have tea, Sally, and you can bring them down to my office," said the tall, bespectacled Eurasian man, who entered from one of the three corridors adjoining the reception area. He extended his hand. "Charles Ong. Greetings, Mr. Aspine, it's a pleasure to meet you. Norman Pell speaks highly of you. How are you coping with our oppressive heat?"

"Thank you, Charles. Please call me Douglas or Doug," Aspine said, as Charles took his arm and led him toward his office.

"How can we help you, Douglas?"

"Well, I'm not an expert in international banking or taxation, but I have read about our infamous Alan Bond, and I've taken some advice from Norman. I was going to set something up in the Caymans or the Bahamas, but I understand the IRS can now access bank records in those countries. If the US government can do it, there's a risk that the Australian government will eventually be able to do the same."

"Slow down, and tell me what you want to achieve. I'll let you know the best methods and countries to achieve your goals."

"Before I continue, is this conversation covered by client-lawyer privilege?" Aspine asked, a look of concern clouding his face.

"Everything we discuss is privileged. You may speak freely."

"I want to create a trust or company or both, that will trade Australian shares on which large profits will be derived. In respect of these entities, I need to be totally hidden. I will of course also need a Hong Kong bank account."

There was a knock at the door, and Sally entered, carrying a tray with the tea, coffee, and biscuits. Charles paused before responding, "If you're so sure of making profits, I presume you'll be using inside information?"

Aspine frowned and took a long sip of his coffee.

"Douglas, it's important that you tell me everything."

"I don't know whether it's inside information, but recent history would suggest there's little risk, and a high probability of large profits."

"That's excellent, Douglas. You probably know that there is no tax payable on profits derived outside Hong Kong. Do you want us to handle your orders?"

"Yes, and I want you to use at least six different Australian brokers, but not Blayloch & Fitch. Not ever!"

"So you want to keep the orders small so as not to alert Blayloch & Fitch because your information's coming from them. Is that right?"

Aspine's face turned red. He hadn't realized his scheme was so transparent.

"You're not the first businessman to come up with something like this." Charles laughed. "Thousands like you have come through these offices."

Aspine felt himself relaxing. "How many have been successfully prosecuted by their domestic tax authorities?"

"As far as I know, none."

"Charles, I'm not a risk taker. I want to add another layer of protection. I want you to instruct your Zurich office to duplicate the structure you're setting up here."

"You're going to trade shares in Australia out of Zurich?"

"No, but I want to transfer the profits earned in Hong Kong to a numbered bank account in Switzerland?"

"Why?"

"I want to make it painful for the Australian Taxation Office, and the Securities & Investment Commission, should they choose to investigate me. It's my understanding that they'd have to set aside client-lawyer privilege, fight you, and obtain a court order from the Hong Kong courts to access the Hong Kong bank account records. Then they'd have to repeat the exercise in Switzerland to access the records to the Zurich bank account. Is that correct?"

"Yes, but the Swiss structure is an overkill, and might I say a waste of money. I'd be humoring you if I was to suggest that you set something up in Zurich."

"Humor me then because I want the added insurance of Switzerland."

Charles laughed. "Douglas, the client is always right. Consider it done. How much will you initially deposit into the Hong Kong bank account?"

"One million Australian dollars."

"Will a shelf company name do, or do you have a name that you'd like?"

"If you can get it, I'd like Mapago. It just came to me."

"Mapago?"

"Make a profit and get out." Aspine laughed.

"I'll see what I can do. I'll have documents drawn up, authorizing us to act, by the end of the day. I'll shoot them over to you for signing. You're in the Sheraton Towers, aren't you?"

"Yes. Thank you, Charles. It's been a pleasure."

It was a moonless night when Craig and Fiona arrived at the noodle bar, appropriately named Café Blah Blah, just before nine o'clock. They strode quickly to the back of the café, and through the rear door into a poorly lit room, set up to cope with the overflow of patrons. The only table occupied was in a dark corner, by a plump, middle-aged woman.

"Shirley, Shirley Bloom?" Craig asked.

"Do you have my money?"

"You'll get it after we find out what you have."

"Then you'll get nothing, young man," Shirley said, starting to stand.

"Give her the damn money, Craig," Fiona snapped.

Craig pulled an envelope out of his jacket, and pushed it across the table while pulling out a chair.

"Don't sit down. I only agreed to you coming so that you could look after the money. You've done that, now please leave."

"What the...That wasn't our deal."

"Buy yourself a coffee, Craig. I won't be long," Fiona said.

Craig mumbled something, and then stomped out of the room. "I need to know that you're not wired, Ms. Jeczik."

"My name's Fiona, and you'll have to trust me when I say that I'm not because you're not going to strip-search me." she laughed. "Besides, why are you so worried about being taped?"

"I might sue for wrongful dismissal and, if it came out in proceedings that I'd leaked those board minutes, it would look bad for me."

"I see. Why did you leak those minutes?"

"Because Douglas Aspine's an egomaniac, who's going to destroy a fine old company."

"Were you fired because he found out what you'd done?"

"I think so. I was told that my position had been made redundant, and I was being retrenched."

"But he employed a new PA?"

"Yes, that's why I'm considering suing."

"What else can you tell me?"

"He charged airfares, accommodation, and gifts for his girlfriend to the company."

"How did he do that?"

"He told me to arrange bookings and send flowers."

"In writing?"

"No, always verbally."

"It doesn't help. If he's found out, he'll say that the expenses were charged to the wrong account. Do you remember the name of his girlfriend?"

"Yes, Charlene Deering, and I have her address," Shirley said, pushing a piece of paper with two names on it over to Fiona.

"There's a second name, Anthony Keen. What does he have to do with Charlene?"

"Nothing. He used to be the company's supply manager until he was demoted. It was rumored that he was the anonymous source who leaked the circumstances of poor old Bert Stuart's tragic death to you. You'll find out a lot more about Aspine and Mercury if you talk to him."

"What else do you have?"

Shirley coughed nervously. "I thought that you'd be able to expose Aspine for spending company funds on his girlfriend."

"Don't you have anything else?" Fiona asked, incredulously. "I pulled strings to get you the ten thousand, and you've given me nothing. Surely you have something else?"

"What about those board minutes?"

Fiona was angry but also sorry for Shirley. She'd had her life ruined by Aspine at an age, and in a not dissimilar way, to what had occurred to her own father. "I want you to contact me if you find out anything else that might be useful, but we're not paying for it. By my calculations, you owe us about eight thousand in information," Fiona said, staring into Shirley's eyes.

Shirley looked down at the table. "I'm sorry. I needed the money, and you made such a big thing about the other information that I gave you."

"You didn't give us anything. We were just the means by which you could hurt Aspine. Keep your ear to the ground and, if you hear anything, call me."

Aspine's business in Hong Kong was complete, and he could not have been more pleased with Charles Ong and Crossley & Leyland. Now he could concentrate on seducing Kelly and spending the next four days between the sheets. It was just after 5:30 p.m. and the heat was stifling when the cab dropped him back at the Sheraton. He immediately buzzed Kelly's room. "Did you go shopping today?"

"It was too hot; I've been in my room reading most of the afternoon."

"Are you hungry?"

"Not really."

"You have to eat. How do you feel about a light snack in the Sky Lounge? Then we could go for a swim in the rooftop pool and cool off."

"Why can't we get a snack around the pool?"

"Yeah, that's fine. Give me five minutes to organize sandwiches and a bottle of Chardonnay, and I'll be with you."

Kelly answered her door dressed in a silk hotel dressing gown with a towel over her arm. "I'm dying to hit the pool," she said.

Dusk was settling on Hong Kong but, surprisingly, there was no-one using the pool. Kelly removed her dressing gown to reveal a yellow string bikini and a taut gym-hardened body which took Aspine's breath away. Her breasts were small but looked firm under the two tiny yellow triangles covering them. She quickly kicked her sandals off and plunged into the pool, seeking relief from the intense heat and the blatant staring of her boss. "It's glorious," she said. "Are you coming in?"

Aspine needed little encouragement and dived into the inviting cool water, freestyling two laps before swimming over to Kelly.

"You're right, it's great."

As if on cue, a waiter appeared with the sandwiches, wine, and two glasses. "Put it on the table and bring the chit over here," Aspine said.

As the waiter knelt by the edge of the pool, Aspine whispered, "If you bring another bottle in half an hour you'll find me very generous."

"Yes, sir."

"Kelly, why don't you pour the wine and bring the sandwiches over to the steps?"

"Why didn't you ask the waiter to do it?"

"Sorry, I didn't think," Aspine lied, longing to see her dripping wet.

He wasn't disappointed. As she bent over the table to pour the wine, her bikini tightened around her bottom, and he felt an intense stirring.

"Here's to us," he said, clinking glasses.

Kelly sipped her wine but did not respond.

Aspine was determined to be patient and not make a move until they were well into the second bottle. "Are you enjoying yourself?" he asked, topping up her wine glass.

"Yes," she replied, but she seemed withdrawn.

Darkness settled over Hong Kong and the lights lit up Victoria Harbor creating a stunning rooftop view. "Let's jump in the Jacuzzi," Aspine said, as the waiter appeared with the second bottle of Chardonnay.

"Put it over next to the Jacuzzi. Come on, Kelly."

She stumbled as she got into the spa, and Aspine smiled, while handing her a fresh, brimming glass. "Cheers," he said, drawing closer.

She felt his leg brush hers and pulled away. His right arm was resting on the tiles behind her. "Douglas!"

"I'm not doing anything. I can't hear over the jets and blowers."

"Maybe we should call it a night?" she said, in a slightly slurred voice.

"Fine, but let's finish the wine first," he said, topping up her glass while lowering his hand, so it was just touching her shoulder. He felt her tense, but she didn't move, and he bent over pulling her toward him, kissing her hard on the mouth. She recoiled as if struck by a cobra.

"No, stop it!"

"What the fuck, you little teaser," he growled, pulling her closer to him, while trying to tear her bikini top off.

"No!" she shouted, her cries drowned out by the thumping of the jets. Desperate, she drove her wine glass through the turbulent water, crashing it into his hardness.

"Bitch!" he snarled, drawing back his fist.

"No, no," she screamed, "I can't, I'm gay."

"You're a fucking dike?" he barked, "but you smiled at me that day at Jeremy's."

"I didn't. You just thought I did. When I accepted the job, I didn't think it included sleeping with you," she yelled, tears streaming down her face. "You bastard!"

"What about when you were in my office with your dress crawling up your thighs. Christ, you nearly winked at me."

"You're a filthy bastard!"

"A fucking dike! I employed a fucking dike. I should have guessed by your weight lifter's body. Are you fucking all the girls at the gym?"

Kelly scrambled out of the Jacuzzi and wrapped herself in a towel.

"You low life. There was nothing for me to do in Hong Kong, was there? You brought me up here so you could get me into bed, didn't you?"

"I want your resignation."

"I have no intention of resigning. If you fire me, I'll have you up before the equal opportunity commissioner, sexual discrimination authorities, and the courts. Then I'll make sure your favorite person, Fiona Jeczik, finds out all about this trip."

"Don't threaten me," he snarled, but his voice was shaky. His head was pounding, and he felt a wall of stress behind his eyes. "We can't work together now."

"Why, because I'm gay?"

"No, because of tonight."

"I can forget what occurred, and you should think yourself lucky that I can. We can still have a formal working relationship," she said, turning and walking toward the elevators.

The rumbling water of the spa compounded his headache while images of the Wanchai bar girls flashed through his mind. He knew what would make him feel better.

The concierge knocked on Aspine's door. "You wanted to see me, sir."

"Come in," Aspine said, motioning to a chair adjacent to a coffee table, which had a small pile of U.S. dollars on it. "I need a girl tonight. Can you arrange it? I want someone young and attractive."

"We don't normally do that, sir," the middle-aged Chinese man responded.

Aspine felt a thudding behind his eyes and downed his third Jack Daniels, but his head still pounded. "But you make exceptions, don't you?" he snarled, picking up the notes, one at a time until there was four hundred dollars directly in front of the concierge.

"We do, sir, but that will only cover the girl."

Aspine knew he was lying but, after all, it was Mercury's money, so he added another hundred and the concierge reached down and put the notes in his pocket.

"Don't send me a dog."

"I'm sure you'll be happy, sir."

Twenty minutes later there was a light tapping at Aspine's door. He opened it to see a smiling, young Filipino girl. She was wearing a black business suit, matching high heels, skirt about five inches above the knees, and a white blouse. Her hair was done up in a bun, and her glasses were shaped like the eyes of a cat. She was petite with fine features, and her smile turned to amusement as Aspine ogled her. "My name's Vanessa. Aren't you going to invite me in?"

"Of course," he said, standing aside while checking her rear.

"Do you like what you see?"

He was taken aback by her confidence but, before he could respond, she said, "I'm an account executive during the day, and only do this occasionally for the excitement. Today's your lucky day. Why don't you sit on the sofa and relax?"

He poured himself another Jack Daniels without offering her anything and parked himself at the end of the couch. She slipped a disc into the sound system, and the sultry voice of Tina Turner echoed around the suite. She stood about a meter in front of him moving to the beat of the music, put her hands up to her head, undid her bun and her long black hair cascaded to her waist. Then she took her jacket off, waving it briefly around her head before throwing it across the room. Slowly she undid the buttons of her blouse, and it fell away to reveal a small black lace bra barely covering her surprisingly large breasts. Aspine reached out for her, but she deftly danced away. "You'll spoil it." she laughed, shimmying out of her skirt, revealing a tiny waist, a tinier G-string, and long, darkly tanned legs. He drained his glass in one gulp and refilled it in one motion. His

head was pounding, and he didn't need the teasing or the dancing —
he just needed sex, desperately.

Gyrating in front of him, she reached behind her back and
unhooked her bra. She moved forward and leaned over as if to place
her voluptuous breasts in his face, and then recoiled in shock as
Aspine reached up and groped them roughly. "What are you doing?"
she shrieked.

"Don't scream," he snarled, backhanding her hard. She fell to the
ground in front of him and, with one hand clenched tightly around
her breast, he tore her G-string off with the other.

"Condom, condom," she whimpered.

"Fuck!" He'd nearly forgotten. He opened his wallet and threw a
packet on the floor next to her. "Put it on with your mouth, and be
careful."

Fifteen minutes later his headache was gone, replaced with self-
loathing and disgust. Not because of what he'd done, but because of
his need for hookers, and he cursed Kelly. He could hear the Filipino
girl sobbing and washing her bruised body in the bathroom. "Hurry
up, I want you out of here," he shouted.

Aspine woke early in the morning and buzzed Kelly as if nothing had
occurred in the pool or his room. "Get us out of here and back to
Melbourne as fast as you can."

- 24 -

AS SOON AS Craig Chisholm told Charlene Deering that he was Fiona Jeczik's producer, she'd agreed to meet him. Now, as she sat opposite him in a coffee lounge in Chapel Street, he was stunned by her beauty, and wondered what she'd ever seen in Aspine? She was surprisingly open, telling him about the abortion, the apartment, the MGB, the clothes, and how she'd been Aspine's mistress. Despite her willingness to help, and her hate for Aspine, she knew little about his business practices.

"He must have discussed the business with you at times," Craig pushed.

Charlie closed her eyes, and placed her hands under her chin, trying to recall any business conversations, before shaking her head. "He loathes Mercury's former CEO, Harry Denton."

"Why?"

"He said he was an interfering old fuddy-duddy."

"Anything else?"

"Sorry, no. Oh, there is one other thing. He hates your boss, and if he could get away with killing her, I'm sure he would."

"Fiona's made many enemies who are big on threats, but they've never amounted to anything."

"No, it's worse than that," Charlie said, relating what had occurred the night she'd gone to the wine bar. "He punched me, but he thought he was punching Fiona."

"Bastard!"

"Then he raped me." she scowled.

Craig mused that they'd known that Aspine was a bastard but, despite Charlie's willingness to help, she'd given him nothing. "Did he talk about his wife?"

"Only that she was always whining about not having enough money to pay the bills or spend on their children."

"Did she know he was paying for your apartment, and the MGB?"

"I doubt it. I was tempted to anonymously let her know after he kicked me out, but I didn't see any reason to hurt her. I have a question for you."

"Shoot."

"Why is Fiona so intent on bringing him down? It can't just be ratings."

"It's a long story. One day, when I have more time, I'll tell you. Suffice to say she's had some personal experience dealing with the Aspines of this world."

"It was nice to meet you, Craig," Charlie said, standing up. "If I can do anything to help bury the bastard, please call me."

The only available flight out of Hong Kong was via Sydney, which had turned a nine-hour trip into eleven hours. Aspine was jet-lagged and grumpy when Brad called and insisted on seeing him at the Docklands. He'd intended to spend the day in the office, and cursing, he snatched his keys off the desk. As he drove out of the car-park, it was drizzling, and the roads were greasy. Stuck in slow moving traffic crawling through the city blackened his already dark mood. Thirty minutes later he pulled up opposite three partly completed high-rises all erected to level five. The sites were hives of activity, and he mused that Jack Gillard's trip to Las Vegas had been well worth it. His thoughts were interrupted by a morose looking Brad Hooper, who was holding two construction helmets. "What's so urgent, Brad?"

"I want to show you some apartments," Brad responded, walking toward the nearest building.

"Just tell me what's on your mind," Aspine said, tired and annoyed.

"You'll see soon enough."

Aspine followed Brad up the stairwell to the first floor, along the corridor, and into a two-bedroom apartment. "Listen," Brad said, knocking on the wall to the adjoining apartment.

"What am I listening for?"

"The walls are paper thin. I could put my fingers through them. The quality of the Richmond apartments wasn't great, but they were masterpieces compared to these. There are runs and blotches in the paintwork, and the taps and door fittings look like they came from a secondhand shop. Christ, we've increased prices and forgotten about quality. How does that work?"

"So, you're whining because you can't sell them."

"No, but we're selling to the suckers who believe the editorials and our bullshit advertisements. But I'm telling you, it's going to blow up when things get tough."

"Why?"

"Because when those suckers try to sell, they'll lose up to a hundred and fifty thousand an apartment. That's unless you're going to buy every pre-owned apartment that comes on the market." Brad sneered. "You've got Brian Eppel designing solely on cost, Jack Gillard putting them up so fast that he's forgotten about quality, and that new supply manager is sourcing cheap, second-rate fittings out of China."

"Unless you've been appointed to do my job, design, construction, and supply aren't your concerns. All you have to do is fucking sell."

"Doug, we can sell around the thin walls and hidden construction defects, but you've gotta fix the finish. A million dollar apartment with a shitty paint job and cheap and nasty fittings is a hard sell — even for me."

Aspine smiled. Brad wasn't worried about the structural integrity of the apartments or the customers — he just wanted to make sure that sales were easy to make and that the visible defects were fixed. He'd been worried that Brad was going soft or, worse, becoming honest. Now his faith in sloth and greed was restored. "I'll get Jack to touch up the paintwork, and make sure that he pays more attention to the finish in the future. I'll also talk to Brian about redesigning the fittings, but I'm not changing anything that's already been finished."

"If you make them half presentable we'll sell 'em. We've already sold most of the completed apartments, but there are only so many wood ducks."

"I've told you before, don't call our customers that." Aspine frowned. "I have to get back to the office."

Craig Chisholm called Anthony Keen, who point blank, refused to meet with him and denied leaking any information about Bert Stuart's death. Keen sounded nervous and anxious to end the unwanted call. Aspine's threat had worked a treat.

Sir Edwin was unusually inquisitive when Aspine called. "What were you looking at in Hong Kong, Douglas?"

Aspine's mood hadn't improved, and he felt like responding, 'None of your fucking business', but curbed himself. "I was exploring joint venture opportunities with some of Hong Kong's builders who'd contacted me."

"To build apartments in HK?"

"That's right."

"How did your discussions go?"

"No good. I decided they weren't worth pursuing. That's why I came home early. I didn't want to waste any more time up there."

The relief in Sir Edwin's voice was apparent. "Good decision. Let's not spread our resources too thin and, besides, it's hard to make money up there. I'm surprised you didn't stay a little longer. You could use a few days break."

"I'm too busy for breaks. I'd rather spend my time at Mercury."

"Don't overdo it. We don't want you to burn yourself out."

"Fucking stupid old goat," Aspine muttered after he'd hit the disconnect button.

Craig related the conversation that he'd had with Charlie to Fiona. "I'm sorry, he's a first-rate bastard all right, but there's nothing new that we can use."

"Of course, there is. He violently attacked and raped her."

"She didn't go to the police, and our legal people will never let you air anything that'll lead to a successful defamation action against the channel. You can't prove anything, there are no witnesses, and even if Charlie wanted to take action, it's probably too late now."

"Can we show that he paid for her car and apartment? Can we prove that when he'd finished with her, he had the car repossessed, and kicked her out of the apartment?"

"Plenty of businessmen have mistresses and affairs on the side, but we don't pursue them. You can't run that, all it will do is hurt his wife."

"Can't?" Fiona said coldly. "I'm going to bring this animal down and when we air the story, who knows how he'll respond or what mistakes he'll make? When does the inquest into Bert Stuart's death start?"

"Next week," Craig groaned.

"Let's turn up the heat on the coroner, and run something that ensures he hands down an adverse finding about Mercury and its lack of compliance with the Occupational Health & Safety legislation. At the end, I'll raise Charlie, and Aspine's treatment of her, so the public, and the coroner, get to know the true character of Mercury's CEO."

"What about his wife?"

"An innocent victim caught in friendly fire, but who knows, she might be glad that we're exposing him for the slime that he is. Our ratings have stalled, so make sure there's plenty of publicity before we go to air."

Aspine never worked with his door closed, but that was before he knew that he was working next to a dike, who could hear every word of every conversation and call that he made. He no longer liked or trusted Kelly, but he was stuck with her, without the slightest possibility of getting into her pants. He pressed the button on his desk and barked, "Get Kurt Metzger and Steve Brogden to come and see me," pressing it again before Kelly could reply.

Five minutes later there was a light knocking on his door. "Come in," he yelled, cursing Kelly yet again. "Shut the door and grab a chair, Kurt. You're doing a great job, Steve. My accounts people tell me you've managed to reduce the prices of all our primary materials. How's Anthony taking his demotion?"

"Thank you. He's been quite helpful."

"He hasn't been disruptive or undermining you with other employees?"

"If anything, he's been supportive."

"But he must have said something to you when you were screwing the prices down of suppliers who'd previously been stitching him up?"

"I changed many suppliers, and all Anthony said was to make sure that I didn't lose continuity of supply for a few dollars."

"Shit!" Aspine growled, catching Kurt's eye and noticing the hint of a smile. "What's funny, Kurt?"

"Nothing, Douglas."

"I want you to get rid of him today."

The mirth in Kurt's eyes disappeared. "You want me to fire him?"

"In case you don't know, it's one of the HR manager's responsibilities," Aspine said sarcastically, enjoying the worry etched on Kurt's face. "Work out a termination amount that'll stop him from taking legal action."

"But you don't have a reason to terminate his services. He's financially independent, and he'll sue on principle."

"I don't have a reason?" Aspine snarled, nodding toward Steve. "This man's saved the company a fortune, and I want to reward him. I can't so long as I'm paying the wages of two supply managers. That's fucking reason enough!"

"Yes, but it would've been easier if he'd caused Steve trouble."

"I'm sorry I can't make your job fucking easier. Don't make me do it for you, or we'll end up with two HR Managers, and we wouldn't want that, would we, Kurt?"

"No, Douglas," Kurt replied, getting out of his chair.

When Wes Bracken called, he sounded agitated. "Douglas, Jeczik was on Channel Sixteen's morning show, saying that she's going to expose a prominent businessman's double life. They've been advertising Monday night's *Your Family Today* non-stop."

"Why do you think it's me? Hell, she's digging up dirt every night on some poor bastard. She's got nothing new on me."

"She said he was ruthless and headed up a large public company. Are you sure she hasn't dug something else up?"

"Every public company CEO is ruthless. If it's me, she'd be telling the world."

"No, she wouldn't. It's all about ratings. It'll be the last segment of her show, and half of Australia will tune in just to see who it is. If anything, she'd lose audience numbers by disclosing who it is now."

"Nah, it's not me. She'd never describe me as prominent."

"She's using that description for ratings. It's not a backhanded compliment. I'll see if I can find out if it's you."

"Do that, Wes," Aspine said. Despite his bravado, he felt ill.

- 25 -

CRAIG TRIED ONE last time to convince Fiona not to air the segment about Charlie, to no avail. "You'll hurt his wife and kids. Why do that? Just run the rest of the story. There's no need to bring the smutty part up."

Fiona was uncompromising. "I'm going to run everything as planned. Who knows what we'll find out from the jilted wife after she knows about the mistress? I'm going to make this bastard's life a misery."

Aspine sat in Mercury's boardroom waiting for the ad break to finish, and for the bitch's face to reappear on screen. Instead, a photo of Bert Stuart in full military regalia and medals appeared, accompanied by maudlin music. "Fuck!" Aspine cursed, knowing he was the 'prominent businessman'. The camera panned to Fiona's grim face as she outlined the circumstances surrounding Bert's death. Sitting opposite her was Andrew Lawson from the Construction Employees Union. "Mr. Lawson, did the company's negligence result in Bert Stuart's death?"

"That's for the coroner to determine, but any workplace death needs to be thoroughly investigated."

"Do you expect the coroner to make any recommendations in his findings?"

"It's not unusual for recommendations to be made so as to ensure accidents like this do not recur."

"I know that. I was thinking more of recommendations that may lead to action being taken against the company and its directors."

"You mean criminal action?"

"Yes. Isn't it about time that the people responsible for workplace deaths are held to account? Didn't Mercury terminate the services of a number of its safety officers immediately before the accident?"

"We've been campaigning for harsher penalties and–"

Fiona interrupted. "Isn't it about time our law enforcers sent a message to these highly paid fat cat directors by incarcerating them, when they fail to look after their workers' safety?"

"Bitch," Aspine gasped, "she's trying to have me jailed."

"Yes. Blatant negligence resulting in death or injury should result in those responsible being jailed. After the first director or manager is locked up, I'm sure there'll be a quantum improvement in the safety of our workers."

"You need an example?"

"Yes."

"Perhaps after the coroner concludes his deliberations this week, you'll have one. Thank you, Mr. Lawson."

Aspine drew himself closer to the screen, his face flushed with rage.

The camera cut to Fiona sitting behind a desk with a black folder in her hand. "We thought that you might like to know about the double life of Mr. Douglas Aspine, CEO of Mercury Properties. Until quite recently he was paying for an upmarket apartment, MGB, interstate trips, and expensive clothing for his mistress of three years. Then he grew tired of her and stopped making payments, without having the common decency or courage to tell her. The first she knew was when real estate agents commenced action to evict her, and a finance company left a repossession notice on her MGB's windscreen. Obviously, Mr. Aspine wasn't satisfied with just getting rid of her, he needed to degrade, and embarrass her as well. It seems that he gets rid of his former girlfriends in the same way that he gets rid of his loyal long-serving employees." As she'd been talking, pictures of the block of apartments, the swimming pool, and the red MGB flashed across the screen. The cameras panned back to Fiona, her eyes, small slits and her lips curled in a sneer of disgust, as she signed off.

Aspine was stunned and overcome by a desire to kill the woman whose face mocked him from the small screen.

Aspine ignored the incessant ringing of his cell phone as he drove to the nearest hotel. His head was splitting as he tried to fathom the effect that the bitch's revelations would have. The hotel was quiet, and he ordered and belted down a Jack Daniels. The stinging spirits brought immediate relief, and he ordered and downed another. His chest was warm, and his mind was clearing. *What business is it of anyone else if I have a mistress? Plenty of CEOs have mistresses. No, that isn't a worry, but the possibility of criminal action and jail emanating from the inquest into Bert Stuart's death is.* Barbara and the kids didn't enter his mind. He sipped his third shot slowly, savoring the smoothness of the amber liquid, before putting twenty dollars on the bar. The last thing he needed was to get caught exceeding the limit on the drive home. He drove slowly, planning what he'd do in the morning to balance the pressure on the coroner. "Bloody hell!" he exclaimed. His driveway was blocked by five near-bursting plastic bags. He got out to move them and noticed one of his Armani suits crumpled against the transparent plastic. Another bag contained his shirts mixed with ties and shoes. "What the fuck's going on?" He hadn't noticed Barbara come out of the front door until she was no more than three steps from him. Her eyes were red, and her face was tense and drawn.

"You mongrel, I want you out of here."

"Christ, Barbara, what are you talking about? Have you gone mad?"

"You bastard, you blamed me because we couldn't pay the school fees, and yet you were renting an apartment, and leasing a car for your whore," she said, kicking one of the bags. "It was her car in the driveway that night, wasn't it?"

"You've known that I've been having affairs for years. What difference does tonight make?"

"It was more than an affair. You jeopardized the future of your kids and their education so that you could have a little plaything on the side. My friends said you were a rake. Now it's public knowledge. Get your stuff in the car and get out."

"What about the kids?"

Her laugh was tinged with sarcasm and pain. "Since when have you been worried about the kids? You'll have a letter from my lawyers tomorrow. Please go."

"Where am I going to find somewhere to sleep at this time of night?"

"I don't know, and I don't care," Barbara sobbed angrily, before storming into the house.

Aspine had no trouble getting a room at the Hilton but slept restlessly, tossing and turning most of the night. When he arrived at the office in the morning, it was uncomfortably quiet, and his staff found it hard to make eye contact. "Get me Max Vogel and then find me a two-bedroom fully furnished rental apartment or townhouse around Hawthorn or Kew," he shouted at Kelly, before closing the door to his office.

"Good morning, Douglas."

"Max, did you see that woman's show last night?"

"Yes. Jeez, why's she got it in for you so bad?"

"I don't know. I'm worried that she may have influenced the coroner."

"Your worries are ill-founded."

"That's easy for you to say. It's not your ass that they'll haul off to jail if you're wrong. Tell me, did you dig anything up on that truck driver?"

"Nothing that'll help. He had a few problems when he was younger, but hasn't had so much as a parking fine in the past eight years. He's a family man, he's not on drugs, and he's a moderate drinker. I'm sorry, but we're not going to be able to stick him with anything."

"Tell me about his problems."

"He has an assault conviction, a drunk and disorderly, and an offensive behavior. He also ran up the rear of another car while driving an uninsured vehicle. It took him five years to pay the damages, but he paid every cent — not many do that. Bear in mind that these incidents occurred before he turned thirty, and he's nearly forty. There's nothing we can use at the inquest."

"I understand, Max. If you find anything out before then, let me know."

Aspine's next call was to Wes Bracken. "Wes, it's Douglas Aspine. I want you to leak a story to the press, preferably the *Herald-Sun*. Now take down the details, and make sure you get it right."

As Aspine put the phone down, Kelly buzzed to say that Sir Edwin Philby, Jeremy Smythe, and Duncan Milgate had called. They could wait; he had to attend to more important matters. "Get me Phil Kendall at the bank."

"How can I help you, Douglas?" Kendall asked.

"I want you to transfer the balances of my personal accounts to an account in Hong Kong. I'll fax the details to you in the next ten minutes."

"You're not happy with our service?"

"I'm perfectly happy. I'm acting on the advice of my tax accountants," Aspine lied. "Can you make the transfer immediately?"

Kendall sounded relieved. "I'll initiate the transfer the minute I receive your fax."

"Thanks, Phil." Aspine didn't know if Barbara's lawyers would seek to freeze his bank accounts but, if they did, they'd find they were too late.

Duncan Milgate sounded sympathetic when Aspine finally called him, but he was clearly worried. "Douglas, we've had an avalanche of calls from concerned clients. They don't like it when the CEOs of companies they've invested in, have their dirty washing aired on television. Worse, the shares are down 20 cents this morning."

"Duncan, I can't control Fiona Jeczik. That show last night was a beat-up, but there's nothing I can do. If I take legal action, it could drag on for years."

"I agree, but you need to be more careful about how you handle your extra-marital activities. We have a lot of old money clients, and they don't like it when these things become public."

"I see. It's okay to do a bit of extra-marital fucking, but it's not okay to get caught."

"Getting caught is not a problem — getting exposed is. You need to be extra careful because that woman seems to be paying you close attention."

"Don't I know it," Aspine mumbled.

"On a more pleasant note, you might like to invest fifty thousand in a small uranium explorer, Clean Energy Limited. The shares are trading at 50 cents. We expect them to more than double in the near term."

"I'd like to, but I don't have any loose cash."

"You're not even going to take your usual fifty percent? Surely you can put your hands on twenty-five thousand?"

"Thanks, but I'll pass."

"You're a strange man, Douglas. A lot of easy money is going to be made on this one. You will, of course, keep it to yourself. I'd hate to see the shares rushed because of loose lips."

"I never talk to anyone about the information you give me. I hope I'm in funds when you next call with a recommendation."

"I'm pleased to hear that. I'll be in touch."

The day's gotten a lot better Aspine thought. He reached into his jacket pocket, pulled out his prepaid cell phone, and punched in Charles Ong's direct line number.

"Charles Ong, speaking."

"It's Douglas Aspine. I've just transferred another three hundred thousand into Mapago's account."

"Yes, I've been notified."

"Good. I want you to invest eight hundred thousand in Clean Energy Limited. Use at least half a dozen brokers, and tell them to buy in small quantities, with a maximum price of 60 cents."

"I'll instruct them to be discreet. Call me in twenty-four hours. I'll let you know at what price you were filled."

Sir Edwin Philby was peeved. "Douglas, I called you hours ago, and you're only just returning my call?"

"Get off your high horse. I had some personal problems that needed urgent attention. I thought you might have guessed."

"Don't take that attitude with me. I've been getting flak from the institutions. Some of them are talking about selling their shares. Can't you be more discreet in your personal life?"

"If you don't like it, Ed, you can always fire me, and see if your precious institutions get the same profits and increase in share price that I've delivered."

"I wasn't critical, I was just suggesting you be a little more careful," Sir Edwin said, in a placatory tone.

Aspine smiled. *Sir Edwin had groveled when his bluff was called.*

It was now 'Douglas Aspine's Mercury Properties.' Everyone else was irrelevant. "I'm busy. Call me when you want to talk about something other than my personal life."

The following morning Aspine awoke in the luxurious townhouse that Kelly had rented for him. He mused that her taste in townhouses was better than her taste in sex. She'd also arranged the delivery of newspapers, and he gloated over the article on the third page of the *Herald-Sun* headlined, 'Inquest to examine tipper driver.'

It stated that the driver who'd reversed his truck over and killed Bert Stuart, had previously been involved in a major road accident, and had a number of criminal convictions for drunkenness and apprehended violence. *Wes Bracken had done well.* The story was also covered by the radio stations and the evening television news. If the coroner was influenced by the media, he now had more to consider than what the bitch had said about jailing negligent directors.

Kurt was surprised at how low the seating in the Ferrari was, and it felt like his bottom was scraping along the road. "Douglas, you don't have to attend the inquest. You haven't been called."

"I'm not staying long. I'm only here as a mark of respect to Bert Stuart's widow and family," Aspine lied. Wes Bracken had insisted that he make at least a token appearance. "I'll drop you at the front of the court, find a car-park and meet you back here."

"There's a car-park right next to the court."

Aspine had no intention of parking where the press could trap him. "I'll find a meter on the other side of the road and walk back."

Five minutes later Kurt glanced up and saw Aspine on the other side of the road. The traffic cleared, and he started to cross when an old white Ford that'd been parked on the side of the road pulled out and accelerated at high speed directly toward him. At the last second Aspine caught a glimpse of white haze coming directly at him. He jumped back but was still struck, and hurled high into the air, before crashing to the road with a sickening thud.

-26 -

"DOUGLAS, DOUGLAS, ARE you all right?" Consciousness and the pain that goes with it quickly returned. His right leg was pounding, and when he reached down, he felt warm blood oozing from above the knee. He looked up and saw the clear blue eyes of Harry Denton only inches away.

"Are you all right, Douglas?"

"Harry, as long as you don't try and give me fucking mouth to mouth, I'll be fine. What happened?"

Kurt rushed across the road. "I saw it. My God, someone tried to kill you."

The television crews at the inquest now had a bigger story and pushed closer. Aspine propped himself up on one elbow and tried to get to his feet.

"Don't move," Harry ordered, as he pulled out a small Swiss army knife and cut his pants away to reveal a gaping bloody wound. One of the cameras focused directly on the seeping gash from no more than a meter away

"Fuck off you parasite," Aspine shakily slurred. He'd lost a lot of blood, and the color was draining from his face.

The wail of ambulance sirens drew closer. Within three minutes Aspine was being conveyed at high speed to St Vincent's Hospital.

Two homicide detectives who'd been standing at the front of the court followed Kurt across the road and heard what he said. "Did you get a look at the driver?" Bill Muller asked, flashing his badge.

"No, it was all too quick."

"Was it a man or a woman?"

"I don't know. I was watching the car."

"What make was it?"

"And old Ford. It was dirty white."

"Are you sure the driver intentionally tried to run down the poor gentleman?" the younger detective asked.

"I'm certain," Kurt responded.

"Do you know him?"

"He's my boss, Douglas Aspine."

"Does he have any enemies?"

Harry laughed. "Thousands."

"And who are you?" The thickset, heavy-jowled Muller asked.

"Harry Denton. I serve on the same board as him."

"Scott, are you getting all this down?" Muller asked, addressing the younger detective.

"What do you mean thousands?"

"Don't you read the newspapers or watch television, detective? This is the man who runs Mercury Properties."

"Shit. It's the prick who sacked everyone and kicked his mistress out of her apartment, without even telling her," Scott said. "You know, Bill, the guy in the chariot cartoon."

"Yeah, yeah, I know who you're talking about now. Let's get a list of suspects."

"Your partner's notebook isn't big enough." Harry grinned.

"You seem to be enjoying yourself. You didn't have anything to do with it, did you?"

"If you're drawing up a list of people, who can't stand Douglas Aspine, put me at the top, but I'm not into violence, detective. I wasn't being flippant about the number of enemies he has, though. Countless people hate him."

"What about you?" Muller asked Kurt.

"I don't hate him, but what Harry says is true. He's taken on the workers, unions, management, customers, and suppliers. He's made a lot of enemies."

"You left out his fellow directors, his former mistress, Bert Stuart's family and friends, and probably his wife," Harry added.

"So he's not Mr. Popularity. That doesn't mean he's fair game for some nutter to kill," Muller growled.

"I hope you still feel the same way after you've met him." Harry smiled.

The two detectives finished giving evidence at the Coroner's Court late in the afternoon. "Scott, let's go and visit Mr. Aspine in hospital."

"Jeez, Bill, you're keen. You're getting transferred to the drug squad in two weeks. Why do you want to get involved in something that you won't be around to finish?"

"I don't, but I've been thinking about this guy. I want to see if he's as big a prick as the media makes out. Come on, let's go."

St Vincent's was a hive of activity, but the nurse on reception knew immediately where Aspine was. "Ninth level, west-ward. With the number of calls we've had, you'd think he was a movie star or something."

As they stepped out of the elevator, they heard a loud, angry, male voice. "Get me my clothes and a walking stick. I want to get out of here."

"Mr. Aspine," a distinctly Asian female voice said, "you can't leave. Don't you understand, any pressure on your leg might pull the sutures out?"

"Looks like we've found him." Muller grinned, as they walked into the ward. The doctor was Chinese, young, pretty and petite. She looked tired and unaccustomed to dealing with the likes of Douglas Aspine.

"If I'm forced to stay I want a private room, bathroom, phone, computer, internet, and television."

"We're not that type of hospital."

"Get me transferred to The Avenue Private then," Aspine said, noticing Muller and Bishop. "Hey, if you don't mind, this is a private conversation,

"Mr. Aspine, there's nothing private about your conversation," Muller said, flashing his badge. "I'm Bill Muller, and this is Scott Bishop. We're from homicide."

"Homicide? I was hit by a car while crossing the road. What's that got to do with you guys?"

"We have witnesses who say the driver intentionally tried to run you down."

"Bullshit!"

"Are you saying you don't have any enemies?" Scott asked.

"For fuck's sake, Sonny, everyone has enemies, but how stupid would you have to be, to try and take someone out in front of the Coroner's Court? It was an accident, pure and simple."

Scott felt himself turn red with a mix of embarrassment and anger. "If it was an accident why didn't the driver stop?"

"How would I know? Maybe he was pissed. Maybe the car was stolen. Maybe he was running late for work."

"Did you get a look at the driver?"

"Is this ask a stupid question day?"

"Your human resources manager is convinced that the driver was waiting for you to cross the road, and tried to kill you," Muller said.

"Kurt, Kurt, Kurt," Aspine sighed. "Do you remember Sergeant Schultz in Hogan's Heroes, Detective? He was a well-meaning, bumbling German, who drew the wrong conclusions on everything he was involved in."

"You don't think much of him do you?"

"Nah, I've never had a great opinion of Sergeant Schultz. Look, why don't you go and find some real criminals, instead of wasting your time investigating a mere accident?"

"We'll do that, Mr. Aspine," Muller said, dropping his card on the bed. "If you think of anything that you might have overlooked, call me. Come on Scott, let's go."

"There's one thing you can do for me."

"What's that?"

"Can you check, or get your mates to keep an eye on my Ferrari. It's parked down from the Coroner's Court, and I'd hate for anything to happen to it."

"Stupid, arrogant prick," Scott muttered, as they reached the elevator. "I'd like to put a dirty big dent in his precious Ferrari."

"He's arrogant all right, but not stupid. He knows someone tried to kill him, and he's got his reasons for not wanting us to get involved."

"What reasons?"

"I don't know, but experience tells me that when victims don't want help from the police, they're usually scared something they're up to might be uncovered."

"You think Aspine's up to no good?"

"I think he's hiding something."

The elevator doors opened, and Muller's breath was taken away by the stunning features and flawless olive skin of the Eurasian woman who alighted, holding the hand of a pimply faced nervous looking young man.

"How come guys like him always seem to end up with girls like her?" Scott grinned.

"Girls like her? Jeez, Scott, when you get a little older you'll realize she's a one off."

"W-we ca-came as so-soon as we cou-could," Kerry said. "We cou-couldn't get a ba-baby sitter. Ho-how are you feel-feeling?"

"I'm all right. I got twenty-seven stitches in my leg, but it's nothing," Aspine said, with false bravado, all the time eyeing Jasmine. She was wearing a simple emerald green silk dress that clung to her body.

"The radio newsreaders are saying it was a hit and run driver, and that police suspect it was an attempt on your life," Jasmine said.

"The driver didn't stop, but the suggestion it was attempted murder is absurd." Aspine laughed. He was enjoying her concern. She hadn't sat down, and as she bent forward, he glimpsed her small, firm, unrestrained breasts. *What did she see in Kerry?* She was the most beautiful woman he'd ever set eyes on, and even in his weakened condition he felt a stirring in his groin.

"Why? Didn't some of the retrenched employees threaten you?"

"You-you did get so-some nast-nasty messages on your-your cell phone," Kerry said. His stuttering was worse than usual, his pimples were angry, and Aspine thought he could smell alcohol.

"And they joked on the radio about the women in your life who'd like to see you dead. It was demeaning," Jasmine said. "I'm sorry that Barbara and you have broken up."

She's naïve, honest, forthright and outspoken, in the way of a child. And she's delightfully charming and provocative.

"I don't have any women in my life, and I'm sure it wasn't an ex-employee. It was probably someone who had a little too much to drink, made a mistake, and didn't stop for fear of getting caught driving under the influence."

"Kurt told us that if you hadn't jumped back, you might have been killed," Jasmine persisted.

"Kurt exaggerates." Aspine smiled. "I've been in here long enough. Kerry, see if you can find some crutches. Then, if it's not too inconvenient, you can drive me home."

With the help of Kerry and Jasmine, Aspine hobbled to his front door. "I won't invite you in. I'm tired and going straight to bed."

"That's sensible," Jasmine said. "You need to rest. Goodnight."

"Thank you for helping. I'll see you in the morning, Kerry."

He half hopped, half limped over to the bar and poured himself a Jack Daniels, and then propped himself up on the sofa. Someone had tried to kill him — he knew it — but he wasn't breathing a word. *The last thing I need is police involvement in my personal affairs or speculation in the financial markets that I might be on borrowed time. Why was Harry so close when the car-park was on the other side of the road? Was he following me, and if so, what had he expected to find?* He was tired and wanted to relax, so his thoughts turned to Jasmine. He smiled. He was sure that he was going to have his way with her.

"I feel sorry for him," Jasmine said. "He's an evil man who needs to find our Lord."

"Why do you say that?"

"He cheated on his wife, disgraced his children, demeaned his mistress, and he's in denial about someone trying to kill him."

"Are you some kind of psychiatrist now?" Kerry growled, taking a corner a little too sharply.

Jasmine placed her hand on his knee. "He's not trying to make you do something that you shouldn't, is he?"

"Why would you say something like that? Of course not!"

"I've never seen you drink before, but now you smell like brandy most of the time."

"Leave me alone. I occasionally have a glass or two to help me relax."

The car became silent and the tension built, until Kerry blurted, "I'm sorry. I'm under pressure. It'll be over soon, I promise."

"Why don't you resign and find a job that allows you to spend more time with the boys and me? We don't need the money, and if we have to sell Mansfield, it won't be the end of the world," Jasmine said, lightly stroking his face.

"I can't. I can't resign now, but hopefully, I'll be able to soon."

"I don't understand."

THE CAB PULLED up in front of Mercury's offices, and Aspine gave the driver a large tip for helping him up the stairs. The pain killers had worn off in the early hours of the morning, and the pain was so intense that he'd been unable to get back to sleep.

As he hobbled past Kelly's office, he threw his keys on her desk. "My car's out in front of the Coroner's Court. Get it picked up and brought back here."

"How are you feeling this morn–?" Before Kelly could finish, he shut the door to his office.

It was 7:00 a.m. in Hong Kong, but Charles Ong answered his phone after two rings.

"Hello, Charles, it's Douglas Aspine."

"Douglas, we managed to buy one and a half million shares in Clean Energy for prices between 49 and 58 cents. The average price paid was 53 cents, and they closed at 65 cents. You're already one hundred and eighty thousand in front. Well done."

"Thanks, Charles."

Kelly entered Aspine's office and placed a large envelope on his desk. "This was just dropped off by courier."

He knew what was inside it. "Get me Max Vogel."

As he waited for Vogel, he tore open the envelope and cursed. Barbara was spending his money on one of the city's largest firms of bloodsuckers. The letter was what he expected, and sought details of all his assets, warned against any disposals, and demanded an outrageous monthly allowance.

"I have Mr. Vogel for you."

"Douglas, how are you feeling? I didn't expect you'd be at work today."

"I'm a little queasy, but I'll live. Max, Barbara's got Carnegie & Yze acting for her. They've couriered me a five-page letter. I'm instructing you to tell them to fuck off."

"It's not something frivolous that you can sweep under the carpet. I'll have to respond, and I'll need your help with the detail."

"Stall them. It's something that I can settle with Barbara but now is not the time. She needs a few days to calm down and see reason."

"You're not hiding or disposing of assets are you?"

"No, I'm not."

"I wish I could believe you."

"What's that supposed to mean?"

"You leaked that information I gave you about the truck driver."

"What if I did? I don't remember you saying it was confidential."

"I told you that we couldn't use it. I thought that was enough."

"It wasn't, and I'm glad it was published. It helped balance what that bitch said about me."

"The coroner and his staff didn't get their positions by being fools. They'll know that you or someone acting for you leaked it and, let me tell you, they'll take no account of it."

"We'll see about that," Aspine said, growing tired of his whining lawyer. "I'll fax Carnegie & Yze's letter to you. Send a response that buys me some breathing space."

Aspine cursed Fiona Jeczik. She'd caused all of his problems and, if it weren't for her, Barbara wouldn't be trying to steal half his assets, he wouldn't have lost Charlie, or needed to be at Bert Stuart's inquest, and he wouldn't have been nearly killed. He felt dizzy, and a wave of anger coursed through him. His leg was throbbing, and a small amount of blood seeped through his pants. He punched Tom Donegan's private number into the prepaid cell phone, and a raspy voice answered, "Yeah."

"Tom, it's Douglas Aspine."

"What took you so long? Do you want me to find out who tried to kill you?"

"No," said Aspine, sweating heavily.

"You've got no labor or union problems, so how can I help you?"

"I want you to dig up everything you can on Fiona Jeczik, and Barry Seymour."

"Everything dirty, you mean. Why are you interested in Seymour?"

"He's CEO of Channel Sixteen."

"I know, but he's not firing the bullets. Why go after him?"

"A little heat about his private life might cause him to rein in the bitch. Better still, he might fire her."

"You're treading on dangerous ground, and there's no way she's going to get fired. She's their star performer and knows it — so does Seymour."

"Just do as I tell you!"

"Calm down, Douglas. Who do I bill?"

"Mercury, of course."

"Labor negotiations and relations?"

"That's right. Get back to me — pronto."

Aspine was stark white, and his shirt was soaked in perspiration. "Kelly," he shouted. "Get me a doctor, and tell him to bring plenty of pain killers."

"You shouldn't be here."

"Get me a bloody doctor. I'm all right."

Fifteen minutes later Kelly showed a young doctor into his office. "Douglas, this is Dr. Stewart."

"Doc, I was in an accident yesterday and had a few stitches in my leg. It's hurting like hell. Can you give me something for the pain?"

"I know; it was on last night's news," Dr. Stewart said, as he took Aspine's blood pressure and pulse, before kneeling to check his leg. "You're in no condition to be here. You should be home for a few days with your leg elevated."

"I'm too busy, Doc."

"You don't seem to appreciate the severity of your wound. Without rest, it could become infected and gangrenous, and you know what that means."

"You're not serious."

"I'm deadly serious," the doctor responded, flicking the point of a large injection. "This might hurt for a second or so."

"It's fine. Thanks, Doc."

"I'm giving you prescriptions for painkillers and sleeping tablets. Get them filled and go home."

Aspine pressed the button on his desk. "Kelly, I need you to get some prescriptions filled, and then get me a cab. I'm going home to rest up for a few days." *Fuck running the risk of gangrene.*

Harry Denton sat in his car watching Aspine being helped into the rear of a cab and wondered what could've been so urgent at Mercury as to require his attention when so badly injured. The cab pulled away, and Harry started the engine of his Holden and followed, feelingly more than a little stupid. He'd had the same feeling when the police asked him if he had seen the driver of the car that struck Aspine, and he'd said 'no'. He had no idea who the little man with the bald head and large glasses was, but in an instant, he'd made up his mind that he hadn't seen anything. Harry had a strong conscience, but it was on holiday, and who knew what Aspine had done to that man? Harry did not have to drive for long before the cab stopped out in front of a townhouse in one of Kew's more exclusive locations. He watched the cabbie help Aspine to the front door, and presumed that he'd been too ill to stay at work. Harry sat behind the steering wheel and let the engine idle, feeling even more stupid.

As Aspine entered the townhouse, he sensed that someone was inside. "Who's there?" he shouted. There was no response, but as he hobbled down the hallway, he thought that he heard the back door close. He felt dizzy and fought back a surge of nausea. When he reached the door, it was securely locked. *Maybe I'm hallucinating?* He walked back down the hallway and noticed that the door leading from the basement garage to the stairs was open. He tried to remember whether it had been open when he'd left for work — he was convinced it hadn't. Nothing appeared to be missing, but perhaps the intent of the break-in hadn't been theft? He staggered back to the front entrance, threw the door open, and stared at the Holden parked fifty meters away. Wasn't that Harry Denton's car, and wasn't that Harry sitting behind the wheel? He closed his eyes tightly and when he reopened them the car was gone. *What are the painkillers doing to me?* He limped down to his study, looking for something out of place or missing. Then he noticed it — the phone wasn't in its cradle — someone had been in his study. Exhausted, he hobbled into his bedroom, falling on the bed, and collapsing into a troubled sleep.

Harry noticed the man wearing a tracksuit run onto the street from the rear of the townhouses and thought it strange that he was carrying a small black case. Perhaps he was just running late for an appointment? A few minutes later Aspine had appeared at the front door of his townhouse, looking distressed and concerned. Harry, hit the accelerator hard, hoping that he hadn't been seen. He surmised that perhaps Aspine had disturbed the man breaking into his townhouse

Images of Fiona Jeczik disrupted Aspine's sleep and he tossed and turned, breaking out in a heavy sweat. She was leading a mob, intent on stoning him to death, and, no matter how fast he ran, he couldn't get away. She disappeared for a few minutes, and he fell into a deeper sleep, only for her to reappear as a judge wearing a black mask. He awoke soaking wet with his leg throbbing, screaming, "No, no, leave me alone." He rubbed his eyes and stared at the clock — it was 3:00 a.m. He'd slept for more than twelve hours, but still felt totally washed out. He forced himself out of bed, removed his shirt and underwear, and threw off the damp sheets. As he put on his pajamas and changed the sheets, it became clear to him — crystal clear — the burglar was a snitch hired by Fiona Jeczik, to look for embarrassing or incriminating private papers. *Bitch!* Then he remembered the phone, and it hit him — she'd also had his apartment bugged. *Bitch! Why is she trying to bring me down?* After swallowing two painkillers and a sleeping tablet, he felt a little better. Then he recalled that someone had tried to kill him. *Surely the bitch wouldn't try and kill me? Maybe it was the would-be murderer who broke into my townhouse?* He resolved to call Tom Donegan in the morning, before flopping back into bed, angry, frustrated, and worried.

"Tom, it's Douglas Aspine."

"That was quick. Sorry, the woman's clean. She's ambitious but blemish-free. She has an alcoholic father, being looked after in an exclusive private nursing home that must be costing her a fortune. She visits him at midday every Friday without fail. We don't have anything on Barry Seymour yet, but I wouldn't get your hopes up."

"I wasn't calling about her. I want you to get your best security people out to my townhouse. I want it swept and made secure, totally secure, and I want it done now."

"I can make your place as secure as Fort Knox for ten thousand. I'll add it to Mercury's account for labor relations. What happened?"

"Someone broke in yesterday. I knocked off early because of my leg and disturbed him."

"You caught him?"

"No, but I scared him off."

"But you don't think he was a burglar?"

"No! I think he was looking for dirt."

"Shit! We'll need to sweep and secure your car and office too," Donegan said, "and Douglas, be careful about what you say, and where you say it, from now on."

"Can you provide me with a discreet device that will enable me to record telephone calls?"

"That's easy, but don't forget, by law you have to inform the other party that you're recording the conversation."

"When can you get your security people here?"

"This afternoon. I'll give them the recorder to give to you."

"Thanks," Aspine said, silently cursing. He'd planned to call Brad and Kerry, but they'd have to wait until he was sure his townhouse was clean. As he was contemplating this, his prepaid cell phone rang, and he hobbled out the front door saying, "Hello, Vic."

"How'd you know it was me?"

"You're the only person who has this number. How's business?"

"Steady, and we're making good money from the sales we're getting. It was a good idea of yours to fix up the pricing."

"It was. What is it you're looking for?"

"I could have been phoning to pass the time of day, or inquiring about your health."

"But you're not," Aspine responded, growing impatient.

"No. Do you have any interest in acquiring four hundred acres of surplus land we have in Melton? We've had it rezoned residential."

"Why do you want to sell? Why aren't you developing it?"

"We've got nearly a thousand acres out there. I just want to trim our exposure."

"I could be interested," Aspine said nonchalantly, smelling the blood of a desperate seller.

"For speedy settlement we could let you have it for what we paid, plus holding costs, and the expenses of rezoning."

"How much would that be?" Aspine asked, surprised that Garland would admit that Vicland had liquidity problems so early in the negotiations.

"One hundred and fifty million."

Aspine's immediate reaction was to say bullshit, but he curbed himself. "Fax the titles, development plans, and everything else you've got to me, and I'll let you know if I'm interested."

"When will you be able to give me an answer?" Garland croaked.

"Forty-eight hours," Aspine responded, knowing that Garland was desperate for cash.

"It's a great deal."

"Sure, Vic."

- 28 -

ASPINE SLEPT WELL knowing that he was totally secure. The technicians had swept his townhouse, checked the phones, and found no bugs. *Perhaps I imagined that I heard someone, in the same way, I imagined seeing Harry Denton. Maybe it was the painkillers* he thought. His leg had stopped hurting, and he decided to follow the doctor's advice and take another day off.

Aspine was pleased when Brad called and broke up his boredom. "Hello, Doug, how's the leg, and is it true that someone tried to top you?"

"I'm okay, and it's rubbish. It was an accident."

"Sorry, but the talkback jocks are speculating about which one of your enemies it might've been. Their words, not mine."

"What did the share price close at yesterday?"

"It's been falling ever since Jeczik's show, but it totally tanked after your accident. It closed at $3.50."

"Fuck! Those talkback jocks are spooking the market. That's bloody terrible." *My new options are worthless, and those I was initially allocated have fallen by a million dollars.*

"Tell me about it. It's costing me big-time."

"How are sales holding up?"

"We've sold everything that's been completed and half of what's available off-the-plan."

"At last some good news."

"Perhaps. We've sold on deposits as low as a hundred dollars, one hundred and eighty-day settlements, subject to finance, and most of the off-the-plan stuff has been courtesy of insurance bonds. We might have problems too."

"What problems?"

"Well, you know the façade of the center building at Docklands was meant to be gold."

"It is."

"Some of the early off-the-plan buyers are saying that brass isn't gold, and they're talking about a class action to rescind their contracts."

"Shit! They don't have a leg to stand on, but the last thing we need is bad publicity. It'll drive the share price down further."

"I do have some good news. I've sold six of the apartments that we've been financing, for a little over three million. I don't know how you got our competitors to increase their prices, but it's lifted the value of our pre-owned apartments."

"I knew that if we propped the market up for a while, it'd turn in our favor," Aspine said, breathing a sigh of relief. "How are Vicland's apartments selling?"

"Strongly, the pricks have been selling against us by shit-canning what they're calling our crepe walls. They're aggressive, tough, and fiercely competitive. It's good; they've sold everything, and don't have much in the pipeline."

"Is that right?" Aspine asked, puzzled. *It didn't fit the profile of a company beset with liquidity problems.*

Aspine knew he had to convince the police to drop their investigation. He found Bill Muller's card in his wallet and called him.

"Muller speaking," a terse voice answered.

"Detective Muller, it's Doug Aspine. I was in a car acc–"

"I remember you, Mr. Aspine. How can I help you?"

"The unfounded rumors going around about the accident are unsettling my employees."

"Are you sure they're unfounded?"

"Detective, I told you it was an accident, and that's what it was."

"Yes, you did say that. Look, I can't control public opinion."

"No, but you can help tone it down."

"I'm not with you."

"I'd like you to release a statement saying that there were no suspicious circumstances and that you're closing your file."

"I can't do that. Hell, even if it was an accident, it was still a hit and run."

"Bill, can I call you Bill?" Aspine asked, oozing charm. "I understand, but couldn't you make a release saying it's no longer a homicide matter?"

"Why's it so important?"

"I told you. My employees are unsettled, and their work's being disrupted by bloody talkback jocks and rumor mongers."

"I can't help you."

The phone went quiet. "Are you still there?" Muller asked.

"Understand this," Aspine snapped, dispensing with any semblance of charm. "My public relations people will issue a press release tomorrow, stating that the police have no evidence that the accident was an attempted homicide."

"You can't do that."

"Watch me. If you have any evidence, you'll be able to repudiate the press release but, if you don't, you'll be pushing shit uphill. If you're right, which you're not, the culprit might relax after he reads the newspapers, and make a mistake that'll help you catch him."

"You can get yourself into serious trouble interfering in police business."

"Detective, you probably earn about seventy thousand a year. That's half what I make in a week so don't threaten me. If you commence any action against me, my lawyers will make your life miserable. Are you getting my message?"

"Don't make a mistake or I'll come down on you like a ton of bricks," Muller said, kicking the side of his well-worn desk hard. He knew he'd been put in his place — he also knew how easy it would be to hate the obnoxious Douglas Aspine.

"I don't make mistakes." Aspine laughed derisively.

Aspine's call to Wes was short, and he told him exactly what he wanted released to the media.

"Have you cleared this with your lawyers?" Wes asked.

"If I cleared everything with them I'd get nothing done. Say the police have no evidence to suggest it was anything other than an accident. It's simple and straightforward. All you have to do is get it out there."

"Why's it so important?"

Fuck, Jeremy told me that Wes was bright. "My employees are upset by the unfounded rumors. I want to ease their concerns," Aspine lied.

The four hundred acres that Vicland wanted to sell in Melton was prime land, but the one hundred and fifty million dollar asking price was, in Aspine's view, way above the odds. Garland sounded tentative and nervous when he answered his prepaid cell phone.

"Vic, I've been considering your offer," Aspine said, without announcing himself.

"Douglas?"

"Yeah, who else would it be, or are you hawking the land to everyone?"

"No, I haven't offered it to anyone else, which doesn't mean I won't."

"If you do, I hope you don't tell them that it cost you a hundred and fifty million because we both know that's bullshit."

"You're not interested?"

"Not at that price."

"I'm prepared to consider something a little less. Make me an offer."

"It's worth no more than eighty million!" Aspine heard coughing and spluttering. "Are you still there, Vic?"

"Are you stupid?" That's a ridiculous offer."

"It wasn't an offer. I was just telling you what it's worth. I might be prepared to go slightly higher, because by redrawing your development plans, we can add value."

"It'll want to be a lot higher. A lot, lot, higher!"

"I'm going to make you one offer. You can take it or leave it. I'd like to get my hands on the land, but I'm not getting drawn into prolonged haggling."

"Make your offer."

"One hundred million, subject to checks on title, and rates and planning."

"That's absurd." Garland laughed, with a barely perceptible hint of nervousness, which didn't escape Aspine. "I might be prepared to accept one hundred and fifteen million."

Aspine didn't respond. As each second passed the tension grew, the only sound being Garland's heavy breathing. "Douglas, Douglas, I didn't hear your response," the old man muttered, his breathing labored.

Aspine waited another thirty seconds. "Look, if my offer's unacceptable, why don't you see if Apartco or Urban are interested? I'm not falling over myself to buy undeveloped land. I'd prefer to concentrate on high-rises."

"Make it one hundred and five and you've got a deal."

"No can do, Vic. One hundred's it!"

"You're screwing me blind."

"You came to me. I don't care whether I buy or not."

"Can you settle in twenty-one days?"

Aspine smiled. *I was right. Vicland's desperate for cash.* "I made my offer based on settling in sixty days. That gives the lawyers plenty of time to do their checks, and prepare contracts."

"You won't consider early settlement?"

"No."

Again the conversation lapsed into silence, and Aspine pondered how much he could knock off the price for early settlement.

"I need early settlement," the old man nervously blurted.

"Vic, if you're prepared to accept ninety-five million, I'll help you with early settlement."

There was a gasp followed by a sudden exhaling of air. "You want five million to settle thirty-nine days earlier — you bastard, you low bastard."

"I'm not forcing you to sell. Make up your mind — do we have a deal?"

"Yes, you thieving bastard, we have a deal. My lawyers will be in touch."

Aspine placed his hands behind his head and gloated — the pain from his leg had mysteriously vanished.

With all the excitement Aspine had forgotten about the quarterly results, but sales had been strong, and he knew there would be a healthy profit. "Carmen, put me through to Kerry," he said to the receptionist.

"He called in sick this morning, Mr. Aspine, and said he wouldn't be in today."

"What's wrong with him?"

"He didn't say."

Kerry works a hundred hours a week and never takes sick days — what's wrong with him? Aspine recalled him reeking of alcohol at the hospital and wondered whether it might have something to do with his illness. *God, the last thing I need is an alcohol-dependent financial controller.*

The morning newspapers contained articles stating that the police had uncovered no evidence to suggest that the accident involving Mercury Properties Limited's CEO, Mr. Douglas Aspine, was anything other than that — an accident. They went on to say that Mr. Aspine had fully recovered from minor injuries, was in good health, and had resumed his duties at Mercury. Some of the radio and television stations devoted fifteen seconds to reporting the story. Aspine thought, *the media loves the sensationalism of bad news, and hates the boredom of good news. Wes mightn't be overly smart, but he has excellent contacts in the media.*

Aspine flicked to the financial pages of the *Herald-Sun* and saw a prominently positioned article headed, 'Clean Energy in major uranium discovery.' The share price had gone through the roof and closed at an all-time high of $1.20. He sat motionless, dazed at the enormity of his profit, which was fractionally short of a million, and resolved to sell as soon as the market opened. Blayloch & Fitch's information had, as usual, been impeccable.

- 29 -

THE CAB DROPPED Aspine at the office just after nine o'clock; he was elated to see the red monster gleaming in the early morning sun. He had missed it and was glad that there'd be no more cab rides. His eyes scanned the car-park, and he breathed a sigh of relief when he saw Kerry's car. He half skipped, half hopped up the stairs, nearly knocking Kurt over. "Get out my way, Kurt."

"I'm sorry, Douglas."

"I was joking. Don't they have jokes in Germany?"

Kurt ignored the jibe. "I need to see you. Anthony Keen was furious when I dismissed him. He said some terrible things about you."

"Sticks and stones might break my bones, but words will never hurt me." Aspine grinned. "He hates me, and knew you fired him on my instructions."

"He said he'd like to see you dead."

"Come down to my office."

Kurt reached for a chair.

"Don't sit down, this will only take a minute. I want you to understand that I was in an accident, not an attempted homicide. No-one tried to kill me, and what Anthony Keen said, is what employees say about their bosses when they get fired."

"After the shock wore off, I remembered seeing the driver. He was bald and was wearing big glasses. He definitely tried to run you do–"

Aspine interrupted. "No, he fucking didn't. He lost control and panicked after he hit me. It wasn't intentional, and I want you to stop saying it was. No more!" *Was it Bert Stuart's son John?*

"Yes, but–"

"No buts. Christ, I'd know if someone was trying to kill me. No-one is, and I don't want you running around saying anything different. Don't waste the police's time either, and don't tell them you can describe the driver because you can't. Now, tell me what you paid Keen?"

"Two year's salary."

"You were too generous, but I can live with it. You made sure that he has no grounds to sue. Well done."

"He was angry; his eyes were rolling with rage. He despises you."

"So do many others. They're all talk, and so is Keen. Forget about it."

"Yes, Douglas," Kurt said, backing out of the office, his face filled with doubt.

After the stock market had opened Aspine called Charles Ong to get a price on Clean Energy. The stock had bounced at the open and was trading at $1.50. He was nearly one and a half million in front. He'd never anticipated making such a killing and was euphoric, but also anxious to sell — who knew how long the price would hold?

"Congratulations, Doug, you've jumped on a hot one."

"I want to sell, Charles."

"Everything?"

"Yes. I don't want to push my luck."

"Why don't you sell half and let the balance run? Huge buy orders are coming into the market, and it's trading at $1.55. It could go to five dollars."

"It could also go to ten cents. Have you forgotten what Mapago stands for?"

"Make a profit and get out. Okay, Douglas, I've got your message loud and clear,"

"There'll be nearly three million in Mapago's account after you've sold Clean Energy. Transfer two million into my Swiss bank account."

"As I told you, your money's safe in Hong Kong, but if you want me to make the transfer, I will."

"I do, Charles. Goodbye."

"Kerry, come and see me," Aspine barked into the intercom.

A few minutes later Kerry knocked at the door. "Come in," Aspine said, knowing he had only one employee who'd tap so feebly at his door. "Take the weight off and tell me the good news."

"Go-good new-news?"

"Yes. Brad tells me that we've sold all available apartments. We must've had a great quarter."

"We-we ca-came in fi-five million b-behind bud-budget."

"Impossible." Aspine frowned.

"Th-the aud-auditors won-won't let us take up any more of the prof-profits on those three inc-incomplete office build-buildings."

"Why? You told me that when they were nearly completed, we could take up the budgeted profit, less some provisions for finishing costs."

"Tha-that's right bu-but they've over-run their fin-finish dates, and the auditors are saying they can't b-be sure wha-what the final costs will be."

"Fuck! How much profit would we have brought to account on them?"

"Four-fourteen million."

Jack Gillard's responsible for completing the buildings on time and on budget. The fucking dopey prick's taken his eye off the ball! "So we would have been nine million in front of budget for the quarter?"

"Ye-yes."

Kerry seemed more nervous than usual; his skin was sickly white, his acne had flared up, he was sweating heavily, and appeared to have aged. "What was wrong with you yesterday?"

"I-I had-had a touch of the flu," Kerry responded, turning bright red.

Aspine watched as Kerry squirmed in his chair. He had all the symptoms of a full-blown alcoholic. "I'm sorry to hear that. I know you're putting in massive hours. After the half yearly results are complete, why don't you take a week off and head up to Mansfield? You could use a break."

"I-I'd like that," Kerry said, brightening up a little, "b-but wha-what are we going to do about the figures? We-we've go-got nine-nineteen mil-million hidden in the fir-first quarter, and we're down another fi-five million in the second."

"Do the auditors know what the overall result is?"

"No-no they-they've been con-concentrating on the office build-ings, an-and some of the apart-apartment sales where the dep-depos-its have b-been less than a thousand dollars. Do-do you wan-want to talk to them about the off-office buildings?"

"I don't know anything about accounting, so no; I don't want to speak to them. Can you put through an adjustment for twenty-four million that they won't be able to detect?"

"You-you said you would-wouldn't ask me to do that ag-again," Kerry said, nearly in tears.

"I didn't think I'd have to, and it's not twenty-four million; it's only ten because we've got the profit in the office blocks when they're completed."

"No we-we have-haven't. There mightn't b-be any profit after the cos-cost over-runs."

"That's not true, and look what'll happen if you don't make the adjustment. It'll be obvious that you cooked the books. Hell, by Christmas our profit will more than cover the adjustment. It's not like we're cheating or lying — we're just borrowing some future profits to flatten out this half's result. We'll look back in a year's time and laugh about it."

"I-I ho-hope you're right. I nearly for-forgot, the aud-auditors are also look-looking at the loans we've made to Balmoral Finance Company."

Aspine felt the hairs on the back of his neck stand up. "In what way?"

"One of them said he'd like to see Bal-Balmoral's balance sheet."

"Would it help if I asked for some of our monies back?"

"It-it would-wouldn't hurt."

"I'll get 'em to transfer three million into our account today," Aspine said, giving silent thanks to Brad.

"I-I'm nerv-nervous, Douglas. I-I feel si-sick with worry."

"Kerry, you told me you could outsmart the auditors, and you know that I'm going to make enough profit to ensure this little adjustment is behind us by Christmas. Relax, don't worry."

"I-I'll try."

"I'll talk to Jack about the remaining costs on the office buildings. In the meantime make the adjustment twenty-five million," Aspine said nonchalantly. "It's a nice round figure and easily remembered."

After Kerry had left his office, Aspine shouted, "Kelly, find Jack Gillard and tell him to come and see me now. I don't care what site he's on, I don't care who he's with, and I don't care what he's got planned. Just get him in here."

Kelly had obviously conveyed the tone of the message because within fifteen minutes Jack Gillard was at his door. "Sit down, Jack," he said, not looking up. "What's the status of the three office blocks in Queens Road?"

"They're nearly complete."

"They were meant to be finished before the end of June."

"Yeah, they've overrun a bit because of the concentration on finishing the Docklands apartment blocks."

"Why? The project managers on the office blocks have got their own teams. What the fuck does the Docklands have to do with not finishing the office blocks?"

"We lost labor at the Docklands, so we borrowed some from the office blocks."

Aspine groaned and held his head in his hands. "You took workers off uncompleted projects and failed to meet deadlines. Whose bright idea was that?"

"Mine. The office blocks were nearly finished, and we were going to have surplus labor. It seemed silly to be hiring workers at the Docklands."

"Silly? I'll tell you what's fucking silly. Not finishing on time and within budget. The auditors are saying that because of the over-runs, they mightn't be profitable."

"Bean-counters," said Jack, perking up. "What would they know? I'll bring the office blocks in on budget or damn close to it."

"Damn close to it? You're worrying me, really worrying me. What are the costs going to over-run by?"

"I can't tell you exactly. We've had problems with the sewerage and commissioning the air conditioning."

"Christ, it's your business to know — it's what I pay you for. When are we liable for liquidated damages?"

"Not until the end of September."

"Six weeks! Six weeks! That's all you've got to fix your fucking mess. And Jack, I want to talk to you about your bonus. I'm going to let you keep your job — for six more weeks! That's your bonus — now get the fuck out of here and get those buildings finished."

Aspine felt the stress building behind his eyes and the onset of a migraine. The stitches in his leg started to tighten, and he could feel them pulling around his quad. He'd never worried about telling Kerry to fudge the figures because he'd known that future profits would be more than enough to hide the false accounting. His focus had been on the apartments; he'd taken his eye off the office blocks, and Jack Gillard had let him down. Now all he could do was pray that they'd be finished within six weeks, and still be profitable. He crashed his fist down onto his desk. "Fuck you, Jack."

Kelly buzzed and said, "I have Duncan Milgate for you."

- 30 -

"HELLO, DUNCAN. HOW are you?"

"I'm well, Douglas. How are the half-yearly figures looking?"

"We'll do marginally better than consensus forecasts."

"No nasty surprises?"

"No."

"That's good. I'm pleased."

"How does the business look going forward?"

"We might do a little better than budget by year's end, providing the economy holds up."

"I understand. The last thing you'd want is an increase in interest rates. Inflation appears under control, so I don't think you need worry. The share price is up ten percent today."

"I didn't know. I don't look at daily share prices."

"I think the market liked the news that you're not on a hit list."

"I'm not with you," Aspine lied.

"It was in the newspapers this morning. It seems the police have no evidence of attempted homicide."

"I could have told them that."

"Yes, Douglas. Do you remember my recommendation a few weeks back?"

"Vaguely, I can't recall the company's name."

"Clean Energy Limited. You didn't mention it to anyone else did you?"

"Of course not. Why?"

"There was heavy buying of the shares after we spoke, and they were sold today. The price more than doubled, so someone's made a nice profit."

"Hell, it sounds like I missed a great one. How do you know?"

"The brokers who did the buying were the sellers. You don't need to be Einstein to know that there was a leak. It's disappointing because our clients had to pay a significantly higher price to get set. Anyhow, we'll find out who it was, and remove them from our list of preferred clients."

"Perhaps it was just coincidence?"

"With one broker, yes, but in this case, there were six. The clear intent was to hide the buying. It was amateurish."

"How will you find out who it was?"

"We have our ways. We'll pressure the smaller brokers into telling us who placed the orders with them. Once we know that, we'll find out who the buyer was."

I'm not worried. I have no apparent connection with Mapago. I'm not a shareholder. I'm not a director. They won't find out it was me.

"I hope you don't come up against a corporate maze."

"It won't make any difference. Once we find out who instructed the brokers, we'll find out who the buyer was. We can be very persuasive."

"I'm sure you can."

"We have another company that we think you should invest in: Cyber-Games Ltd. I've put you down for fifty thousand dollars. Are you in?"

"I'm having some marital problems and my cash is tied up for want of a better description. I can't come up with more than twenty-five thousand."

"Sorry to hear it. You're going through a rough patch, what with your accident, that Jeczik woman and now your marriage."

"Tell me about it."

Aspine put the phone down and immediately rang Charles Ong on his prepaid cell phone, relating what Duncan Milgate had said, without mentioning Cyber-Games.

"He's bluffing, Douglas; it's nigh on impossible to trace you."

"Nigh on impossible?"

"Blayloch & Fitch, are very powerful and have a wide range of contacts."

"Yes, but they'd have to have contacts in Crossley & Leyland to find out about me."

"They might have."

"Christ, you're making me nervous."

"Don't worry. I'll delete all references to you from the computer, and take your files home with me for safe keeping. Even if they have contacts, they won't find anything."

"Thanks, Charles."

The board meeting to review the half-yearly figures was subdued and even Harry Denton was quiet. Aspine still had the stitches in his leg and was walking with a pronounced limp. *Perhaps Harry's feeling sorry for me* he pondered.

"An excellent result, Douglas," Sir Edwin said. "Are you going to confirm earlier guidance to the market for the full year?"

"Thank you. Yes, I'll confirm full year increase of thirty percent."

"The office blocks were due to be completed by the end of June. What's happened?" Harry asked.

"Completion's slightly overdue. There's nothing to worry about."

"They were the last contracts I negotiated as CEO. Remember there's a liquidated damages clause that takes effect at the end of September."

"Yes, I know. They'll be finished and handed over before then."

"We declared an interim dividend of 8 cents last year. I think we should increase it to 10 cents this year," Stan Pettit said.

"As you know, I'm opposed to paying any dividend," Aspine said. "We need to conserve our cash; we've got a ninety-five million dollar settlement on the Melton property coming up later this month."

"Our shareholders expect increased dividends when the company's doing well. I agree with Stan. We should declare an interim dividend of 10 cents," Sir Edwin said.

"I don't know why Vic Garland sold you that Melton property for such a bargain price? It concerns me," Harry said.

"Vicland must have liquidity problems. I don't think Vic had much choice but to sell."

"Vic Garland mightn't appear in *Business Review Weekly* as a billionaire, but he most certainly is. He could've personally fixed any of Vicland's liquidity problems," Harry responded.

Aspine frowned. "Maybe Vicland's land supply bank had grown too large, and he was looking to reduce it."

"Maybe," Harry said, without conviction.

"Are there any other matters anyone would like to raise?" Sir Edwin asked, pleased the meeting was running so smoothly.

"I'd like to inform the board of my intention to exercise my options," Aspine said. "I'll need to borrow monies, and then sell some of my shares to cover the loans and income tax on the profit on the options conversion."

"That's great. I take it you'll be supporting the declaration of dividends from now on." Harry grinned.

"I won't dignify that comment with a response, however, I'd appreciate it if you'd sign my half yearly bonus check, Sir Edwin."

"It's my pleasure, Douglas, and again my congratulations on delivering another superb result."

"Hear, hear," William Claymore added, making his only contribution to the meeting.

Mercury's shares had climbed to $4.40 on controlled buying in the morning session. Aspine knew that it was Blayloch & Fitch's clients buying, courtesy of inside information provided by Duncan Milgate. Just after midday, Kelly faxed Mercury's results to the Stock Exchange showing a thirty-one percent increase in half-yearly profit, with guidance for more of the same for the full year. As expected, the market embraced the result, and heavy buying in the afternoon pushed the shares to an all-time high of $4.90.

Aspine called Phil Kendall and told him that he'd like to borrow eleven million so that he could exercise three and a half million options. Kendall immediately agreed, saying that he'd be at Aspine's office at ten o'clock the following morning with the documents, and a bank check made payable to Mercury.

Barbara wasn't keen on seeing her estranged husband but had agreed when he said that he only wanted to discuss the children's welfare. She had been reluctant to see him without her lawyer, but he'd been persistent, and she'd relented. She looked like she'd been working out hard in the gym, her arms were toned, and she gave off an air of vibrancy and confidence.

"You're looking great," he said.

"I can't say the same for you," she said, looking at his leg.

"I'm fine; the stitches come out later this morning."

"Is it true that someone tried to kill you?"

"You know the media. They'll say anything so long as it sells. It was an accident, that's all."

"So, what are your concerns about the kids?"

"First, I think we should sort the property settlement out."

"No! You said you wanted to see me about the children. I agreed on the condition that the divorce and property settlement weren't discussed. You're not going to cheat me out of what's rightfully mine, and my lawyer's going to be with me for those discussions."

"I'm trying to save legal fees. Those bloodsuckers will bleed you dry if you're not careful, and we both know it's me who'll be paying them."

"No, I'm not discussing settlement without my lawyer," she said, putting her fingers into her ears. "Please leave."

"I'm trying to save the kids from grief. I thought you'd want the same."

"What's the property settlement got to do with the kids?"

"If your bloodsucker comes after me, which he will, some of your past might surface."

"Don't threaten me. I'm not the one in this family with a past, but even if I was, there's nothing you could do about it." She scoffed. "Haven't you heard of 'no fault' divorce?' You should talk to your lawyer."

"I haven't briefed one and don't expect that I'll need to. I just don't want to have to bring up the fling you had with your old boyfriend, Jamie Wallace while I was slaving away in Sydney."

"You bastard, I went to the Wallaces' dinner party, that's all, and you know it."

"I wonder what Sue Wallace will think when she finds out that you've got the hots for her husband."

"You're a filthy liar, but you don't scare me. You can't bring up any of your lies and slime in the divorce proceedings. After twelve months separation, I'll have all the grounds I need to have you out of my life permanently. I'm going to take you for every cent that I can."

Aspine ignored what she'd said. "And what about that young tennis coach you had it off with? What was his name? Maurice wasn't it?"

"He was only a young boy, you scum. Get out of my home."

"And then there was the assistant professional at the golf club who gave you all those lessons. I'm sure he did more than improve your swing," Aspine smirked.

"Get out," Barbara screamed, tears of anger running down her cheeks. "You can't tell your disgusting lies in court."

"Who said anything about court? Can't you see the articles in the dailies, 'Which estranged Malvern wife is having it off with a prominent Toorak plastic surgeon?' Or 'Malvern's Mrs. Robinson seduces boy tennis coach.' Can you see the evening current affairs programs airing 'Separated wife of CEO lusted after younger men?' I wonder what your snobby girlfriends would think, not to mention Sue Wallace."

"Get out, get out! My lawyers will stop you from circulating that horrible filth."

Aspine didn't move. "I won't circulate it, but the people I pay will. They won't specifically name you, everything will be by innuendo, and there's nothing your dopey lawyers can do to stop them, without disclosing that you're the unnamed party. Do you want that?"

"Even you wouldn't stoop that low."

"In case Sue Wallace and your girlfriends can't work out who the scarlet woman is, my people will send emails from anonymous Hotmail accounts naming you. You know what they say, if you throw enough shit some always sticks," Aspine said, through thinly drawn lips.

"You, you wouldn't do it," Barbara stammered. "The kids would never forgive you."

"I don't want to, and I don't want kids telling ours that their mother's a whore. Mark's too young to cope, and can you imagine how embarrassed Jemma would be with her girlfriends? I'll pay you one and a half-million and sign the house and car over to you unencumbered. It works out to nearly two and a half mil. I'm being extremely generous."

"No, I won't accept. Only last month you were boasting about making more than five million this year, and you expect me to take less than half of that, for the twenty years we've been together. No, I won't! I won't!" Barbara said, sobbing uncontrollably.

"Yes, you will, because if I walk out of here without your agreement, we'll be at war, and people get hurt in wars. You'll be lucky to have any friends in a year's time, and the kids will disown you. I'll instruct my lawyers to prolong the proceedings, and in the meantime, you won't get a cent. Do you want that? I don't think so. Let's agree and get on with our lives."

"I want monthly maintenance too!"

"Trevor's grown up, Jemma's about to turn eighteen, and with one and a half million in cash, you'll have plenty to look after Mark for the next four years."

"You're eve-even cheat-cheating your kids. I-I hate you. I fel-felt sorry for you when you we-were hit by that car. Now I wis-wish you'd died."

"Do we have an agreement?"

"Yes, now get out. I never want to set eyes on you again."

Aspine smiled cruelly. "Make sure your bloodsuckers don't send me any more threatening letters. Max Vogel will confirm what we've agreed. Goodbye. Have a nice life."

"Bastard!"

As Aspine drove away, he knew that he could move onto his next phase of his wealth creation without having to worry about Barbara.

In contrast to their first meeting, this time, Aspine didn't keep Phil Kendall waiting.

"Phil, good to see you," Aspine said, grasping his hand like he was a long-lost brother.

"Good morning, Doug. I'll go over these documents with you, and get your signature. Then I can let you have this," Kendall said, holding up a check made payable to Mercury Properties Ltd, for eleven million three hundred and seventy-five thousand dollars.

Aspine laughed.

"What's funny?"

"That check's a hundred times larger than what you wouldn't lend me eighteen months ago. Ironic, isn't it?"

"I thought we'd finished with that."

"We have. I'm sorry," Aspine said, without sincerity. "Bear with me, Phil. I have to make a call that's nearly as important for you as it is for me."

"Duncan, it's Douglas Aspine. What are our shares trading at?"

"There's been strong demand and the last trade went through at $5.20."

"That's great. Sell three million shares at market."

"Why are you selling so many?"

"I have to repay the bank's loan of eleven million, and tax of four million."

"The tax won't be anything like four million and, besides, you've got a year to pay it. You only need to sell a little over two million shares to repay the bank. You can sell more when your tax falls due."

"Duncan, I've told you about my other problems, and that I have no money, so just do what I've asked you to," Aspine snapped.

"If you insist, Douglas. Don't forget to lodge the appropriate notices with the Stock Exchange."

"I know."

"Problems?" Kendall asked.

"No Phil, just a stockbroker who likes hearing his own voice."

I've made nearly seven million from the options, but after paying tax, and the divorce settlement of two and a half million, I'll be lucky to end up with two million. Fuck! I've been far too generous with Barbara. If only I didn't have to pay tax and her. It's so unfair. Lucky I've got three million salted away in Hong Kong and Switzerland. I'll have to increase it while Blayloch & Fitch still trust me. I'd better call Charles Ong while I'm still in their good books.

- 31 -

"**CHARLES, IT'S DOUGLAS** Aspine. I want you to buy a million shares in Cyber-Games Ltd. They're trading at $1.02. If necessary, you can go to $1.15 to fill my order."

"I assume this is another Blayloch & Fitch recommendation?"

"Yes."

"Don't you think it'd be prudent to wait for another recommendation a little further down the road?"

"I thought about that. What if they find out that it was me who traded Clean Energy? I won't be on their preferred client list any longer, and won't be getting any more tips. No, I want to buy what I can, while I can."

"They'll be pissed off, and they're sure to intensify their efforts to find out who's abusing their information."

"I know. I want you to instruct a local broker and swear him to secrecy. Then get him to place orders through three smaller Australian brokers none of which are based in Melbourne. I want to make it as difficult as I can for Blayloch & Fitch to find out who's behind the buying."

"I understand, Douglas. Call me tomorrow, and I'll let you know if your order's been filled."

Max Vogel was subdued when he related the coroner's findings to Aspine. "You're going to have to improve the control of vehicles on your building sites and quarries. You should do it immediately."

"Yes, of course. What about criminal action?"

"The coroner found that Bert Stuart partially contributed to his demise by removing his hearing aid. He made no recommendations regarding criminal action against the company's executives."

"Hallelujah! Hell, Max, why are you so downbeat? That's great news."

"Stuart's son, John, took it very hard and abused the coroner. He called you a murderer. It was one of the most violent outbursts that I've ever witnessed in any judicial forum. I'd be careful if I were you."

So it was John who tried to kill me. "Don't worry; I'll be on guard. God, that's great news and an enormous relief. I thought you could be fighting to keep me out of jail."

"I still might. There's still some possibility of criminal action, and there'll certainly be a civil suit."

"Cheer up, Max. I'm not worried about civil proceedings, and the coroner's buried any chance of criminal charges."

"I hope you're right."

Aspine's cell phone vibrated. He didn't recognize the number on the screen, but the caller's voice was refined. "Mr. Aspine, it's Hamish Gidley-Baird from Sainsbury & Co. You applied for the Genilab position through one of my partners."

"Hell, Hamish, I'm surprised you don't know that I already have a job," Aspine sarcastically responded.

"We're aware of that. We know all about you, Mr. Aspine. You've done an incredible job at Mercury, and we have a client who could use your services."

"A public company?"

"Yes."

"I'm on a lucrative package."

"We're prepared to significantly exceed your current remuneration."

"I don't think so, but thanks anyhow."

"I'll give you my private line and cell phone numbers. Call me if you'd like to meet."

"I'm flattered, Hamish, but I've got a job to finish."

"You should at least see what we're prepared to offer. Don't be shy about calling if you have a change of mind."

"I won't."

Tom Donegan rarely displayed emotion but could barely contain his excitement when he called. "Douglas, I have some information about Barry Seymour that I'm sure will interest you. When can we meet?"

"Why don't you tell me over the phone?"

"I have a few documents that I think you'll want to see."

"Fuck, Tom, tell me what you've got."

"Jeez, calm down. He borrowed heavily to take control of Channel Sixteen nearly thirty years ago, but it was losing money — heavily."

"He couldn't have been getting dividends, so how did he pay the interest on his loans?"

"He embarked on a slash and burn campaign, sacked half the workforce and turned the losses into profits."

"Bloody hypocrite!"

"I wouldn't say that because he's not the one who's going after you. Anyhow, when he eventually needed more staff, he hired some of the employees he'd gotten rid of, on a contract basis at half the rates they'd previously been paid. The unions went apeshit, but then went quiet."

"He paid them off?"

"Yeah, but that's not all. Channel Sixteen hired helicopters for its news team, and one crashed, killing the pilot and four researchers."

"How does that help me?"

"They denied any liability in respect of the deaths of researchers because they were all *supposedly* independent contractors. Obviously their insurers instructed them not to admit liability, and there was an almighty shit fight that ended up in the Supreme Court, where the judge found against Channel Sixteen. Not only that, he was scathing in his judgment and condemned the company, and its management, for its bloody-minded and uncaring attitude to the families of the deceased. I've got a copy of the judgment if you're interested."

"Oh, I'm interested, very interested." Aspine laughed. "That's fantastic."

"There's more. He was involved in a messy divorce and not only disowned his wife but their only daughter. The girl became drug addicted in her early teens, and she's been in and out of drug rehabilitation clinics ever since. According to his ex-wife, he hasn't seen the girl in fifteen years, but he pays for her treatment."

"More likely pays for her to remain hidden so she won't embarrass him."

"I thought the same."

"Do you know where she is?"

"Yeah. Why?"

"I might want to get some pics of the girl and the clinic she's in."

"The media won't gang up on their own, not at ownership level anyhow. You're not going to get the mainstream media to run with this. It's yesterday's news," Donegan croaked.

"You don't understand the power of the internet, Tom. When the time is right, I'll anonymously get into half a dozen chat rooms with the story and pics of the girl. I'll make it today's news. Did you find out anything more about that bitch Jeczik?"

"Nothing, she's squeaky clean. As I told you, she visits her alcoholic father at the Fairhills Nursing Home every week. He can barely put two words together."

"Maybe I should visit. I could gift him a bottle of Jack Daniels."

"Be careful, you've seen how dangerous she can be."

"I was joking. Can you get me the name of another Fairhills patient, preferably comatose?"

"I'm not with you."

"I might like to visit my new found friend at the same time the bitch is visiting her drunken old man."

"She won't be intimidated."

"We'll see. Keep digging. Everyone's got skeletons. You just haven't found hers yet. Talk to her old boyfriends. They're always a rich source of spleen."

"Mr. Bracken's been holding for over five minutes," Kelly said. "He sounds stressed."

"What's up, Wes?"

"Douglas, do you remember asking me to prepare press releases on your land acquisition in Melton?"

"I'm not bloody senile. Of course, I do. Get to the point."

"I had a call from a close contact in Canberra. You're going to have problems. It seems that the land you've acquired is the habitat of a rare and endangered species of rat. The Minister for the Environment is going to hand down a decision in the next four weeks ensuring their survival."

"They're going to stop my development for a fucking rat?"

"It's a behind the scenes deal that the Federal Government's doing with the greenies to stick it up the State Government. It's what you and I would call a rat, but to the greenies, it's the smallest native marsupial."

"I know who the fucking rat is," Aspine snarled, thinking about Vic Garland. "Who else knows?"

"It's hush-hush. The Federal Government's keeping a lid on it, pending a major announcement on development by the Victorian Premier. The Feds will make their announcement later on the same day, and it'll be designed to make the Premier and State Government look stupid."

Aspine had no doubt that Vic Garland knew what the Feds had planned when he'd sold him the Melton land at a seemingly bargain basement price. *Old bastard!* Mercury's share price would be smashed when the Minister made his announcement.

"Wes, listen to me carefully. You didn't tell me anything about endangered rats or the land at Melton. Do you understand? We never had this call."

"What call?" Wes laughed.

I've still got 500,000 shares in Mercury worth more than two and a half million. After the Minister's announcement, I won't get half of that, and I'll be lucky to still have a job. If only I wasn't a director I could sell without making an announcement to the market. If I sell it'll be treated as a lack of confidence in Mercury, and I might face insider trading charges later, Aspine thought. He felt trapped and waves of anger coursed through him. Vic Garland had sucker punched him. Any hope of numerous non-executive director positions in other public companies had been killed. He felt a pounding in his temples and another savage migraine coming on.

Kerry Bartlett knocked nervously on Aspine's door. His eyes were red, and he looked exhausted. "Come in, Kerry," Aspine snarled, still thinking about Vic Garland while fighting to soften his tone. "I wanted to talk to you about your bonus."

"I-I-I've-"

"Try and relax, Kerry. I've authorized a half yearly bonus of a hundred thousand to compensate you for the enormous effort you've put in. I've exercised my options, and I suggest you do the same. I'm sure you know that your profit's around seven hundred thousand."

Kerry's demeanor hadn't improved and, if anything, he looked sicklier. "I-I ha-have some b-bad news."

"That can wait. Do you want me to ask Phil Kendall to fund the exercise of your options in the same way he did for me?"

"It-it's not imp-important."

"Of course, it is. I'll get Phil out tomorrow morning." Aspine's head ached, but he ignored the pain knowing that he had to make sure Kerry exercised his options.

"All-all right," Kerry mumbled, without enthusiasm. "Doug-Douglas, the cos-costs on the office bl-blocks have blow-blown out. Th-the four-fourteen mil-million profit that we thought we had has tur-turned into a loss. We-we're in troub-trouble."

Aspine couldn't conceal his shock. "How can that be? Are you sure?"

"I-I'm certain."

"What can we do?" *Fuck Jack Gillard. It's his fault.*

"I-I can't th-think of any-anything, I-I'm so-sorry."

"It's not your fault. I'm not an accountant but why can't you allocate the additional costs to the other partly completed projects? That way the office blocks will still appear profitable, and our little problem will be solved."

"Lit-little prob-problem? We-we've fake-faked the figures by twenty-five million, and we-we've just los-lost fourteen that we thought we were going to get back. I-I might be able to trans-transfer some cos-costs, but eventually, they'll come ba-back to bite us."

"If you can push the costs out to next year, we'll make enough additional profits to hide them. We need breathing space." Aspine said, placing his hand on Kerry's shoulder. "I'll never let you down, mate, trust me."

No-one had ever called Kerry 'mate' before, and while his gut was twisting, he felt affection and loyalty for Douglas Aspine that bordered on love. "Thank you, Doug."

After Kerry had left, Aspine put his arms on his desk and rested his head on them, praying that it would stop throbbing.

Wes Bracken's call about the endangered rats on the Melton land had sealed Aspine's future, and cost him millions. It was not in his nature to turn the other cheek, and he intended to extract retribution. He carefully connected the recording device to his phone and punched in Vic Garland's direct line number.

"Hello," a gruff, testy voice answered.

"Vic, it's Douglas. How are you?"

"Why are you calling me on this line?"

"Fuck. I forgot. It won't make any difference this one time."

"Hmmph. What do you want?"

"My salespeople are complaining. They say they're selling against heavy discounting at the Docklands. You told me you could control apartment pricing," Aspine said, flicking on the recorder.

"We haven't discounted, and I've told the principals at Apartco and Urban what they should be charging."

"Yes, but do they listen to you?" Aspine scoffed.

"Listen, sonny," Garland growled, "as far as apartment pricing goes, they do exactly what I tell them."

"How often are you in contact with them?"

"Regularly. I'll call them, but I think your salespeople are whining because they're being outsold. What do you expect when they've got to sell crepe walls?" he laughed disdainfully. "I'll call you in a few minutes."

Aspine didn't have long to wait. "What's wrong with your prepaid? When I called, it went to message bank."

"Sorry, Vic. My battery ran out," Aspine lied.

"Jesus, how slack are you? I've spoken to my contacts at Apartco and Urban. As I thought, there's been no discounting."

"So they're charging the prices they agreed with you?"

"I just said that, didn't I?"

"I don't understand."

"It's simple. Apartco, Urban, and Vicland are holding the agreed prices. I'm warning you, don't start discounting or we'll launch a price war that'll kill you," Garland growled.

"I won't. By the way Vic, what's your full name?"

"Why do you need to know?"

"My PA's sending out invitations to a Mercury function, and wanted to know if your full name is Victor?"

"Don't invite me. Those bloody functions are a waste of time. Tell her to take Vic Garland's name off her list because I won't be there. Goodbye."

Aspine broke his prepaid cell phone into two parts and cut the sim card into small pieces that he'd dispose of in public rubbish bins. As far as he was concerned, it had never existed. He placed the recording device in his jacket pocket and patted it. Vic Garland was about to be hit by a bombshell which would rob him of a lifetime's respect — together with a large amount of his cash. His headache had disappeared, and he felt clear-headed and sharp. This had never occurred before without sex, but then again, what he was about to do to Garland, was far better than sex.

Aspine couldn't call Max Vogel fast enough. "I need to see you first thing in the morning, Max. I'll come to your office."

"Douglas, I have other appointments. I can't see you until the afternoon."

"Cancel them, this is urgent."

"I can't, D–"

"Fucking lawyers! Christ, Max, I'm your biggest client."

"You're not, you know, but I'll fit you in at eight o'clock," Vogel sighed.

- 32 -

SLY & VOGEL OWNED a small three-level period building at the Paris end of Collins Street that'd been extensively refurbished. The furnishings and décor were expensive but understated. The reception was unattended when Aspine arrived, and he thumped the bell.

"Good morning, Douglas," the slim, urbane, graying lawyer said, extending his hand.

"Hello, Max. Thanks for seeing me."

"Come down to my office," Vogel said, walking down the corridor. "What's so urgent?"

"You'll see in a second," Aspine replied, taking the recorder from his pocket and playing the Garland recording.

"Shit! That's dynamite, but I don't understand why you've kept it, or why you're playing it?"

"I want you to give it to the ACCC."

"You want to give it to the Competition Commission? Have you gone mad? They'll bury you. What have you got against Vic Garland? The penalties could be tens of millions."

"I wasn't involved in the price fixing. I increased Mercury's prices, and the others followed. Then Vic Garland called and told me that he'd put me out of business if I discounted at the Docklands."

"But Mercury still benefited from the absence of genuine competition. Why do you want to blow the whistle on Garland? Does it have something to do with the Melton land deal?"

"I'm not out to sink Garland, and it's got nothing to do with the land."

"Why then?" Vogel asked, starting to lose patience.

"Is everything I tell you privileged?"

"Yes."

"So you can never give evidence against me?"

"That's what I said."

Aspine explained the creation of Balmoral Finance Company Pty Ltd, and how it had been used to prop up the prices of pre-owned apartments.

Vogel groaned, "I wondered how Mercury's apartments were holding their prices when I read those advertisements, but what does it have to do with Garland?"

"The ACCC has a history of granting immunity to the first whistle-blower in a cartel, doesn't it?"

"Yes, with the consent of the Director of Public Prosecutions; but how does that help you with Balmoral?"

"Simple. I want you to approach the ACCC and DPP and negotiate my immunity, including an all-embracing indemnity for all and any breaches of the Trade Practices Act that I may have inadvertently committed. I also want you to ensure that they can't share any information I provide, or that they might discover, with the Securities and Investment Commission."

"Inadvertently? You're asking me to go to the ACCC and tell them I have a client with evidence unlawfully gathered, of extensive price fixing in the building industry, who'll provide that information if he's granted a watertight immunity."

"Unlawfully gathered?"

"You can't tape a conversation without the other party's knowledge and use it as evidence."

"I knew that," Aspine lied. "I thought it might whet the antitrust regulator's appetite, though."

"I think you know far more than you're telling me. The tape more than establishes the grounds for a full investigation, and I'm sure the ACCC's investigators would love to have it."

"Good. I doubt the ACCC will find out about Balmoral but, if they do, I want to be fully insured. It should be easy for you. After all, lawyers are trained to prepare all-encompassing documents designed to protect their clients against unforeseen future pitfalls. Do you think you can pull it off?"

"You must think I can, or you wouldn't be here."

"Max, make your first overtures to the ACCC today and get a draft indemnity prepared. However, I don't want to provide any statements or evidence for another two weeks."

"Why?"

"I can't tell you, but I want you to personally handle this matter. No delegating. If it leaks out before I'm indemnified, I'll be deep in the shit."

Aspine smiled as he walked out onto Collins Street. *Vic Garland doesn't know what's about to hit him. Old bastard! I'll instruct Wes to issue press releases on the day the ACCC indemnify me, that'll make me look like an unfortunate victim, and Garland a bully and a rogue.* Before going back to the office, he visited a Vodaphone dealer and paid cash for an essential tool — another prepaid cell phone. He wanted no record of buying the prepaid or of his calls to Charles Ong.

Aspine knew that he couldn't sell his remaining five hundred thousand shares in Mercury without creating suspicion, leaving himself open to insider trading charges once the Melton disaster became public. It was against this background that he decided to make an off-market transfer of his shares to Barbara. He would lodge the requisite forms with the Stock Exchange, making it clear the transfer was to his wife. Hopefully, those who made their money by analyzing such announcements would not consider it a sale, but rather a change of ownership within the family.

"I don't want bloody shares," Barbara screamed down the phone. "You said it'd be cash, and you'd sign the house and car over to me."

"The deal's changed. You're now getting five hundred thousand shares worth more than two and a half million, and taking over the mortgage on the house, and the car loan. It's more than what we agreed, so I don't know why you're whining."

"I don't want to own shares in any company that you're involved in, and I can't repay the loans with them."

"Sorry, that's not my problem."

"You force me to take shares, and I'll sell the bloody things."

"I wouldn't do that if I were you," Aspine gloated, knowing that Barbara would do exactly the opposite.

"I'm selling!"

"You'll regret it."

He crowed at his cunning. *I've managed to get two and a half million for shares that are soon going to be worth half that, without selling them. Better still, Barbara will say, if questioned, that I tried to talk her out of selling.*

Aspine knew he had to find another CEO's 'position before the shit hit the fan. With this at the forefront of his mind, he called Sainsbury & Co.

"I'm surprised but pleased to hear from you, Douglas," Hamish Gidley-Baird gushed. "What made you change your mind?"

"I haven't, Hamish, but I thought I should at least listen to your proposal. When can we meet?"

"Can you come to our offices?"

"I don't think that would be wise."

"No, you're right, sorry I didn't think."

"Where do you live, Hamish?"

"Beaumaris."

"You must pass Finz, the fish restaurant and bar on Beach Road on the way home. Let's meet there tonight at seven o'clock?"

"That's fine. It'll allow me to get away from the city a little earlier than usual."

"How will I know you?"

Gidley-Baird laughed. "Don't worry, Douglas, with the exposure you've had in the newspapers and television, I'll know you. Make yourself comfortable when you get there. I'll do the looking."

Vic Garland's treachery had messed with Aspine's head but, he didn't forget to call Charles Ong, to ensure that his ill-gotten profits were still accumulating.

"Douglas, we bought one million shares in Cyber-Games at an average of $1.10. They opened at $1.35 this morning, and there's been heavy buying since."

"Thank you, that's good news."

"Blayloch & Fitch know the Clean Energy orders came from this firm."

"How do you know?"

"Someone within the firm has been prying into Mapago."

"Shit!"

"Don't worry, I've made sure there's nothing to find, but they're persisting. If I were you, I'd give it a break after you've closed the Cyber-Games position."

"I will. After I've closed, I'll transfer everything into the Swiss bank account. If the Cyber-Games shares perform to expectations, I'll have over four million in Zurich."

"You won't get any more protection there than you have in Hong Kong."

"You're probably right, Charles, but I like muddying my tracks. Goodbye."

Finz was quiet, and Aspine took a table near a beachside window. "Will you be dining with us this evening?" the waitress asked.

"I'm not sure. I'd like a Jack Daniels while I think about it."

"Certainly."

It was nearly dark, but Aspine still caught glimpses of the ocean through the ti-treed foreshore and heavy Beach Road traffic. He pushed his drink from hand to hand pondering what the night might hold.

"A penny for your thoughts," the tall, blonde-haired man said.

"Hamish? It's good to put a face to a voice. What would you like to drink?"

"Douglas, it's a pleasure to meet you. I'll have a dry white."

"If you'd rather avoid the house whites, I'd be happy to share a bottle with you."

"Thanks, but I'm only having one glass. I want to get home to see my kids before they go to bed, and I'm hoping to get to the gym a little later."

"You want to cut through the small talk and get down to business."

"That's right. We already know what we need to about you, so why don't I brief you about our proposition."

"Go for it."

"Our client is a major drug developer and pharmaceuticals

company. It has brilliant chemists, scientists, and researchers, but a poor record of selling its products. Most of the marketing is via license agreements with large US companies."

"Who cream off most of the profits leaving your client, Philmont Pharmaceuticals, with the dregs. Is that a fair summary?"

"I didn't think it'd take much for you to work out who our client is and, yes, you're right. It's a staid old company, and two of the Philmont family are still on the board. It has no debt, it's asset-rich and has been overpromising and underdelivering for years. The family still own more than thirty percent, and if they didn't, it would've been taken over years ago."

"Who are you acting for?" Aspine asked, sipping his whiskey.

"I'm not with you?"

"Who's the catalyst for a new CEO? Is it the family or the institutions?"

"The third generation of the family would like to sell, but not while the share price is languishing at less than net tangible asset backing."

"They want someone to kick it into shape and then they'll sell out. That's hardly an attractive proposition for the incumbent CEO," Aspine said, thinking it was perfect.

"They realize that, and there'll be a generous early termination sum built into the remuneration package."

"Why don't you give me the details of the package, because what you've said so far holds no appeal," Aspine lied.

"You're going to earn seven million with Mercury this year. With the Philmont package you'll make ten million plus," Gidley-Baird said, his light blue eyes glazing over at the size of the numbers. "This is a terrific opportunity."

"I don't think so. If I accepted would your client indemnify me for legal costs and damages in the event of Mercury suing me for breach of contract?"

"We anticipated that would be a concern, and should your former employer litigate, our client is prepared to fully indemnify you."

"Former employer? You're getting a little ahead of yourself. If you know so much about my current package, you'll be aware that if I accept your offer, I'll be sacrificing a half yearly bonus of three million," Aspine exaggerated.

"Douglas, Philmont's package is vastly superior to Mercury's, and you won't be sacrificing anything. On the contrary, you'll be benefitting."

"Perhaps. Do you remember the 'golden handcuffs' used by Bond Corporation to secure its executives, and ensure that they couldn't work for competitors?"

"Bond Corporation collapsed, and golden handcuffs went out of vogue years ago."

"That's not right; the National Bank used them quite recently."

Gidley-Baird looked flustered. "What's your point?"

"If your client's prepared to offer me a five million dollar signing on fee, it will make the balance of the package considerably more attractive."

"A five million dollar pair of golden handcuffs?" Gidley-Baird gasped.

"Yes."

"I'm not sure if my client will be that generous, and I'm not sure I want to ask."

"Generous? When I was appointed at Mercury, its shares were trading at $1.80. They're now $5.20 — that's an increase of nearly two hundred percent in less than two years. If I can do that with Philmont, the value of the family's investment will increase from six hundred million to two billion, and you're quibbling about a mere five million." Aspine smiled, all charm.

"I'll check with my client and come back to you, but I'll need to give them an undertaking that you'll accept before they'll even countenance making such an offer."

Aspine sat for a long time, apparently deep in thought. "Let them know that I'm prepared to execute a contract this week, and commence within six weeks. I will, of course, want the five million as soon as I sign, which will not be refundable, should they later change their minds for any reason. I want you and your principals to understand that acceptance will be a big decision for me, given what I'll be giving up at Mercury."

They shook hands at the front door. "I'll call you. Thanks for taking the time to see me, Douglas."

"It was nice meeting you, Hamish."

Aspine let out an almighty whoopee as he walked across the car-park. He was confident that he'd soon be receiving an offer from Philmont.

-33-

ASPINE SLEPT RESTLESSLY but woke from an early morning drowse with adrenalin pumping through him. He'd spent most of the night plotting his exit from Mercury, and devising plans by which he could tidy up any loose ends that might see him end up in jail. The traffic was surprisingly heavy and, as he crawled along Punt Road he called Brad Hooper telling him to be in his office at 9:00 a.m.

Brad had moved from browns to blues, and Aspine thought he looked more like a merchant banker in his navy blue pinstripe suit than a hard-nosed apartment salesman. "You're looking prosperous, Brad."

"It's my manager's garb. What is it that you want to see me about?"

"I want to thank you for a job well done. You've sold nearly everything."

"I told you I could sell."

"Yes, and I'm rewarding you with a mid-year bonus of three hundred thousand." Aspine smiled.

"Shit, that's unexpected. Do I get options as well?"

"No, but you should exercise your four hundred thousand options. When you do, you'll make a tidy eight hundred thousand."

"What's going on? Why do I need to exercise them now? After tax, I'll only be able to afford to keep a hundred thousand shares."

"I never said this, but if I were you, I wouldn't keep any."

"Something's going down. What's happening? Fill me in," Brad said, his face filled with apprehension.

"I can't, but don't worry, I'll look after you. I want you to call Phil Kendall at the bank and tell him you want to exercise your options. He'll handle the funding. Sell your shares at the same time."

"I don't like the sound of this. What are you up to? Has it got anything to do with those fucking apartments I've been buying? I'm not going down for that."

"No-one's going down. You might have to take an extended holiday, but you'll have plenty of spending money to enjoy yourself. Do as I say, Brad, and I'll take care of you. Now get out of here and call Kendall."

That's another loose end tied up. I could've told Kurt Metzger and Jack Gillard to exercise their options too, but the dumb Kraut nearly got me thrown in jail over Bert Stuart's death, and Gillard goofed up the completion of the office blocks. They don't deserve any special treatment, and they can't hurt me. Bad luck for them!

Gidley-Baird's call came just before midday. "My principals are prepared to consider making an offer in the terms that we discussed last night, subject to one change. If you accept their offer, but later renege on your undertaking, you will return their five million plus another three million in damages. Before making a firm commitment, Helen and Phillip Philmont would like to meet you."

"Why do they want to meet me? You said you knew all you needed to know? If they ask me anything about Mercury, I won't be able to respond, because I won't breach confidential information entrusted to me," Aspine said, anxious to ensure that he'd have no difficult questions to answer.

"They want to know more about you as a person. They were moved by what they saw as your softer side."

"Softer side?"

"Yes, your work with the National Homeless Foundation. They know you're not afraid to make tough decisions, but were also impressed to see you helping the needy."

Aspine smiled. *I couldn't care less about the poor and the homeless, but it's great that others think I do.* "It's important to give something back to the community, Hamish."

"I agree, Douglas. Helen lives in Toorak and wondered whether you might be available at ten o'clock tomorrow morning?"

"I'll be there. If I pass inspection, when can I expect an offer?"

"I'll courier it to you tomorrow afternoon, with an acceptance in the form my principals require. I'm sure you'll want to take legal advice before signing. Upon execution, I'll ensure that I'm in a position to complete the agreement."

"You'll have a bank check for five million?"

"Yes."

"All going well, I'll complete on Friday morning. If need be, can you attend my lawyer's offices?"

"Yes, Douglas."

The Sting echoed around Aspine's office, and he glanced at his cell phone's screen and cursed. "Yes, Barbara, what is it?" He snarled.

"It's Trevor," she sobbed. "He tested positive for driving under the influence of drugs this morning. The police have locked him up."

"Fuck! Where? How can he have tested positive in the morning? What is he, a bloody pothead?"

'He's at Flinders Street Police Station. Can you go and get him?"

"I ought to let him rot, it'd teach him a lesson. How long have you known that he's been using dope?"

"I-I didn't," she sniffled.

"Christ, he's using it under your nose, and you don't know. What kind of mother are you?"

"After you left he moved into a flat with his girlfriend. He's nearly nineteen and has his own life."

"I never left, you kicked me out."

"This is not about you, you selfish bastard. Are you going to help him?"

"I suppose I'll have to."

The desk sergeant at Flinders Street was courteous and helpful. "Yes, we do have a Trevor Aspine in custody. Hold on," he said, nodding to a young constable, "we'll get him for you."

Two minutes later the constable returned with Trevor. His hair was shoulder length, he had a three-day growth, his clothes were dirty, and he looked like he could use a good wash. "Hello, Dad," he said, grinning nervously.

Aspine ignored him and looked over at the desk sergeant. "Is there somewhere I can talk to my son in private?"

"Show them to an interview office, constable."

The door hadn't fully closed before Aspine backhanded Trevor and he crashed into the wall. "You stupid fucking crack-head."

"Da-Dad, I smoked a little bit of pot. It was noth–"

Trevor never finished before another backhand slammed into his face, drawing blood.

"Dad, it's no big deal."

The sound of the slap that followed echoed around the small room.

The door was flung open, and Aspine felt a strong hand on his shoulder. "What's going on here?" He shrugged the hand away and turned in blind fury, his right fist cocked.

"Why don't you throw it?" Detective Bill Muller said. "I'm not like your son, Mr. Aspine. I'll hit back."

"Da-Dad."

"Shut-up, you've caused enough trouble you bloody drug addict," Aspine snarled. "So you're involved, are you, Detective Muller?"

"No, I was here when the highway patrol brought him in. I never knew he was your son. If you hit him again, I'll charge you with assault, and all your money won't help you then."

Aspine was angry and fighting to regain control. "I'm sorry. I hate drugs, any form of drugs. I'd like to line up all the drug dealers and shoot them."

"What do you think Jack Daniels is?" Trevor sneered.

"He's right you know, Mr. Aspine."

"Don't you fucking dare take his side."

"Why don't you take him home? He knows he's done the wrong thing, but it's not like he's committed mass murder," Muller said, trying to placate Aspine.

They got into Aspine's car, and he said, "Where do you want to go, Trevor?"

"You can drop me back at my car." Trevor scowled, the side of his face red and swollen

"Is that smart?"

"I got done at ten this morning, and the arrow barely moved."

"Ten o'clock? How can you get caught that early? Do you wake up smoking the shit or something?"

"Haven't you ever had an all-nighter? I didn't get to sleep until six o'clock."

"Why'd you leave home?"

"I gotta girlfriend, and we're gonna backpack around Asia next month. We shacked up in a flat to get some privacy."

"I hope you're using protection."

"She's on the pill. My mouth's hurting. Can we drop the small talk?"

"What'd your Mom think about you leaving home?"

"She was okay. After you left, Jemma, wanted to move in with her boyfriend, but Mom had a fit. Said she was too young, and Jemma got really upset. Mom's worried about money. She told us that you cheated her out of the cash you promised, and gave her some shares that she's sold but hasn't been paid for."

"I didn't leave, and those shares were worth three million," Aspine snarled. "How's Mark?"

"He misses you, and he's hurting because you don't call or see him anymore. You really are a prick, aren't you?"

"Don't talk to me that way or you'll get some more of what you just got."

"If you ever hit me again, I'll fucking deck you. I didn't hit back today, but the next time I will."

Aspine glanced at his son. His right cheek was blue, he was biting his lower lip, and his eyes were filled with anger. "Sorry, I overreacted, I hate drugs. You be careful in Asia. They hang druggies up there."

"I know, I'm not stupid."

"Pack your suitcases and make sure you've got tamper-proof locks on them. You know the dealers plant drugs in them if they're left unatt–"

Trevor cut him off. "I'm not naïve. Let me out at this intersection. My car's around the corner."

Helen Philmont's house was the size of a medieval castle, and it was no surprise when the front door was opened by a maid wearing a white blouse and a perfectly pressed black skirt. "Mr. Aspine, Ms. Philmont's expecting you. She's on the phone, but she won't be long. Can I get you anything?" she asked, leading him into a sun-drenched room with large glass windows that overlooked a perfectly mani-cured lawn tennis court.

"No thanks," he responded, taking a chair and picking up a maga-zine from the coffee table.

Ten minutes elapsed and there was no sign of Helen, and he became annoyed. He had plenty of time on his hands, but that wasn't the point — he didn't like being insulted, especially by people who needed his services.

"Hello, Douglas," she said, as she strolled into the room. She was diminutive, late twenties, and wearing jodhpurs, riding boots, and a starched white blouse. Her dark black hair was pulled severely back from her forehead and contrasted with her porcelain white skin and, while not a ravishing beauty, she was certainly attractive.

He extended his hand. "Helen, it's a pleasure to meet you. Where's Hamish and will your brother be joining us?"

"I told Hamish I'd prefer to meet you without him, and Phillip has other matters to attend to. How do you have your tea?" she said, ring-ing a small gold bell.

"I'll have coffee, thanks."

"A shame. I thought you might have more civilized tastes," she sniffled, "but with your business history, I should have known better."

He felt himself turn red but didn't say anything. *Helen Philmont's a first-rate snob who probably hasn't had a decent fuck in years. Maybe she plays on the same team as Kelly?*

"How do you justify asking for five million as a signing on fee? It's a real cheek."

"You need me far more than I need you," Aspine said, gambling that he was right. "I can increase the value of your family's invest-ment in Philmont by at least a billion dollars over the next two years. For that, five million seems reasonable — almost too reasonable."

"Would you downsize the company in the same way you did at Mercury?" she asked, ignoring his response.

"Yes."

"I thought so. We, the family, might have to appear to be critical of you — in fact we may have to publicly admonish you. Would that upset you?"

"You want me to crack the whip, make the hard decisions, and ruthlessly turn the business around, but you don't want to be seen to be condoning it."

"Exactly," she said, not flinching. "You didn't answer my question."

"You can say what you like, do what you like, and even fire me if you like, but not without paying me five million upfront."

"The golden handcuffs?"

"Yes."

"We've discussed your request with our lawyers, and I want you to know the handcuffs will be cast iron, and you won't have the keys — well not for at least two years. You would be dangerously underestimating us if you think that we'll pay you five million, only to have you resign six months later. If you withdraw your services for any reason other than death, incurable illness or dismissal within the first two years, you will have to return the signing on fee in full and pay us damages of three million. Is that acceptable?"

"Yes."

"Good. Tell me about the work you do with the National Homeless Foundation."

Aspine went into great detail, exaggerating his role and the time that he spent at board meetings and other functions, knowing Helen Philmont would be impressed.

She paused. "If you had to put a value on the work you do for the foundation, would it run to half a million dollars?"

"I'd like it too," he lied, "but it's probably between fifty and a hundred thousand. Why do you ask?"

"We want you to resign from the board. We'll give the NHF one hundred thousand annually, and send a letter giving you the credit for our donation. We don't want you to become distracted from turning Philmont around."

"You mean you don't want me to become distracted from increasing your family's wealth by a billion dollars."

"At least a billion," she said. "Do you have any questions?"

"Some your family members work in the business. If I have to get rid of them, will there be any restrictions on their dismissal?"

"I expect that they'll be the first to go, but Phillip and I won't be able to support you. Do you understand?"

"Yes, you don't want any dirt on your hands?"

"Correct. I have to get changed for tennis now," she said, dismissing him.

On the way back to the office Aspine used his prepaid cell phone to call Norman Pell on his direct line. "Norman, I want you to send your final account to Mercury in the next few days."

"You didn't call me about that."

"No. I want you to transfer two months interest in separate payments to Mercury, and the balance of the account at the end of October."

"You're leaving?"

"Yes, and I want you to transfer Balmoral's registered office from your premises to another address."

"You mean fictitious address don't you?" Pell laughed.

"Yes."

"Somewhere like 920 Pier Street, Geelong or 500 Bay Road, Queenscliff."

"I take it those addresses don't exist."

"If they do, they're under fifty fathoms."

"ASIC will still talk to you about Balmoral. What will you say?"

"Five hundred companies have their registered offices at my office. I couldn't tell you the names of hardly any of them. With Balmoral, I'll have a signed resolution changing the address of the registered office, and I'll have copies of invoices I've rendered for providing registered office services, which will have been paid in full — by internet transfer, of course."

"Good. What about your dummy director?"

"And his dummy address. They'll never find him and even if they do, he has the mental competence of a six-year-old. Don't worry; I had a lot of experience with bottom of the harbor tax schemes when they were in vogue. Do you remember them?"

"Sorry. No."

Pell laughed. "They got their name because the principals of these tax evading companies dumped all their records in the Sydney Harbor. We're not going to be that crude, but all roads regarding the formation and management of Balmoral will lead nowhere."

Another loose end tied up.

As Pell was talking, *the Sting* tone emitted from Aspine's cell phone. "Sorry, Norman, I have to go."

"Hello, Douglas. Congratulations. You must have impressed Helen. I have an offer I'd like to courier to you. Where should I send it?"

"Send it to Max Vogel, Hamish. I'll let him know it's coming."

"The offer's not precisely what you wanted. Helen's lawyers have included a number of nasty clauses about early termination you may not like."

"What about the five million?"

"I have a bank check made payable to you in front of me."

Aspine laughed. "That's good. It'll make those nasty clauses a lot more palatable. I'll call you after Max has looked over the offer. Keep tomorrow morning free."

- 34 -

COLIN SARLL WAS a bitter man. After the bank had terminated his services, he applied for jobs with other banks, finance companies, and financial planners only to receive rejection after rejection. No-one told him that he was too old, but at fifty-four, he knew he was virtually unemployable. His bank payout of four hundred thousand was enough to pay off the mortgage and leave him a little over one hundred and fifty thousand — to live on for the rest of his life. The long-planned overseas trip with his wife of twenty-seven years was canceled, and she'd walked out, taking his two teenage children, the furniture, and most of the money with her. The house was cold and empty without his family, but soon that wouldn't be a problem — his wife's lawyers had advised him that it was to be sold and that she would be claiming all the proceeds. He was a defeated man and had no intention of contesting his wife's claims. The last time they had spoken, she'd told him that he was a loser and had been all of his life — worse, she'd shouted it in front of the kids, and any respect they'd once had for him was dashed in a few vicious minutes.

He was sitting on the one wooden chair his wife had left him. It was cold, and his fingers were numb, but the oil on his hands felt good — it had been over thirty years since he'd done his national service, but he hadn't forgotten how to clean a rifle. The five-shot bolt-action Winchester was soothing, and he rested the butt on his shoulder, stared down the scope, and imagined the cross hairs were focused on Douglas Aspine's head. He'd hidden the Ford in the garage and hadn't used it since that day at the Coroner's Court. The hood was dented, and the passenger side head light had been smashed. He'd been too scared to get it repaired — besides, he didn't have the money. He wouldn't miss a second time, and a thin smile creased his mouth at the thought. Once the house was sold and the last of his scant assets were signed over to his wife, he'd kill Douglas Aspine, and then turn the rifle on himself.

- 35 -

THE NORMALLY URBANE Max Vogel was furious, and barely glanced at the letter from Sainsbury & Co, before putting it back in the envelope and re-addressing it 'Private and Confidential, Douglas Aspine, Mercury Properties.' "Douglas," he shouted, down the phone, "don't you understand I can't act for you and Mercury. I have a conflict of interest. I'm not sure that I don't in respect of the ACCC matter, but I certainly do regarding the job offer."

"What do you think?" Aspine asked, ignoring his concerns.

"I hardly looked at it. I can't and don't want to comment. I'm having it couriered to you."

"Is it onerous?"

"Not if you fulfill your obligations but, if you don't, the penalties are severe," Vogel responded, immediately wishing that he hadn't. "I didn't read the letter, the offer or the form of acceptance in their entirety. If you're considering accepting, you should seek independent legal advice."

"Consider accepting? Didn't you see the part about the five million signing on fee? I don't know what you're worried about; you'll soon be able to act for me without breaching your precious ethics."

"Why do you say that?"

"Mercury's not going to retain you after I'm gone. Anyhow that does n't matter. How are your negotiations with the ACCC progressing?"

"They're receptive. I've sent them a draft indemnity that they're considering. They'll be back to me early next week."

"And it covers me against any form of legal action?"

"Yes, Douglas," Vogel groaned.

Aspine carefully read the offer and acceptance. They did no more than reflect the representations made by Gidley-Baird and the pompous

Helen Philmont. The five million and the pending disastrous news about the Melton land deal were compelling reasons for him to call Hamish. "I've signed the acceptance. I'll be in your office at nine in the morning to make the exchange."

"Congratulations, you've made a wise decision. I thought we were going to meet at Sly & Vogel?"

"Max has something else on that he can't cancel."

"Okay, I'll see you in the morning. Oh, Douglas, taxation hasn't been deducted from the check. I'll need you to sign an undertaking to meet any and all tax liabilities on the payment."

"No problems, Hamish. See you in the morning."

Aspine grinned, it wasn't every day that he got to walk down Collins Street with a bank check for five million in his pocket. He had his passport, driver's license, and a rate notice that would provide him with enough evidence to open a new bank account — he had no intention of letting Phil Kendall know what he was doing. He entered 101 Collins Street and caught the elevator to the twenty-sixth level, the offices of the Macquarie Bank. Ten minutes later he'd deposited the check, paid for a quick clearance, and handed a letter to one of the clerks that authorized the transfer of unlimited sums to the account of Mapago Pty Ltd in Hong Kong.

The drive to the Fairhills Nursing Home was relaxing, and Aspine gloated about how he'd managed to turn a certain disaster into a magnificent victory. He arrived just before midday and parked the Ferrari at the end of the car-park, in a row where it was concealed, and strolled over to the veranda of the home and waited. Five minutes later, a bright yellow Audi pulled into the car-park, and Fiona Jeczik got out. Aspine quickly entered the reception. "I'd like to see Mrs. Dunstall," he said, using the name of a patient that Tom Donegan had given him.

"Are you related to her?" the nurse behind the counter asked, stifling a yawn.

"I'm her nephew."

"She's in room 115. Five doors down the corridor on the right. Poor lady."

"Thanks." As he walked along the corridor, he noticed that the rooms were numbered and that the patients' names were on the doors. He knocked gently on the door to Mrs. Dunstall's room, and when there was no answer, he pushed it open. The woman in bed was old, frail, and showing no signs of life. There was a tube projecting from her throat, and he guessed that she was force fed. He sat in the visitor's chair, wondering how Tom Donegan had so accurately managed to ascertain the state of her health. Ten minutes later he left the room and walked out onto the veranda — sure enough, the bitch was sitting with her back to him, talking to an old man in a wheelchair. "Good afternoon, Ms. Jeczik, fancy meeting you here."

She turned abruptly, open-mouthed and shocked. "What are you doing here?"

"I have a close friend who's a patient." he smiled, but his eyes were cold and hate filled. "Are you going to introduce me?"

She was shaken. "This is my father. Unfortunately, he rarely speaks."

"What's wrong with him?"

"None of your damn business," she responded, recovering her composure.

"Sorry, I'm here quite often, and if it'd help, I'd bring him a gift."

"He wants nothing from you. Please leave."

"I was thinking of buying him a bottle of Smirnoff or Johnny Walker, but metho's probably more appropriate."

"You bastard!"

"Ms. Jeczik, do you know that alcoholism is hereditary? Do you drink?"

"If you don't leave, I'll call a nurse," she said, trying not to tremble.

"I'm going." he grinned. "You like dishing it out, bitch, but you sure don't like receiving it. You keep going after me, and I'll expose your old man for the drunken disgrace that he is. Then there's your boss. Why don't you ask him about helicopters, drugs, and daughters? Now you have a nice day."

Aspine drove slowly down the driveway savoring the look of shock and horror on Fiona Jeczik's face. *Why can't every week end like this?*

In all her years of exposing crooks and bullies, Fiona had never been physically confronted before, and she trembled uncontrollably. She knew that he'd been lying about having a friend in the home and was sending a message that he could hurt her. What did those questions about Barry Seymour mean and how damaging were the answers?

Aspine spent the weekend planning to tie up the last remaining loose ends before his imminent departure from Mercury. He was confident that by the time he departed, he would have covered all bases.

When Duncan Milgate called, he was blunt and angry. "Someone bought over a million shares in Cyber-Games and drove the price up before our clients could get fully set. Do you know anything about it?"

"That sounds like an accusation to me."

"The buying came out of Hong Kong. You were up there recently, weren't you?"

"Yeah, looking for joint venture partners."

"Do you know anything about a company called Mapago?"

Aspine froze. "No. Why?"

"That's the name of the company that bought the Clean Energy shares. A lawyer's nominee company did the buying, but the bank account of Mapago was debited with the contract note amounts. It was so bloody amateurish."

"It wasn't me. Christ, how do you get access to someone's bank account?"

"We've got someone inside the firm of lawyers. We don't know who's behind Mapago yet because their computer records have been tampered with, but it's only a matter of time."

"I want to sell my shares in Cyber-Games. What price are they?"

"It's too early, they're trading at $1.70. They're going higher."

"Sell them. I resent your aspersions, Duncan."

"We've narrowed it down to three, and you're one of them. I hope it's not you, Doug because we can be nasty enemies. Goodbye."

As Aspine put the phone back in its cradle, he mused that Duncan Milgate hadn't given him a new share recommendation. Clearly he was on Blayloch & Fitch's black list.

The week dragged on, and Aspine became worried that the ACCC indemnity wouldn't be received before the Minister announced his ruling on Melton.

When Max Vogel called, he couldn't answer fast enough. "They've granted you full immunity, Douglas, but, if you withhold any information, they'll rescind it."

"Yeah, but they're not expecting a full confession are they? They have to ask the right questions."

"Are you worried about Balmoral?"

"Yes."

"If they ask you anything about Balmoral, you'll have to answer, fully and truthfully, or your indemnity will be of no use. Do you have to tell them about Balmoral without being asked? Certainly not."

"Good. I'm happy with that. Max, the ACCC have a history of leaking to the media. I don't want to read, 'Whistleblower Does Deal' in the newspapers, so let them know, no leaks and no publicity. I want this kept hush-hush."

"I can ask. They might hold off for a few days, but you're not going to be able to keep this quiet and, Douglas, they want to interview you, and they want to do it now."

"Stall them; I need a little more breathing space."

Aspine didn't put the phone down, instead, he punched in Marcus Easton's private number. "Marcus, it's Douglas Aspine. I have a real scoop for you. Can you meet me for coffee in half an hour? I'd prefer somewhere discreet, not the city."

"What's it about?"

"I can't say over the phone."

"I'm flat-out, Douglas, so I hope it's worthwhile. There's a coffee shop in Burke Avenue, Camberwell with a little car-park opposite it. No-one will see us there. I'll be there in thirty minutes."

"You'll thank me after you hear what I have to say."

- 36 -

"UNBELIEVABLE," EASTON SAID. "You were told that you'd be put out of business if you discounted your selling prices?"

"That's right."

"When?"

"Right after you published your article about pricing and the quality of our apartments. It upset some influential people and our competitors increased their prices."

"But you won't tell me who made the threat."

"I can't run the risk of a defamation action, Marcus. It's unwise to defame a billionaire."

"It was Vic Garland."

"I can't comment."

"You just did," Easton said, scrawling furiously. "Are you sure the ACCC's going to launch an investigation into the building industry?"

"I'm positive."

"And there's a cartel comprising Apartco, Urban, and Vicland fixing apartment prices?"

"That's what I said."

"And they tried to force Mercury to join them?"

"Yes."

"Why did the ACCC approach you?"

"Sorry, I'm sworn to confidentiality. Be careful about who you name."

"I will. I'll mention the ACCC, the building industry, and that the prime mover behind the price fixing is rumored to be a billionaire with powerful political connections."

"Will you run it this week?"

"Are you joking? Front page, tomorrow morning."

"Remember, you mustn't quote me or even hint that we've spoken."

"Don't worry, it'll be 'sources within the industry'." Easton grinned.
"Thanks, Marcus."
"Thank *you*."

Aspine sat in the car-park gloating. He would look innocent, and the victimized party in Easton's article, whereas the ACCC, would have painted him as an active participant who'd rolled over. The loose ends were coming together nicely, and his only worries were Kerry Bartlett and Blayloch & Fitch. He'd have to handle Kerry with kid gloves, or he'd likely make a full confession that'd put them both behind bars for ten years. And if Blayloch & Fitch's clients lost heavily on Mercury's shares, there'd be hell to pay, and they'd almost certainly go after him. Somehow he had to tip them off before the pending Melton disaster became public.

Fiona Jeczik wasted no time in confronting her boss with Aspine's accusations.
"I won't be blackmailed by Aspine, Fiona," Barry Seymour said.
"Did you deny liability when those poor people were killed in that helicopter crash?"
"I didn't want to. I had no choice. Our insurers threatened to remove all cover if we admitted liability. I should've stood up to them."
"Yes, you should have," Fiona agreed, struggling to hide her disgust.
"We all make mistakes. It was a long time ago. I was young, the circumstances were different, and our lawyers were adamant that I shouldn't oppose the company's insurers. After the litigation, I made significant personal payments to the families. I'm not remotely similar to Douglas Aspine if that's what you're thinking."
"What about your daughter?"
"I don't care to discuss my personal and private relationships with you."
"Don't you understand? If I continue to pursue Aspine, you won't have any privacy. All of your dirty washing will be aired."
"The other channels and newspapers won't run it.'
"They don't have to," Fiona sighed. "He'll release it into the internet chat rooms, and it'll develop a life of its own. From there it'll go to

talkback radio, and then the mainstream media will have no choice but to air it."

"I'll have to cop it on the chin." Seymour grimaced. "I don't want you to back off on your exposé to protect me."

"Thanks for your support," Fiona muttered. Despite what Barry had said, she felt sorry for him and, and knew he'd be badly hurt if she kept pursuing Aspine.

"Are you going to move your father?"

"No! I won't be intimidated. I've ensured that he has around-the-clock security. Our slimy friend won't be slipping him any alcohol."

"Be careful. When you corner a rat, it's at its most dangerous."

Before reading Saturday's newspapers, Aspine put the recording device next to his land line and cell phone. The front page of *The Australian* carried the headline, 'Collusion and Coercion' and stated that the ACCC was investigating massive pricing rorts in the building industry. Aspine reveled, and while it was only eight in the morning, he called Max Vogel at his home. "Max," he shouted, "the bloody ACCC's leaked the investigation to the press. Didn't you talk to them?"

"Of course, I did."

"Well, it was meant to be kept hush-hush. I'm bloody annoyed."

"I don't know why the journo was kind to you. When I read it, my first thought was that you leaked it."

"That's absurd. I wanted it kept confidential. You know that. It either came out of your office or the ACCC."

"It didn't come from my office; I can assure you of that."

"Talk to the ACCC, find out what happened, and let them know I don't want any more leaks," Aspine said, well satisfied that he'd muddied the waters. *Now all I have to do is wait for the inevitable call.*

Fifteen minutes later Aspine's cell phone rang, and he hurriedly attached the recorder to it. "Hello," he yawned.

"What have you done?" Vic Garland shouted.

"Who is this? What time is it?"

"It's Vic Garland. What are you up to with the ACCC?"

"What are you talking about? Talk sense." Aspine yawned loudly.

"Have you read today's *Australian?*"

"Jesus, Vic, I'm still in bed. You woke me. What are you on about?"

"Well get out and buy it. The ACCC's launching an investigation into price fixing in the building industry, and Mercury's the only company smelling like roses. If you're behind this, I'll bury you," Garland snarled.

"Vic, I don't know what you're talking about. I'll shower and go out and buy it."

"Don't worry about showering. Get out and buy the bloody thing. If you've double-crossed me, you'll live to regret it."

"Why would I?"

"Call me back on my prepaid cell. What happened to yours?"

"Sorry, I left it at the office," Aspine lied.

"Jesus, how incompetent are you?"

Aspine replayed the conversation, smirked in satisfaction, and then deleted everything after, 'If you've double-crossed me you'll live to regret it'. *You old bastard,* Aspine thought, *you screwed me, and if anyone's going to have regrets, it'll be you.*

Aspine called Charles Ong and instructed him to sell Mapago's shareholding in Cyber-Games, for a profit of nearly eight hundred thousand. With the Philmont monies, there'd be more than six million in the Hong Kong bank account, after the shares in Cyber-Games were settled. "Transfer the balance of the Hong Kong account into the Swiss account, and then close the Hong Kong account. I won't be using it again."

"You'll have more than nine million in Switzerland. Would you like me to invest it in a secure deposit?"

"No thanks, I'll leave it in the Swiss account," Aspine lied. "Are the moles in your firm still looking to see who's behind Mapago?"

"Yes, and it's getting worse."

"How?"

"The auditors supposedly want to look at the file."

"Is that unusual?"

"Yes, with a new client it's almost unheard of."

"Can you hold them off for a few more days, Charles?"

"Yes."

"You sound like you're no longer concerned about Blayloch & Fitch?"

"I'm not. What can they do, other than remove me from their list of favored clients? I'm not worried about them."

Max Vogel was angry when he called. "The ACCC's bloody angry with you, Douglas."

"Why?"

"They say it's obvious who leaked, and that you're playing games blaming them. They said if it happens again they'll rescind your indemnity."

"It wasn't me."

"Yes, Douglas," Vogel said, his voice dripping with sarcasm. "They want to see you tomorrow morning."

"I can't, I have other appointments that I can't cancel."

"They didn't ask, they demanded. It's serious. If I were you, I'd treat it that way. Don't stuff them around."

"All right, but I want you with me."

"That's not a problem."

"Can it be at your offices?"

"I don't see why not. I'll arrange it for nine in the morning."

Aspine wasn't worried that he'd breached Blayloch & Fitch's trust, after all, regarding ethics and morals, he saw no difference between them and himself. However, he was concerned about how vengeful they might be if their clients' sustained large losses on Mercury. Mindful of this, he called Duncan Milgate, who was terse. "Yes, Douglas, what do you want?"

"That's hardly a friendly greeting."

"We don't like it when our confidence is abused."

"Maybe I can do something to restore your confidence."

"I doubt that."

"I thought you were smarter than that, Duncan. I'm disappointed in you."

"Don't talk in riddles," Milgate snapped.

"That's the way we usually talk, isn't it?"

The phone went quiet for twenty seconds before Milgate asked, "How's Mercury traveling?"

"The penny's finally dropped."

"You didn't answer my question."

"Yes, I did. You didn't seem to hear my answer."

"We should sell Mercury?"

The phone went quiet again before Aspine finally said. "It's been a pleasure doing business with you."

"Goodbye. Oh, and Douglas, thank you. I know you did it out of self-interest, but in terms of your future, it was a wise decision. Do we have much time?"

"No. Goodbye, Duncan."

Aspine breathed a sigh of relief. Another loose end had been tidied up.

Blayloch & Fitch immediately started selling, and by the end of the day, Mercury's share price had fallen from $5.00 to $4.70.

The two men seated at the board table in Sly & Vogel's meeting room were fresh-faced and appeared too young to hold positions of seniority with the ACCC. "Mr. Aspine, I'm Simon Youle, and this is Graham Stoddard," said the taller of the two, extending his hand. He nodded to the recorder on the table. "We're going to record this interview."

"That's fine. I have a recording of my own."

"Yes, we've heard it."

"No, I have another one that I'm sure you'll find interesting."

Max Vogel was perplexed and annoyed. "What recording?"

"It's a call I received on Saturday morning."

"Don't you think I should have heard it before now?" Vogel growled.

"Don't worry, Max, it's more of the same."

"Let's get basics out of the way," Youle said. "Please state your name and position?"

"Douglas Aspine, CEO, Mercury Properties."

"How long have you held that position?"

"Nearly two years."

"When were you first approached about fixing the price of the apartments, and by whom?"

"Vic Garland, about a year ago. You'll be able to trace the call to my office, and that'll tell you the date."

"What about other calls from Mr. Garland?"

"He purchased prepaid cell phones for himself and his contacts in Apartco and Urban. I don't know whether you can trace them or not, but he called me on my cell phone and told me he was using his prepaid."

"Did you ever call him?"

"Yes, but only to negotiate the purchase of a large tract of land in Melton."

"Did you call him on his prepaid phone?"

"I can't remember, but I can tell you the number," Aspine said, pulling out his pocket diary. "0400 244 309."

"Do you have a prepaid cell phone?"

"No, I have nothing to hide."

"Did you ever contact Apartco or Urban?"

"No, and I have no idea who Garland's contacts in those companies are."

"Did he threaten to break Mercury if you reduced prices?"

"You've heard the recording."

"Answer the question please, Mr. Aspine," Youle said, tapping his long, slim fingers on the table.

"Yes, he did."

"How did he propose to do it?"

Aspine sighed and rolled his eyes to the ceiling. "Unless I toed the line, Vicland, Apartco, and Urban would engage in a marketing and price war, designed to put Mercury out of business."

"Do you have any other evidence, such as letters, memos, and minutes of meetings?"

"No, only the recordings."

"Was anyone else ever present while you were talking to Mr. Garland?"

"No, would you like to listen to the second recording?"

"Before we play it, I'd like you to turn your recorder off," Vogel said.

"It's all right, Max," Aspine said.

"Please turn it off," Vogel said, staring daggers at Aspine.

Youle reached out and flicked his recorder off. "Let's hear it."

Max Vogel looked nervous as the recording echoed around the room. When it was finished, Aspine asked, "What do you think?"

"Mr. Garland seems to think that you leaked to *The Australian*. Did you?" Youle grinned.

"No, I didn't. Why would I?"

"It's obvious; you wanted to paint yourself in the best possible light. We're not fools, and you'll be doing yourself a favor if you don't forget it. Let's go back on the record," Youle said, turning his recorder back on before Aspine could respond.

The Federal Minister for Environment & Heritage, the Right Honorable Brian Gleeson, called a press conference in Canberra, to announce that he was blocking development of a large tract of land in Melton, Victoria, to save a rare and threatened species of marsupial related to the kangaroo. His announcement was greeted with howls of outrage from the Victorian premier, who said that the minister and the marsupial were both rats.

Mercury's shares were trading at $4.40 when the announcement was made, but within fifteen minutes they were $3.90 and in free-fall, as shareholders rushed to sell.

Kelly sounded stressed. "What's happening? The phone's going crazy. I have Sir Edwin, Harry Denton, Max Voge–"

Aspine cut her off. "I'll talk to Sir Edwin. Tell the others I'll call them back."

"Have you heard, Douglas?"

"Yes, I've just got off the phone from one of the institutions."

"God, the shares are trading at $3.10 and tanking. What happened? Who did the due diligence before we committed to buying that bloody land?" Sir Edwin demanded, unable to keep the panic from his voice.

"Max Vogel's firm, and they would've checked everything known at the time. You can't expect them, or me, to know about pending confidential government decisions."

"Vic Garland knew, that's why he sold to you, for what you thought was a bargain price. Has this got anything to do with that ACCC investigation?"

"How could it? I only found out about the bloody rats in the last hour. I doubt Garland knew. He got lucky."

"That's bullshit! Vic Garland's a hard man, who's spent most of his life stitching others up."

"Ed, I didn't hear you complain when the Melton land acquisition was raised."

"I relied on you. I'm not being paid seven million a year to manage the company. You are!"

"It sounds like you're running for cover when I need your support."

"Can we use any of the land?"

"I don't know. I'll find out."

"Ninety-five million," Sir Edwin groaned, "ninety-five million dollars. The institutions, if there are any left as shareholders, are going to go crazy. I'll have to convene a board meeting for tomorrow morning."

"I thought you would. I'll know more about the government decision by then."

"Hmmph, shutting the gate after the horse has bolted, are we?"

"Let me know what time the meeting is, Ed."

"Don't forget that you have to keep the market fully informed. You'll need to lodge a statement with the Stock Exchange."

"I know. Do you think there's anyone who doesn't already know?" Aspine grunted.

"Helen Philmont's been calling every five minutes. She sounds angry." Kelly said.

"I'll call her, but I'm not available to anyone else for the rest of the day. Take messages."

"Helen Philmont, please."

"Who's calling?"

"Douglas Aspine, returning her call."

"You bastard!"

"I beg your pardon."

"And so you bloody well should. You took our money, knowing you were going to get sacked."

"I knew, and know nothing of the kind."

"You're joking. There's no way Mercury can keep you and maintain credibility, but you knew that didn't you?" she snapped. "We can't make you CEO of Philmont Pharmaceuticals."

"You already have and, if you maintain your nerve, I'll reward you with a billion dollars in the next two years."

"You're a pariah. The top end of town is already making jokes about you. 'Would you sell a block of land to this man? I'd love to.' If we employ you, we'll look stupid."

"As I said, you already have."

"We're withdrawing our offer, and want our five million back."

Aspine laughed. "You're not getting your money back, and if you withdraw your offer, I'll sue you. Thanks to you, I've got plenty of money for legal fees, and if you lose, which you will, you really will look stupid."

The line went quiet. "Helen, you're pissed off because other members of your family are going to criticize you for employing me. I can add a billion to your coffers. What happened with Melton could've happened to anyone."

"No, it couldn't. Vic Garland outsmarted you, and he's letting everyone know. We don't want to alienate him by employing you; he's an influential and powerful man."

Aspine felt a surge of anger. "He won't be for much longer, I can promise you that. Helen, I intend to take up my position as agreed. Forget Garland and think about the billion. If you support me, you won't regret it."

"I mightn't have a choice," she muttered, "but I don't like it."

Aspine was amazed when Vic Garland answered his prepaid cell phone — why hadn't the old fool got rid of it? "Hello," the gruff voice said.

"You sold me a pup, Vic, or should that be a rat-infested piece of dirt?"

"I don't know what you're talking about."

"Yes, you do, and you're boasting about it around the city. You're going to pay big time for your treachery."

"Ah, that's why you conned the ACCC into launching their sham investigation."

That's a strange choice of words. Perhaps the old bastard's recording the call. "I didn't know about the fucking rats until an hour ago. I don't know what you're on about."

"Bullshit!"

"I haven't even started on you yet, Vic. You're going to live to regret the day you fucked with me," Aspine snarled, before cutting Garland off.

"Sir Edwin said to let you know that the board meeting is at nine o'clock in the morning," Kelly said.

- 37 -

THE MOOD IN the boardroom was somber. "I've called this board meeting because–"

"Ed, we all know why we're here," Harry interrupted "Let's get on with it. What can we salvage, if anything?"

"I've been told that the ruling covers a little over one hundred acres, but there's going to be noise and disturbance restrictions over the remaining land," Aspine responded.

"We're going to drop forty to fifty million plus costs. Vic Garland saw you coming." Harry sneered. "And you thought Vicland was overstretched."

"Does this have anything to do with the ACCC investigation?" Sir Edwin asked.

"Nothing," Aspine lied. "The ACCC approached me about price fixing, long before I knew about Melton."

"Is that right?" an incredulous Stan Pettit asked. "I checked to see who was selling our shares before the Minister's announcement, and your friends, Blayloch & Fitch, were heavy sellers."

"You knew and tipped them off," Harry said, glaring at Aspine.

"How could I have known?"

"Do you still have your shares?"

"I don't know," Aspine mumbled.

"You don't know. What kind of answer is that?" Harry growled, his steely blue eyes staring right through Aspine.

"I transferred them to my wife as part of my pending divorce settlement. I told her not to sell. I don't know whether she listened to me."

"She didn't," Stan said. "I followed through the notice you lodged with the Stock Exchange. She sold almost immediately."

"So you got out losing nothing," Harry shouted. "What a fix-up.

You and your mates get out, and everyone else is left holding the can. You know you can go to jail for insider trading."

"I've done nothing wrong."

Harry laughed. "You've lost fifty million, tipped your mates off, slipped out yourself, and yet haven't done anything wrong? Ed, we have a duty to our shareholders to call in ASIC and the Stock Exchange to investigate our former CEO's actions."

"I agree."

"Hear, hear," William Claymore piped up.

"It has to happen," Stan Pettit said.

"What do you mean former CEO?" Aspine snarled, angry that Ed had turned on him.

"You've got no choice but to resign," Harry growled. "It's the only decent thing you can do."

"I'm not resigning over one deal that's gone awry. Jesus, Harry, you'd have resigned twenty times, if the penalty for making a mistake was the loss of your job."

"I never lost fifty million in one transaction. If I had, I wouldn't have sold my shares, and left everyone else in the lurch. We want your resignation."

"You forget, I have a contract that still has over a year to run, and by my calculations, it's worth ten million."

"That's including bonuses, and I think it's safe to say you've seen your last bonus," Harry scoffed. "You can resign, and save what little honor you have, or we can sack you, but either way you're going today."

Aspine had hoped it would come to this, and he fought back the impulse to smile. "Are you supporting Harry, Ed?"

"I'm sorry, Douglas,"

"So, I'm the scapegoat?"

"A scapegoat's someone who's blamed for others' mistakes," Harry said. "You're no scapegoat."

"I'll sue."

"And so will we," Harry said, "to recover your mid-year bonus that should've never been paid."

"We don't want drawn-out litigation," Ed said.

Ah, the soft voice of reason. "I won't resign."

"You're fired then," Harry shouted. "Get out."

"Who's going to run the company?" William Cleary asked.

"I will, until we find someone else," Harry snapped, angry that the question had been asked.

"Hold on," Sir Edwin said. "Unfortunately, he's right; he does have a contract, and we'll have to pay him something, even though the honorable thing to do, would be to resign."

"I'm not resigning."

"So much for honor," Harry snorted.

"One year's salary," Ed said.

"No, no," Harry shouted, "give him nothing."

"It's nowhere near enough," Aspine snarled, "I'll see you in court." *Another two million. It's about the best I could hope to get, but why not try to put some icing on the cake?*

"You just lost fifty million! Your fancy lawyer's not going to be able to hide that. You're the company's lawyer, Stan," Harry said, glaring at Aspine. "That's right isn't it?"

"It won't make any difference, Harry. Ed's right. He has a contract and, if we terminate it, we'll have to compensate him. It's better to make a clean break, rather than dragging it through the courts and media for ages."

"Why is it that when anyone else messes up they pay for it, but when it's a public company CEO *he* gets paid?" Harry bellowed, thumping his fist on the table.

"Douglas, if you want to maintain any credibility in this town, you'll resign."

"I'm staying, Ed."

The room went quiet, and the tension started to build. Aspine tapped his fingers on the table and smirked while Harry looked like he'd explode. Stan Pettit broke the silence. "You've heard our chairman's offer. Take it or leave it?"

"No!" Harry shouted.

"It's not en–"

"In that case, we'll let the courts determine your level of compensation if any. I move we dismiss Mr. Aspine without compensation." Stan said.

"I'll second that." Harry grinned.

Fuck! I overplayed my hand. I never expected Stan to be the one to call my bluff. "I want the minutes to record that I wanted to remain as CEO, but at the board's request, and to avoid protracted litigation, I reluctantly tendered my resignation."

"Without compensation?" Sir Edwin mocked.

"I'll clear my office of personal belongings while you prepare my letter of resignation and check," Aspine said, ignoring Sir Edwin's remark.

"Ed, go with him. Stan and I will get the paperwork done."

"I don't think that's necessary, Harry," Sir Edwin said, miffed that he'd been spoken to that way.

"You employed him; you sang his praises, so now you make sure it's only personal items that he takes," Harry growled.

"Worried that I'm going to pinch the stationery are you?" Aspine sneered.

Aspine didn't look back as he gunned the Ferrari through Mercury's gates for the last time. Fifteen minutes later he was at the Macquarie Bank depositing his termination check. He strolled out onto Collins Street and was pondering the few remaining loose ends he had to tidy up when one of them called. "Doug, there's a rumor doing the rounds that you've been sacked."

"That's bullshit, Brad. I resigned."

"Are you in trouble?"

"Why would I be?"

"You know, about buying those apartments at inflated prices with the company's cash."

"No, I've got that covered, but it'd help if you were to go on an extended overseas vacation in the next few weeks. You have more than enough cash, and I'm sure Stacey would enjoy the sights of South America."

"I'm rolling in it thanks to you, and I've always wanted to see Argentina and Brazil, but I'll be going by myself. Why would any guy in his right mind take his girlfriend to Rio?"

"You're a great salesman, Brad. I'd like to work with you again when you get back."

"You sound like you already have a new position."

"I don't, but by the time you return I will. When are you going to resign?"

"Later this week, as a mark of loyalty to you and, besides, they tell me Harry Denton doesn't like paying salesmen." Brad chuckled.

"We'll have to catch up for drinks or dinner before you head off on your travels."

"Sounds good, Doug. Let's make it soon."

It was early afternoon when Aspine arrived at his travel agent's office in Armadale and booked a first class return flight with Qantas to Los Angeles. She'd been surprised by the brevity of his trip, but he explained that he was going to see an old friend and four days was more than adequate.

The final *loose end* was going to be the most difficult, and require the most deceit. "Put me through to Kerry Bartlett."

"Yes, Mr. Aspine," the receptionist responded.

"Kerry."

"Wha-what ar-are we go-going to do?"

"Settle down. There's nothing to worry about," Aspine said, having never heard Kerry stutter that badly before.

"We we-we're go-going to ja-jail. Wha-what am I go-going to do now you-you're not here?"

"Calm down. You're blowing things out of proportion. No-one's going to jail. If you hold your nerve, we'll be fine."

"Har-Harry Den-Denton's call-calling in the au-auditors, to do a sp-special audit."

Shit! I didn't anticipate that, but I can't let Kerry know I'm worried. "And they won't find anything, Kerry. Can you come around to my house tonight? I told you I'd never let you down, mate, and I meant it. Is seven o'clock okay?"

"I-I'd li-like that. See you to-tonight."

"Keep your chin up. It's nowhere near as bad as you think." *I should've known that Harry would call in the auditors. I hope Kerry's as clever as he'd said he was.*

Aspine hadn't been in a Flight Centre travel agency before. It was far larger than the agency he used, and travel brochures adorned the walls. "Can I help you, sir?" A fresh-faced trainee agent asked, flicking the hair from her forehead.

"No thanks, I'm only browsing."

"Is there any country, or way of life that appeals?"

"When I find a suitable destination, I'll be back to book," he said, tucking brochures on US domestic routes and the Caymans under his arm.

Aspine spent hours on the internet, checking out the banks licensed to do business in the Caymans. The history and backing of the Royal Bank of Canada appealed to him, so he called and asked to be put through to the manager.

Almost immediately a man with a distinctly English accent said, "Phillip Carradine speaking. How can I help you, Mr. Aspine?"

"I'd like to establish an account with your bank; I'll be in Miami next Tuesday. Could I fly down and see you on Wednesday afternoon?"

"I'd be delighted to see you. Will you need us to establish legal entities?"

"Probably. Yes."

"And will you want to deposit monies into the accounts immediately?"

"Yes."

"You'll need to stay at least one night. I'll book you into the Hyatt, Seven Mile Beach."

"Thank you, Phillip."

"Let me have a contact number or email address."

The line went quiet before Aspine said, "I'd prefer not to at this stage. You'll understand why after we've talked."

"I already do. That's fine, Mr. Aspine. We have many clients who require absolute privacy. I look forward to seeing you on Wednesday."

Aspine pocketed his prepaid cell phone and smiled. He was about to close another *loose end.*

Fiona Jeczik devoted three minutes of her program to Douglas Aspine's unexpected departure from Mercury, revisiting what she cynically described as his disruptive, negative achievements. She'd spoken to Harry Denton in the afternoon, and he was one of the few businessmen that she genuinely liked, and he'd accidentally on purpose, let a few things slip. "So what is this man's legacy?" she concluded. "Is it the pain and suffering that he inflicted on his workers and their families? Is it the near destruction of a fine company? Is it the massive salary, bonuses and benefits that he received, or is it the fifty million dollar loss that he incurred as a result of a hasty and ill-thought-out property acquisition? Douglas Aspine's CV will say that he resigned. Let me assure you, he did not. I am reliably informed that the board of Mercury Properties demanded his resignation. Why they paid him a year's salary is totally beyond me," she said, shaking her head. "Let's hope that this man is never again appointed CEO of one of our conservative, and well- managed companies." The music to finish *Your Family Today* came on, and the cameras panned away from her. She was well satisfied with her response to Aspine's crude attempt to intimidate her.

Aspine heard the front door chimes but found it hard to drag himself away from the television. He was shaking with rage, knowing that his visit to Fairhills had had no impact. The bitch must have thought that he was bluffing — she'd soon learn that he wasn't. "Good evening, Kerry," he said, struggling to regain his composure. "Come in."

"Hel-hello Doug-Douglas. I'm so-sorry ab-about today."

He smelt of spirits, his shirt was stained, and his pimples were a sickly yellow.

"Don't worry about me. I'll rebound, and when the time is right, I'd like you to join me in my next position. You're a first-rate financial controller."

"Wh-what am I go-going to do about the twen-twenty-five mil-million?"

"I thought you said that the auditors would never find it."

"I did bu-but th-that was be-before I knew they-they'd be sp-specifically looking for an-anomalies. An-and I th-thought we'd be rev-reversing it against fut-future profits. Th-there's no profit in the off-office bl-blocks."

"Can't you reverse five million in the September quarter's accounts, and another five million in December, and keep doing it until the books are kosher again?"

"If I d-do th-that the prof-profits will look terr-terrible."

Who cares about profits? I'm no longer CEO, and my bonuses are in the bank. "Can't you add the first five million to the losses on the office blocks?"

"You-you don-don't und-understand. It's har-hard to hide what I-I've done with-without profits. I wis-wish we'd nev-never done it."

Aspine poured himself a Jack Daniels. "Would you like one?"

"You know I-I don-don't dri-drink."

Shit. He's an alcoholic in denial. "Sorry, I forgot. Kerry, if you stay at Mercury for another year, you'll be able to undo all you've done, and no-one will be the wiser. I know you're smarter than those bloody auditors. If you remain positive, with time, this little problem will solve itself."

"I do-don't know."

"No matter what happens, I want us to remain mates. I'm going overseas for a few days, but I'm not fleeing the country." Aspine laughed. "Kerry, you're welcome here anytime. I'm not going to let you down, mate, not ever!"

"Th-that's goo-good to know," Kerry said, a picture of misery. "I'm s-so wor-worried about the sh-shame that I'll br-bring on my fam-family and fr-friends if we go to ja-jail."

"Jail? We're not going to jail. Come on, get a grasp; in a year's time, we'll look back and laugh about this. If you think you've got a problem, I want you to come and see me, and we'll talk it through to a solution."

"Th-thanks."

"Don't thank me," Aspine said, as he put his arm around Kerry's shoulders and walked him to the door. "That's what mates are for."

I'll have to nurse Kerry through the next year. He's the weak link and will require a lot of attention.

Charlene Deering was jubilant. She'd just finished watching *Your Family Today*. "Bobby," she yelled, "do you remember that asshole I was dating? He got fired. Whoopee."

"The prick who has that DVD of you, whose townhouse I broke into?" the tall, dark-haired man, with the towel wrapped around him, asked.

"Why'd you have to bring that up? I'd almost forgotten about it. Jeez, you stink of chlorine. Go and have your shower."

"I was about to when you called. If you were cleaning pools all day, you'd stink too."

"I wish you'd got that DVD," Charlie moaned.

"Me too. Do you want me to try again?"

"I'd do anything to get it back."

"Maybe he's forgotten about it?" Bobby said.

"He never forgets about things he can hurt others with."

- 38 -

THE FLIGHT TO Los Angeles was uneventful, and Aspine slept for nearly ten hours. He was traveling light and, once he'd cleared customs, he made his way to United's counter and booked a flight to Miami, paying cash. At Miami airport, he made a booking to Grand Cayman Island.

The Cayman Airway's stewardesses were stunning, brown skinned, long-legged young girls with welcoming smiles, which was a nice change from the guys on Qantas, and the boilers on United. He hadn't been to the Cayman Islands before and knew little about them, other than the intricacies of their banking systems. They represented the fifth largest financial center in the world, outpaced only by New York, London, Tokyo and Hong Kong. There were tens of thousands of corporations with registered offices and more than six hundred banks with branches and offices in the islands. There was no personal income tax or capital gains tax, and corporations did not attract company tax, goods and services tax or bank debits tax. The banks at one time had been as secret as the Swiss but, more recently, the IRS had been able to access bank accounts, and the attraction of the Caymans as a tax haven had diminished. For Aspine, this was no longer a worry as, if the Australian Tax Authorities ever investigated him they'd first have to get past his lawyers in Hong Kong, then the bank in Hong Kong and finally past the bank in Zurich. In the unlikely event of this occurring, he'd have plenty of time to move the monies he was about to transfer to the Caymans.

As the plane commenced its descent, he looked out of the window at the tiny island below. The flight path took them over crystal clear ocean water, and white sandy beaches before the pilot made a bumpy touchdown and the passengers burst into applause. He'd experienced the same occurrence in the U.S. many times. It amused and unnerved him, to think that the pilot was being applauded for doing no more than his job.

He cleared customs, and half a dozen dark-skinned kids fought to carry his bags, but he shooed them away and went looking for a cab. There wasn't a cloud in the sky, the heat was oppressive, and he was sweating profusely. "Hey, Mon, are you looking for a taxi? I got air conditioning." The bearded, overweight man standing next to the old blue Chevrolet said.

"Where's your cab?"

"What do you think this is, Mon?" The driver said, patting the Chevy's hood. "Where are you going?"

"Do you know The Royal Bank of Canada, Georgetown?

"Yes, Mon."

The road from the airport to Georgetown carried an assortment of old cars that had seen better days. The air conditioning in the Chevy wasn't working, and the fan circulated hot uncomfortable air, but Aspine didn't complain. The taxi driver talked incessantly, but Aspine couldn't understand him and merely grunted when he thought that it was appropriate. As they turned into the main street of Georgetown, he was struck by the modern buildings. The traffic was heavy and, as the cab crawled along, he felt sweat pouring down his chest. "Five minutes, Mon," the driver said.

Aspine entered the bank and was hit by the chill of air conditioning. Within five minutes he was sitting in Phillip Carradine's office, sipping iced tea. Carradine was tall and distinguished looking for someone who was still on the right side of forty, and unmistakably English. "Phillip, I want a corporate trustee and a trust set up. Can you organize the documentation?"

"The bank, through one of its nominees, can act as trustee."

"No thanks," Aspine said bluntly. "I want to be able to look after my own affairs. Discretion, privacy and, might I say, secrecy are paramount. I want to be able to access the account via the internet, and to transfer monies in and out by the same means."

"That won't be a problem. Do you have a company name and how much will your initial deposit be?"

"I like the name Phoenix or a derivative thereof, and nearly ten million Australian dollars."

"Do you intend to continue to hold Australian dollars?"

"No. I want you to convert to U.S. dollars. I want no communications from the bank unless I initiate them in person. When I do, I want you to ask me for a primary password before communicating any information. I'll create a secondary password over the net to authorize account transactions. You will hold all records and statements. Is that acceptable?"

"Perfectly. Do you have a primary password in mind?"

"Yes, Jasmine1."

"Very good, Douglas," Carradine said, glancing at his watch. "I'm terribly sorry, but I have another appointment and, unfortunately, I'm not free for dinner tonight, which is rather embarrassing."

Aspine breathed a massive sigh of relief. The thought of spending the night with the pompous Philip Carradine was far from tantalizing. "There'll be another time."

"I'm sure there will. I'll organize to have you dropped at your hotel and picked up in the morning. Is nine o'clock suitable?" Carradine said, picking up the phone.

"Yes, thank you."

The Hyatt Regency Grand Cayman was an upmarket, low-rise hotel positioned on Seven Mile Beach. Carradine had booked him into an ocean view executive suite, with spectacular views of the beach, the yachts and cruise boats lolling on the glittering blue sea. The beach was a hive of activity with people, swimming, and walking while the kids played cricket and soccer. The Hyatt had a bar on the beach appropriately named the Beach Bar, and he headed off for an early evening drink.

"Why don't you try dark Jamaican rum, Mon?" The barman asked.

"I'll have a Jack Daniels, with a sprinkling of water."

"You don't know what you're missing, Mon."

"And I've no intention of finding out." Aspine laughed, downing his whiskey in one gulp.

"Can I get you another?"

"I'm going for a walk along the beach. I'll have a thirst by the time I get back."

The sun was sinking behind the horizon, and its remaining rays bounced off the water's ripples, creating a kaleidoscope of color. Island girls frolicked in the shallows in their tiny thong bikinis, catching the last of the sunlight. They had lithe, toned bodies, flashing white teeth, and inviting smiles. Such was their beauty that he found it hard to concentrate on any one of them. "Hey, watch out, Mon," the young girl lying on the sand said.

"I'm sorry, I wasn't watching." She was about twenty-five, with sun-bleached blonde hair, a broad cheeky smile, tiny nose, and the golden brown skin that all the natives seemed to have been blessed with. Her bikini top was bright yellow, and he could see the matching thong under her white shorts.

"You nearly trod on me." she giggled. "What accent is that?"

"I'm Australian."

"Aussie, Aussie, Aussie, oi, oi, oi," she said, bursting into laughter. "I watched the Sydney Olympics on the telly. What were you looking at?"

"The ocean and the setting sun."

"Not the pretty girls?"

"I might have been." he grinned. "What's your name, and can I buy you a drink or perhaps dinner?"

"My name is Simone. Are you trying to pick me up, Mr. Aussie?" she asked, her big brown eyes glistening with mirth. "Where are you staying?"

"The name's Doug and I have a suite at the Hyatt."

"We could go to the Beach Bar and have a few drinks if you like."

"You've been there before?"

"Who hasn't?"

As they strolled along the beach, he couldn't believe how easy she'd been to pick up. If all the girls in the Caymans were like her, maybe he'd think about relocating. The bar had filled, the music was thumping, and the dance floor was full of writhing bodies. They managed to get a table near the bar, and the barman winked knowingly at him. "What'll it be, Mon?"

"Jack Daniels neat and an ale."

"Red Stripe," Simone interrupted.

"Yeah, Red Stripe," Aspine repeated, not knowing that it was the national beer.

"So what are you doing here, Mr. Aussie?" she said, taking a large swig from the bottle of Red Stripe.

"I have some banking business."

"How long are you staying?"

"Only tonight."

"Oh," she said, looking disappointed. "Can I get myself another beer?"

"Of course," he said. He'd hardly touched his whiskey.

"What room number will I put it on?"

"Hang on," he said, looking in his wallet, "308."

She came back with two bottles of Red Stripe. "Saves me getting up again." She grinned. "You want to dance?"

"Sure, if you like."

The floor was crowded, and she gyrated in front of him totally uninhibited, oblivious to anyone else. He felt her breasts brushing up against his chest and her pelvis thrusting into him. He was sweating heavily but enjoying the pleasant throbbing in his groin. After about ten minutes she said, "Let's have a drink." She downed the second bottle and knocked the top off the third. "I have to go to the little girls' room."

"No wonder," he replied, still sipping his whiskey.

As she left the bar, a strapping bald Jamaican followed her. "What room is he in?"

"308."

Aspine felt good. She was a lovely looking young girl and better still, she wasn't a prostitute. He wasn't drinking heavily because he didn't want to spoil what he knew was going to be a fantastic night.

"Did you miss me?" She giggled, taking a large swig from the remaining bottle of Red Stripe.

He laughed. "Would you like to see my suite? It has some great views."

"So you want to show me the views?"

"Let's go." he smirked.

They entered his suite, and she kicked off her shorts revealing a thong bikini that left nothing to the imagination. He flicked through his wallet and found two condom packs and threw them onto the bed, before putting his arms around her, and kissing her passionately. Her lips were wet and warm, and her tongue darted in and out of his mouth. He started to remove her bikini top, but she pulled away. "What's wrong?"

"We'd better get the business out of the way before we start." she smiled. "It'll be two hundred dollars for an hour or five hundred all night."

"You're a hooker! You bitch, I kissed you," he shouted, spitting on the carpet. "I'm not paying anything." He grabbed her with one hand while trying to pull her thong down with the other.

"No," she screamed.

"Shut up," he yelled, placing one hand over her mouth while raising the other as if to punch her. "Shut up."

He was interrupted by a sharp knocking on the door. "It's hotel security, open up."

"Don't say a word." he glared at her.

"What's the problem?" he asked.

"We've had a complaint about noise coming from your room, sir. Please open the door or I'll unlock it myself."

He picked up her shorts, throwing them at her. "Put them on," he whispered.

"Hold on," he said, grasping the door handle, and turning it slowly.

The door crashed open, knocking him down. He felt an enormous hand tighten around his throat and lift him off the floor until he was staring into the raging eyes of a huge black man. "What you doing with my wife, Mon?"

Aspine was terrified. "I...I didn't know. She told me she was a hooker."

"What'd you say about my wife?" the man growled, tightening his grip and crushing Aspine's windpipe. "What's he talking about, woman?"

"It's not true, honey. I had too much to drink, and he forced me up here."

"If you touched my wife, I'll kill you, Mon. Did he touch you, woman?"

"Yes," she sniffled, pointing to the scratches and red marks around her thighs, where Aspine had tried to pull her thong down.

"You raped my wife." The big man's eyes narrowed, and he drew back his fist.

"No, no, I didn't. Tell him."

"You saved me, honey. You got here just in time, but he still hurt me."

"Go downstairs and get 'em to call the police, woman. We'll see how you like a Cayman jail, Mon."

"I didn't do anything. She never told me that she was married, and I never forced her to come up here."

"Are you calling my lady a liar?"

Aspine was panicking. He couldn't afford to be stranded in the Caymans. If he didn't get back home to hold Kerry's hand, he'd probably break down and confess. "No, I'm not. Look, is there anything I can do to stop you from calling the police?"

"You're not trying to buy my lady's honor are you?"

"No, it's all a big misunderstanding. If I hurt you, I'm sorry, Simone. Please don't call the police."

"What you think, woman?"

"I'll have to see a doctor," Simone sobbed, suggesting her leg had been torn off at the hip.

"Let me get my wallet," Aspine said, pulling away from the man. He took out two, one hundred dollar bills, and handed them to Simone, but the man grabbed his wallet and emptied all the notes into his hand.

"What's this funny colored money?"

"Australian dollars."

"You can keep them," the man said, dropping the notes on the floor. "Come on, woman, we're leaving. You should think yourself lucky, Mon. If I'd got here ten minutes later, you'd be dead now."

Aspine sat on the bed, massaging his neck and cursing. He knew that it'd been a scam, but he couldn't afford to call their bluff with the police. They'd stolen a little over eight hundred U.S. dollars from him, but there was nothing he could do about it.

"Did you see any of our nightlife, Douglas?" Phillip Carradine asked.

"No, I had an early night," Aspine said, trying not to think about what had happened. "Are the documents complete?"

"They will be when you've signed them before a witness. We couldn't get Phoenix, so the name of your new company is Seven Mile Phoenix."

"I'll sign now, and you can witness. Then I'd like access to a computer so that I can make a transfer into the account."

"I'll show you to a private room where there's a computer ready to use. We'll be able to confirm receipt of the funds within an hour. Will you wait?"

"I'll have to. I've left myself short of cash. I'll need to withdraw a thousand dollars."

He logged into the Swiss National Bank and punched in the numbers that Charles Ong had given him, and Mapago's account appeared on screen showing a balance of just under ten million dollars. He hit transfer and typed in the details of The Royal Bank of Canada and the account number of Seven Mile Phoenix. He filled in the amount, leaving only one hundred dollars in the Swiss bank, pressed confirm, and was asked to type his password again. Almost instantly the account balance was reduced to one hundred dollars. *Another loose end tidied up. I no longer have to worry about Charles Ong stealing my money.*

He sat chatting to Phillip Carradine, sipping iced tea and eating chocolate biscuits, while awaiting confirmation of the receipt of funds. Forty-five minutes later a young clerk knocked at the door and handed Carradine an envelope and a piece of paper that he glanced at before handing it to Aspine. "Confirmation of your deposit, Douglas, and there's a thousand dollars in the envelope."

"Thank you, Phillip," Aspine said, anxious to get out of the Caymans.

"It's been a pleasure," Carradine said, rising and extending his hand. "I'll arrange a car to take you to the airport."

"Thank you."

The air conditioned Mercedes was more to Aspine's liking, but on the short trip to the airport, he resolved, despite the climate, the beaches, and the beautiful girls, never to set foot in the Caymans again.

Kerry Bartlett was under severe stress, and at times, Mercury's accounting and administration staff seemed to be outnumbered by auditors. They plied him with questions, which he somehow managed to answer, or which he fobbed off by saying that he had to complete the third quarter's results for the board. At the end of each day, he knew that they were only one question away from finding out what he'd done, and he sweated in the knowledge that they might ask that question the following day. Harry Denton was a totally different CEO to Douglas Aspine. He spent most of his time on the company's building sites, or he was interstate with the branch managers, or he was out at the quarries. Brad Hooper had resigned and the slick talking, freewheeling salesmen that he'd employed soon followed. They quickly realized that Harry Denton wasn't going to pay them the tens of thousands in commissions that they'd earned under Brad. Harry was overseeing what was left of the sales team but, despite, his age, the long hours, and pressure, he was thriving. There was a new culture in the company, not based on greed and while Kerry had little to do with Harry, he found himself liking and respecting the older man. Harry had asked him when the quarterly figures would be ready, and did he have any idea of what the result would be? "Fi-first we-week in Nov-November, and no I don't," he'd responded. On two occasions he'd gone to Harry's office on the verge of confessing and telling him what he'd done, but Harry hadn't been there. In the rare times he was, he was surrounded by managers asking him questions, or on the phone receiving progress reports from site managers. Kerry craved brandy at the end of each day but was too scared to leave until after the last auditor had left. Then he'd rush to the hotel, drink a bottle or more of Remy Martin, and crawl home hours later, racked by self-pity and guilt.

"What's wrong, honey?" Jasmine pleaded. "Tell me. It'll help."

"Nothing," he slurred.

She knew something was wrong, but the more she probed, the more he clammed up. "It's that job, isn't it?"

"No, no, it's not."

"Has it got something to do with Douglas Aspine getting fired?"

"No, leave me alone. It's nothing."

"Honey, you can always leave. I'd rather you worked forty hours and were happy, than this."

"I can't."

"You can't resign?"

"You don't understand. Leave me alone," he said, staggering down to the study.

"It's Douglas Aspine, I know it," she screamed in frustration.

-39-

HARRY DENTON LOVED Mercury Properties, the industry, the people and, most of all, the employees. He flourished running the business again, and he sensed that the staff were hugely relieved that Aspine had gone. His inherited PA, Kelly, couldn't type and couldn't make a decent coffee, but she knew the business and nearly every deal that Aspine had done backwards. She was quirky, competent and helpful. He suspected that she had little time for Douglas Aspine, but she didn't bucket him. Harry admired her loyalty and confidentiality and hoped the new CEO would retain her services. Kerry Bartlett was another matter. He had a severe case of acne, was nervous, stuttered badly but, worse, his body reeked of spirits. Harry had seen the signs of alcoholism before and thought it was a shame. Kerry was highly qualified, obviously bright, had a young family, but was an alcoholic. To date, the auditors had not detected anything untoward in the figures, and Harry was starting to think that his earlier misgivings might have been ill-founded.

Aspine called Helen Philmont on his return from the Caymans. She didn't mince words. "We haven't decided whether we're going to sue you or hire you."

"You've already hired me, and I'm starting on the first of October."

"No, you're not. If you start, the earliest it will be is November. We don't want it to look like you already had the job when that deal at Mercury blew up."

"You mean you don't want it to look like I conned you. I didn't; I had no idea that deal with Vic Garland was about to go sour. I promise."

"I don't want you to call me again. I'll instruct Hamish Gidley-Baird, and you can deal with him in the future," she snapped angrily.

"You sound like you're losing it. If you try and shaft me, I'm going to sue you for early termination."

"If you haven't started you can't be terminated, and don't threaten me. If we take you to court, we'll make your life hell."

"Bullshit! You're not going anywhere near court. Your family's not going to like it when they find out that you've parted with five million from its coffers. How do you think you're going to look when I swear on affidavit that you asked me to fire family members? No, you want to keep this as quiet as possible. I have an offer from you on your agent's letterhead, and I'm more than ready to sue them and you. I'll reconfirm my availability to commence on the first of October in writing. You're not weaseling out of this."

"Talk to Hamish from now on," Helen Philmont snarled, slamming down the phone.

Kerry Bartlett's head was splitting from another session with Remy Martin the previous night, when he walked into his office. Two auditors were sitting in the visitors' chairs waiting for him. "Good morning, Kerry, we're having a little difficulty understanding some entries in the last year's accounts," Richard Creland, the dapper special investigation manager with Kravis & Cooke, said.

Kerry glanced down at the work paper, and his heart skipped a beat. "Wha-what's the prob-problem?"

"It seems that costs have been taken out of completed buildings, and added onto part-completed buildings."

"I-I'm sor-sorry," Kerry said, sweat seeping from his armpits.

"Well, in this entry here," Creland said, pointing to the work paper, "you reduced the cost of the completed building in South Melbourne by four million, thus increasing the profit on it by the same amount. Then you added the costs to the part completed Richmond building."

"Tha-that's be-because costs were charged inc-incorrectly to South Melbourne in the fir-first place. I'm sure I wen-went over it with the au-auditors at the end of the year," Kerry mumbled, unable to hold Creland's gaze.

"I thought so." Creland smiled, "but we've been unable to find any backup documents or evidence to support the entry."

"I'll hav-have to hun-hunt through my files. I hav-have a few meet-meetings this morn-morning. Will this after-afternoon be all-all right?"

"That'll be fine. Oh, we'd also like to have a look at the Balmoral Finance file."

"I-I'll let you hav-have it at the same time that I give you the wor-work papers."

"Thanks," Creland said, walking to the door with his junior close behind.

Kerry closed the door, took a huge breath, held his head in his hands and whimpered. He knew that he was off to jail in the morning. He tried to regain his composure but, as he left his office to go to the toilet, he felt a hundred eyes staring at him. He splashed cold water on his face and looked at his reflection in the mirror — bloodshot eyes, the worst acne he'd ever had, flaky pallid skin, and severe and unsightly dandruff.

He didn't return to his office, but crept out to the car-park, continually glancing over his shoulder. The drive to Mansfield took a little over two-and-a-half hours, and he wept uncontrollably all the way. He drove past hotels, for the first time in months, having no desire to feel the stinging taste of brandy burning his throat. He stopped at the town's fish and chip shop and ordered a hamburger and chips. While he was waiting, he walked to a nearby pharmacy. He felt calm, relaxed and in control, feelings that'd become totally foreign to him over the past eighteen months.

It was a bright, sunny, early spring day, the birds were chirping, and the towering gums were starting to break out in brilliant red flowers. As he drove down the twisting dirt track toward the house, the sun's rays bounced off the lake. He didn't go into the house but instead, walked around the property, touching the fences and barn, before eventually sitting on the end of the jetty and looking down at his reflection in the water. His thoughts turned to Jasmine and the two boys, the tears welled up, and he started to choke. "Why was I so stupid?" he mumbled. The sun began to drop and the chill late afternoon air reddened his cheeks. Surprisingly, he felt hungry.

He went back to his car, grabbed the cold hamburger and chips and entered the house. He put the food in the oven and turned on the house heating, before wandering around looking in the rooms. It was far more homely than it had been the day that they'd bought it. He sat on the lounge, feet on the ottoman, munching on his dried-out hamburger and overly crisp chips. Finally, he picked up the phone.

"Hello."

"Jasmine, it's me."

"Hi honey, are you going to be early tonight?"

"No, I'm up at Mansfield."

"Why?"

"I needed a break, and it's so peaceful up here."

"Why didn't you take us?"

"Sorry, I needed to be by myself, but I'd like it if you came up tomorrow," he said, fighting the choking in his throat.

"We'll come up first thing in the morning."

"Don't bring the kids. We need to have some time by ourselves."

"Are you all right?" Jasmine asked, her voice filled with concern.

"I'm fine, but tired."

"Do you want to say hello to the kids?"

"No-no, not now. I hav-have to g-get some sl-sleep."

"Love you, honey."

"Love you to-too."

"See you in the morning."

Kerry flicked the television on and watched the news. Mercury's shares were still falling and had closed at $2.40. The weather presenter said Victoria was going to be basked in sunshine tomorrow, and he was glad that Jasmine wouldn't have to drive on wet, slippery roads. He went into the bedroom, took a duvet and pillow and threw them on the floor in the family room before going down to his study. Ten minutes later he went into the kitchen and poured himself a large glass of water, which he placed next to the pillow. He pressed hard on the cap of the bottle of sleeping pills he'd bought at the pharmacy, and tipped them all into his hand. He crammed most of them into his mouth and took a huge gulp of water, before shoving the rest in and finishing the glass. He pulled the duvet up around his shoulders and rested his head on the pillow, tears streaming down his cheeks. "Forgive me, Jasmine, please forgive me."

Jasmine had arranged for the boys to sleep at a friend's house so that she could get away early. She'd called Kerry at nine o'clock the previous night, but he hadn't answered, and she'd guessed that he was in a deep sleep. She left home at seven in the morning; the low easterly sun coming through the windscreen making it difficult to see. She drove slowly and didn't arrive in Mansfield for three hours. The dew was still on the ground as she drove down the dirt track. Kerry's car was covered with condensation, and there was no sign of life. Suddenly she had misgivings but immediately admonished herself for being so silly. Her fears quickly returned when she found the front door locked, and she panicked, fumbling to find the key. She pushed the door open, and Kerry was lying motionless on the floor, a duvet pulled up around his chest. She knew he was dead and was hit by the odor of stale brandy coming from his kidneys and liver. "Why?" she screamed. Body fluids had seeped from his eyes, mouth, and nose, and when she pulled the duvet away, the back and front of his pants were soaked, giving off a vile smell. She dry retched violently as she gently placed the duvet back over him. "Why? Why?" she moaned. There was an empty bottle of sleeping pills and a glass next to the pillow on which his head was resting. She stroked his cold face gently, fighting back the tears. "Who made you do this, my darling? What will I tell our boys?" Then she noticed the unsealed envelope on the other side of the pillow. There were two letters inside it, and she slowly read the top one. 'My darling, Jasmine, you will soon learn of the dreadful mistakes that I have made. I was weak, and I can no longer live with the shame of what I have done. I love you, and I'm sorry that it had to end this way. Don't ever tell the boys how I died. It's the coward's way out. Tell them that I loved them with all my heart. If God is forgiving, one day I'll see you in heaven. All my love, Kerry.' The second one contained details of a bank account with over seven hundred thousand dollars in it, which he said that he'd been too scared to tell her about. 'Don't spend it, because you may have to return it,' the note warned. In death, as in life, he had not sought to blame anyone else. She put the letters back inside the envelope and pushed it to the bottom of her bag. No matter what her husband had done, he was innocent in her eyes, and to the rest of the world, his suicide would not be accompanied by a final message to the living. She fought for composure as she dialed 000 and told the operator what had occurred. Five minutes later she heard the wail of police sirens coming down the dirt track. A heavyset, middle-aged detective from Mansfield, with large jowls and a kind face, jumped out of the passenger's side of the first vehicle and walked briskly over to the house. Jasmine took one look at him, and all her forced self-composure evaporated. She slumped into his arms and wept uncontrollably while he beckoned his partner to enter the house. A few minutes later, the second detective came out of the front door, slowly shaking his head.

Within two hours, news of the suicide of Kerry Bartlett reached those in the know, and shares in Mercury sold off in huge volumes, driving the price down to $2.00. As hysteria took over, shareholders rushed to sell their holdings. The shares continued to plunge, but the bidders dried up. At the close of the market, the asking price had fallen to $1.20, but the only bidders were bottom feeders, offering $1.00. Bad news drives share prices down, but uncertainty causes them to go into free-fall. No-one knew why Kerry Bartlett had committed suicide and the 'not knowing' triggered panic.

The detectives were kind and sympathetic, but surprised when they couldn't find a suicide note. They suggested that Jasmine stay in Mansfield overnight and drive back the following day, but she desperately needed to be with her boys. Dusk was rapidly approaching as she left the township and started the long, lonely drive back to Melbourne. Her mind was numb as she struggled to imagine what life would be like without Kerry. They'd been together since school, and she'd never known another man. Tears poured down her cheeks and she wondered what he had done that was so terrible. Had he embezzled the seven hundred thousand dollars that he'd mentioned in his note? And if he had, why? He'd been earning a large salary and bonuses; they lived comfortably and had virtually no debts. Try as she might, she couldn't imagine any act that he might have committed, that would lead to him take his life. Sorrow turned to anger when she thought about him leaving the boys without a father, and leaving her without a husband. "How could you have done it?" she wept in exasperation. The road was dark as she drove through the small town of Yarra Glen and caught a glimpse of a café where they'd enjoyed coffee and cakes only three weeks earlier. It brought a new rush of tears — tears of self-pity. What would she do without him? How could she go on? "Why didn't you talk to me? Why didn't you tell me?" she sobbed. The one thing she was sure of was that Kerry's problems had started the day that he'd joined Mercury Properties.

Aspine was shocked to hear of Kerry's demise and then terrified. What had he said in his suicide note? Had he blown the whistle? Any small concern that he might have felt for Kerry disappeared in a haze of thoughts of self-preservation. Why hadn't Kerry spoken to him? What had triggered such a terrible act? He watched the early news on Channel Ten and was surprised to hear the newsreader say the police had been unable to find a suicide note. At six o'clock he flicked to Channel Sixteen, who'd rushed a crew to Mansfield, and there was footage of the detective in charge being interviewed. "Yes, it's tragic," he agreed.

"Do you know why he did it?"

"Unfortunately, we've been unable to locate a suicide note."

"Isn't that unusual?"

"Very."

"Could it have been foul play and not suicide?"

"No."

Aspine's mind turned back to Kerry's demeanor and personality, and he smiled. He was one of those rare types who took the blame for everything, someone given to self-admonishment, someone unlikely to burden others with what he saw as his mistakes. There was no suicide note because Kerry, right up until his death, had determined that he was the one at fault. He'd been weak and needed to be punished by making the supreme sacrifice. Aspine's mind worked furiously, because, if there was no suicide note, he was off the hook. Better still, anything found by the investigators at Mercury could be blamed on Kerry without the possibility of repudiation. *The final loose end had been tied up, and I'm safe from prosecution.* "Thank you, Kerry," he murmured, "and God bless you."

Harry Denton aged ten years on the news of Kerry's death. He knew exactly why he'd taken his life and grieved for him. The evening prior, the auditors had informed him of the anomalies they'd found, and that Kerry had not returned after leaving for some meetings earlier in the day. Harry read the personnel file on Kerry, talked to Kurt, and made discreet inquiries. Kerry had had a brilliant mind, had been deeply religious, had a beautiful, devoted young wife and two sons, and had been a non-drinker before joining Mercury. He'd also been shy and nervous and, while Harry hated to label him with the word, he'd been *weak*. The saying, 'the devil made me do it,' flashed through Harry's mind, and the Phoenician features and sneering face of Douglas Aspine laughed at him. Harry knew Aspine had murdered Kerry, as surely as if he'd bought a gun and shot him. His heart was heavy, as he thought about the young widow and the two poor little boys orphaned from their father. Harry admonished himself; he knew Kerry had been a heavy drinker, but he hadn't made any effort to counsel or help him. The joy that he'd felt about managing Mercury again had made him blind to the plight of others. On Sunday, he would pray to the Lord for forgiveness and, in the meantime he would bleed for the loss of one so young.

- 40 -

JASMINE DIDN'T WANT to put the boys through the trauma of a funeral procession, followed by the lowering of a casket bearing their father's body into the cold ground. Instead, she chose to hold an early afternoon service in the Renowden Chapel at the Necropolis, Springvale, where mourners could bid Kerry a last farewell. The chapel only seated fifty, but it was intimate, and Kerry had had few friends. She stood at the door, dressed in a long black dress and veil, her eyes red and swollen from tears and lack of sleep. Mourners paused and told her how sorry they were, or what a fine man and father Kerry had been, and that the pain would eventually go away. She was stoic and charming but yearned for the dreadful day to end. The little man with gray hair and intense blue eyes had been warm and yet deeply affected, but she didn't know who he was. "How did you know Kerry?" she inquired.

"My name's Harry Denton. I'm looking after Mercury until they find someone else."

"Mr. Denton, Kerry liked and spoke highly of you. I'm glad you could come."

Aspine had wrestled with himself about attending the funeral. He didn't like funerals and didn't see any need to go, but was worried about how it would look if he didn't. He wondered whether Jasmine blamed him for Kerry's death. He sat in his car waiting for two o'clock to come around so that he could slip quietly into the chapel. He walked toward the entrance of the chapel, looking down at his feet.

"Douglas, it's good of you to come."

He looked up in surprise. "Jasmine," he said, kissing her on the side of the veil. "I don't know what to say. I feel your loss so badly."

"Thank you. Are you coming back home? I'm having a small wake

314

for family and close friends, and Kerry considered you one of his closest."

"I felt the same way," he lied, surprised by Jasmine's warmness. "I'd be pleased to come."

He was entering the chapel when he heard Jasmine cry out. "Raj, you came," and throw her arms around a tall, fair skinned Indian man in his early thirties. He was strikingly handsome, with a strong jaw, penetrating brown eyes, and jet black hair. His suit was finely tailored, fitting him like a glove, and his black shoes shone. He seemed to be a man of affluence.

"I'm sorry, my precious sister, it is a sad day, and my heart goes out to you. Where are the boys and how are they taking it?"

"They're in the chapel with a close friend. I think they're still struggling to realize that their Dad's gone," she said, taking his hand. "The service is about to commence."

Aspine watched Jasmine and the Indian man walk down the aisle to the front of the chapel, and sit down next to her children and another woman. He wondered who the man was.

A close family friend delivered the eulogy and spoke of Kerry's many excellent qualities. There were no other speakers and the service finished with the mourners filing past the open coffin for one final glimpse of Kerry. Jasmine saw no point in prolonging the boys' pain. She asked her friend to take them home while she went to the front door of the chapel where she could thank the mourners for their attendance.

Aspine wasn't looking forward to the wake, and he drove slowly to Glen Iris. The house was a neat old weatherboard in a peaceful, tree-lined street. Sometimes the Ferrari was totally inappropriate; he parked around the corner and walked two hundred meters to the house. Jasmine mingled with her friends and relatives, trying to keep busy by serving drinks and finger food. She'd removed her veil, her face was drawn, and there were blemishes on her cheeks. "Can I get you a drink, Douglas? We have some alcohol, but I don't know what it is."

"I'll have a cup of tea, thank you." As she turned, he said, "I'll come out to the kitchen with you."

"Thank you for coming. Kerry idolized you," Jasmine said, as she waited for the jug to boil.

"He was a splendid young man."

"Douglas?"

"Yes."

"Do you know why he did it?" she asked, her eyes welling up.

"I'm sorry, I don't," he said, taking her hand and squeezing it gently. "If there's anything I can do to help, please don't hesitate to ask."

"Was he doing anything dishonest?"

"Not that I know of. Why do you ask?"

"There's a bank account with seven hundred thousand dollars in it, and I don't know where it came from."

"Don't worry. I can put your mind at ease. Kerry converted some options into shares and then sold them. I remember him saying that the profit was about seven hundred thousand. He didn't do anything illegal or dishonest."

"That's a relief," Jasmine responded, wondering why Kerry had said that she might have to repay it.

"Do you need money?"

"Oh, no, you misunderstood. I don't care about the money, but I'd be disappointed if Kerry had done something dishonest to attain it."

"I don't know of anything that Kerry did that could be construed as dishonest," Aspine said, choosing his words carefully.

As Jasmine poured tea, the tall Indian man came into the kitchen. "Douglas, I'd like you to meet my brother, Raj."

"I'm pleased to meet you, but I wish it was under different circumstances," Aspine said.

"It's sad. You were Kerry's boss, weren't you?"

"Yes, up until about a month ago, when I left the company. I'd forgotten that Jasmine had a brother."

"I'm based in Singapore, and unfortunately rarely have time to visit."

"How long are you here for?"

"I go back tonight."

"Oh no," Jasmine cried. "Do you have to go back so soon?"

"I'm sorry. I have to make a presentation to the cabinet tomorrow. I must attend."

"Do you consult to the government?" Aspine inquired.

"No, I'm a businessman but, as you know; business and government are closely linked in Singapore."

"I wish you could stay," Jasmine begged.

"I'll come back down again as soon as I can."

"I should be going," Aspine said. "I don't want to intrude on what little time you have. It was nice meeting you, Raj. Jasmine, if there's anything I can do, please call me."

Two weeks after Kerry's funeral, Aspine received a phone call from Ken Sturt, an ASIC investigator. "We'd like to talk to you about the affairs of Mercury Properties Limited, Mr. Aspine."

"Will I need an attorney?"

"Only if you think you'll need one, but yes, if you'd like representation, feel free to bring your lawyer."

"I have nothing to hide," Aspine said. "I'll come alone."

"Do you know where we are?"

"You're in La Trobe Street from memory."

"That's right. Is ten o'clock tomorrow morning convenient?"

"Yes, I'll be there."

Aspine received two calls from Jasmine. The first was quite formal, and she'd sought his help and advice regarding the administration of Kerry's estate. He had wondered why she hadn't asked her lawyer. Perhaps she was still distraught and confused. The second call was late at night. She seemed stronger, more in control, and not at all cold or formal. She talked about the boys, their school, how they missed their father, and not knowing what the future held. Aspine let her talk, only occasionally responding. He was surprised and pleased that she was using him as a strong shoulder to cry on. Two hours later she apologized for taking so much of his time. "That's okay, Jasmine," he said. "Would you like to catch up for coffee?"

"I'd like that."

"Is Saturday morning convenient? There's a quiet little place on the corner of Mathoura and Toorak Roads."

"That'd be nice. Eleven o'clock?"

"I'll see you then."

The irony of her turning to him in her moment of need was not lost on him. Perhaps they could satisfy each other's needs, he thought, the sides of his mouth turning up in a wicked smirk.

Mercury was a hive of activity for all the wrong reasons. The auditors were still trying to ascertain the exact size of the discrepancy, investigators from the ACCC were looking at the pricing of apartments, and investigators from ASIC were looking at false reporting, insider trading and fraud. Harry knew who the perpetrator of all the company's sins was, and he didn't hold back. He intended to see that Douglas Aspine went to jail for a long time.

Aspine was shown into a small room at ASIC, equipped with extensive audiovisual equipment. A few minutes later, a small young man with striking red hair introduced himself. "Mr. Aspine, I'm Ken Sturt. We spoke on the phone. This is my assistant, Karen Lacey. We'll be recording," he said, in a matter of fact way.

"That's fine," Aspine said, eyeing the girl up and down. She was pretty in a mousy sort of way and didn't look like she was long out of university.

"Mr. Aspine, Mercury's auditors, have detected large scale accounting falsifications. What do you know about them?"

Aspine gasped. "Was Kerry embezzling the company? God, I can't believe it. Is that why he took his life?"

"No, to the best of our knowledge he wasn't an embezzler. Please answer my question."

"I don't know anything." Aspine scowled.

"Are you sure of that?"

"Of course, I am."

"Why would Mr. Bartlett do it?" Karen asked.

"I don't know. I have no idea what he did. It comes as quite a shock."

"Some of the accounting falsifications related to shifting costs from completed buildings to uncompleted buildings. Did you know about it?"

"Christ, Ken, I'm not an accountant. How could I have known?"

"You did benefit from it, though," Karen said.

"I knew nothing about any false accounting until I walked into this room."

"You received large bonuses based on the profitability of the company, didn't you?" Sturt asked.

"And it also increased the value of your options," Karen chimed in.

Aspine looked at the ceiling and sighed in exasperation. "You're not listening to me."

"You signed the company's accounts didn't you?"

"Yes, I did, but I told you, I'm not an accountant. I would've signed anything, and don't forget, the chairman, Sir Edwin Philby, signed them as well."

"You sold most of the shares you acquired by way of conversion of your options almost immediately."

"Yes, with the full knowledge of the board. I had to repay loans I'd taken out to acquire the shares, and I needed to set aside my tax."

"And your wife sold the rest."

"Ex-wife, and I told her not to sell."

"Knowing that she had no choice but to sell because she had no money." Karen sneered."

"Did you tip Blayloch & Fitch off, before making the announcement to the market about the Melton land?"

"No, I had no knowledge or information until the Minister made his announcement."

"You do understand that you can go to jail for insider trading?" Sturt snapped.

Aspine didn't respond. Instead, he tapped his fingers on the table while blowing air through his lips in a silent whistle.

"What do you know about Balmoral Finance Company Proprietary Limited?" Karen asked.

"It's a company we deposited surplus monies with at a high interest rate."

"Is that all you know?"

"Yes. What does this have to do with the false accounting entries?"

"We're not sure. Did you ever talk to, or have dealings with, anyone from Balmoral?"

"No, Kerry, handled the investing of our surplus cash."

"Let me tell you about Balmoral," Sturt said. "Its registered office is at the bottom of the ocean, its sole director is mentally retarded, and the monies deposited with it have been used to finance the acquisition of apartments previously sold by Mercury in the Docklands."

Aspine's mouth was agape. "I'm staggered, I had no idea."

"Your sales manager Brad Hooper, set up a number of companies to buy the apartments on his behalf."

"Brad did that," Aspine said, gazing at Sturt in amazement. "Why?"

"We thought you might be able to tell us."

"Well, I can't."

"Hooper was running advertisements for Mercury, stating that its pre-owned apartments were increasing in value or, at worst holding their own. Would that have anything to do with it?" Sturt asked.

"I don't know," Aspine said, holding his head in his hands. "Maybe Brad was building a property portfolio. Is that illegal?"

"Every transaction on the bank account of Balmoral was made through the internet. Don't you think that's strange?" Karen asked.

"Everything you've told me has been strange. I can't believe it. Have you asked Brad about Balmoral?"

"We're trying, but it seems that he's traveling in Paraguay, and we've been unable to contact him. Do you still maintain that you don't know anything?" Sturt asked, not trying to hide his sarcasm.

"How many times do I have to tell you?"

"It's funny, you're the main beneficiary, but you don't know anything," Karen said.

Aspine didn't respond for nearly a minute. He frowned, then he looked enlightened, then deep in thought, and finally unsure. "There are others who benefited. Kerry and Brad also received performance bonuses and were granted options. I wonder ..." he stopped.

"Go on," Sturt said.

"I don't want to speak ill of the dead, but Kerry suicided, and Brad's disappeared in South America."

"Are you saying they put this scam together?"

"I don't know. You seem to be accusing me, but I haven't committed suicide or disappeared in another country that doesn't have an extradition policy with Australia," Aspine said, staring directly into Sturt's eyes.

"We'll need to talk to you again, Mr. Aspine. You're not planning to leave the country are you?"

"No, but if I do, you'll be the first to know," Aspine said, as he stood to leave.

"What a liar," Karen said.

"Yeah, but it's not going to be easy to prove. He's exactly what Harry Denton said he was. We need to find Brad Hooper."

"But even if we do, Ken, it'll be his word against Aspine's."

"Are you sure you didn't miss anything with Balmoral?"

"The agreement's signed by Kerry Bartlett and the transfers were authorized by him. There's not one piece of paper bearing Aspine's signature."

"What about that shifty accountant, Norman Pell?"

"He said he knows nothing. He has hundreds of companies using his premises as their registered office. He doesn't remember Balmoral, says he has no responsibility and doesn't know why the company changed its registered office. Balmoral paid his invoices over the net."

"Keep digging, Karen."

"Stan," Harry shouted down the phone. "I want you to sue him. Let's force him to repay those bonuses that he stole off us, and get the profit that he made on those options off him."

"Slow down, Harry. There's nothing we can do until we've got restated financial accounts. Until then, we won't know what the profit really was. And we won't be able to do anything about the profit on the options until we know if Aspine was behind those falsified accounts."

"We know."

"Knowing and proving are two different things."

"I'm desperate to nail this guy, Stan."

- 41 -

IT WAS A sultry Saturday morning. Aspine arrived early at the coffee shop to ensure he could get an outside table. He spread the *Financial Review* out in front of him and gloated about the article on page three. The principals of Apartco and Urban had confessed to entering into a price fixing arrangement with Vicland. Vic Garland continued to deny any involvement in the scheme, but he was now isolated and without credibility. *You did me over you old bastard, but you're paying for it now.*

"What's so amusing?"

He looked up and gasped. Even dressed in casual clothes she was stunning. She was wearing a white, short-sleeved top, black jeans, and wedge heeled sandals. Her hair was pulled back in a ponytail, and she removed her oversized sunglasses. "Hello, Jasmine," he said, standing and kissing her on the cheek. "No, there's nothing funny in the paper. I was miles away. What are you having?"

"Cappuccino, please."

"You look tired. Aren't you sleeping?"

"I've been tossing and turning most nights. I still don't understand why Kerry did it, and I've had so many people wanting to talk to me."

"Like who?"

"A young girl, Karen Lacey, from ASIC, came to see me and asked a lot of questions."

"What about?"

"She wanted to know if Kerry had been having problems at Mercury. I told her that he never discussed his concerns with me. I wish he had, but he didn't. He was having problems, though, wasn't he?"

"I didn't know it at the time but, yes, he must have been. ASIC told me they've found some anomalies in the accounts," Aspine said, looking concerned.

"Are you sure it has nothing to do with the seven hundred thousand dollars?"

"I was positive, but I'm not sure now. What am I saying? Of course, I'm sure. Sorry. Who else wanted to talk to you?"

"Fiona Jeczik came and saw me yesterday."

Aspine tensed but kept his voice calm. "What did she want?"

"She wanted to know what Kerry had said about you. I told her that he idolized you, and she didn't like it. Why does she hate you so much?"

"I don't know. She attacks me on her television show at every opportunity."

"She said the pressure you put on Kerry was the reason that he took his life. I asked her to leave," Jasmine said, placing her hand over his. "I know it wasn't you."

That Jeczik bitch! "I'd give or do anything to bring Kerry back."

"I know you would."

"How are the boys holding up?"

"It's hard to tell, but they seem to have blocked the pain out. They didn't see much of their Dad in the past two years, and in some ways it's cushioned their suffering," she said, glancing at her watch. "I'm sorry, I have to pick them up. I'd like to stay in touch until this dreadful business is sorted out and I know what Kerry did."

"I'd like that. Feel free to call me anytime."

"You're kind," she said, standing on tip toes to kiss him on the cheek.

As she walked away, he focused on her tight, curved butt, and felt a familiar stirring in his groin. He'd never wanted a woman so much. *I know what's being said about me, and I don't trust Jasmine — not yet. Maybe she isn't as smart as I thought, or perhaps Kerry spoke so highly of me that she's become a convert.*

Mercury's shares finally stabilized at $1.20. Harry Denton reluctantly made some presentations and, while the brokers didn't like what they heard, they trusted him, and when he said that the company was getting back on its feet, they believed him. Sir Edwin Philby's reputation was in tatters, and he was asked to resign from two other public company boards. The institutions were baying for his blood. He called Jeremy Smythe and castigated him for recommending Aspine. "You did a terrible job, Jeremy."

"Ed, it wasn't my f–"

"Sir Edwin to you," Philby interrupted. "It's not good enough. We paid you a lot of money, and you obviously didn't do the checking that you should have. The man has no character."

Jeremy was as annoyed as Sir Edwin. He'd lost Mercury's business, and Aspine had cheated him out of fifty thousand. "It's easy to be wise in hindsight. You were singing his praises three months ago."

"I despise the man. I'll be lucky to retain any board seats after this."

"I'm not in love with him myself. I've lost a lot of good clients."

"And so you should have," Sir Edwin retorted, slamming down the phone.

It took Aspine less than two hours to enter half a dozen chat rooms, using the pseudonym 'good guy', and spill the beans on Channel Sixteen's CEO, Barry Seymour. He raised everything from how Seymour ignored the families of his employees who'd perished in a helicopter crash, to disowning and committing his drug-afflicted daughter to a rehabilitation clinic. Seymour was a low-profile CEO, but was known to be extremely wealthy, and the trolls on the internet picked up the story and ran with it. Aspine embellished and added to what Tom Donegan had told him, suggesting that Seymour had unnatural sexual desires. When he clicked off, the chat rooms were running hot. In the morning, the story took on a life of its own and was the prime topic on talkback radio. Barry Seymour was belittled, and big business and its owners were chastised. *Maybe that'll slow the bitch down, but, if it doesn't, what I do next, definitely will,* Aspine gloated.

Gidley-Baird was evasive when Aspine called him. "No, Douglas, you can't start with Philmont on the second of November. We think it would be better if your commencement date was pushed out to the second of January. We need to give the heat in the media about you a chance to cool down."

"Fuck that! I have an executed contract. Make no mistake, Hamish, if you try and blow me off, I'll sue you, your firm and Philmont,

"That would be most unwise on your part. Once this matter becomes public, the family will have no reason not to sue you. You conned me, and you conned them, but you're in no position to be making threats. Be patient, and the appointment will go ahead, albeit that it'll be a little delayed," Gidley-Baird drawled, apparently unaffected by the threats.

"I'm going to want three month's back pay on the second of January."

No-one crossed Vic Garland and got away with it; he was determined to have his revenge. Despite his troubles with the ACCC, he continued to lobby state and federal members of parliament to ensure that Aspine was prosecuted under the Corporations Act. He was pleasantly surprised when Helen Philmont called and, when she mentioned Douglas Aspine, he had no hesitation in agreeing to meet her. His chauffeur came around to the rear door of the Bentley, and he gingerly alighted and shuffled toward the front door of the large Toorak mansion, tapping on it with his newly acquired walking stick. "Mr. Garland," the young girl said, "it's good of you to come."

"Helen?"

"That's me," she said, taking his arm, and leading him to the sun room.

"You were a baby the last time I saw you. Your family and I go back a long way, and your deceased grandfather Eric was a great friend of mine."

"Yes, I know. Would you like coffee or tea?"

"No, thank you. I'm running short of time in more ways than one." he laughed. "What do you want to tell me about that scum, Douglas Aspine?"

Helen explained everything that had occurred with Aspine, including the job offer and the five million.

"You're not a good judge of character, are you?" Garland said, his eyes twinkling.

"It's not funny."

"I didn't say it was. You wish you'd never laid eyes on Aspine, don't you? And of course, you'd like to get your five million back."

"Can you help?"

"I'm sure I can." Garland smiled.

"Can you keep it confidential?"

"From the public, and other members of your family?"

"Yes, Mr. Garland."

"I'll try, but I can't make any promises. It might become nasty."

Fiona Jeczik had struck up quite a friendship with Harry Denton. She liked his honesty, sincerity and caring nature and, of course, his total disdain for Douglas Aspine. They sat, comfortable in each other's company, in a coffee shop at the bottom of a medium-rise office building in Kew.

"How's your boss?" Harry asked.

"The publicity, particularly about his daughter, hurt him badly."

"Did he tell you to ease up on Aspine?"

"On the contrary. He knows it's impossible, but he'd like to see Aspine incarcerated for the death of poor Kerry Bartlett."

"So would I. What do you make of the widow seeing so much of Aspine? It's not three months since Kerry died, and they seem to be spending an awful lot of time together."

"It's strange. I interviewed her shortly after Kerry's death and was blunt about what I thought Aspine had done. She defended him; said that Kerry had idolized him, and wouldn't hear a word against him."

Harry shifted uncomfortably in his chair and felt himself going red. "Do you think she was having an affair with Aspine, and that's why Kerry took his life?"

"No, I don't think she's terribly bright, and by defending him, she sees herself as being loyal to Kerry's opinion."

"He would've overwhelmed Kerry with his lies. He was a bright young man, but weak. Aspine employed him because he knew that he could be easily manipulated. I'm sure of that."

"Have the ASIC investigators said anything about prosecuting?"

"No, I don't think they have much evidence, and it won't surprise me if he walks."

Fiona smiled. "I'm about to help them."

"You're going to run another exposé?"

"Yes, we're going to run a show on all the coincidences, and draw the conclusion that the circumstantial evidence warrants prosecution."

"Good."

"Maybe; ASIC isn't an authority that usually responds to pressure from the public," Fiona said, standing up to leave. "If I don't see you before, Harry, have a wonderful Christmas, and don't let Mercury get between you and your family."

"Same to you, Fiona, and let me offer you the same advice about Channel Sixteen."

Ken Sturt from ASIC was under extreme pressure, as those above him lobbied hard to ensure that Douglas Aspine was charged for his many misdemeanors. Someone with political connections was exerting heavy pressure on his bosses, and they were doing the same to him. He was worried, because the evidence against Aspine was mainly circumstantial and sketchy and, other than the signed financial accounts, did not include one document that bore his signature. Despite this, a summons was about to be issued, charging Aspine with falsifying company records, misleading and deceptive conduct, failing to keep proper books and records, and a variety of other offenses under the Corporations Act, to be heard in Melbourne Magistrates Court. Sturt knew that Aspine would almost certainly mount an 'aw shucks' defense, so-named as a result of the many CEOs in America who used the defense, 'Aw shucks, I didn't know, I'm not an accountant,' to exonerate themselves from their misdemeanors. There would be a committal hearing, before a magistrate who would determine whether ASIC had enough evidence to have the case kicked up to a higher court where a jury of 'twelve good men and women true' would determine Aspine's fate. Corporations law was complex and not something that magistrates had expertise in, and they almost always referred the hearing of the offenses to a higher court. It was the 'almost' that worried Ken Sturt, because ASIC's evidence, without Brad Hooper, was weak, and on rare occasions, magistrates had been known to throw charges under the Corporations Act out of court.

- 42 -

"SAINSBURY & CO," THE receptionist answered.

"Put me through to Hamish Gidley-Baird," Aspine growled, peeved that he was still being given the runaround.

"Who shall I say is calling?"

"Aspine, Douglas Aspine. Christ!"

"Hold on, sir."

"You're looking for a start date are you, Douglas?" the raspy voice asked.

The voice was vaguely familiar. "I want to talk to Hamish Gidley-Baird."

"I bet you do."

"Who is this?"

"You disappoint me, Douglas. I'm the new owner of Sainsbury & Co. I thought you'd be pleased to talk to me."

"Vic-Vic Garland? Is that you?"

Garland laughed. "I take it that you're calling about the Philmont position? Sorry, the offer's no longer on the table, and we'd like our five million back."

Aspine was trembling. He'd never anticipated this turn of events but knew that if you took on a billionaire in court, you couldn't win. "What is this?"

"It's payback time, Douggy. This morning I instructed my lawyers to recover the five million plus damages. I've also called in a few political favors to see that you get your just desserts."

"You won't win," Aspine snarled, with false bravado.

"Maybe not but, before it's over, the legal fees will bankrupt you. I may even have the satisfaction of seeing you being led away in chains. Oh, I nearly forgot, Hamish sends his regards." Garland chuckled.

Aspine slammed the phone down, Vic Garland's laughter ringing in his ears.

Brad Hooper's email was buoyant about his travels in South America and the girls in Paraguay, Brazil, and Venezuela but, after nearly five months away, he was becoming homesick. Aspine responded carefully, informing him that investigators from ASIC and the ACCC wanted to talk to him and it would be for the best if he came home, and faced the music. He knew what Brad's reaction would be, but if ASIC obtained an order to seize his computer, all they would find was a responsible email.

Under the mature and honest leadership of Harry Denton, shares in Mercury climbed back to $2.00, as the market came to the realization that the company was not going to fail. The institutions had forced Sir Edwin Philby to resign in disgrace, and Harry found himself in the rare dual position of acting chairman and acting CEO.

Fiona Jeczik used *Your Family Today* to unleash a scathing attack on ASIC, and its failure to bring Douglas Aspine to account for rorting Mercury and misleading the market. "A young man lost his life because he was manipulated, perhaps forced, into acting against his will," she said, through pursed lips and, narrow flashing eyes. "Thousands of small investors lost their savings while the fat cats bailed out. What is ASIC doing about it? When is it going to act to bring the culprit or culprits to justice?"

Aspine watched in a cold rage. His exposure of Barry Seymour had obviously had no impact. *Bitch! She'll soon have reason to regret starting her crusade.*

Jasmine seemed to bear Aspine no malice. They saw each other regularly for coffee, dinner, and sometimes a movie. He offered to take the boys with them on Sunday drives, but she declined, and he still hadn't met them. He thought this a little strange but he didn't persist, happy to be with her by himself. He was very careful to be on his best behavior. Occasionally he put his arm around her waist to help her through a crowd or took her hand as they were crossing a road. He ached to take her in his arms and crush her lips against his, to feel her warm body and the touch of her skin on his. But Kerry had not been dead six months, and he knew that she'd be offended if he moved too quickly. He surmised that it was like having a rare fish hooked on the end of a line, which needed to be coaxed in gently if it was to be landed. The greeting and farewell kisses that had been on her cheek were now on her lips, and she showed no sign of being upset. It was a slow, frustrating process, but he was positive that she was worth it. She told him that she didn't believe the stories about Kerry being coerced, and was openly annoyed that the media wouldn't let it go. Aspine smiled. It was strange to think that she was the only ally he had.

The chiming of his front door bell was incessant as if someone was holding the button down. He flung the front door open to see a shabbily dressed man, his finger still on the button. "Get your finger off that."

"Douglas Aspine?"

"Yes. What do you want?"

"You've been served," the man said, handing Aspine a sheaf of documents, before rapidly departing.

Aspine flicked open the Summons and cursed Fiona Jeczik again. It had been only seven days since her last hatchet job, and ASIC had responded by filing numerous charges under the Corporations Act against him.

When Aspine drove into the Fairhills Nursing Home car-park, he noticed the sedan with the signage ADF Security on its doors and wondered whether Jeczik was having her father guarded. He parked at the end of the car-park, took a box of chocolates from the passenger's seat, tore the cellophane off, and entered the reception foyer. He asked to see Mrs. Dunstall, saying that he was her nephew, just as he had on his earlier visit. As he ambled down the corridor, he saw a security guard dozing in front of the door to room 109, a door that strangely didn't bear a patient's name. He was certain that the bitch's father was in that room. Nothing had changed when he entered Mrs.

Dunstall's room, and the old woman in bed appeared comatose. He pulled out his prepaid cell phone and punched in the nursing home's number.

"Good morning, Fairhills Nursing Home."

"It's John, from ADF Security. I need to talk to the guard. It's urgent."

"Hold on. I'll have to go and get him."

Aspine poked his head out of the door and watched the receptionist shake the guard awake. As the guard started to walk toward reception, Aspine strode down the corridor and entered the room. As expected, Fiona Jeczik's father was in bed, eyes open but unseeing. Aspine took the lid off the chocolate box and placed it on the breakfast tray next to the bed. Fifteen seconds later he walked through the reception foyer unnoticed. The guard and receptionist were engaged in animated conversation.

Aspine waited until he was forty kilometers away from the nursing home and punched Channel Five's number into his prepaid cell phone, and asked to speak to the producer of *The Front Page*. "Who's calling?" a young female voice asked.

"Never mind, I have a major story for you. Fiona Jeczik's alcoholic father is running amok in Fairhills Nursing Home. You need to get out there."

"Who is this?"

Aspine hit the end button.

It was early afternoon when the director of Fairhills called Fiona Jeczik, and she reacted immediately. She sped along the roads leading to the nursing home, and forty-five minutes later, accelerated hard up the long tree-lined driveway, past the car-park, screeching to a halt in front of reception. She flung the door open, surprised to see Channel Five's cameras focused on her. "What is this?" she snapped.

"Did your father try to kill one of the nurses?" a barely-out-of-school young female reporter asked, thrusting a microphone into Fiona's face.

Fiona tried to push past the reporter and cameramen, but they closed ranks, blocking her. "Is it true that he's an alcoholic, and you've had him locked away out here for years?"

"Get out of my way," she shouted, pushing one of the cameramen aside.

The director of the home, the receptionist, and the security guard were waiting in the foyer. "What happened?" Fiona barked. "Where's my father?"

"Calm down," the tall, distinguished man said, "everything's under control."

"Don't tell me to bloody calm down, Julius. Who tipped the media off?" She scowled, eyeballing the receptionist. "What happened?"

"Someone left a box of chocolates in your father's room, and he ate—"

"Get to the point, he's allowed to have chocolates. They're not the reason he suddenly became desperate for alcohol."

"They were liquor chocolates. You know the type, a thin layer of chocolate enclosing whiskey, brandy, and rum. Your father ate the whole box."

"But how could he have got them? You were outside his door all the time." She glared at the security guard. "Weren't you?"

"Yes."

"What about when you went to the toilet?"

"I use the toilet in your father's room."

"So you never left my father's door today?"

The security guard shuffled his feet nervously, his large belly jiggling, and ran his hands through his scraggly, long hair. "I left for about two minutes. Julie," he said, nodding to the receptionist, "told me that I had an urgent call from work but, when I got to reception and picked up the phone, there was no-one there."

Fiona groaned, "Did you call your work?"

"Yes, and there was no-one looking for me," he said, turning crimson.

"Where's my father now?"

"We've sedated him," Julius said. "For one so frail and old, his strength was truly amazing."

"How's the nurse?"

"She's recovering. She'll be okay. When your father tried to break out of the room, he slammed her head with the door."

"I'd like to see him."

That night Aspine crowed as he watched and recorded *The Front Page*. Channel Five had had a camera positioned at the front gate of Fairhills, and they'd captured Jeczik swerving through the gates, speeding up the driveway and coming to a screeching halt. Then they'd shown the confrontation with the young female reporter, slowly dragging it out with close-ups of the bitch's face, ugly with rage. Aspine was exultant and replayed it repeatedly before going to bed.

It was 8:00 p.m. but it was February, and with daylight saving it wouldn't be dark for another hour. The early evening lights flickered through the window as Fiona sat in Barry Seymour's office, watching a replay of *The Front Page*. "Have you filed a complaint with the police?"

"No, it's pointless. I can't prove it was Aspine and, even if I could, there's no crime in giving someone a box of chocolates."

"There is if he knew your father was an alcoholic."

"He mocked me about it, so he knew all right but I can't prove it."

"I think you should drop your crusade. Your father could have been killed today, or he might have killed someone else."

Fiona's eyes were red, and she bit her lip. "No, I won't. If I do, he wins."

"It's not about winning or losing. It's about your safety and that of your father. The public knows what Aspine is, and he'll shortly be doing a long stretch in jail. I want you to drop it, Fiona. He's not worth it."

"Are you ordering me to stop?"

"Yes, but when has that ever made any difference to you?" he laughed.

"He hurt me today. I've looked after my father as best I can, and now it looks like I discarded him and stuck him in a home."

"I know the feeling."

"I'm sorry, I forgot about your daughter."

"It's easy to be judgmental of others when you don't know the full circumstances. Your father's lucky to have a caring daughter like you. I want you to stop your campaign against Aspine. He's a dangerous man and, the closer he gets to jail, the less he has to lose by hurting you."

"Thanks for your concern. I'm not promising anything, but I'll think about it."

- 43 -

A MURMUR WENT around a packed Melbourne Magistrates Court as Douglas Aspine entered, accompanied by Murray Bowden, Queen's Counsel, his junior, Alexander Humphrey, and Max Vogel.

Ken Sturt looked around, and a wave of nausea swept over him. Bowden was a brilliant QC with a rapier wit, who reputedly could not be retained for less than twenty thousand dollars a day. It was rare for Counsel as eminent as Bowden to appear in the lower courts, and his presence told Sturt that today was going to be far more than a routine hearing. Worse, the magistrate, Clifton Bond, was one of the few of his brethren who had some expertise in corporate law. Sturt would have far preferred a magistrate who knew nothing about companies, as this would have ensured referral to a higher court. ASIC, through the Public Solicitor's office, had instructed the pompous Stuart Thistlewaite, Senior Counsel, who was attended by his junior, Penny Aldridge.

Aspine sat next to Bowden at the front of the court and turned to peer over his shoulder. The puny bank manager Colin Sarll, was there, as was his old boss Bob Dwyer, Harry Denton and Sir Edwin Philby, who were sitting on opposite sides of the court. Vic Garland sat in the front row, surrounded by suits who Aspine presumed were his lawyers. Shirley Bloom sat at the back of the court, and Charlie sat two rows in front of her next to a young man he didn't recognize. Andrew Lawson and two of his union cronies parked themselves in the middle row. Tim Farmer and Neil Widge sat together, gloating in anticipation. A second buzz went around the court as the diminutive, but charismatic Fiona Jeczik strode into court and took a standing position against the rear wall. They'd all come to see him get his comeuppance — all except Jasmine, that was, who gave him a warm and encouraging smile, which he returned with a wink.

"All rise," the clerk shouted, as Magistrate Clifton Bond entered the court and took up his position on the bench, before gesturing with his hands for the court to be seated.

"Mr. Bowden, to what do I owe the honor of your attendance in my humble court?" He smiled.

"Your Worship is generous," Bowden responded, touching his forehead in a theatrical manner. "I appear for the defendant, Douglas Aspine."

"And I appear for the crown, your Honor," Stuart Thistlewaite interrupted. He was fat, with three chins, pale white skin and a six strand comb-over that accentuated his hair loss.

"Mr. Thistleweed." Bond frowned, peering over the top of his thin framed Armani spectacles.

"Thistlewaite, your Honor."

"Why are you repeating what I said?" Bond said, his pudgy fingers tapping impatiently on the bench. "Are you ready to proceed?"

Ken Sturt noticed Bowden smiling, and the queasiness that he'd felt earlier returned.

"Yes, your Honor," Thistlewaite replied, before presenting a long and monotonous recital of the charges.

"Thank you, Mr. Thistleweed. You may call your first witness."

"I call Mr. Ken Sturt."

"Mr. Ken Sturt," the clerk shouted, as Sturt walked toward the witness box. For the next hour, Thistlewaite asked questions and received answers that he'd rehearsed with Sturt. They went over the false accounting entries, Balmoral Finance Company, and Thistlewaite produced originals of Mercury's financial accounts, signed by Aspine.

"Would you like to cross, Mr. Bowden?"

"Thank you, your Worship." Bowden rose, stretching his long legs, and running a manicured hand over his slicked down hair. "Mr. Sturt, how long did you say you've been working at ASIC?"

"Six years."

"And where were you before that?"

"I was an auditor with two international firms of accountants."

"So you're a qualified accountant and experienced investigator?"

"Yes."

"Is it fair to say that there's usually a significant amount of documentary evidence in most cases of white collar crime?"

"Yes," Sturt murmured, knowing exactly where Bowden was going.

"So in the case of the false accounting entries, did you find any documented evidence to support the charges against my client? Did he process the false entries, or issue written instructions to others directing them to do so?"

"No, but—"

"Just answer my questions, Mr. Sturt," Bowden interrupted. "Were there any minutes, memos or notes from my client evidencing his involvement in the falsification of the company's books?"

"No."

"Did you talk to anyone who heard my client issuing instructions to others regarding the false accounting entries?"

"No, but he was the CEO of Mer—"

"Mr. Sturt, just answer my questions. So am I to understand you do not have any documentary evidence against my client?"

"He signed the company's financial accounts."

"Did Sir Edwin Philby, and the company's auditors, sign the same set of financial accounts?"

"Yes, but—"

"There are no buts, Mr. Sturt. Why hasn't Sir Edwin Philby been charged with the same offenses that you've charged my client with?"

"He's not an accountant and could not reasonably be expected to understand complex accounting nuances."

"But the auditors are, and they signed off on the financial accounts, so presumably they did not detect the falsifications. My client is not an accountant, so I'll ask you again, why is he being treated differently to Sir Edwin Philby?"

"Sir Edwin, in his role as chairman, was not responsible for the management of the company. Douglas Aspine was."

"Would it be fair to say that your office has been placed under extreme pressure by outsiders to launch this action? And isn't it based on vindictiveness rather than fact?"

"Not that I know of," Sturt muttered.

"Your Honor, I'd like to move for the dismissal of all charges against my client, and an order for costs against the Crown," Bowden said.

"I'm inclined to agree," Magistrate Bond replied.

A gasp of dismay went around the courtroom, and Stuart Thistlewaite jumped to his feet, protesting, "Your Honor, counsel has not refuted the evidence."

"What evidence?" Bond replied, looking at Thistlewaite with disdain. "That's your problem, Mr. Thistleweed, you don't seem to have any evidence."

Thistlewaite ignored the insult. "Your Honor I must prot—"

Bond cut him off. "Mr. Bowden, I'm not prepared to make a ruling yet. Carry on."

"As you wish, your Honor." Bowden nodded deferentially.

"Mr. Sturt, in reference to Balmoral Finance Company do you have any checks signed by my client?"

"No."

"Any check requisitions?"

"No."

"Did my client sign the agreement between Mercury and Balmoral Finance Company?"

"No."

"Are there any memos, notes or letters that link my client with Balmoral Finance Company?"

"No."

With great theater, Bowden turned to Magistrate Bond, palms uplifted as if to say, 'What more do I have to do?' "I move for dismissal of all charges."

Bond picked up his gavel and hammered it on the bench. "All charges are dismissed, and I'll sign an order for costs against the Crown."

Thistlewaite was on his feet but, before he could speak Magistrate Bond bellowed. "Sit down, Mr. Thistlewaite; I'm disgusted that you could come into my court so poorly prepared."

Aspine glanced around, and the first face he saw was Fiona Jeczik's. She was shaking her head in disbelief. Shirley Bloom looked like someone had kicked her, and Vic Garland was engaged in furious conversation with the suits surrounding him. Harry Denton appeared impassive, and his cold blue eyes momentarily sent a shiver through Aspine, before he broke into a huge grin and watched Harry's face redden. Jasmine looked happy and relieved and gave him a radiant smile. He shook hands warmly with Bowden. "Thank you, Murray, it's a relief to put this behind me."

"I wish they were all that easy, Douglas."

"You told me that the Director of Public Prosecutions can override the magistrate and still bring charges against me."

"Yes, he can, but he won't. For the DPP to act there needs to be at least a probability of conviction. Unless they unearth substantial documentary evidence or find some witnesses, you have nothing to worry about."

"They won't find either." Aspine smiled confidently.

As Aspine walked down the stairs, there were little groups clustered on the footpath. They'd come to see him committed, but he'd defeated them, and he made no attempt to conceal his smirk. Harry Denton, Fiona Jeczik, and Charlie looked like they'd been to a funeral and were talking about the bereaved. There was no sign of Channel Sixteen's cameras. Shirley Bloom looked like she was asking Andrew Lawson and his off-siders for advice. Vic Garland was gesticulating angrily with his hands to Bob Dwyer as the suits looked on. "I didn't know you two knew each other but, then again, you've got a lot in common." Aspine laughed. "You've both been done over by me."

Garland looked like he was going to explode. "Make the most of it, because you won't find it that easy when my lawyers take to you."

"Is that right? Murray Bowden doesn't think it'll be much of a problem."

"You'll need more than a smart mouthpiece next time." Garland coughed, his face red with anger and exertion.

"Take it easy, Vic, I'd hate for you to die before I have the satisfaction of crushing you in court." Aspine laughed.

"Piss off, you bloody spiv," Bob Dwyer snarled.

"You're not looking well either, Bob. Have you thought about retiring?" Aspine sniggered, before walking over to Jasmine, who was standing by herself. He hadn't noticed Colin Sarll standing in the shadows glaring at him.

"I'm glad that's over," she said.

"Me too. Let's have lunch."

Despite it being early April, the weather was warm, and the outdoor restaurants in Hardware Lane were doing a thriving business. They found a table at a small Italian restaurant and ordered lasagna and salad. Aspine was dying for a Jack Daniels, but when he was with Jasmine, he didn't touch alcohol. "I thought you'd be having a celebratory drink." she smiled.

"Do you make a habit of reading minds?"

"Let's buy something we can share."

"You don't drink alcohol."

"I've never tasted it, but I think I'd like to try some today." she giggled. "Why don't you order something for me?"

Aspine caught the eye of a waitress and ordered a Jack Daniels and a screwdriver.

"I can't taste the alcohol," she said, "but I like the orange juice."

"Be careful; three of those and I'll be carrying you home."

"I might like that." she smiled.

He felt her foot brush his and wondered if it'd been an accident. "You're a good friend," he said.

"Oh, is that what we are? Good friends?" She finished the screwdriver and was picking at her lasagna.

"I think the alcohol's going to your head, Jasmine."

"I'm sorry, I'm being silly. You're not as happy as I thought you'd be."

"I'm relieved that the court action is over, but I haven't worked for seven months, and I'm unlikely to get another job in this town. Worse, I'm not getting any younger," he said, taking a long sip of his whiskey.

She didn't respond immediately but, instead, took his hand and squeezed it. "Do you remember my brother Raj?"

"Of course."

"He's built quite an empire in Singapore and was heavily involved in the acquisition of Optus and Tru Energy in Australia. He's always on the lookout for undervalued companies with good cash flows."

"I'm sorry, but how does that help me?"

"He's going to open an office in Sydney or Melbourne, specifically to search for badly managed and undervalued companies. He's looking for an Australian-based manager. Would you like me to talk to him?"

"That'd be helpful," Aspine said, visibly brightening.

"I'll call him tonight. Now I'd like another yummy corkscrew, please."

"Screwdriver." Aspine laughed. "I think one is more than enough when you have to drive."

"But I feel fine."

"Maybe next time, when I'm driving. Come on, I'll walk you to your car," he said, taking her arm. When they reached the car-park, he bent down and kissed her lightly on the lips, and she responded firmly. He put his arm around her waist and felt her body through her thin silk dress. "You're driving me crazy."

"Am I?" she giggled.

Colin Sarll had gone to court expecting Aspine to be committed, but the bastard and his slimy barrister had managed to worm their way out of the charges. Sarll's house had been sold and in ten days' time it would be settled, and he'd no longer have a roof over his head. He cradled the five-shot Winchester like it was a baby, oiling the barrel for what must have been the twentieth time. His mouth turned up in a grim smile in the knowledge that he'd be dead within ten days, but so would Douglas Aspine.

Vic Garland's lawyers had told him that the civil case to recover the five million would be easy once Aspine had been convicted of the charges he faced under the Corporations Act. Now he'd walked free, and Garland wanted to bring the civil action on without delay. The bastard had mocked him and Garland wanted blood.

Harry Denton watched Jasmine give Aspine a brilliant smile in the front of the court. What was wrong with her, he wondered? Had she been having an affair with him? Was that the real reason poor Kerry had committed suicide? He'd joked with Stan Pettit that Aspine was like Satan and, being a religious man, he now wondered whether he was the devil incarnate. For some strange reason Harry felt that if he watched Aspine closely enough, he'd eventually make a mistake.

Aspine's cell phone rang and the screen lit up with Barbara's name, and he wrestled with whether he would answer or not. "Yes?"

"Mark's been sent home from school for fighting," she shouted angrily. "He has a black eye, a bloody nose, and a chipped cheekbone. I hope you're proud of yourself."

"What are you talking about?"

"The other kids at school were calling you a crook and a sleaze, so he went to your defense."

"Shit."

"God knows why. You never call, and you're always too busy to see him."

"Get off my back. You know I've been in court and haven't had any time."

"No time for your kids! Why don't you listen to yourself? How long's it been since you spoke to Jemma?"

He didn't answer, but Barbara wasn't going to let a silence build. "She's leaving home and moving into a flat with her boyfriend."

"Well, stop her."

"How? She's eighteen. Oh, sorry I forgot you haven't seen her for nearly two years. I wish they'd locked you up and thrown the key away." she sobbed angrily.

He hit the end button cutting her off. Her whining had given him a headache.

- 44 -

JASMINE SOUNDED EXCITED, but Aspine couldn't make out what she was saying.

He heard her yell, "Jack, turn the telly down, Mommy's on the phone."

"Sorry, Douglas, the boys have everything on full blast."

"I know, I have a few of my own." he laughed.

"I told my brother about you, and he's keen to meet with you. Can you have dinner with him in Singapore this Friday night? He will, of course, reimburse your airfares and expenses."

"I most certainly can, and thank you. I'm lost for words."

"SQ 638 departs Tullamarine at 10:10 and lands in Singapore at 16:45, allowing you plenty of time to freshen up before dinner."

"Thanks again. I'll book as soon as I get off the phone."

"Douglas?"

"Yes, Jasmine."

"Would you like to stay with me this Thursday night?"

He felt a tightening in his chest, and he struggled to keep his breathing normal. "I'd love to. Are the boys going to be home?"

"Of course not, silly." she giggled. "I have a girlfriend who's looking after them. I thought we could go out and have a nice dinner and a few of those yummy screwdrivers."

He laughed. "I thought you were meant to be a non-drinker."

"I am. I don't think drinking flavored orange juice counts. Truly, I didn't feel anything at lunch."

"Maybe you're right." he smirked. "We'll find out on Thursday night."

"I don't want you driving. Why don't you come to my home? We'll get a cab."

"I like driving."

"I'm not going to drink by myself," she said, sounding miffed, "and if you're driving, you won't be able to drink. Maybe Thursday night isn't such a good idea."

"Hey, slow down. If you want to get a cab, then we will," he said, desperate not to do anything that would ruin a night in the cot with her.

"You're so good to me. Don't forget to pack your suitcase. You have to be at the airport early on Friday morning."

For the first time since Kerry took his life, Jasmine felt at peace with herself. Instead of shopping at her local supermarket, she drove to Camberwell and threw a box of condoms into her trolley. She was looking forward to Thursday night. She had a few other items to pick up in the city, and then she'd be fully prepared.

It had been a cold, wet, unseasonal day, and the heater in Colin Sarll's old white Ford didn't work. In the two hours he'd been parked in front of Aspine's townhouse, he hadn't seen any sign of life and didn't know whether he was home or not. As he watched from the back seat, the garage door started to open, and the Ferrari entered from the street. There was no time to shoot, but if Aspine went out again, he'd need just one clean shot.

Harry Denton parked two hundred meters down the street from Aspine's townhouse in his wife's Corolla. He felt stupid and didn't know what he was doing, or what he was trying to find. He too saw the Ferrari enter the garage, but paid no attention to the old white Ford parked directly opposite.

Aspine had decided to spend the weekend in Singapore so, in addition to his suit and business shirts, he threw in some casual clothes for the flight and a few days sightseeing. There were two side combination locks on his suitcase, and he made sure that he had a set of anti-tamper seals with him. He knew that he couldn't be too careful traveling to South East Asia. It was dark when he reversed the Ferrari out of the garage.

Colin Sarll was cold, hungry and alert. He'd left the driver's side window open, and the front seat was now saturated with the constant rain. He rested the Winchester across the bench seat, so the end of the barrel rested on the front door and took aim. As he started to gently squeeze the trigger, an elderly couple walking a playful golden retriever blocked his line of vision. They were about twenty meters away, and he shouted, "Get out of the way," more to himself than to them. The Ferrari was now on the street, and he realigned the barrel of the rifle but, as he did, the old couple scurried across the road, spoiling any chance of him taking a shot. In a flash, the Ferrari was gone. Sarll didn't notice the blue Corolla take off after it. He'd been waiting for nearly four hours and a few more hours in the cold wouldn't hurt. He got out of his car and casually strolled over to Aspine's townhouse, took a rubbish bin and placed it directly in front of the garage door. When Aspine got home, he'd have to get out of the car and move the bin, and that would be the last thing that he'd ever do.

Because of the rain and wet roads, the traffic was heavy, and Harry had no trouble keeping the Ferrari in sight. The big red car turned into a quiet street in Glen Iris, and now Harry knew exactly where Aspine was going. He couldn't understand it, and he felt ill and angry. The widow was obviously without morals. He watched as Aspine drove under the carport of the weatherboard house and took a suitcase from the boot. What was he doing? Harry's first thought was that Aspine must be moving in with her, but he quickly dismissed it. He'd need more than one small suitcase, and the house would need to be a lot more palatial. Perhaps they were going on a holiday together? Harry parked the Corolla a hundred meters down the street, and sat, waited and watched, feeling a little more stupid each passing minute. Fifteen minutes later a yellow cab pulled up in front of the house, and Aspine and the widow climbed into the back of it. Neither had any luggage, and Harry scratched his head, totally confused. Should he follow the cab, wait where he was, or go home? He decided to wait but had no idea why. It was as if something or someone was driving him to pursue what he knew was an exercise in futility.

Jasmine was dressed in a simple black dress with thin shoulder straps, black high heels, a smart jacket, and an imitation pearl necklace that accentuated her skin color. Her hair cascaded over her shoulders, and she wore no makeup, other than soft pink lip balm. The Hyatt was warm, and she handed her jacket to the waiter and smiled at Aspine, placing her hand over his. "I wish you could come to Singapore with me," he said. "You could see your brother, and we could spend the weekend together."

"If I didn't have the boys, I would. Don't worry, there'll be other times."

The waiter brought their drinks, they clinked glasses and Jasmine said, "Here's to the future, and may we both get all we deserve in life."

"That's a strange toast." he laughed, as he watched half her screwdriver disappear. "Take it easy, we've got all night. I don't want you getting sick."

"With these?" she scoffed, holding up the glass and draining it.

"Tell me more about your brother."

"We're opposites. Right from boyhood he craved power, and later this became a craving for money, which I couldn't care less about."

"Money is power."

"Unfortunately, that's true. Anyhow, he made powerful friends in business and government in Singapore and started to build an empire. He's very private, but a recent article in an influential Singapore business magazine described him as one of Asia's newest billionaires. It's obscene, isn't it?"

"More like impressive." Aspine grinned, looking at the empty glass in front of her.

They had oysters Kilpatrick for their entrée. Jasmine seemed happy and babbled on constantly as the alcohol diminished her inhibitions. The speed with which she was drinking was even affecting him. He'd lost count, but guessed that he'd knocked over at least six Jack Daniels, and felt a little woozy. Her speech was clear and lucid. He was surprised that she'd managed to consume so much, and remain coherent.

"What time will you have to leave for the airport in the morning?" she asked, as the waiter set down another round of drinks.

"If I'm away by seven, I'll have plenty of time."

"What would you like for breakfast?"

"You." He laughed.

"You say the nicest things." she giggled, surreptitiously tipping her screwdriver on the carpet under the table. "I love these screwdrivers," she said, holding up the empty glass. "But really, what would you like for breakfast?"

"Coffee and orange juice will be fine."

"I'll wake you at half past six. That'll give you more than enough time to shower and shave."

He chuckled. "I'm an early riser, and with you next to me I'll be awake long before then."

By the time her barramundi and his steak arrived, he felt decidedly worse for wear, and yet she continued to chatter, seemingly unaffected by the screwdrivers.

"Do you feel like dessert?" he slurred.

"Just one more screwdriver, and coffee please. Then I'd like to go home."

He hadn't touched his last whiskey. "That's fine. Excuse me, I have to go to the little boys' room."

As he staggered away, she reached over and picked up his glass, bent down as if to scratch her leg, and sprinkled a fine white powder into the whiskey. She gently shook the glass from side to side, ensuring that the powder was totally dissolved, before placing it back on the table.

"I didn't order you another one," she said, nodding to the glass in front of him. "Here's to the future, and may we both get all we deserve in life."

"Thass the second time you've proposed that strange toast," he slurred, as they clinked glasses and he watched her down another screwdriver. Little did he know, that while he'd been gone, she'd ordered orange juice.

"Drink up," she said, urging him to finish the last of his whiskey.

The weather had deteriorated when he staggered onto Collins Street, using her as a prop. He felt dreadful, his head was spinning, and the cold air made it worse. She hailed a cab and somehow maneuvered him into the back seat.

It had been close to four hours since the yellow cab had pulled away from the house. Harry had been turning the engine on every fifteen minutes and letting the heater run while continuing to curse his stupidity. The bright headlights of another cab blinded him for an instant before it stopped in front of Jasmine's house. He wound his window down and heard her angry voice. "Come on, come on," she said, as she tried to drag Aspine out of the cab. "Help me get him inside," she demanded of the driver.

"I don't get paid to help drunks get inside their houses. I'll help pull him out, and that's it."

"There's twenty dollars in it for you if you help me get him into bed."

"Fifty and it's a deal," the cabbie responded.

"Yes, yes," she said impatiently, "please help me."

The cabbie climbed out from behind the wheel. "I'll get him out, but get ready to get under one arm. He's too big for me to get into the house by myself."

"I'll prop the front door open," she said.

A few minutes later Jasmine and the cabbie were each under an arm, half dragging, half lifting Aspine through the front door and onto the bed in the master bedroom. Jasmine paid the cabbie his fifty dollars.

"Thanks, lady. I feel sorry for you, being married to something like that."

"He's not my husband," Jasmine snapped.

Harry had seen drunks before, but never anyone as drunk as Douglas Aspine. His first feeling was one of disgust, but there was something not quite right — something was not as it appeared. He didn't know the widow well, but he'd never heard her speak an angry word, yet she seemed almost manic. He drove away slowly, puzzled by what he'd seen.

Jasmine knew that Aspine would be knocked out for hours and would be difficult to wake in the morning. She undressed him, throwing his clothes all over the room, before maneuvering him between the sheets. She opened his wallet and went through the compartments, finding two condoms. Her purchases at the supermarket had been superfluous. She tore the wrappings off and threw them on the floor, taking the condoms out to the kitchen where she tipped a little plain yogurt into each, before crinkling them up and dropping them on the bedroom floor. She tried to open his suitcase, but it was securely locked — it would have to wait until the morning. She undressed in Jack's bedroom, changed into a sexy black chemise, and carried the clothes that she'd been wearing into the master bedroom, scattering them around the floor. It was nearly two o'clock when she finally crawled into Jack's bed, having set the alarm for six.

It seemed that she'd barely closed her eyes before the radio alarm woke her, and she hastily turned it off. She was nervous and scared. What would she do if he woke in the next twenty-five minutes? She had been too busy the previous night to be scared, but the next ninety minutes would be the most difficult. She crept into the master bedroom at six-thirty and climbed into bed next to him, barely daring to breathe. Five minutes later she nudged him. "Wake up, Douglas, you've overslept."

He stirred, but his eyes remained closed.

"Wake up," she said, pushing him hard in the kidneys.

"Wassup?"

"You have a plane to catch, and you're running late."

He forced his eyes open. There were clothes strewn all over the room, a lacy black bra was next to his underpants, and two used condoms were on the carpet. He couldn't remember anything after the Hyatt.

"You have to get up and shower. I'll make coffee," she said, jumping out of bed.

His head was pounding, but he liked what he saw. "Come back to bed for a few minutes."

"You're insatiable." she laughed. "You make love all night, but still want more. I'll be here when you get back from Singapore."

Jasmine threw a dressing gown on before going to the kitchen and putting the kettle on. A few minutes later she heard Aspine stagger down the hallway to his suitcase and open it. He took out a change of underwear, sports shirt, casual shoes, socks, slacks and his toiletries bag. As Jasmine heard the bathroom door close and the sound of the shower, she moved quickly, taping a small plastic bag, to the side of one of the concealed compartments inside his suitcase.

"Hurry up," she yelled. "It's after seven o'clock."

He lumbered into the kitchen, and she handed him a coffee. "You're looking a little better," she said. "I'll get your clothes from the bedroom."

"They can stay here until I get back," he replied. He felt terrible. He'd checked his wallet in the bathroom, and the condoms were no longer in it, so he knew he'd had sex with her — he just couldn't remember anything about it.

"You forget that I have two young boys," she said, handing him an armful of clothes. "You'll have to take them with you."

She heard the suitcase being opened and his toiletries bag and the soiled clothes being placed in it. A few seconds later she heard it click closed, and she breathed a long sigh of relief.

"Can you drive me to the airport? I feel rotten, and I'm sure that I'm still over the limit."

"I'm not feeling too well myself," she lied.

"Please."

"Oh, all right," she smiled. "After all, you did look after me last night."

He groaned, *where was the fun in sex if you couldn't remember it the following day?*

"What are those things on your suitcase?" she asked, as they walked out the front door.

"Anti-tamper seals. Jasmine, I'm trying hard not to be rude, but please don't talk," he said, holding his head.

"Poor, Douglas."

She found the Ferrari surprisingly easy to drive and was more than pleased not to have to talk. "You may as well keep the car and pick me up on Monday."

"It's a nice car, but I don't want it in my driveway. I'll get a cab home."

"Park it in Qantas Valet parking then. Are you going to have coffee with me before I leave?"

"Sorry, I can't, I have to get back to pick the boys up."

The Valet attendant booked the car in, and they stood together waiting for the receipt. He bent down and kissed her on the lips, but she didn't respond. "Are you annoyed with me because I asked you not to talk?"

"No, I don't feel very well."

"I know the feeling."

"I do hope you get everything you so richly deserve. Give my love to Raj."

As he took the escalator to the international check-in counters, he wondered about her strange choice of words, but not for long. His head was hurting too much to think.

Harry Denton had been mesmerized by what he'd seen the night before, and now he sat in front of Jasmine's house in the Corolla, wondering what had gone on in there the previous night. The Ferrari was gone, and there was no sign of life. Harry was about to leave when a yellow cab pulled up in front of the house, and Jasmine got out. He was more confused than ever, but she wasn't the target of his interest, so he drove away.

Colin Sarll was famished and nearly frozen. He'd dozed during the night, but the rubbish bin remained where he'd put it, so he knew that Aspine hadn't returned home. He had no money for food and had expected to be dead by now.

Jasmine boiled the sheets and vacuumed and cleaned her house until it was spotless. She was glad that she had found nothing belonging to Aspine. It was nearly ten o'clock when she called Raj. "Everything went to plan. The plane departs in fifteen minutes."

"Well done. How are you feeling?"

"Hollow. It won't bring Kerry back."

"No, but it will bring his killer to account. I'm coming down to Melbourne for a week when this is over."

"I'd like that. Call me as soon as you hear anything, Raj."

- 45 -

SQ 238 TOUCHED DOWN at five in the afternoon, Singapore time. Aspine had traveled business class because he didn't want Raj to think he was a spendthrift. It hadn't been as comfortable as first class, and he'd dozed off and on during the nine-hour flight, racking his brain trying to remember what had occurred the previous night. He'd slept with the most beautiful woman that he'd ever set eyes on and couldn't remember anything. *Well, next time I most definitely will.*

He cleared immigration and collected his suitcase from the carousel, expecting to breeze through customs.

"Do you have anything to declare, sir?" The young Singaporean asked.

"I filled the declaration in," he responded testily.

"Did you pack your suitcase?"

"Yes."

"Was it ever out of your sight between the time you packed and the time you checked it in?"

"No."

"Did you affix the anti-tamper seals?"

"Yes."

"And have they been tampered with?"

Aspine glanced down at his suitcase. "Obviously not," he growled.

"Are you aware that bringing drugs into Singapore is a crime, punishable by death?"

"What is this? I'm running late for an appointment with one of your country's most influential businessmen."

"Please remove the seals and open your suitcase."

"How long is this going to take?"

An older customs officer joined the younger man. "It's routine, sir. We'll be as quick as we can."

The younger man put on a pair of cotton gloves and began to slowly empty Aspine's suitcase.

"You're not going to find anything," he snarled, angry because he was being needlessly held up. "Why do you think I use anti-tamper seals?"

The suitcase now appeared empty, and his clothes and toiletries were on the bench in front of them. "Are you going to re-pack my clothes?" he scowled.

They ignored him and concentrated on the suitcase carefully checking the compartments as if they were expecting to find something. Suddenly the younger man gestured excitedly to his superior. Aspine looked at the small plastic bag taped to the inside of one of his suitcase's compartments and froze. "What is this?" the older man demanded.

"I don't know. I've never seen it before."

The younger officer removed the bag, and two police officers positioned themselves directly behind Aspine. The sweat seeped from him as he wrestled to understand how the bag had got there.

The older officer opened it, carefully placed his index finger inside and tasted the white powder. "Heroin," he exclaimed.

There were now half a dozen police officers behind Aspine and, at a sign from the customs officer, they seized and handcuffed him.

"No!" he screamed. "It was planted. It's a frame-up."

His protests fell on deaf ears, and the police dragged him through customs, before hurling him into the back of a waiting police car. Remarkably, TV crews, reporters, and photographers appeared to materialize from nowhere to capture every second of the unfolding drama.

Aspine was half led, half pushed into a small room at Changi Police Station. A small, middle-aged Singaporean sat behind a simple wooden desk. There were two wooden chairs on the other side, and Aspine was shoved into one. The little man nodded at one of the police officers. "Take the handcuffs off, Corporal," he said, in perfect English.

"I'm Inspector Tan Tack Tong, Mr. Aspine. Would you like coffee, tea or water?" he asked as if they were about to share a drink at their local club.

"I want to get out of here," Aspine shouted. "This is a frame-up. I never put that stuff in my suitcase."

"Everyone who sits in that chair tells me the same story." Tan smiled.

"I'm telling the truth. I hate drugs."

"But you know a lot about them and Singaporean laws."

"What are you talking about? I know nothing."

"The mandatory death penalty applies to those who bring more than fifteen grams of heroin into our country. You brought exactly fifteen grams, so you will not be executed. I think you know our drug laws very well."

"I did not put that bag in my suitcase."

"Didn't you tell the customs officers that the suitcase was never out of your sight and that you affixed anti-tamper seals to it?"

"Yes," Aspine groaned. He remembered that he'd opened it for a change of clothes and his toiletries in the morning but didn't want to say anything, because, if he was wrong, he'd alienate his only chance of help in Singapore. "I came up here specifically to meet with one of your country's most influential businessmen, Mr. Raj George. Can you contact him for me?"

"You know Mr. George?" Tan asked, looking surprised. "Corporal Koh, could you please call Mr. George?"

"You'll soon see that I'm telling the truth."

A few minutes later Koh returned to the room and whispered in the inspector's ear.

"Mr. George knows nothing about any meeting with you," Tan smiled. "He said that your name is vaguely familiar and that he may have met you on one of his numerous trips to Australia."

"Lying bastard," Aspine bellowed. "He and his whore of a sister framed me."

"Enough," Tan said menacingly, barely raising his voice, eyes narrowing and his mouth turning up in a cruel sneer. "You are a liar."

"I'm not. It's a fucking frame-up!"

"Let me tell you the penalty for bringing fifteen grams of heroin into our country. Twenty years to life with little chance of remission. You'll be close to seventy before you get out of Changi prison if you live that long." Tan smiled. "You thought you were smart bringing in that quantity of heroin, but you will find that being incarcerated in Changi is a fate worse than death."

What had she said? *'I do hope you get everything you so richly deserve.'* "I want to see the Australian Consul and a lawyer. Until then, I'm not saying anything."

"You've already said more than enough."

The following morning, every television station and newspaper in Australia carried the story of Aspine's arrest in Singapore.

Jasmine Bartlett read the front page of the *Herald-Sun* with satisfaction. "I have avenged you my darling," she said, a photo of Kerry in her hands.

Vic Garland felt fifteen years younger. "What a pity they're not going to hang the bastard," he said, to no-one in particular.

Colin Sarll felt cheated at first. His plans for Aspine, and his suicide were ruined. As he absorbed the news, the loathing bottled up inside him dissipated. He had kids who he loved dearly, and the thought of taking his life, and leaving them without a father made him ill. What had he been thinking? He needed a meal, a shower, and a good sleep. On Monday morning he'd find a job, even it was only sweeping streets. He was a re-born man.

Detective Bill Muller was amazed. No wonder law-enforcement officers were cynical and distrusting. He remembered Aspine bashing his son for smoking marijuana, and his vehemence toward those who peddled and used drugs. The newspapers reported that Aspine was claiming that the heroin had been planted in his suitcase but, then again, everyone caught with drugs said that.

Harry Denton was confused but had an inkling of what might've happened. He called Fiona Jeczik, who was elated, and organized to meet her for coffee in Armadale. He explained in detail what had occurred on the previous Thursday night. "You followed him and then sat out the front of her house for nearly five hours?" she said, incredulous.

"I know," Harry responded, turning red.

She placed her hand on his forearm. "Don't be embarrassed, your motives were good."

"I think she planted the heroin in his suitcase."

"Where would she have gotten it from?"

"I don't know."

"I thought she wasn't very bright."

"I know, Fiona. You were wrong. That was the impression she wanted to create."

"You're only guessing."

"Yes, but why would he take the risk with only fifteen grams? Its street value is twelve to fourteen thousand dollars. He made millions at Mercury."

"What you say makes a lot of sense."

"I think the fifteen grams was intentional. She wants him to spend the rest of his life in Changi, knowing that she put him there." Harry said.

"I love it. What are you going to do?"

"Nothing, but I'd like to have a word with her to satisfy my curiosity."

"A guilty, horrible, despicable dreg of humanity incarcerated for a crime that he didn't commit. I was happy when I heard the news this morning. Now I'm euphoric."

"You hate him, don't you, Fiona?"

"Don't you?"

"I'm a religious man."

"Think about an eye for an eye, and a tooth for a tooth, Harry. Besides, everything you've surmised is circumstantial, and the Singaporeans won't listen to anything you have to say."

"I know. I don't think anyone can help Aspine. She did what the ACCC, ASIC, Vic Garland, you, I and many others couldn't. She destroyed him."

"God bless her," Fiona smiled.

The Australian Consul told Aspine that Teo Boon Wan was the finest and most expensive criminal lawyer in Singapore. They sat facing each other in a small visitors' area in Changi prison. "I have read the statements made by the customs officers and police, Mr. Aspine. It seems that they have a watertight case against you," he said, running his long delicate fingers through his oily silver hair.

Aspine related everything that had occurred since Jasmine told him that her brother wanted to meet him for dinner in Singapore.

"Did you call, Mr. George?"

"No."

"Pity. Proving you'd made contact with him would've been helpful."

"Did he pay for, or reimburse you, for airfares and expenses?"

"No, but he said that he would, or at least his sister told me that he would. She also said he was going to book a room at the Mandarin Hotel for me."

"I've already checked. There was no room booked in your name. In fact, there is nothing to connect you in any way to Mr. George." Teo's spectacles slipped down his nose, and he looked at Aspine over the top of them. "Mr. Aspine, in the thirty years I've been acting as a defense attorney, I've never seen a stronger prosecution case."

"I'm innocent. How many times do I have to tell you that I was framed?" Aspine ranted.

"If what you say is true, those who framed you have done a remarkable job. Have you thought about pleading guilty?"

"Are you mad? Listen to me. I have over nine million dollars in the Caymans. Get me off and half is yours."

"You're in Singapore, Mr. Aspine. All the money in the world won't help you, and if, as you say, Mr. George is involved, the amount that you have is a mere pittance."

"I never brought that heroin in. I hate drugs but, even if I was a peddler, why would I waste my time bringing in fifteen grams worth only twelve thousand dollars? It's madness."

"The prosecution will say that you brought in a small amount to avoid the death penalty. If you plead guilty, I may be able to get you a twenty-year sentence, which might be further reduced to fifteen years with remissions. If you plead not guilty, you'll most likely get life."

"No!" Aspine screamed. "No!"

"I'm sorry, Mr. Aspine," Teo said, standing to leave, "but, in the absence of new evidence, you're going to spend a minimum of twenty years in Changi."

- 46 -

JASMINE AGREED TO meet the lawyer from Singapore, and freely admitted that she'd had dinner with Aspine the night before he went to Singapore. He'd got shockingly drunk and couldn't walk when they arrived back at her home. She'd had no choice but to let him sleep at her home, but she most definitely had not shared the same bed with him. Yes, she did remember him bringing a suitcase into her house in the morning for a change of clothes and toiletries. No, he had not brought his suitcase in when he arrived to pick her up. Why would he? It was not a romantic dinner, and there was no plan for him to stay overnight. She had gone out to dinner with him because she had questions about Kerry's estate and death, which she wanted to ask him. Yes, she had driven him to the airport shortly after seven o'clock in the morning because he was still too drunk to drive. He was disgusting. No, she hadn't touched his suitcase or put anything inside it. Why would she?

Barbara knew that he'd been framed, but she no longer cared. He'd hurt her too badly, and she'd long ceased to have any feelings for him. Trevor was somewhere in South East Asia with his girlfriend, and she had not heard from him. Jemma was besotted with her boyfriend and had moved in with him. She'd hardly seen anything of her father for two years, had no sympathy for him and had adopted her boyfriend's surname. It was only Mark who fretted, pined and fought for his father. Barbara's heart went out to him, but she knew with time these feelings would diminish and eventually disappear.

Harry called Jasmine, and she agreed to have coffee with him at a little shop around the corner from her home. He arrived early and, as she approached, he stood and pulled a chair out for her. She was a breathtakingly beautiful young woman. They exchanged small talk while they waited for their coffee.

"I know what you did," Harry said, sipping his latte.

"I'm sorry, I don't understand."

"I followed Douglas Aspine to your house that night. I saw him carry his suitcase into your house."

"Why, why did you follow him?" she asked, trying to remain composed.

"I was hoping I'd unearth evidence of some crime or clandestine activity. I was still out the front of your house when you arrived home."

Her face lost color. "Why?"

"I'm old-fashioned, and I couldn't understand why you were with the man who was responsible for your husband's death. Then I heard the way you berated him when the cab driver helped you carry him inside. You'd been making out that you liked him, but you really hated him."

"I don't know what you're talking about," she said, standing to leave.

"Please sit down and hear me out. I mean you no harm."

"All right, only for a minute."

"I wanted to meet with you today, to apologize."

"Sorry, you're confusing me."

"When you started seeing Aspine, I was thoroughly disgusted with you. I thought you may have been having an affair with him, and that was what sent your husband over the edge. I'm sorry."

"Oh."

"Don't worry; I don't intend to say a word to anyone. I know how difficult it must have been for you to do what you did."

"I never slept with him, if that's what you mean," she said, defiantly.

"I'm pleased to hear that, but that's not what I meant."

"Oh," she said, turning bright red. "Harry Denton, you're a lovely man. I wish Kerry had worked for you."

"Thank you. If you ever need to talk to anyone, please feel free to contact me. You're a brave, clever and loyal lady. I admire you. What you did can be our little secret."

"But I didn't do anything." she smiled, standing up. "Douglas Aspine got caught taking heroin into Singapore. I had nothing to do with it. End of story."

"As you wish," Harry said, returning her smile.

Detective Bill Muller's transfer to the drug squad often involved him in looking at footage recorded by CCTV devices positioned around drug areas in Little Bourke and Bourke Streets, Melbourne. He was skimming through some footage, looking for a particular dealer who'd been under surveillance, when he saw something that caused him to hit the rewind button. Even with sunglasses and a scarf wrapped tightly around her hair, she was stunningly beautiful and unmistakable. He slowed the footage and zoomed in on her, and the Asian dealer whom with she was negotiating. She opened her handbag and handed him a large wad of hundred dollar bills. He looked around nervously before giving her a tiny plastic bag containing what looked like white powder. A few seconds later he handed her a slightly larger plastic bag also containing white powder. Muller zoomed in on the second bag and guessed by relating it to the size of her hand that it might well contain fifteen grams of heroin. He puzzled over what might have been in the smaller bag, not knowing that it was a powerful knock-out drug. He'd been following the case closely in the newspapers and knew Aspine was claiming that Jasmine and her brother had framed him. There was no evidence to support this, and Aspine's claim was deemed preposterous and no more than the ranting of a guilty man. Bill Muller had been amazed when Aspine was caught with heroin because he'd witnessed his obvious hate of drugs. Now he knew that Aspine had been telling the truth. Muller was a good policeman, fighting with his conscience. He knew that Aspine had ruined countless lives, had driven Kerry Bartlett to suicide, had stolen millions of dollars and was arrogant and a bully — he also knew that he should disclose his findings. Aspine would walk free and the fraud charges that he should have been found guilty of had already been thrown out of court. He wouldn't pay for driving Kerry Bartlett to suicide and, worse, Kerry's widow may find herself in serious trouble.

If Muller could've wiped the hard disk, he would have, but no-one else would watch the footage, and even if they did, without his knowledge, all they'd see was a routine drug deal. Bill Muller hit a button and the screen in front of him turned black — he'd not seen anything that warranted further action on his part. He was comfortable with his decision knowing that he would've never forgiven himself had he helped Aspine.

Aspine had aged terribly in the year since his arrest. He'd lost ten kilograms, his jowls were sunken, his hair was gray and his pallor was yellow. Now he stood in the dock waiting to be sentenced.

"Twenty years to be served in Changi prison," the judge intoned.

Aspine gasped, slumped over and clutched his throat. "I want to appeal the judgment and the severity of the sentence."

"I wouldn't if I were you, the sentence may be increased." Teo gratuitously smiled. "I thought that you'd get life."

"You mean that I got less than what I so richly deserved?" Aspine snarled, the irony lost on Teo.

Reviews:

Good, bad or indifferent are important for readers and authors alike. The Amazon links are:

U.S. http://a.co/bO3FqKb
U.K. http://amzn.eu/7n88WNS
Canada http://a.co/d8EvLmU
India http://amzn.in/j8XL1AI

Other Books By Peter Ralph